GREGORY BASTIANELLI

SHADOW FLICKER

This is a **FLAME TREE PRESS** book

Text copyright © 2022 Gregory Bastianelli

FLAME TREE PRESS
6 Melbray Mews, London, SW6 3NS, UK
flametreepress.com

US sales, distribution and warehouse:
Simon & Schuster
simonandschuster.biz

UK distribution and warehouse:
Marston Book Services Ltd
marston.co.uk

Publisher's Note: This is a work of fiction. Names, characters, places, and
incidents are a product of the author's imagination. Locales and public names
are sometimes used for atmospheric purposes. Any resemblance to actual
people, living or dead, or to businesses, companies, events, institutions, or
locales is completely coincidental.

Thanks to the Flame Tree Press team, including:
Taylor Bentley, Frances Bodiam, Federica Ciaravella, Don D'Auria,
Chris Herbert, Josie Karani, Mike Spender, Cat Taylor,
Maria Tissot, Nick Wells, Gillian Whitaker.

The cover is created by Flame Tree Studio with
thanks to Nik Keevil and Shutterstock.com.
The font families used are Avenir and Bembo.

Flame Tree Press is an imprint of Flame Tree Publishing Ltd

flametreepublishing.com

A copy of the CIP data for this book is available from the British Library
and the Library of Congress.

HB ISBN: 978-1-78758-678-9
PB ISBN: 978-1-78758-676-5
ebook ISBN: 978-1-78758-679-6

Printed in the USA by Integrated Books International

GREGORY BASTIANELLI

SHADOW FLICKER

FLAME TREE PRESS
London & New York

To Jim and Pam for introducing me to the wonderful woman who became my wife, and for taking us to a special island off the coast of Maine

CHAPTER ONE

The dandelions almost killed the old man.

Melody Larson hauled her laundry basket out to the clothesline late one Saturday afternoon that spring. The forecast promised a warm sunny day and hadn't disappointed. A slight breeze curled over the hills to the northeast on Kidney Island and Melody liked to believe it came from the Bay of Fundy and not from those infernal wind turbines about a thousand yards from her farmhouse.

She waited as late in the day as possible before coming outside to hang the laundry so the sun would be higher in the sky and she could avoid the shadow effects the rotating propellers of the turbines cast over the landscape. She didn't want to step outside the house till then, not that it was any better inside. As Melody began hanging the sheets she had stripped from her bed, she thought how much she desired to slip back under them once they were dry. The seven hundred-thread-count Egyptian cotton sheets provided her the most comfort these days. Drying them under the warm sunshine and cool salty air of the island became something she looked forward to after the long winter. The clothes dryer never left them with that same feeling of comfort.

Of course the comfort she pined for under those sheets in her bed pertained to sleep, much to the chagrin of her husband, Myles, who hoped for something more he'd rather enjoy in those soft threads, but it was not what Melody desired. And the sleep she so craved had been difficult to come by these days. The soft grinding as the wind turbines went through their rotation pierced her veil of sleep, leaving her exhausted every morning.

As she clipped each end of a sheet to the rope line with a wooden clothespin, she spied her elderly father in the middle of the backyard and smiled. He still worked as hard on the Darrow farm as she remembered growing up here, even though their agricultural output had shrunk to a fraction of what the old man and his father and grandfather before him had built up on the island. That made her sad thinking of it, but she still managed to smile seeing him tending to the land even well into his seventies.

Tyrus Darrow carried two objects as he shuffled in a slow halting pace across the lawn of the backyard. In his left hand he held a steel pail by its thin handle. His right hand grasped a long metal implement used for digging dandelions out by their roots. Every time he came to an outcropping of the yellow flowered weeds, and there were no shortages of them scattered throughout the green grass, he'd set the pail down and stick the bottom of the tool into the ground around the leaves of a dandelion. He stepped on the metal foothold at the base, allowing the tip to dig into the ground under the plant's roots. He rocked the tool back and lifted, its prongs pulling up the weed.

Of course, Tyrus didn't think of the plant as a weed. To him it was sustenance. The greens he'd wash and bundle up to sell at the family farm stand at the end of their property by the road. The yellow heads of the dandelions would go into the barn where he'd put them into the press to make dandelion wine.

It was probably the last bit of joy Melody's father got out of what remained of their farm, and she watched him with a touch of sadness. The hum from the wind turbines reminded her of what they gave up. Not that the sound didn't annoy her, but its constant vibration in her ears served as a reminder that it was she who had convinced Tyrus to sell the acreage they could no longer maintain to Aerosource, the energy company that installed the turbines. Her father met her suggestion with reluctance, but at his age she thought it would really only be her future that would be affected by the decision.

How wrong she had been about that.

Melody continued pinning sheets and pillowcases to the lines, this time the bedding from her two kids. She kept one eye on her father, knowing his footing wasn't quite what it used to be. She always dreaded the possibility of him taking a tumble and cracking his fragile bones. He seemed strong enough to have many years left in him, but still she worried.

Once Tyrus filled his pail to the brim, he brought the bucket over to the picnic table on their back patio, setting it down on top and laying the tool on the ground beside it. She watched as he began separating the yellow dandelion heads from their stems and putting them in one pile, the greens in another.

Melody smiled and reached down to grab another pillowcase. Her gaze only left him for a second. When she straightened up and clipped the pillowcase to the clothesline, she glanced over at the patio. Her mouth opened; her eyes widened.

Tyrus sat at the picnic table with the pile of dandelion heads in front of him. He plucked one yellow flower out of the pile and popped it into his mouth.

At first, Melody wasn't sure she saw correctly. Maybe he had pulled some kind of snack out of his pants pocket, nuts or something. But as she watched, pausing from her chore, she saw him pick up another dandelion head and stuff it into his mouth, his jaws churning as he chewed.

"Dad?" Melody stood stunned, not comprehending what her eyes observed. Her mind tried reasoning that maybe he enjoyed the taste of dandelions before, or maybe he always sampled the latest crop to make sure it suitable for wine making. But as she watched, he continued stuffing dandelion after dandelion into his mouth, his eyes a vacant stare as if in some kind of trance.

"Dad!" she cried, running across the yard, calling out again though he acted as if he didn't hear or see her. By the time she got to the picnic table, she had no idea how many of the dandelions he had stuffed in his mouth, but the pile in front of him had been nearly depleted.

He began choking.

"Dad!" she screamed at his side, taking hold of his right arm, which tried to reach out and pick up another dandelion despite his gagging sounds. "What are you doing?"

His head turned, face still gripped in a dazed expression and becoming flush as he looked up at her. His face bulged out like a squirrel whose cheeks were stuffed with nuts, his mouth opening to reveal a yellow morass coating his lips and tongue. He tried to speak, but only emitted choking sounds. His eyes looked glazed.

Melody began shaking him. "Spit it out!" she cried, no, yelled at him.

He sputtered, his Adam's apple bobbing in the floppy skin of his neck. He attempted to cough, but only a muffled sound came out. His face drained of color.

"Jesus, Dad!" she squealed. Panic took hold of her. She pounded on his back and he hunched over but the choking sounds persisted. Melody got behind him, bringing her arms around him and making a fist with her right hand and wrapping her left hand around it. She felt around for the middle of his paunch and then leaned into his back. With all her strength, she pulled her arms back, driving her fist into his gut.

His body lurched up off the seat from the force, but the gagging sounds persisted.

"Please God," she said in a less-panicked voice. *Please help me.* She pulled her fist in again. His body jerked and she thought she heard a gurgling sound from his throat. *Again*, she thought, bracing herself, worried if she didn't get his airway cleared, he would pass out and topple off the table, taking her with him.

She tugged hard, ramming her fist into his gut with all her might.

A sound erupted from his open mouth followed by a geyser of a yellow sticky coagulated substance that spewed across the top of the picnic table.

Tyrus Darrow's shoulders slumped, and as Melody relaxed, the muscles in her arms, back and legs that had been bracing herself behind him let go; the old man pitched forward, his head falling to the tabletop, his face landing in the gooey yellow mess.

Behind them, the sound of the wind turbines continued to whirl and hum.

CHAPTER TWO

Oscar Basaran pulled into the driveway of the Darrow farm on Haven Road late in the day. He felt weary after the long journey from Boston to Kidney Island, but after a short afternoon nap at the Tides Hotel to shake off the road lag and also settle his stomach from the ferry ride, he decided to get to work without wasting time.

The sun began its descent, dragging some of the August heat with it, but as soon as he stepped from the air-conditioned rental car into the hot air, he started to perspire. As a kid, he'd been used to the hot air growing up in Turkey, but thirteen years of living in Boston enabled his reliance on air-conditioning in the summer and his body adjusted.

The farmhouse looked old, as many of the houses he'd seen on the drive. But just before he reached it, he'd passed a new development under construction, Pickett Fences Estates, with several homes completed, and the shells of half a dozen homes underway and signs advertising many additional lots available. It surprised him since all the information he researched showed the population declining on the island. And now with the Aerosource concerns, there might be more reasons for the development to be in jeopardy.

But that's why he had been sent here, he thought as he strode to the front door, to get to the bottom of the problems and see if there were any justification to the complaints. Aerosource didn't think so, but he didn't work for them. Not exactly.

★   ★   ★

One month earlier, he sat in Mason Helleson's office on the seventeenth floor of the Aerosource building on Seaport Boulevard in Boston. The firm, one of the leading companies of wind turbines in the Northeast, established wind farms across upstate New York, throughout Massachusetts, off Cape Cod and several other places, including Kidney Island in the Penobscot Bay off the coast of Maine.

Helleson stood tall, his head topped with short white hair, his creased face belying a man in his late sixties, shoulders broad. He kept in shape for a man more than twice Oscar's age and it made him somewhat intimidating as Helleson stood by the expanse of glass windows looking out over the Seaport district. Oscar sat nervously in a seat before the man's desk waiting to find out why his insurance company sent him to one of its biggest clients.

The older man cleared his throat.

"Renewable energy is what everyone wants," Helleson said. "It's what the world needs." The man turned to look at him and Oscar nodded. "Wind power is the most affordable zero-emission energy source available. But while we're trying to do what's best for our planet, there remain stumbling blocks."

"I'm sure," Oscar said, though he wasn't really. He felt like he needed to hold up his end of the conversation.

Helleson strode over to his oversized desk and sat down behind it, but in no way looked any less imposing than when he stood. "You have no idea why you were sent here, do you?"

The man's teeth when he smiled ratcheted up Oscar's nerves. "No, Mr. Helleson, I don't."

"Call me Mason."

Oscar nodded, but wouldn't feel comfortable doing that.

Helleson's brows furrowed as he eyed Oscar. "Oscar isn't your original given name, is it?" he asked.

"No," Oscar said, squirming a bit in his seat. "I Americanized it when I became a naturalized citizen. It's originally Ozgur."

Helleson reflected on this for a moment and smirked. "I've been informed by your firm that you are one of their best insurance investigators."

"I'm glad they think so."

"This should be a fairly routine inquiry," Helleson said. "A handful of interviews and that's about it."

Oscar leaned forward. "And whom am I interviewing? And what am I asking them?" The mystery of the assignment annoyed him.

Helleson chuckled, but it didn't have a cheerful sound. "Ever hear of 'shadow flicker'?"

Oscar leaned back in his chair. "No." Didn't sound familiar to him.

"Not surprised," Helleson said with a wave of his hand. "It's mostly nonsense. But the people living near our wind turbines on Kidney Island seem to think otherwise, and they've hired an attorney to represent them in a claim against Aerosource."

Now it began to come clear to Oscar. He nodded, but waited for Helleson to continue.

"Shadow flicker is what's being termed the effect of the shadows and reflections cast over the land by the propellers of the turbines. Residents who live nearby claim it's affecting their health and that the combination of the shadow flicker and the noise vibration contribute to headaches and sleep loss and a myriad of other symptoms."

"And does it?" Oscar asked, wary of the response.

"Nonsense." The old man leaned forward on his desk as he spoke, but now settled back in his chair. "This comes up with every turbine we place throughout the Northeast. There's always some neighborhood group that wants to gripe about it. It's more a case of NIMBY if you ask me."

"Not in my backyard," Oscar uttered to himself.

"Research and studies have been done over the years about this issue and it's never been determined that there is a direct link between the turbines and health issues. Hell, fossil fuels are the real health problem, with carbon dioxide, sulfur, nitrogen. Everyone's worried about climate change, and our company is doing something about safe energy, and a handful of complainers in a few locations try to stir up trouble."

"So where do I come in?" Oscar asked, wondering why his own firm didn't apprise him of what they expected of him.

"Because of this claim filed by the attorney, we need an independent investigator to interview the residents who live near the turbines. Find out what health issues they really believe are happening." He put his hands behind his head and leaned back in his chair. "That's all. Fairly simple."

★   ★   ★

And as Oscar knocked on the wooden front door of the Darrow farmhouse, that's what he hoped it would be. Simple. He didn't know at the time how far from that it would be.

When the door swung open, he was greeted by a dark-haired woman who would under most circumstances be considered attractive, even if not for the silver strips of hair, like dull tinsel, that streaked through the very dark locks that fell to her shoulders. But weariness clung to the features of her face, leaving creases, bags and a blotchy complexion that staunched her good looks.

"Yes?" she asked, looking at him through droopy eyes.

"I hope I'm not bothering you, m-miss." He had been about to say *ma'am* but corrected himself in time. "My name is Oscar Basaran. Would you happen to be Melody Larson?"

"Yes."

"I hope I haven't caught you at an inconvenient time."

She held tight to the door, almost afraid to yield it to him.

"I'm from the Freedom Insurance Company and I'd like to ask you some questions if you don't mind."

"Questions?" She eyed him with suspicion. "What kind of questions?"

"I'm conducting an investigation about the health concerns you've been experiencing." Standing at the doorstep he could still hear the hum of the turbines and sympathized with its annoyance. "Because of the turbines."

Realization settled on her face. "Oh, yes, of course." The door opened a bit more.

"Would this be an okay time?"

She nodded. "Yes, yes. Do come in." She swung the door wide and gestured with her arm. "Forgive the clutter."

He entered into a small hall. A coatrack with a bench stood up against one wall, muddied boots and sneakers piled under the bench. A couple of yellow rain slickers hung from wooden pegs above the bench.

"I'm sorry to show up unannounced, but I've kind of had this case thrust upon me without much notice."

Melody tried to smile, but only managed a less than valiant attempt. "I'm just glad someone wants to listen to us." She wiped a hand across a furrowed brow. "It's just been so frustrating."

"I understand."

She led him down the hall and into the kitchen and to a small round dining table where she offered a seat. He set his briefcase down, opening it and retrieving a yellow legal pad and a pen.

"Would you like some coffee?" she asked.

"Oh, not necessary," he said. "But don't let me stop you from having some."

"Coffee I don't need," she said, taking a chair opposite him. "I'd be up all night."

He sensed frustration in her comment.

"My lawyer didn't mention anyone would be coming by to take a statement," she said.

Oscar paused. He could have continued and thought it would make things much easier to let her believe her attorney sent him, but his conscience got the better of him and he didn't want to start off on the wrong foot.

"My insurance firm wasn't hired by your attorney," he said.

Her eyes narrowed. "I don't understand."

"My insurance firm represents Aerosource." He braced for reaction.

Her face stiffened. "You work for Aerosource?"

"Not exactly," he tried to correct. "My firm is the insurance carrier for Aerosource. I'm here to evaluate your health claims."

"You want to know if I'm making this all up?" She pursed her lips.

"Oh, no." He shook his head. "That couldn't be further from the truth. My firm just needs me to document your concerns, so we have a better understanding of the issues involved." He doubted he assuaged her feelings.

"My father nearly died," she said, her voice stern.

"Died?" Oscar didn't know what she meant.

"Did the other man tell you what happened this spring?" Her hands clamped together.

"No," he said, not sure what other man she meant. Was she talking about Mason Helleson? No, he couldn't imagine someone in his position would have actually reached out to her or her attorney. He'd have people for those tasks. "I don't know anything about that. All I know is that you and some of your neighbors are having health concerns you feel are related to the wind turbines and this thing they call 'shadow flicker'. And I'm here to find out what those concerns are."

Melody drew in a deep breath.

"My father is an old man," she began. "But he always had all his faculties." She paused. "Until they put up those damn turbines. Ever since, he's had problems." She leaned forward in her chair, her eyes narrowing. "We've all had problems. But his scare me." She leaned back.

Oscar felt the need to write something down, but she hadn't really told him much. Still, the look on her face and the tone in her voice made his hands sweat, and the pen felt slippery in his grip.

"The doctor in town said my father is starting to exhibit periods of dementia. But I don't believe it."

"You don't."

"No. He's been having sleepless nights and bouts of forgetfulness." She shook her head. "That man used to be sharp as a tack. But, now..." Her eyes drifted off.

"And you don't think the doctor's assessment is accurate?"

"This spring, my father sat down outside and began eating a bucket of dandelions till his mouth was so crammed he couldn't even breathe." Tears formed at the corners of her eyes and she wiped them away.

"But he's okay now?" Oscar asked, concerned.

She glared at him. "I don't think he'll ever be okay."

He jotted this down. "And you think the turbines have had this effect on him?" He didn't get the correlation.

She pounded a fist on the table, causing him to jump. "It's every goddamn day!" Her voice hitched.

Oscar gave her some time to compose herself.

"When the sun comes up in the morning, no one wants to go outside. It's like torture."

"Because of this flicker?"

She nodded. "Have you ever seen it?"

He felt ashamed he hadn't done more research beforehand. "No, I confess."

"It's a nightmare. I get the most awful headaches. I can't sleep. And that constant hum. It never goes away." She leaned in again. "Even when the blades stop turning, which is rare, I swear I still hear the sound in my head."

Oscar began to wonder if something else wasn't going on with Melody Larson.

She slumped in her chair. "It exhausts me, dealing with it. I can't imagine how a man my father's age manages." She shook her head. "It's not dementia he's suffering. Or if it is, it's been brought on by those damn turbines."

"I'd like to talk to the rest of your family," he said. "If that's all right with you."

She eyed him with caution, trying to judge whether she should trust him.

"My father is resting right now," she said, "And I don't want to disturb him when he does get the chance to sleep. My husband's working. He picks up shifts down at the beverage store because...." She paused. "Well, this farm doesn't make the money it used to. It's fallen on hard times." She laughed, or rather chuckled, but it made a sarcastic sound. "That's the reason we sold a lot of our land to Aerosource a couple years back, to help us get out from under our financial problems." She looked at him with distant eyes. "How's that for irony? We gave them the land they needed to build those damn turbines, and look what it's doing to us."

This was another fact Helleson never mentioned to him.

"I'd like to come back when this shadow flicker takes effect, if that's okay?"

She smiled, but it wasn't a pleasant smile. "That's the only way to understand what I'm talking about."

He put his notepad away in his briefcase and stood. "Then I won't bother you any more today, but I can come back in the morning."

She escorted him to the front door. As he was about to leave, he remembered something she said earlier and turned.

"You mentioned something about another man?"

She nodded. "Yes. Someone came around earlier this summer. Same as you. Said he was investigating our claim against Aerosource. Asked a lot of the same questions you did. Said he'd come back and talk to us some more."

"And did he?" Oscar asked.

"No. We never saw or heard from him again."

CHAPTER THREE

As dusk fell along the north side of the island, Barrett and Letty Granberry began the process of herding their cows into the barn. The old couple maintained a small herd and mostly sold their milk products to one of the big plants over on the mainland. It gave them a modest income as they advanced into their later years.

Barrett was not quite as old as Tyrus Darrow and for now considered himself fitter than most men in their late sixties. Letty too held her own while helping her husband out on the farm. There was a time when the farm stretched out farther than the acreage they owned now, but they too had sold a small strip of land to Aerosource to provide an access road to the turbines. The Granberrys also sold a bigger chunk of land to the developer building the new houses along Haven Road, though progress had slowed on that front, and Barrett blamed the wind turbines.

Barrett heard them now, the soft whisper as their blades turned and the droning hum their motion created. Letty didn't hear so well these days, so it didn't bother her, but it nagged Barrett in the back of his head no matter how hard he tried to block it out.

His border collie, Butch, used to run to the back of the lot and bark at the machines first thing every morning till Barrett would have to get out there and hush him before the damn dog woke up the neighbors. Not that there were any close neighbors. Up the road lived Miss Gallagher and her family, and farther on up was the Darrow farm, where Tyrus, Myles and Melody Larson lived.

The Larsons were the ones who sold the major portion of their property to Aerosource, and if that didn't irk Barrett and Letty. His wife kept telling him the only reason it bothered him was because he didn't get to sell off first when the energy company was scouting for property for their turbines.

Barrett knew what a chunk of change they were throwing around, and he sure would have liked to have gotten in on a bigger piece of the pie. As it turned out, he managed to settle for the little strip he sold that provided the access road. Not as big a sum of money, but it helped offset the losses the farm endured.

He felt fortunate to be able to sell his land south of Haven Road to the housing developer, and he was lucky the sale went through when it did. That project ground to a halt after the turbines went up and all of a sudden that gorgeous country plot of land didn't have the same appeal with those whirling blades in the distance.

And the flicker effect.

Damn! That always spooked Barrett's cows. And Christ if their milk production didn't show it. Of course Letty said how the hell could they be sure that was to blame, and she might be right. It could be just a coincidence, but Barrett didn't think so. That's why he agreed to talk to the attorney fellow Melody Larson wrangled up. As much as he distrusted lawyer folks, he didn't want to miss out on another opportunity to help his farm out. And him and Letty. They weren't getting any younger and he wanted to make these last years as easy as possible.

Letty waved to him from across the field as the cows filed along like orderly students heading in from recess.

"Here she comes," Letty hollered.

The *she* was Myrtle, the only pregnant cow they had in their herd. With the lack of milk production, they felt the need to increase the herd a bit, so they hired one of Hubert Mace's bulls to come over and mingle with the ladies, but Myrtle was the only one who got impregnated. Barrett blamed that on the damn turbines as well.

Letty liked to baby Myrtle and Barrett appreciated that. There was a time when Letty didn't want to keep Myrtle, when she was first born. Myrtle was the only red-and-white Holstein calf they owned and at first Letty wanted him to get rid of it. Generations ago, the red-and-whites weren't accepted by some farmers who felt they were inferior and shouldn't be mixed with the black-and-whites. Letty said they weren't pure because the red-and-white coloring of their coats came from breeding with several different types of dairy cows.

Letty said it was a bad sign for their farm when the calf was born, that it was an unnatural breed. Something was amiss, she warned him. But he convinced her they needed to keep every cow they had to maintain the farm, and eventually Letty came to appreciate Myrtle, especially when she became pregnant.

Letty nurtured her and wanted to make sure everything went smooth come delivery time, and that wasn't far off. The fat cow sauntered down the field heading toward the barn and Barrett drew up alongside it. He walked with Myrtle while Letty made sure the last of the stragglers headed this way.

The barn door stood open as the cows filed in with little prodding. Sometimes Barrett thought they couldn't wait to get away from the whine of the turbines too. As he and Myrtle approached the barn, the cow veered to the left, almost bumping into him.

"Whoa missy," Barrett said, patting her lightly on the rump to redirect her.

But the stubborn cow seemed to have a mind of her own, and moved away from the barn door toward the split-rail fence that rimmed the yard.

"Where you going, little lady?" Barrett asked, taking off his ball cap and scratching his thinning scalp.

The cow started to stumble and he rushed over.

Myrtle lunged forward, toward the fence, dipping her head and ramming it into the upright fence post.

"What the hell!" Barrett rushed over just as Myrtle backed away from the fence, staggering, her legs shaky. Then the cow rammed forward into the fence post again, bending it backward, before she dropped down on her front legs. Blood flowed out from a cut just above her snout.

"Christ, girl," Barrett yelled and reached out to grab her by the scruff of her neck.

Letty screamed something he didn't understand and ran over to them.

"What's got into her?" she cried.

"Damned if I know!" He tried pulling her up and moving her away from the fence. Her eyes looked dazed as the blood ran down into her sweaty nostrils. He removed a red bandana from his back pocket and began to wipe the blood off, trying to see how badly the cut looked.

"Shall we call Doc?" Letty asked.

Barrett shrugged. The wound didn't look too bad, but maybe it'd be a good idea to get the vet out here and see if there might be something else wrong with her. This sudden aberrant behavior scared him.

The two of them managed to guide Myrtle into the safety of the barn and secured her along with the other cows. Glancing back out the door, Barrett eyed the turning blades of the turbines.

CHAPTER FOUR

Kidney Island is nestled in Maine's Penobscot Bay, about a seventy-five-minute ferry ride from the town of Rockland. Earlier in the day, when Oscar first arrived at the island, he marveled at its beauty as the ferry pulled up to the terminal.

Of course he had seen his share of New England coastal towns along the North Shore and Cape Cod, but something about this one struck him as more peaceful. Maybe because once he reached the island, the mainland no longer remained in sight, giving it a sense of remoteness.

He had originally sat in his car for most of the ferry ride, but once away from shore, a wave of nausea swept over him and he stepped out for fresh air. While Oscar was growing up in Turkey, his father had many times taken him out into the Sea of Marmara on an uncle's boat, but Oscar's stomach never acclimated to the rocking motion that always upset him. He felt better with his feet planted on the ground.

But the salty air and constant breeze on the ferry made him feel better and he stood on the upper deck watching the island approach. In a way, he felt grateful for the assignment and the opportunity to get away. It removed him from the doldrums he'd found himself ensconced in for the past several months.

It still struck him odd that Kyle Devitt no longer played a part in his life after three years of what seemed like a blissful relationship. What frustrated him the most, thinking back, was he never noticed the signals. Sure, Kyle's moodiness became apparent, but most relationships suffer bouts of communication lapses. But Oscar never expected to hear what Kyle said when he finally did feel like talking.

The fact Kyle decided to leave him for someone else struck with intense emotional pain, but somehow the fact he decided to leave him for a woman seemed an extreme act of betrayal. And of what else? Dishonesty? Not that he had the affair. But that their whole relationship might have been a sham? Could it be?

But Kyle tried to assure Oscar that his feelings for him had been genuine. Had? Then how could he be in love with a woman?

Kyle tried to explain that he didn't see genders, that he only saw personalities, and the woman he claimed to be in love with was the best fit for him now. The question Oscar's therapist asked him reverberated in his head: What are you angrier about, that he left you, or that he left you for a woman?

Oscar didn't know the answer. Only that he felt angry and frustrated.

And despondent.

So this job and the chance to get away from Boston, the office and his now-lonely apartment came at the right moment in his life. But as the ferry approached the island and the harbor full of small boats moored throughout the calm waters, it reminded him of trips he and Kyle took to Provincetown on the Cape, and Oscar now wondered if even Kidney Island was remote enough.

Back at his room at the Tides Hotel in town, after his preliminary interview with Melody Larson, something nagged at him. Why had Aerosource already sent someone out here, and why hadn't Mason Helleson told him about it?

Oscar called the contact number Helleson provided him and after several rings, which worried him the old man wasn't going to be available, he heard someone pick up.

"Yes?" The voice sounded flat.

"Mr. Helleson," Oscar began, dispensing with calling him Mason. "I've arrived and already got a chance to speak to one of the residents who live out near the turbines."

"Good to hear," Helleson said. "But don't feel you need to check in. Just provide your final report when you've finished your interviews."

"Understood, but that's not exactly why I'm calling." Oscar heard an obvious pause on the other end.

"Yes?"

"Did someone from Aerosource already come out here and talk to some people?"

Now the pause was even longer.

"Is that what you were told?"

"Yes," Oscar said. "By Melody Larson, the woman I spoke to already."

"I see," Helleson said, very matter-of-fact. "We did send someone from the company out there to sort of check on some things."

"I wish I had been told."

"It's of no concern to you and should have no bearings on your assignment." He sounded dismissive.

Oscar scratched his chin. "I just don't want to duplicate any work."

"There's no need to worry about that."

"Oh, no?" *Why not?* Oscar wondered. He already felt a bit foolish in front of Mrs. Larson if he was asking her the same questions. "She mentioned he planned to talk to her some more but never did."

"That's my understanding." Helleson's voice remained flat.

Something didn't sound right to Oscar.

"Do you know why?"

"I don't," Helleson said. "He never finished his assignment."

"How come?" It all sounded mysterious to him.

"The man in question never returned to work at Aerosource."

This made no sense. "What do you mean, never returned?"

"Meaning we've had no contact with him since he left for the island."

*　　*　　*

Oscar stepped out of Tides Hotel onto Main Street and looked up and down what accounted for the island's business district, on the lookout for a spot to eat.

Kidney Island had a population of only a little over one thousand year-round residents, but the summer tourist season boosted it to more than double that. A lot of that were day-trippers who took the morning ferry over to spend the day and then return on the early evening ferry. With the exception of private boats, it remained the only way to reach the island.

Other summer visitors came from anywhere for a week or two, or the whole summer, either renting cottages and homes on Vrbo or Airbnb, or staying at one of the three bed & breakfast inns or the town's only hotel, the Tides, which overlooked the harbor and featured two dozen rooms.

The only actual town on the island went by the name Loch Raven and featured a small village center at the crux of the harbor. The ocean flowed through a small inlet under Main Street and created a large basin on the other side officially named Loch Raven, but most of the natives referred to it as the Basin. It became a popular spot for kayakers and canoeists who sometimes paddled alongside swimming seals. Rocky outcroppings dotted the perimeter of the basin, often lined with fishing enthusiasts. These were mostly the tourists, as the true fishermen and women on the island, who made a living out of it, took off early in the morning in the many boats in the harbor and didn't return till late in the day with the spoils of their catch: lobsters, cod, haddock and salmon. Fishing remained the lifeblood of most of the island natives though their numbers dwindled.

Along Main Street were businesses the natives needed, the food market, bakery, bank, post office, hardware store, beverage center and bait shop. The rest of the shops catered to the tourists, with gift shops, boutiques, candy and ice cream parlor, bookstore and an art gallery. Only four eateries existed on the island that served both natives and tourists alike and in the summer it often became difficult to get a seat in one of them. The islanders were caught in a dilemma where the summer tourism kept the downtown businesses thriving, though year-round residents couldn't wait for vacation season to end so it would be easier to snag a table at their favorite food joint.

The eateries on the island were the Pizza Pit, the Homeport Diner, the Porthole, and the Raven's Bar & Grill, which served as the only drinking establishment.

The Porthole was across the street from the Tides, so that's where Oscar headed with an aching in the pit of his stomach. He wanted to think it was hunger, but something remained unsettled in his gut since his phone conversation with Helleson. It bothered him that Helleson hadn't told him about the previous investigator. But it concerned him more that the man had disappeared, and worse, that Helleson appeared nonchalant about it.

Was Helleson hiding something? He should have been up front with Oscar. Oscar felt deceived. And what had happened to the investigator? Helleson said the man never reported back to the company. So, either something happened to him on the island...*or what?* Did he just decide to quit his job and not return? And how much information did he get from the neighbors of the turbines? Melody Larson said he never came back to finish the interviews. *What stopped him?*

So many questions.

No wonder his stomach ached.

The Porthole featured a lot of exposed beams and a floor of wide pine boards. Circular tables filled the dining room. A screened-in porch wrapped around the left and back side of the long low building, looking out over the inlet and the Basin respectively. A long counter with stools ran along the right side of the restaurant separating the kitchen from the main dining room.

The place was crowded and the hostess told him he could grab a seat at the counter. There was only one available and he took it. He would have preferred grabbing a table, but a line of people had already begun building up by the door and it felt unnecessary to occupy a whole table for just himself.

Oscar took a stool in the middle of the counter, glad his thin frame allowed him to ease in between two burly men who smelled of fish. He noticed glances cast his way and suspected his olive-colored skin must be a sight not often spotted in these parts. It was certainly more than the usual summer tan of a tourist. His research on the island before the trip informed him that its population was ninety-six per cent white. It shouldn't have surprised him, considering most of the native islanders probably descended throughout the years from the original inhabitants. He had hoped to blend in with the population so his investigations wouldn't arouse curiosity, but that hardly seemed possible given the circumstances.

He opened the menu and glanced over its offerings, with seafood occupying the majority of the items. *When in Rome,* he thought, which then made him wonder if he should have gone to the Pizza Pit instead. His stomach rumbled and now he understood it must be hunger and not the uneasiness of the day's situation.

It had been a long ride up the New England coast from Boston and he only stopped once, around lunchtime to grab something to eat. He stopped in the town of Wiscasset, Maine, on Route 1, where someone at his office recommended he get the lobster roll at Red's Eats. The place was a popular tiny shoebox seafood shack with an outdoor patio larger than the place itself. He got the lobster roll, which overflowed a toasted hot dog bun and tasted fantastic, but certainly hadn't helped his wave of nausea on the ferry ride to Kidney Island.

When he had checked into his room at the Tides Hotel, he had to lie down on his bed for a while to allow his stomach to settle. It didn't help though that the water running from the harbor through the inlet into the Basin actually flowed beneath the hotel where the whole east wing was supported by stilts over the inlet. As he lay there trying to stem the tide of nausea, the actual tide flowed out of the Basin under his room, and though he couldn't feel it, the sound of the sloshing water did not comfort him at all.

His stomach felt fine now, and famished, so he settled on the haddock dinner with a baked potato. As he waited for his order, he reflected on the day, satisfied that even after the long journey, he'd managed already to make contact with one of the families involved in the complaints against Aerosource and happy Melody Larson agreed to let him continue talking to them in the morning.

At least in the early part of the day, he'd get to observe this effect of shadow flicker and have more of an idea of what it was all about. From his research, he gathered the most common complaints were sleep loss, headaches and depression. But with everything he learned from Helleson, the turbines met the thousand-foot setback from residential areas required by law, so he was not sure what the neighbors and their attorney hoped to achieve except maybe some kind of settlement for the aggravation they seemed to endure. It surprised Oscar that Aerosource hadn't already offered the neighbors a cash settlement to make the whole issue go away. It wasn't like they could expect Aerosource to tear the turbines down. From what he read, the three turbines provided more than enough energy to supply the entire island with electricity. In fact, the town managed to be able to sell off the excess energy generated to one of the neighboring islands.

It was nothing but a benefit for Kidney Island, as long as you weren't one of the unlucky ones to live near the turbines.

CHAPTER FIVE

Tatum Gallagher lived next door to Melody Larson's family, although next door on Haven Road did not mean one could see the next house up the winding road since the homes were spread out along the rolling pastures. Tatum's house, its days as a farm long gone, sat between the Larsons' and the Granberrys'.

Tatum slept alone in bed and did not hear the man who slipped into her darkened home. Her teenage son was sleeping over at a friend's house, leaving Tatum alone. As she lay comfortably in bed, the man entered her room quietly and gazed down at her.

The open bedroom window let in a slight breeze that stirred the curtains, but also allowed the hum of the wind turbines to enter. The man pulled the covers off Tatum, revealing her naked pale body glistening in the shadows. Her red hair billowed out, tumbling over the edges of the pillow. He smiled as he undressed, and then slipped into bed beside her.

Tatum squirmed, and then her eyes slit open as warm hands caressed her flesh.

"I didn't think you were coming," she said, her voice stirred from sleep; her eyelids fluttered. She grasped on to the man.

"I can't stay long," he whispered into her ear in a breathy voice. "Rigby's not here, right?" he asked about her son.

"No," she said, still stirring from her rest. "I told you, he's staying at a friend's house."

"Good." The man pulled her body tight to his. "Then there's no need for us to be quiet."

"Oh, Myles."

When their lovemaking romp ended, and Myles pulled out of her, she clutched at him as he rose from the bed, but he slipped from her grasp and began to get dressed. Tatum looked up at him, admiring, even in the dark, the silver streaks that caressed the sides of his dark hair.

"I wish you could stay," she said.

"I do too." He leaned down and kissed her full on the mouth. "But you know I can't."

And just as quietly as he entered the house, he slipped out.

★   ★   ★

Up the road, Melody Larson lay in her bed, awake as usual, when she heard a noise from the front of the house. She sat up. A door? Footsteps? She glanced at the clock and noticed it was eleven twenty-three. Late. Both her children were asleep upstairs. She wanted to be asleep, but knew that was unlikely.

Her window also remained open, trying to cool off the hot August night, but it still wouldn't allow sleep to come. Not with the sound of the turbines.

Her bedroom door opened and she lay back down, closed her eyes and pretended to be asleep. She opened her eyes enough to see the shadowy figure beside the bed. He undressed and slipped quietly under the sheets beside her.

"You got out late," she said to her husband.

"Couldn't be avoided," Myles said. "The store needed help with inventory." He rolled over so his back faced her and in a few minutes she heard his soft breathing as sleep overtook him.

Melody lay there, eyes open, staring at the dark ceiling and listening to the humming from outside.

CHAPTER SIX

Oscar didn't understand what he was dealing with until he saw it firsthand in the morning. On his way to the Darrow farm, he stopped at the end of the driveway near their farm stand and stared out his windshield.

The rays of the sun moved across the sky till they met the spinning propellers of the turbines and were sliced into slivers of light. They swept across the entire sky before him, long sweeping stripes of shadows, one followed by another in a constant strobe-like effect, reflecting off the leaves of the trees and racing across the grassy pastures. With the car window down, he heard the drone of the turbines, a low grinding hum whose vibrations he swore he could feel penetrate his inner ears.

As he continued down the driveway, he spotted a man watching him near a tractor in the middle of a grove of trees. Oscar pulled up in front of the home, and noticed how the shadows fell across the whole house, beating on it like a drum. All the blinds were closed on the windows.

Melody answered the door when he knocked, her face a twist of knots.

"You've picked a good time," she said. Her voice sounded tired.

Oscar stepped into the dark home. "This is when you said to come."

Melody led him to the living room. Bursts of light and shadow shot through the spaces in the blinds, causing him to involuntarily blink. He actually raised a hand to his forehead to shield his eyes to no avail.

"This is...." he started.

"The flicker," she finished. "It's just begun. As soon as the sun is up enough to hit the blades of the turbines."

He already felt a little dizzy as he scanned the room. A small boy sat on the couch smiling.

"This is my son, Troy," she said.

"Hello," Oscar said to the boy, who only smiled. Oscar turned to Melody. "How long does this go on for?"

She shrugged. "It depends on the time of the year. Usually a few hours, till the sun gets high enough to be clear of the blades."

Being in the room for only a few minutes was enough for him to realize how irritating it was; he couldn't imagine being there for several hours. "And outside?"

"Did you see for yourself?" she asked.

He nodded. "I just wondered if being in the sunshine made it slightly tolerable."

Once again she shrugged. "Just a different kind of annoyance." She took a seat on the couch near her son, who leaned into her. He looked about ten.

Oscar took out his notebook and sat in a cushioned chair opposite the couch, the blinds of the front window behind him. "Can I ask him a few questions?"

"Okay," Melody said.

Oscar clicked the end of his ballpoint pen. "Mind if I turn this light on?" he asked, motioning to a lamp on a table beside the chair.

"Be my guest."

He turned the small black knob and the light came on but shed little brightness into the room, obscured as the shadows continued to sweep across the room followed by the flickering flashes of light.

"How can we expect to live like this?" Melody said.

"I understand."

"Do you?" Her eyebrows arched.

God, her face looked drawn, he thought, looking even less attractive than he noticed the day before. "I do," he said and nodded.

She flashed half a smile.

"I want to help, if I can," he said, and meant it. He looked at the boy, who still smiled. "Troy," he began. "What do you think of all this?" He waved his pen around.

"Sometimes it makes me laugh."

It wasn't the reaction he'd been expecting. "How so?" He could barely withhold a smile himself.

The boy glanced up at his mother, who glared down at him with an irritated stare. Obviously that wasn't the answer she wanted him to give.

Troy looked back at Oscar. "It makes the birds dance."

Oscar shifted his gaze to Melody, and then back at the boy. "Birds dance?" He didn't understand.

"The seagulls," the boy said, as if that answered it.

"What about the seagulls?"

The boy turned to his mother.

"Tell him," she urged.

"The seagulls get caught in the shadows, and they dance all crazy like."

Oscar looked at Melody for help.

"He's said it before," she said. "I don't quite know what to make of it." She glanced down at her hands in her lap. Troy grasped one in his own. "I don't go outside myself until it's finished."

Oscar stared back at Troy. "But you go outside and play during the flicker?"

The boy nodded. "It's when I see the birds."

"Not all the time," Melody corrected.

"No," Troy agreed. "Just sometimes."

"And what do these seagulls do?"

Before Troy could answer, the door burst open.

Oscar rose as the man strode in, noticing the stern expression his face held, gray eyes taking him in. He stood over six feet tall, broad shoulders, tanned rugged features and streaks of gray along the sides of his short dark hair that looked a bit mussed.

"This is my husband, Myles," Melody said, still seated on the couch.

"Hello," Oscar said, and introduced himself with an offer of a hand. The man took it with reluctance and Oscar felt the callous roughness of the firm grip against his own smooth palm.

Oscar remained standing. "I explained to your wife what I'm doing here."

"She told me," Myles said. He turned to his son. "Troy, why don't you go outside and play, get some fresh air."

The boy didn't say a word, but with a smile on his face, hopped up off the couch and ran out of the room. The front door slammed.

"I don't mean to intrude." Oscar felt uncomfortable. Surely Mrs. Larson would have said something if her husband objected to his being here.

Myles shot him an intense glare. "Where are you from?"

Oscar halted. "Boston."

"No, I mean where do you come from?" The man's expression remained rigid.

Oscar thought he understood what the man was getting at and maybe should have expected something like this on an island without any diversity.

"Turkey," he answered.

Myles looked baffled, his eyes narrowing, and then shook the confusion from his head.

"No," Myles said. "I meant what company sent you?"

"Oh." Oscar felt foolish now and gave a half laugh. "I work for Freedom Insurance."

The man studied him. "You don't work for Aerosource?"

"I told you he didn't," Melody said. Oscar had nearly forgotten she still remained on the couch in the room.

"Not exactly," Oscar tried to explain. "My insurance company has Aerosource as a client. I'm here representing their interests in the claim against them, just to gather information about the issues you're having with them."

The whole time during the conversation, the stripes of shadow and light continued to flicker throughout the room, giving it the appearance of some fun house exhibit. That along with the nervous feeling that crept into his body, caused Oscar to blink periodically.

Myles waved his arms around the room. "You can see for yourself, can't you?"

Oscar nodded as he glanced about. "Yes, and I'm quite amazed. I understand your annoyance."

"It's much more than an annoyance," Myles said. He gestured to

Melody. "My wife can't sleep. She can't stand being inside or outside during it. Her father has trouble concentrating and now doesn't come out of his room until it's over." He took a deep breath. "And of course it's never over. Even when the flicker is gone, there's still the noise."

"Noise?" Oscar said and jotted this down in his notepad.

"It's not loud," Myles said, shrugging.

"No," Melody agreed.

"But it's constant." He pointed his right index finger to the back of his ear. "It's a low drone that never stops unless the blades aren't turning. A kind of grinding sound that drills its way into your skull." He gritted his teeth as he spoke.

"Do the blades stop?" Oscar asked, thinking in just the two days he'd been on the island, he'd always observed them spinning.

Myles chuckled, but not a cheerful sound, and glanced at his wife. She dropped her eyes. He looked back at Oscar.

"When the wind isn't blowing, the blades stop," he said. Then he flashed a mad grin. "This is a small island. Nothing but ocean surrounds us. There is always an ocean breeze."

Oscar nodded, taking that as a no, and jotted it down in his notes.

"It does stop," Melody said softly, and her husband glared down at her. She raised her head.

"It does?" Oscar asked.

"Sometimes." She glanced away from them, as if her eyes were drawn by some intrusion. "They slow down at times and then come to a stop." Her voice faded. "But even when they do, I still hear the noise in my head."

"It's rare," Myles said to Oscar. "But yeah, it does."

"Tatum's seen it," Melody said.

Again her husband shot her a stern look.

"Is that your daughter?" Oscar asked.

"No," Myles emphasized. "Neighbor."

Oscar remembered the notes he prepared beforehand on the other people involved in the claim against Aerosource. "Oh right, Mrs. Gallagher and her husband."

"Not husband," Myles said. "Not married."

"Might as well be," Melody responded. "Common-law marriage. They've been together for nearly twenty years."

"Dirk Lassiter," Myles added. "They live on the next farm down the road with their son."

"Two sons," Melody corrected in a drifting voice. "They have two boys."

It seemed like Melody would fall asleep. Even in the shadowy light, her eyes looked heavy.

"They lost a boy, Nathan," Myles said. "Last summer. Drowned while fishing on the north coast, place called Crooked Cove. Troy and he were best friends."

Melody looked up at them with sad eyes. "Don't know for sure he's gone."

Oscar was confused.

"They never found his body," she said.

"Washed away," Myles added. "Very choppy waters that day. Constable figures a wave swept him right off the edge of the rocks and took him out to sea. Only found his fishing pole and tackle box." He dipped his head at the thought.

"That's terrible," Oscar said. "Troy must have taken it very hard."

"Yes." Myles nodded. "We all did."

"They didn't find his body," Melody repeated.

Myles lowered his voice so his wife wouldn't hear. "It'll wash up one day, or get hauled up by a fisherman."

Oscar noticed Melody's shoulders slump, and he assumed she heard anyway.

"I hoped to talk to Ms. Gallagher," Oscar said, "but I don't want to intrude on her grieving."

"Maybe that's best," Myles said.

"She'll talk," Melody offered. Her wet eyes gazed up. "She has things she'd like to say."

"Melody," Myles said. "It might be best to leave her be."

Melody shook her head, dark hair bobbing. "She can tell you some very interesting things." It sounded like a plea.

Oscar nodded, but didn't say anything. He wanted to talk to Tatum Gallagher, but sensed the discouragement from Myles Larson, so decided to let it be for now and take care of it on his own. He didn't need these people's permission.

"I hope to talk to the Granberrys too," he said, looking at his notes. "They have a farm down the road as well?"

"Yes," Myles said. "But you may find people here not quite willing to open up to you, considering."

"Considering?" Oscar didn't know what that meant. Because he represented Aerosource?

"You're an off-islander," Myles said. "People here tolerate them in the summer, but that's about it. We're a tight-knit group here. But we don't have a great deal of trust in off-islanders."

"I see," Oscar said. "I just want to be able to document all the problems everyone is having, so maybe there can be a reasonable resolution."

"Take them down," Myles said. "That's the resolution."

Oscar knew that wouldn't happen. *How ironic,* he thought, that it was this family that sold the land to Aerosource for them to build their wind turbines. Didn't have problems dealing with off-islanders then.

"I only plan to be around for a few days, just to get what information I can for my company. Freedom Insurance," he stressed.

"You can talk to me and my wife, but I'd rather you leave the kids alone," Myles said.

"Fair enough," Oscar said. "And what about Mr. Darrow?" he said to Melody. "I'd certainly like a chance to speak to your father."

Melody shrugged. "Maybe later in the day. He rests during...." she looked up and waved her hands around. "During all this."

"Okay. Maybe I can stop by later this afternoon."

"Fine," Myles said, the word coming out exasperated.

"Thank you for your time," Oscar said to both of them.

Myles walked him to the door. Oscar thought the man would follow him out of the house and to his vehicle, but he didn't. Outside the shadows continued to fan down over him as he looked up at the turbines in the distance, looking tall and white like alien machines. Staring at them he noticed the blades on all three towers turned at different rotations. For some reason he thought they would be in unison.

He continued staring, sensing an almost hypnotic effect from the spinning. He pulled his gaze away with some difficulty. As he got in his car, he realized that if he didn't pay attention, he couldn't really hear the noise from the turbines, but now that he concentrated, the low hum drifted down off the hill and into his ears.

Oscar shrugged, started the car, turned around in the driveway and headed out. He spotted Troy on a tire swing hanging from the limb of a giant maple tree beside the long driveway. The boy waved at him and he stopped and rolled down his window.

"It was nice meeting you, Troy," he said.

The boy smiled. "Thank you, mister."

"Call me Oscar." He looked up at the shadows floating across the sky behind the tree and the boy's gaze followed. "Thank you for telling me about the dancing birds."

"They ain't out today," Troy said.

"That's too bad. I'd like to see them."

"That's not the only thing I see in the flicker," Troy said.

"Oh no?" Oscar was curious. "What else do you see?"

"My friend, Nathan."

Oscar blinked. "From next door?"

Troy nodded. "They said he drowned. But I don't think so. I see him sometimes, in the flicker. I think he's stuck there."

CHAPTER SEVEN

"What do you think, Doc?" Barrett Granberry asked as the veterinarian withdrew the blood sample from Myrtle's rear and capped the tube before he placed the vial in a plastic holder and transferred it to his black bag.

Doc looked at him and shrugged.

"It's not mad cow, is it?" Letty asked, her face ruined with worry.

The trio sat around the cow in its stall in the barn. The vet had patched up the cut on Myrtle's snout – it turned out to be a fairly minor laceration – and given the cow a full examination before taking the blood samples.

"I don't think so," Doc said, "but won't know for sure till the lab work gets done." He gazed around the barn. "In the meantime, I'd be sure to keep her away from the rest of the herd. Don't let her mingle with them till I can figure this out." He pulled off his plastic gloves and scratched the back of his head. "Don't see any obvious signs."

Barrett exhaled a deep breath.

"What about the calf?" Letty asked, glancing down at Myrtle's full belly.

"If I didn't know better," the doc said, "I'd say you've got a ways to go. But I know that can't be right." He scratched his head again, as if it made him think better, or if a horsefly had crawled under his gray mat of hair. "She been eating all right?"

Barrett pouted. "Her feed ain't been going down as much as before."

Letty gazed at her husband. "You know why."

The old man shook his head.

"Something else going on?" Doc asked as he packed his bag.

The three of them stood up. Barrett closed the gate to the stall and they left the barn. When they stepped out into the open, the flicker of shadows fell upon them.

"It's that!" Letty said and pointed toward the turbines beyond the pasture.

The shadows swept over the field where the cows grazed.

Doc looked across the field at them and then turned to the Granberrys with a worried look. Without a word he strode across the lawn to the pasture with Barrett and Letty in tow. When Doc reached some of the nearest cows, he halted, as he scanned the animals. He approached one and brushed a hand along the flank of the cow.

He turned to face the Granberrys. "Your cows look malnourished," he said.

Barrett cleared his throat and spat. "They haven't been grazing much."

"I swear that damn flickering disrupts their feeding," Letty said, squinting into the flicker.

"Messes them up, it does," Barrett added.

Doc looked back at the cows and then up into the strobe of shadows flowing over the pasture.

He didn't say a word.

CHAPTER EIGHT

After leaving the Darrow farm, Oscar drove down Haven Road, amazed by how little his sunglasses did to thwart the strobe-like effect coming through his windshield. He reached up and pulled the visor down over the windshield, though it didn't help much either. He drove slowly until he got to the next house and pulled into the driveway.

When he stopped, he opened his notebook and glanced at what he had written in his notes: *Tatum Gallagher, Dirk Lassiter and their teenage son, Rigby.* Next to the note on their son, Nathan, he had written the word: *Deceased.*

Oscar got out of the car and approached the front porch, stepped up onto it and paused at the door. A brass knocker clung to the door. He grabbed it and rapped it down three times. The hollow sound echoed around the quiet home.

No. Not quite.

His ears picked up the low thrum of the turbines in the distance, subtle, but letting him know they were there.

He waited patiently, hands clasping his notebook and rocking back and forth on his heels. He looked over the doorframe, hoping to spot a doorbell, but saw none, so he knocked again, louder. When the last of the echoes from the knock disappeared into the warm breeze, he heard another sound. Laughter.

Oscar stepped off the porch and looked left, across the yard. Beyond the ruins of a former greenhouse, three teenage boys sat in lawn chairs about fifty yards away from the house, their chairs facing the wind turbines in the distance. The shadows of the blades swept across them in a steady pace. He heard them laugh again.

As he walked toward the boys, who seemed unaware of his approach, he sensed an odor wafting toward him, pushed along by the breeze. The smell of pot. He noticed the boys passing a joint amongst them, the sound of sucking air as each one took turns inhaling.

"No one's home," one of the boys said, making him realize they did hear his approach.

The others chuckled.

The boy in the middle seat turned to look back at him. "My parents are working."

Oscar came up alongside the boys, so they wouldn't have to crane their necks.

"You must be Rigby Lassiter," he said to the boy in the middle.

"Guilty as charged," Rigby said, laughing out a wave of smoke before passing the joint to the kid next to him with blond hair down past his cheeks. "These are my buds."

They all broke out laughing at his unintended pun.

The three of them wore sunglasses and as they took turns taking tokes on the joint, they stared up toward the turbines and the splintered rays of sun beaming behind the whirling blades. Rigby's hair was dark as night with thick waves that nipped the tops of his ears.

"My name's Oscar Basaran. I'm with Freedom Insurance Company." He felt no need to explain any further to teens he knew wouldn't care anyway. "I was trying to catch your parents."

"Mom works down at the market," Rigby said, passing the joint to a skinny kid with a buzz cut on his left. "Dad's out on the boat."

"The boat?"

"Lobstering." He got the joint back and he sucked the last intake from the small tip that remained. "He's a fisherman." He laughed. "He goes out fishing." He paused. "Every day." He put down the roach, and took out another joint from a small plastic bag on the ground beneath his chair. He lit it up and took a deep inhale, then passed it to the blond boy. "Besides, he don't live here right now."

"Oh?"

Rigby turned to look up at him. "They're kind of on the splits right now." He shrugged. "Probably just for the moment. They do this a lot."

"I'm sorry to hear that." Oscar thought of his own split from Kyle and knew how much it sucked. And they didn't even have kids involved. He pondered the fact that this couple just lost a child last summer. He'd heard that the death of a child often breaks apart a family.

"Are you trying to sell them some insurance?" Rigby asked, a spacey look on his face.

"No, just wanted to ask them some questions about a health claim they're involved in."

"I don't know anything about that," Rigby said, resting his head back in his chair.

"Want a hit, man?" the buzz cut kid said, hoisting the joint up toward him.

Oscar shook his head. "No thanks." He watched the kids as they continued passing the new joint. *Summer must be boring for teens on the island,* he thought. Nowhere to go. He stood in silence wondering why they were sitting there, staring out toward the turbines. "What are you guys doing?"

All three broke out in laughter, smoke billowing around their heads. Rigby raised his right hand and kind of danced it around in the air in front of him.

"Oh, man," he said. "You gotta try this." He took a puff. "We get high and get flickered." He giggled.

"Flickered?"

"Yeah," the blond kid said. "It's the best way to watch the flicker."

"It's such a trip," Buzz Cut said.

"Out of this world," Rigby added.

Oscar nodded, dumbfounded, but fascinated. "Do you do this every day?"

"Every chance we get," Rigby said and laughed so hard he almost fell out of his chair.

Oscar had enough of the wayward youths. He told Rigby he'd try and catch his mother another time and walked off.

"I'll tell her you stopped by," Rigby said and the three boys burst into laughter again.

Oscar got back to his car and drove off.

Farther down the road he pulled into the Granberrys' driveway shortly after the veterinarian left. The old couple stood outside their barn as Oscar exited his vehicle and approached.

"Hello," he said and extended a hand.

Barrett Granberry stared at the offered hand as if it were some diseased organ.

Oscar withdrew his hand and explained to the old couple who he was and his reasons for wanting to talk to them.

"Freedom Insurance?" Barrett said, brow furrowed, and then looked at Letty with a quizzical gawk. "We make some claim with Freedom Insurance?"

"No," his wife said, not taking her eyes from Oscar. "Never heard of them. Where are you from, mister?"

"Boston," Oscar said. "I know you didn't make a claim with Freedom. Our company represents Aerosource, who you did make a claim against. I'm just gathering information before we can make any kind of payments."

"Payments," Barrett huffed. "Who said we wanted payments?"

"Well, I know—"

The old man cut him off. "Take those down," he said, and pointed behind him toward the turbines in the distance. "That's all we want."

"I understand—"

"I don't think you do, sonny." He crossed his arms in defiance.

"None of that's for me to decide."

"Then why are we even talking to you?" Letty asked.

Oscar felt frustrated. "I'm just gathering information. So we can all better understand the problems everyone here is having."

The pair stared at him with grim faces and did not respond.

Oscar sighed. "If I could just have a few minutes of your time to ask some questions."

"We ain't got time," Barrett said. "This is a farm. We got work to do." He turned to leave.

"Could I just tag along and talk while you work? I promise not to be a bother."

Barrett turned back to glare at him. "Mister, you're already a bother."

As he started to walk away, Letty said something that stopped him in his tracks.

"Tell him about Ash."

Oscar watched the old man's shoulders hunch and then he turned to look back, first at his wife, and then at him. "Come along," he said. "You'll need to keep up with me."

Relieved but still a bit nervous, Oscar followed the old man into the barn. Barrett grabbed a small wooden stool and a bucket and brought it over to one of the cows. He set the stool down and settled onto it. With the bucket on the ground underneath, the old man started stroking the sides of the cow's udder. Then he grabbed one of the cow's teats, clamping the top of it just below the udder between the crux of his thumb and index finger. He did the same with his left hand and began gently squeezing till streams of milk jetted out into the pail. Oscar stood by and watched, amazed at the sight. He hadn't realized there were farmers still doing this by hand.

As Barrett worked milking some of the cows, he spun a story about an old horse they used to have. Ash was a male American Quarter Horse about twenty-seven years old, with a dull black coat that inspired his name. He had been born on the farm and when he was a foal they used him to give rides to kids at school fairs and other such events. As he got older, Letty gave riding lessons to young girls and the occasional boy, but mostly it was the girls who wanted to learn how to ride. She had even given Tatum Gallagher lessons when their next-door neighbor was about twelve.

But as the horse got older, and Letty, the Granberrys decided Ash could just live out his later years roaming the paddock. A saddle hadn't touched his back in at least eight years. Ash was content and deserved it.

Things changed though after the wind turbines went up, Barrett said. Neither he nor Letty had anticipated the problems it would cause. The flicker came as a surprise. Barrett remembered waking up early one morning just before sunrise to make the coffee. As the sun slid up from behind the hills to the north, flashes of light and shadow began bombarding the house. He remembered yelling out for Letty, who was in the bathroom, and she came running. The two of them stood in the kitchen, looking at each other with astonished expressions.

"Letty thought a UFO was hovering over the whole dang farmhouse," Barrett said. "It scared the crap out of us at first." He shrugged. "Now we expect it as a part of our daily routine." He squinted at Oscar. "Not that I don't detest it any less." He spat.

That morning when he went to take Ash out of his stall in the barn, Barrett got as far as the open door when that old horse reared back, rising up on his rear legs, front legs batting the air as if in defense.

"Spooked him good, that flickering did," Barrett said. "I had to pull him by the reins just to get him outside that first day. Hard as dickens. Didn't think I'd make it to the paddock with him, but I managed somehow." He shook his head. "Boy, he ran around inside there, not knowing which way to go. Took him a while, but he finally settled down."

Still, he continued, every day he didn't want to go outside. "Can't say I blame him. Took me and the missus a while to get used to that dang thing. The noise I barely hear anymore, but then my hearing ain't what it used to be."

He said he thought about leaving Ash in the barn until the sun rose above the turbine's reach, but he knew it wasn't good to keep the old boy penned up so long. Still....

"It broke my heart every day to see poor Ash, roaming around in the paddock, every now and then galloping back and forth like he was running from the devil." He spat again.

Barrett said he shouldn't have continued bringing him outside and had just about decided that he wouldn't do it anymore. Let the poor boy stay in the barn till later in the day. But he made that decision one day too late.

The last day he let Ash out of the barn and led him to the paddock, he could see something in the horse's eyes. Not fright, not sadness, they just looked empty.

Barrett had just come out of the barn that day after a round of milking, when he saw Ash running madly back and forth in the paddock. He called to Letty, who came out of the house and stood beside him.

"Bring him back in, Barrett," she said, and he began making his way to the paddock. But before he got there, the old boy ran straight for the back end of the paddock and leapt over the fence.

His eyes locked on Oscar's. "Mister, that old boy hadn't jumped over anything in the last twelve years. But dang it if he didn't kick his legs hard enough to leap clean over that fence." And he kept going, he said. He and Letty ran after Ash, calling him, but that horse ran like the wind.

Barrett had to get his pickup and head north along some of the conservation land roads, but he couldn't pick up Ash's trail. He had gone north and the island wasn't that big. Where could he go? So Barrett came back to the farm and called the constable, just to make him aware. He and Letty figured Ash would turn up somewhere, eventually. It would only be a matter of time. They'd probably hear from a neighbor or something, about poor old Ash wandering around in their yard.

Every time the phone rang the next day, they ran for it in anticipation that it was to say Ash was found. And then one of those times, it was.

Barrett took a handkerchief out of his back pocket and wiped his damp eyes.

"They found poor Ash down among the rocks at the bottom of Crooked Cove." He placed the bandana back in his pocket. "He must have leapt right off the cliff above, to end up in that spot." He looked hard into Oscar's eyes. "What in god's name would make a horse do something crazy like that?"

Oscar didn't know what to say. There was nothing he could say. The whole time he didn't even jot any notes down in his notepad, only listened to the old man's story.

Then Barrett looked over his shoulder, back toward the spinning blades of the turbines and the shadows dancing across his pasture.

CHAPTER NINE

Rigby Lassiter stood with his toes at the edge of the granite and curled them around the lip as if to get a firm grip on the rock before staring down at the greenish hue of the water far below. Exhilaration swept through his body from those toes all the way up the muscles of his legs, swirling around his spine like a whirlpool and eventually tickling the back of his neck.

His body shivered, but that could have been the light breeze in the air that always hung over Kidney Island no matter how hot the August day felt. But Rigby knew that more than the chill caused the goose pimples along the flesh of his bare arms and shoulders. It was the precipice he stood on at the moment and the apprehension about what he planned to do.

He thought the pot he and his buddies smoked earlier in the day would be enough to settle his nerves, but here he stood about to take the plunge he often pledged to commit. The others watched, so he couldn't step away from the edge.

Kidney Island drew a fair amount of tourists in the summer for different reasons. More than half of the island had been committed to conservation land and several moderate hiking trails threaded through the northern portion of the land, offering encounters with a variety of vegetation, gentle wildlife, and fantastic scenic views. A couple of small hills on either end of the island gave more enthusiastic hikers the opportunity to climb to the highest points and look back at the spectacular landscape of the interior. The Basin gave kayakers and canoeists a chance to paddle alongside seals that swam from the harbor under the Main Street bridge and into the large body of water on the other side.

Other tourists came for the serenity of renting one of the houses or cottages that rimmed the coastline and rented bikes for touring some of the local roads. But what tourists didn't come for on the island was a beach.

Because there weren't any. Well, technically, there existed an official state beach on the island. But it was a beach that didn't offer any sand.

The Kidney Island beach consisted of a gravel crescent on the south-eastern shore, not the ideal spot for anyone looking to lie out on a beach towel in the sun unless they didn't mind small rocks digging into their backside. The constant breeze whipping around the island didn't help matters much. And of course the ocean water, even in the height of the summer heat, felt much too cold to be even remotely refreshing.

So if someone did want to enjoy sun and a refreshing swim, they came to where Rigby now stood, the old granite quarry off the appropriately named Granite Road. It hadn't been in operation since the early 1900s, having one time been one of the world's biggest suppliers of granite, and time had now turned it into a freshwater swimming hole.

The rumor had been that around 1907, the crews digging and cutting granite out of the quarry had gone down several hundred feet by that time and finally hit groundwater. Once that happened, the quarry flooded and the crews had to scramble out of the hole, leaving behind equipment and even a couple construction vehicles.

How much truth existed in the story, Rigby had no clue, but most of the island natives believed the story and passed it along. Rigby's friend Evan, the boy with the buzzed haircut, had sworn that earlier in the summer he dove into the quarry from this very same spot and touched the tip of a winch on one of the vehicles.

Rigby didn't know whether to believe him, but if anybody could do it, Evan would be the one. He planned to join the service when he got out of high school, one of the reasons he kept his hair cut military style. He obsessed over the military and wanted to eventually join one of the Special Forces, like the Navy Seals or Green Berets. The dive to the bottom of the quarry had been a challenge to prove he had what it takes.

And now he had challenged Rigby. Why? Rigby didn't know for sure. Evan could have easily goaded Max Pickett, the boy with the long stringy blond hair. But for some reason the target had fallen on Rigby and now he stood at the edge of the highest point on the granite wall on the western end of the quarry near the road.

Off to the left side of the water, the granite formed a wide smooth surface where other sunbathers stretched out on blankets, towels and beach chairs. A series of cut blocks between where Rigby stood and the sunbathers lay led down into the quarry like a set of granite steps. Swimmers walked down these steps into the water, adjusting to the coolness of it before the steps abruptly ended and the bottom could no longer be felt.

Rigby wished he could be over there instead, with the other swimmers who waded off the small lips of granite that rimmed that side of the quarry and splashed around in the water. But no, he had come up here to the high point with Evan and Max. After Evan dove in and climbed back up the rocks to the upper perch, he waited for Rigby's turn.

"Anytime now, Lassiter," Evan goaded.

Rigby felt eyes on him from the others lying out on the rocks across the way. He had earlier spotted his next-door neighbor, Whitney Larson, among some of the teenage girls. It wouldn't do to look afraid in front of her or any of the others. He knew she liked him, and though she wasn't his type, he still felt he needed to prove something in front of her. And the guys.

The granite edge dug into the underside of his toes and he felt the bones in his calves begin to tremble. *It's now or never,* he told himself, bending at the knees and hoping his legs had the strength to push off before he collapsed to the ground.

He sucked in a deep breath and launched himself, regretting it the moment his toes lost connection with the granite. His body formed an arc as he brought his arms out in front of him and put his palms together in the sign of a prayer.

And that's what he did all the way down in the air – prayed.

He sliced through the water, feeling its refreshing coolness flow over his shoulders and down his abdomen before swallowing up his legs. He opened his eyes underwater, pumping his arms and kicking his legs as he drove deeper beneath the surface. The water got colder the deeper he swam, the light penetrating from above growing dimmer.

But he could see something down in the murky depths. An outline of something large. *What is that?*

A flash came, like a bolt of heat lightning, and Rigby shook his head.

What the hell?

Pressure enclosed his lungs.

The flash again, and he could see what looked like an old rusty rig below, some kind of enormous truck.

The flashes struck again and again, as if someone were taking pictures with an underwater camera, and the light hurt his eyes and his skull began to squeeze in. He broke his descent by pushing back with his arms, swinging his legs underneath him and beginning to propel himself up toward the surface.

The cold water gripped his legs like a fist and he had trouble kicking them, relying on his arms to push the water down, his lungs struggling, his brain registering that he might be in trouble. The flashing lights continued. The buzz from the pot wore off and his head cleared. *Is this what it's like to die?* The nerves inside his stiffening limbs pulsed.

Air engulfed his lungs as he broke the surface with a wild splash.

Above, Evan and Max looked down from the edge of the cliff. Rigby tried a smile, but it felt more like the wild gape of a madman. For he felt mad trying this. With eyes from around the quarry watching him, he didn't want to display the panic he still felt coursing through his body. The sun from above felt good and warmed his chilled limbs enough that he could manage a slow crawl to the edge of the rocks.

Once there, he clung to the rocks, treading water, not sure if he had the strength to pull himself up onto them. But he wanted to get out of the water now, so he mustered what strength he had left and managed to pull and drag himself up, scraping his knees on the edge of the rocks. He turned and sat, leaning back on his arms and letting his legs dangle over the edge of the rock.

"Nice job!" Evan yelled. Max smiled beside him.

Rigby had the strength to lift one arm and give them a thumbs-up. He wondered if Whitney and the others from the opposite side were watching. He hoped so.

As he sat catching his breath before thinking of climbing up the cliff to join the others, he thought about the flashes of light. *What the hell happened down there?*

It reminded him of something. Something that hadn't happened to him in a very long time.

CHAPTER TEN

When he left the Granberrys, Oscar didn't know what to make of the stories the old farmer told him, especially when he spoke about his pregnant cow bashing its head into a fence post the other day. Did he expect him to believe the turbines drove a horse and a cow into fits of lunacy and attempted suicide, one succeeding?

Oscar knew as soon as he drove off that there was no way he planned to write that up in his report to Mason Helleson. The man would have him escorted out of Aerosource headquarters and probably get Freedom Insurance to fire him.

At the juncture of Haven Road and Crockett Road, he stopped the car, thought for a moment, and then took an unexpected left onto Crockett. He wanted to see the turbines up close. A couple miles up the road, he spotted the turnoff on the left, a well-graded dirt road. He drove slow, following its curve to the left like a big fishhook. At the end he stopped the car and got out.

There they stood.

He tilted his head back and peered up at the giant towers with their slowly spinning blades. The noise was louder here than below, but still only a steady grinding vibration. The propellers twirled in their own rhythm, none of them spinning in unison. It felt hypnotic as he stared up at the blades and he became dizzy for a second and had to pull his eyes away.

The three behemoths stood in a small clearing in a field at the end of the dirt road, a few small shrubs in the perimeter and then a long grassy field that sloped down beyond. He expected some type of outbuilding or something nearby, but there was nothing, only the three towers alone in the middle of nowhere like lonely giants watching over the island.

He thought of the Martian machines in the book, *The War of the*

Worlds, he read as a young boy, and could almost imagine these machines pulling up from the ground and marching down the slope toward the village center, destroying everything in their path along the way.

The three towering turbines were set up in a triangular pattern, with the middle tower out front of the two flanking ones. Oscar walked out past them till he stood in front of the lead tower and looked down the slope toward the farms along Haven Road and the incomplete housing development.

He spotted the Darrow farm, where Melody Larson and her family lived, noticing the cornfields and rows of apple trees looking tiny from up here. To the left of it he could see Tatum Gallagher's home and its decrepit greenhouse, and farther along, the cows that grazed in the Granberrys' pastures. Or, according to Barrett Granberry, they didn't really graze. At least, not as much as they should be.

Oscar looked up over his shoulder at the tower behind him, craning his neck to see its peak. The blades spun and he could feel their power sweeping over him, as if trying to push him away. Could these things really be causing all the problems these people said they did? And he still hadn't finished talking to them all. It didn't seem possible. They looked like lonely sentinels, efficiently working to provide the power the islanders needed.

He looked back down along the breadth of the island. Trees blocked the view of the Loch Raven village center, but he knew it lay down there along the harbor and he could see the great blue sea beyond dotted with the white speckles of fishing boats. It all seemed peaceful from this view, and beautiful.

He reflected about his former partner. Kyle would love this. He, being the more outdoor type, always dragged Oscar on hikes and excursions to Cape Cod where they would lie out among the sand dunes between bouts of bodysurfing along the crashing waves.

Oscar felt his heart squeeze as he sucked in cool air and wondered if Kyle took his new woman to places they used to visit like the Cape. His fingers tensed and he brought them tight into his palms and then extended them. There's no place for resentment, his therapist had told him. It's like taking poison and expecting someone else to die. That life was over, and the time had come for him to push on with a new path.

That's what this trip felt like to him, a chance to recharge and redirect his life. Mason Helleson hadn't given him a timeline to get the job done, so he could spend a reasonable amount of days here and forget the troubles he left back home. For now.

As he turned to head back to his car, he realized something.

For a brief moment, he hadn't been aware of the noise of the turbines, and had to glance up to make sure the blades were still turning. They were. It felt like he had already become accustomed to the sound, that it wasn't even noticeable. But now that he thought about it, the grinding hum crept back into his ears.

His pace quickened as he went back to his car. When he got in, he put up the windows and turned on the AC, before turning his car around and heading back onto Crockett Road and toward town. A man stood astride a bicycle and watched him as he drove by. The man wore sunglasses and a white construction helmet perched atop his head.

Oscar didn't get a good look at the man, but in his rearview mirror he could see him pedal onto the dirt road leading to the turbines. Perhaps the man worked maintenance for the structures. But why on earth was he riding a bicycle?

He shook his head and pushed the man from his thoughts. Once in town, he parked in the municipal lot beside the harbor and walked over to the grocery store that sported the nondescript name of Island Market. He spotted a middle-aged man in a maroon smock near the customer service kiosk of the store and drew his attention.

"I'm looking for Tatum Gallagher."

The man eyed him up and down and then he glanced over toward the registers at the front of the store. "Are you looking for her for any particular reason?" the man asked. The name tag on his shirt said: *Brock*.

Oscar shook his head. "Private matter."

Brock shrugged. "Not sure if she's around today. Haven't seen the schedule." He turned his back and began chatting to the girl behind the service counter.

Oscar drifted off, picked up one of the store's hand baskets from a display and meandered up and down the aisles. He grabbed some items he thought he'd like to have in his room at the hotel. There was a small fridge in the room. He grabbed a bottle of orange juice, a bag of bagels and some cream cheese. He picked up a six-pack of local Maine Allagash White beer and a bag of potato chips along with a premade turkey sandwich from the deli counter.

When he got to the registers, he eyed the two ladies working at them and chose the lane with the woman who had fair skin and thick red hair pulled back in a ponytail. Her name tag said: *Tatum*.

"You're Miss Gallagher," he said as she rung up his sparse purchases. "Up on Haven Road."

She stopped mid-scan and locked eyes with him. "Who's asking?"

"My name's Oscar Basaran. I work for Freedom Insurance. I visited with some of your neighbors earlier today, the Larsons and the Granberrys."

She continued scanning the last of his items and began bagging them in a brown paper bag. "How'd you know I work here?" Her eyes cast suspicion.

"Your son – what was his name?"

"Rigby?"

"That's right." He nodded with a generous smile. "Said I could find you here."

"That's $27.79. Where'd you stumble upon him?"

He dug a couple twenties out of his wallet and pulled out a business card as well, handing it to her with the cash. It depicted a small headshot of himself along with the company name and his title.

"After talking with the Larsons, I stopped at your house. He was outside with some friends."

"Loafing no doubt," she said, scrutinizing his business card. "Insurance investigator?"

"Yes," he said. "I'm talking with all the neighbors about the wind turbines and the ill effects they have on everyone in their vicinity. As part of the claim you've filed along with the rest."

"About time someone does something about those. Aggravating as hell."

He nodded in agreement. "I'm just here to gather information. Is there a chance we could talk sometime? I'm just here for a few days." How long he really didn't know, or care, but he wanted her to think he didn't have much time.

She shrugged. "I guess. I get off at four. You could meet me at the house then, before I have to start dinner for Rigby. And most likely his mooching friends if they're still around."

"That'd be great," he said, taking his change and picking up his bag. "It won't take long. Just want to give you a chance to voice your concerns."

"Oh, I've got plenty of those," she said with a smirk.

"I'll look forward to it," he said and left. He noticed the man he spoke to earlier, Brock, watching him as he walked out the front doors.

⋆   ⋆   ⋆

After putting his purchases in his room at the hotel, Oscar ate his sandwich along with a bottle of the beer and some chips, and then decided to take a stroll around the village shops to kill time before his drive back up Haven Road. He poked around in a couple of the gift shops, looking at knickknacks priced too high, but it made him think of Kyle Devitt and a lot of the trinkets he always liked to buy at shops like these on the Cape, so he left and continued up the street.

He passed a coffee shop and came to a real estate office. Pictures of listings were pasted on the inside of the window and he perused them. A couple of the homes looked like some of the newly built ones up on Haven Road that he had passed earlier. Some were for sale, others for rent. The prices were a lot higher than he'd expect on the island. *Do people really move here to live*, he pondered, *or is it more of a place to retire to and retreat to a simpler life?* He wondered about whether the turbines had driven down the asking prices of the homes.

He decided to go in.

No bell rang over the door as he entered like many of the other shops downtown. A chubby middle-aged woman with a round face topped with a curly mop sat behind the lone desk in the place looking at a computer screen and moving a wireless mouse around a felt pad with her right hand. Young faces of children stared up from the mouse pad.

"Hello," he said, approaching the desk.

She glanced up with a bright smile.

"I hope I'm not interrupting," he added.

She frowned. "Not likely." She turned the flat screen toward him and he saw a display of solitaire on it.

He laughed.

"We don't get real busy around here," she said, her smile breaking over her plump face again. "With Airbnb and Vrbo taking over most of the rental opportunities these days, I have to hope someone wants to move to a small island off the coast where not much goes on."

"Is there a lot of demand for that?"

"I wouldn't be looking for a red queen if there was." She turned the screen back and stood up. "Polly Stark," she said and extended her hand.

"Oscar Basaran." Her hand was soft and cool.

"What's that? Egyptian or something?"

He grinned. "Turkish."

"So what brings you to our fair island? Looking for a summer getaway home?" She looked hopeful.

"Sorry to disappoint you. Mostly just curious."

Her lips tightened. "What about?"

He explained about the insurance firm he worked for and his investigation about the effects the turbines were having on a small group of islanders. "I was wondering about the development along Haven Road that seems to be at a standstill. And some homes out that way look –" He wanted to say *abandoned*, but chose wiser. "– vacated."

She nodded. "Yes, Pickett Fences Estates," she said. "Gavin Pickett is the developer, and our Board of Selectmen Chairman. Thought he could develop unused farmland and lure retirees out here to an island paradise." She shook her head. "Didn't quite work out that way."

"Was it like that before the turbines went up?"

"I wouldn't exactly say that. I'm not sure people would have been buying those places up there if the windmills weren't there, but it sure as Hades didn't help once Aerosource put them up." She leaned forward. "You can hear them, you know."

"Yes. I've been up there."

"I mean, down here in the village we look up that way and they stand tall in the horizon with their propellers spinning and it don't look like they make a sound. But up close...." She tsked. "Couldn't pay me to live up there."

"I understand." He'd probably got all the information he could out of the woman. Whether he'd use it in his report was unlikely, but it satisfied his curiosity. He thanked her for her time and turned to go.

"Hey, where are you staying, mister?" she asked as he reached the door.

"At the Tides Hotel," he said.

She nodded. "Oh. I thought maybe since Aerosource sent you, they might have rented the place the other guy stayed at."

He paused at the doorway. "The other guy?" The mystery man again.

"Yeah. From Aerosource. Couple of months ago."

"And where did he stay?"

"He rented a small ranch house out on Tolman Road, in the new development. Put down a deposit on the place. Said he planned to stay for a while."

"But he didn't?"

"Nope. After the first month, he didn't stop back in." She shrugged. "Left the island, I guess. Never did see or hear from him again. Had to go up there and find the keys to the place. They were just lying on the counter. He still had food in the fridge. I had to check, you know."

"And he didn't return."

"Nope. Never heard from him again."

CHAPTER ELEVEN

Melody Larson went into the barn to see if her father needed a hand. After his afternoon nap he planned to work on the dandelion press. But when she stepped into the barn, there was no sign of him. The winepress stood in the middle, wooden bucket beneath it, empty. She glanced all around the barn.

"Dad?"

No response. She stepped farther into the barn, telling herself not to panic. Just because he wasn't where she expected him to be, didn't mean there might be something wrong. He was a grown man, not a child, but ever since the incident with the dandelions, she'd been trying to keep a more careful eye on him.

Of course Myles assured her it was the onset of senile dementia. The man was seventy-nine after all. But Melody knew better. Her father loved to tell stories from the past, like the time as a young man in his twenties when he and a couple buddies stole a boat and sailed all the way to the mainland to meet up with some girls at a dance hall.

But ever since the turbines went up, she noticed the slippage in his mind. The stories grew fewer as he grew quieter. He became forgetful. He complained of ringing in his ears. And he began to wander off sometimes. Like now.

Melody sympathized with her father. She felt the effects on herself from the constant drone of the propellers and that damn flicker every day. She couldn't sleep at night, and in the daytime, once she could stand to go outside (not that the flicker was any better inside), she felt herself walk around like a zombie, energy drained, body wrought with exhaustion.

And of course the toll it took on her marriage. She no longer had the energy or the desire for intimacy with Myles and she knew it frustrated him. Hell, it frustrated her. Didn't he realize that? She felt no passion inside herself. How long had it been since she last made love to him? Weeks at least, more than a month…possibly longer? She no longer knew. Time had slipped away from her.

Just like her father slipped away.

Where the hell did he go?

Melody walked farther into the barn and noticed the door at the other end was open a bit. Enough for a scrawny old man to slip through. She spotted the empty wooden peg where the old wicker basket used to hang and knew where she'd find him.

Damn him.

Outside behind the barn, she spied him in the distance, toward the back end of the property where the chicken coop used to be. At one time it had been a large two-story structure, back when the Darrow farm thrived. But slowly over the years, the egg-producing aspect of the farm dwindled. Heck, even when Melody was a wee child, the second floor of the coop no longer held hens, just remnants of straw and feathers. She remembered playing up there with her siblings until her mother would catch them and chase them out, warning them that the old flooring could open up and send them crashing to the bottom.

The coop had been empty most of her adult life and began to rot and became nothing but an eyesore. When they decided to sell the back acreage to Aerosource, the old structure got torn down.

There the old man stood now, basket clutched in the knobby fingers of his right hand, feet planted right in the middle of where that majestic coop once stood. His head tilted up, staring at the turbines in the distance. The humming reverberated in the air.

"Dad?" she said as she sidled up beside him. He did not turn. She reached down and clasped his free hand in hers. "Let's go back to the house."

"I came out to get some eggs," he said, not turning to look at her. "But I couldn't find the chicken coop."

She rested her cheek against his bony shoulder. "I know, Dad." She squeezed his hand, not too hard. "It's gone. We tore it down, remember?" Her eyes gazed up at his.

"God darn," he said. "Could have sworn it was here yesterday."

"Let's go back to the house," she said. "I'll make you a cup of tea."

He shook his head, slow, but she couldn't tell if it was in response to her offer, or from thoughts churning around in his drifting mind. "When did they put those up?" he asked, not taking his eyes from the turbines.

"Two years ago," she answered, gazing toward them herself.

She had been the one who convinced him to sell the land. The money had been good and enabled them to keep running what meager aspects of the farm they had left. Corn, cucumbers, peppers, green beans and zucchini in the summer, apples and cider in the fall. And of course, Dad's dandelion wine. But what price had it cost them? Melody had no idea the effect those blasted things would have on her family. It felt as if the twirling propellers were slicing off pieces of their lives.

And she could be blamed. Well, she and Myles. He had been very convincing about the proposal. If they hadn't accepted the offer, Aerosource would have found some other spot on the island for the turbines and they would have missed their chance at a tidy profit that would have cost them nothing.

But it had cost them. In fact, every day it elicited a payment from them, in their comfort, their health, even their sanity.

"Let's go, Dad." She tugged on his hand and began leading him back down the hill toward the house.

CHAPTER TWELVE

Before leaving to drive to Tatum Gallagher's place, Oscar decided to call Mason Helleson again. It nagged at him that Aerosource had sent someone else out here, but it bothered him even more that people didn't know what happened to the person.

It took an inordinate number of rings before Mason answered.

"Yes, Mr. Basaran?"

"Hi, Mr. Helleson." He still couldn't bring himself to call the man Mason. "I keep hearing from people about the man you sent over here earlier and can't help but wonder if I'm retracing the same steps." That's only what partially concerned him.

"Have no fear," Mason said, clearing his throat. "The man we sent had entirely different duties than the one you are performing. You are strictly investigating the claims from those living in close proximity to the turbines. That's all."

"I see." Not really. "So, what was he doing here? If you don't mind my asking." He felt sure Mason did mind.

"It's not really a concern you need bother with. The man we sent was an Aerosource scientist, merely collecting data and such." He pronounced data with a long 'a' as if making it sound more scientific.

"But he did talk to the same neighbors as I am?" That's what bugged Oscar the most. He got the feeling these people didn't want to talk to him and maybe it had something to do with how the Aerosource man treated them. He sensed the bitterness with the company and didn't appreciate being affected by the fallout.

Mason drew in a deep breath that hissed over the line. "Our man might have collected some input from the neighboring residents, but certainly not the depth that we need from you in order to proceed with this insurance claim against the company. I assure you that the duties you are performing are highly necessary."

Oscar mulled this over. "That's reassuring."

"How is the process going?"

"I'm making progress," he replied, wondering if he really were. "I'm meeting with another family in a little while, in fact."

"Good to hear," Mason said. "Looking forward to seeing your report."

He felt Mason was going to ring off. "There's just one thing I was wondering."

"Yes?"

Was that exasperation he heard in the man's voice?

"What happened to your scientist? How come he never returned to Aerosource?"

"That's a personnel matter," Mason said. "But to put it bluntly, when the man failed to complete his assignment and report back to the company, his employment was terminated."

"But didn't you wonder what happened to him?"

"The energy business is a highly competitive industry. Some people jump ship when lured by a lucrative offer from a competitor. We made valiant efforts to reach our man, but to no avail. What became of him after we terminated his employment is of no concern to me."

Seemed harsh, Oscar thought. "I see. I guess I wondered if anyone worried some mishap might have befallen him."

"Maybe he fell off the ferry," Mason said.

It sounded like a joke, but his tone gave no indication of that. Oscar didn't know how to respond to the comment.

"All I know," Mason continued, "is that we sent him to Kidney Island to perform a job, and then we never heard back from him. That negligence for whatever prevented him from his duties is inexcusable."

"So, I take it no one is really worried about what happened to him after he got here."

"No, Mr. Basaran. We are only concerned with you."

As Oscar drove out on Haven Road, he reflected on his conversation with Mason. An unsettling feeling wormed its way into his thoughts. He doubted Mason told him the whole truth about the missing scientist. It didn't all sound believable. Swayed by another energy corporation like some double agent in a spy organization? Really? Did a solar power company convince the scientist to defect to their side? It sounded preposterous.

Mason was holding something back from him. But why? Could there be something more to what was happening on this island than what he had been led to believe? It gave him an uneasy feeling, making him believe he didn't belong here. The more he tried to ascertain the facts of what effects the turbines had on these people, the more he had to try and distance himself from Aerosource. He sensed how much these people despised the company. At least the ones who lived near the turbines. Oscar even half convinced himself he didn't work for them. And he didn't. Freedom Insurance paid his salary, not Aerosource.

Coming the opposite way down Haven Road pedaled the man wearing the white construction helmet on the bicycle. Oscar had suspected earlier the man worked for Aerosource. Maybe he should stop and talk to him.

But why did he ride a bicycle? Did the company not provide him with a vehicle? The guy couldn't possibly be regularly stationed on the island. There wouldn't be much of a need for a permanent maintenance worker for the turbines. They couldn't malfunction or break down that often. He should have asked Mason if someone else from the company were here.

As he slowed going by the bicyclist, the man looked at him, his eyes hidden by dark sunglasses. Oscar watched him through his rearview mirror as the guy pedaled down the road, and then continued on his way. A short while later Oscar pulled into the driveway of Tatum Gallagher's home.

A porch rimmed the front of the house and he stepped up onto it as he had earlier this morning to knock on the door. A feathered dream catcher hung from a hook in the porch ceiling at one corner, twirling in the breeze. The front door opened and Tatum Gallagher stood before him, no longer dressed in her grocery smock, but instead in a fitted blue blouse tucked into her jeans.

Her red hair, the color of soft clay, spiraled down across her shoulders, a few curls drifting over her freckled chest above the V-neck of her blouse. She had a figure Oscar appreciated as attractive for a woman and tried to imagine how his former partner saw the opposite sex. Did Kyle appreciate the curves of a woman more than his own lean frame? As much as Oscar could admire Miss Gallagher's attractiveness and appeal, it stirred nothing else in him. Had Kyle just evolved in a different way from himself? He claimed gender did not make a difference to him, but Oscar would probably never understand it.

"Hello," Tatum said, pulling him from his thoughts.

"Thank you for taking the time to see me."

She nodded and gestured to some wicker chairs on the porch. "Mind if we sit here? I've been cooped up all day in that cold supermarket, I feel the need to soak up some warmth." She had a fractured smile.

"Not at all."

She led him to the chairs. "Would you like a cup of coffee or something?"

"I'm good," he said as he took a seat. "But go ahead yourself."

She shook her head, her red locks bouncing. "No. I'm fine."

Oscar took his yellow pad out of his briefcase. "As I mentioned at your store, I'm just talking with the neighbors who've had some issues with the turbines, getting their statements."

Tatum shivered as if the mere mention of the turbines caused a chill, or perhaps it only came from a slight breeze drifting across the porch, sending the dream catcher in a slow rotation.

"It's funny," she began. "Everyone else on the island reaps the benefits of the power Aerosource provides, but it's only a few of us who'd like to put a stop to it."

"Is that what you want?"

She tilted her head as she gazed at him. "If only they had been more up-front about the annoyance those things cause. They could have placed them farther away."

"But your neighbor sold them the land, the Larson family."

She nodded. "Yeah. I guess they beat us to it." She gestured out toward her land and the crumbling greenhouse. "This has been even less of a farm than theirs. We certainly could have used the money. Maybe I wouldn't be stuck working at the grocery store. I inherited this farm, just like the Larsons did, but I couldn't make anything of it."

Oscar felt the conversation was getting off topic, but he remembered this woman had lost a child a little over a year ago. Maybe he ought to let her spill out her thoughts and he'd sort through them later. "Did you have any help? Your husband?"

She laughed. "Dirk and I have been together for seventeen years, but we never did get married. I guess you could call me his common-law wife."

"What's Dirk's last name?"

"Lassiter."

He jotted it down.

"I'd like to talk to him sometime if I could."

Again she laughed. "Good luck with that." She sighed. "We haven't actually been together, not for nearly a year, not since...." Her voice trailed off.

It ventured into uncomfortable territory, but Oscar knew it couldn't be helped. "I heard you lost a son. I'm terribly sorry."

She nodded. "Nathan. He was only ten. It's hard." Her words were lost in a deep swallow. She shrugged. "Dirk don't talk about it much."

Oscar didn't know how to get things back on track. "So, Dirk doesn't live here anymore?" It was the feeling he was getting.

She shook her head, and then her eyes drifted off to the left, toward the turbines.

"He couldn't stand those things anymore," she said. "I wanted to think it was losing Nathan that drove him off, but he kept saying he couldn't stand what those things were doing to him."

This was more what he came for, Oscar thought. "What did he claim they did to him?"

"Headaches. The constant humming mostly and the flicker through the early part of the day when he was home. He said it drove him batshit. So he moved into town with his fishing buddies." She glanced at him. "That's what he does for a living now. Used to paint houses, but now works on a lobster boat a buddy of his owns. Sleeps on his couch rather than here in my bed."

He could sense the bitterness.

"He comes by for dinner sometimes, and to see Rigby when he's around, which as teenagers go isn't often. But he won't stay here. He won't wake up in the morning here, even though he's usually up and gone before the sun rises now." Her eyes narrowed. "That's when it's the worst. In the morning."

Oscar remembered experiencing it with Melody Larson, and that was only for a short while.

"As soon as that sun comes up," she continued, "it begins." She stared out toward the hill. "Sometimes it seems the noise gets louder when the flickering starts, but I know that can't be so." She laughed. "It's no surprise it drives Dirk crazy."

Oscar wrote furiously to get everything down. He thought about this morning and Tatum and Dirk's other son, Rigby, sitting out with his friends getting high and…what did they call it? Getting flickered. Funny how they experienced it in a much different way than Dirk Lassiter.

Oscar looked up from his writing at Tatum, whose eyes seemed glazed as she appeared lost in her thoughts.

"And what about you?" he asked. "How are you affected by the turbines?"

Her eyes grew intense and her lips drew open in a mad grin. "You'd think me crazy if I told you."

"Not at all. It's what I'm here for."

She stared at him, hesitating. He sensed her mind tried contemplating whether she could trust him."

"Trust me," he assured her.

She looked away, her lips tightening, but still not saying anything.

"I only want to help," he said.

She cocked her head and gave him a sideways glance. "It only happened once."

He didn't know what she meant. "What?"

She bit down on her lower lip, as if trying to keep something she'd regret spilling out of her mouth. Then she laughed and shook her head.

"Tell me," he urged, anticipation crawling up inside him.

She closed her eyes as if guarding herself from what she was about to say to him.

"I've seen time stop."

The point of Oscar's pen almost tore through the paper of his legal pad as he bore down on it. Her comment startled him. Had he heard correctly?

"I beg your pardon?"

She stared back, eyes frozen, mouth hanging open as if her tongue wanted to reach out and retract her words.

"I saw time stop," she repeated, and it made no more sense than the first time. Her head dipped. "I can't believe I'm even telling you this."

Oscar watched her eyes for the tiniest hint of jest. "I don't think I understand," he said when it became apparent none was forthcoming.

"Everything on the island –" she raised her hands and spread them, "– I mean, everything I came upon, stopped." She looked at him with an expression of total seriousness. "Except for me."

"Stopped?"

She nodded. "It happened last year, about a month after Nathan drow— I mean, went missing. I was here in the morning and came outside to the flicker going really strong. So strong, my eyes started to hurt. I wore sunglasses, like I usually do during the flicker. It helps a little. Not enough, but some. Rigby sat on the rider mower cutting the lawn. But I couldn't hear the motor all of a sudden. He just sat there on the mower, not moving. I thought maybe he ran out of gas, or it conked out on him. So, I yelled to him, asking what was wrong." She brushed a lock of hair away from her face. "But he didn't answer. And he looked…odd. I mean he was just sitting on the mower, not moving. I thought maybe he was sick or something. So I ran over to him and…."

Oscar waited for her to continue, thinking some logical explanation for her story was forthcoming.

"And?" Oscar prodded.

"He was frozen." She looked away from his eyes, as if embarrassed. "Like he was in some kind of trance. I mean, his eyes were open, but there was no life in them. His hands gripped the wheel. It felt like looking at a picture."

He could see her imagining the memory in front of her.

"I grabbed his arm and shook him." She gazed at Oscar with a look of fright and shook her head. "But nothing. It had no effect on him. I thought it might be…well, Rigby was prone to epileptic seizures when he was young. But he's been on medication and hasn't had one in years. And anyway, they weren't like this. But ever since the turbines and the shadow flicker, Dirk and I worried that the flashing lights would trigger it again. And that's what I thought happened."

"But that wasn't it?" Oscar asked.

She shook her head. "The smoke from the exhaust on the mower hung in the air behind the exhaust pipe. Just floated in the air, like a tiny cloud."

Oscar didn't know what to say, so he didn't try to say anything.

"I ran back to the house to call for help, but the phone line was dead. No, not dead. Just nothing there. No dial tone, no nothing. So I grabbed my car keys and got in my car. But it wouldn't start, so I started to panic and ran down the road to the Granberry farm and…."

"Were they home?"

"Outside, in the field." She looked at him with an intense glare. "But they weren't moving either. Barrett Granberry stood before a feed trough, with a bag in his hand, and just like Rigby, he was frozen. And so was his wife. And the cows in the field." Her voice rose in a pitch. "I don't know. I felt like I was going mad."

Oscar stared at her, watching her expression and wondering that exact thing. It would be easy to attribute it to her state of mind since the recent loss of her child. That would send anyone temporarily over the edge. How could it not?

"So what did you do?" he asked.

"I continued down the road, stopping at some of the other houses. But everywhere I stopped, if someone was there, they weren't moving. The mail truck was stopped on the side of the road, the mailman extending a hand with a bunch of envelopes ready to place them in an open mailbox, but not making it." She shook her head as if to shake the vision out of it. "That's when it dawned on me. Time had stopped. At least for everyone but me." Tatum looked at Oscar. "I notice you're not writing any of this down."

Oscar glanced down at the blank page on his lap. No, he hadn't written down any part of her story. How could he? Her tale stunned him, but he couldn't take it seriously. It certainly wasn't anything he could present to Mason Helleson. (*You must take down the turbines Mr. Helleson, they are messing up time.*) No. He couldn't report this. He didn't know what to say to Tatum.

"That's okay," she said, as if reading his thoughts. "I don't expect you to believe me. Dirk didn't want to either. He's the only other person I told. He blamed it on the flicker. It's been driving him crazy, no reason he shouldn't think it would do the same to me. I think what I told him led to his decision to move out. I think he might have been more disturbed by me than the turbines."

"I wouldn't say you're crazy," Oscar offered, though deep inside he thought that might be a possibility. "It's just hard to believe a story so… unreal."

She nodded. "I've tried to think what else could explain it. But I could move around and no one else could."

"What did you do?"

"I ran back home. My main concern was Rigby. I lost one boy, damn if I was going to lose another."

The thought crawled into Oscar's mind about what the young Larson boy said yesterday, about seeing Nathan Lassiter in the flicker. He wanted to ask Tatum if she saw any such thing, but thought it wise not to feed into her delusions. The woman sounded too close to the edge.

"I went into the house," she continued, "and tried to call for help again, but the phone was still dead. No dial tone. All I could hear was a hum. But it wasn't from the phone. It came from outside. It was the turbines. The humming sound they make was even louder than usual, maybe because it was the only sound around."

"But they were working?" Oscar asked. "The blades were turning?"

"I went outside, where the sound got even louder. They were spinning. I stared, watching the flicker throw its shadows everywhere. And then all of a sudden, the sound of the lawn mower roared. And there was Rigby, riding across the lawn on it, and he waved at me, as if nothing had been wrong."

She spoke slowly, her eyes still lost in the memory.

"And a few minutes later, the mailman pulled up out front of my house and put stuff in my box. As if everything were normal again."

She had a delusion, Oscar thought, brought on by grief, depression, and just maybe, triggered by the flicker effects of the turbines. That made him think of something.

"But the turbine blades were spinning the whole time?" he asked. "While everything else was stopped?"

"Yes," she said. "I heard the humming. It was the only sound. But I just remembered something else."

"What's that?"

"When time stopped, I do remember seeing the turbine blades turning."

"Yes?"

She gazed at him with a look of remembrance.

"But the blades were spinning backward."

CHAPTER THIRTEEN

Tatum wasn't sure she should have told the insurance investigator about the incident last year. She doubted he believed her anyway. Probably thought she was some crazy island girl. She hoped she didn't make things worse for the neighborhood's claim against Aerosource. But what's done is done, she told herself. It probably was the wrong thing to do. She should have known better.

Like she knew better than to tell Dirk about the visit. He wouldn't appreciate knowing she told the guy about her experience. It would make him angry. He came over to have dinner with her and Rigby, like he often did. He had an open invitation. This was still his home too. Sort of. He helped pay the bills all those years while they were raising their two boys so she owed him dinner at least.

Of course, she was indebted to him in a way she could never repay. He rescued her all those years ago in her greatest time of need. And he helped raise Rigby from day one, even though he wasn't the boy's real father.

If she closed her eyes, she could almost picture the face that fathered her oldest son. He had been a summer visitor, a college graduate student named Braydon Lane, who worked at the university's marine research station on the west side of the island. She met him in town one day while enjoying the last summer before her senior year in high school.

The attraction was instant on both sides. Braydon's dark looks charmed her, and his smile. There weren't a lot of ways to entertain oneself on the island, but they managed to make the best of it. And when he had time off from his research, and she had the day off from working at the market, they sometimes took the ferry over to the mainland and she loved it.

He wasn't her first, but the grown-up passion he showed her put those other high school boys to shame. Tatum fell in love, real adult love, not like a school crush. And his smarts and looks swept her off her feet. She felt he could be a way to get off the island for good.

Toward the end of the summer, she got pregnant. Panic set in. God, her father would be so angry. She cried for days, alone in her room. She didn't dare tell anyone. Not any of her friends, not even her closest ones.

But she told Braydon. At first he seemed disappointed in her, and she felt terrible. "I'm still in school," he said. "My studies are important to me." And she cried. But he comforted her, pulling her head to his shoulder, soothing her.

"We can make this work," Braydon told her. "When the summer internship ends, you can leave the island with me."

"Really?" she said, the words filtered through heavy sobs.

"Yes," he assured her. "We'll get married and get an off-campus apartment." He rubbed her shoulders. "I'll keep going to school. We'll figure it all out."

Her whole world lit up with the possibility. The burden eased from her hunched shoulders. This would bring what she always wanted, a chance to get off this island and live a normal life with the rest of the world. She threw her arms around him and hugged him tight, whispering in his ear that she'd never let him go.

Braydon made her promise to keep the pregnancy and their plans quiet till the end of the summer and she agreed. Her dad would fight it every step of the way, for sure. She secretly packed her bags and kept them hidden under her bed for the last couple weeks of the summer. She wrote a long letter to her parents that she planned to leave behind for them. She would give them some time for the dust to settle and then call them to let them know where she was living.

When the day came, she had one of her friends drive her to the docks where she arranged to meet Braydon. She settled on the bench by the loading area for the ferry, two suitcases by her side. And she waited.

And waited.

Braydon never showed. As the last of the ferry passengers and vehicles boarded, the tears streamed down her cheeks. She watched the boat pull away from the dock, taking all her dreams and hopes with it, and it dawned on her, as she held her right hand to the slight bulge in her belly and the mistake growing in there, that she would probably never leave this island.

"Are you okay?" came a voice, and she turned, wiping tears from under her eyes.

Dirk Lassiter stood before her.

She knew him from school, of course. It was hard not to with a school that small. But he sat at the back of the class, the bad boy who couldn't care less about learning. He looked good, in a rough sort of way with his blond locks flowing down over his ears and the slight stubble on his chin. And blue eyes that looked gentle as he gazed down at her with concern.

Tatum burst into tears and he sat down beside her, brushing the hair away from her face.

"Did you miss your ferry?" he asked, looking down at her bags. "No need to worry. There'll be another one later today."

She laughed. Just the idea that he thought she cried this much over a missed ferry. Then she cried some more. And with those tears, her story spilled out in a gushing wave.

And he listened, with sincerity in his eyes and sympathy in his caress as he rubbed his rough hand up and down her back. He told her how much of a crush he always had on her, something she had never noticed or realized. He said he would take care of her if she let him, and help raise her baby.

She looked deep into those blue eyes and saw a sign of hope and relief from the mess she had made of her life. She felt desperate and reached out and clasped his hands in hers.

It wasn't love, not right away, but he was true to his word and after graduation, they moved into an apartment in town. She survived the wrath of her father and gave birth to a beautiful dark-haired boy with dark eyes. She settled into her life with Dirk Lassiter, who after high school became a fisherman.

After all the dreams she had for so many years about escaping this island and the limited life it provided, she ended up with a fisherman. There would be no escape for her.

She never heard from Braydon again and she never understood how someone could wipe clean the slate of a child and have no interest at all in what he helped create. Dirk always feared that Braydon would come back and take Tatum and Rigby away from him. But as the years went on, and they had Nathan, their child together, those worries became less for him. And for her. This was her life.

And when her parents passed, and she inherited the farmhouse, they moved in together as a family. Tatum and Dirk never officially got married, but they were a family as much as any other. And they never told Rigby about his true father.

What could she tell him? She knew nothing about him herself. And that was never more apparent than when Rigby was diagnosed with epilepsy. What else had Braydon passed down to her son? There was no way of knowing, his heritage an unknown. And Tatum was happy to keep it that way. No need to tell Rigby. They were a family.

But things began ripping them apart. And it all started with the turbines. The shadow flicker affected Dirk the most. It angered him, annoyed him, made him feel helpless. It disrupted their daily lives and she felt powerless against it.

After that day Nathan went off to go fishing and never came back, nothing was ever the same.

Dirk moved out shortly after that. He didn't blame it on Nathan's disappearance, but she knew better. He told her it was the flicker, that he couldn't stand it anymore, but she knew better. It was an excuse and it made her feel abandoned. He came around at times, like this very evening when he stopped over to have dinner with her and Rigby. She allowed him because she felt grateful he still wanted to see the son he raised, even though he wasn't his. She sensed the concern he had for the boy, and that stirred her heart.

"It was nothing," Rigby said, still at the dinner table while Tatum cleaned up the dishes.

"What do you mean nothing?" Dirk asked, tempering his tone as best he could.

Tatum dropped some plates into the sink and came around behind her son. "If it's happening again, we need to know."

Rigby shrugged. "It's not. I just saw some lights flashing, that's all."

"Underwater?" Dirk probed.

"When I got deep." His eyes showed guilt.

"I don't like you diving in that quarry," Tatum said, gripping his shoulder like she wanted to hold on to her boy. "I've told you before."

"We're just enjoying the summer," Rigby said, looking up at her. "Just having fun."

Dirk's eyes gazed up at Tatum. Nervous eyes. "There couldn't be any lights under the water," he emphasized.

"If it was a seizure," Tatum stressed, "even a little one, we need to tell the doctor."

"It wasn't. It just felt like…." His voice trailed off.

"Like what?" Dirk asked.

Tatum sensed he didn't want to offer his thought.

"Please, tell us."

"It felt like the lights from the flicker. Flashing."

Dirk's eyes shot up at Tatum's. Now they looked more than nervous. Anger? Fear even?

"You let us know if something like that happens again," Dirk said. "Do you understand me?"

Rigby nodded.

"Okay."

"Can I go now?' the boy asked.

"Where to?" Tatum asked.

"Hang out. Staying at Max's house tonight." His eyes ping-ponged from one parent to the other. "If that's okay."

"Sure, baby," Tatum said, rubbing his shoulder.

After he left in the pickup truck, Tatum crossed her arms over her chest and stared at Dirk. "What are you thinking?"

"I just don't like it," he said. He walked over to the window and gazed out.

She knew what he looked upon, could hear them thrumming as the sun dipped down.

"I think you both should move into town."

She laughed. "Where? Move in with you and Jumbo at Brownie's?"

Those were the pair he worked the lobster boat with, that Brownie owned.

"We could find somewhere else."

"This is our home," she said, anger flaring up. "Where you're supposed to be."

"You know I can't."

She didn't know if she wanted to kick him or kiss him. Damn. She walked out of the kitchen and down the hall to the bedroom. He followed.

Once there, he grabbed her and pulled her to him. And she did kiss him, hard on the mouth, and his hands began pulling at her clothes, dropping them to the floor at her feet by the side of the bed. His calloused hands felt rough on her tender skin, making her squirm beneath his touch.

Tatum helped him pull his shirt off, and he tossed it behind him. Before she knew it, his pants were down; he spun her around, bent her over the side of the bed and plunged into her from behind. She gripped the sheets in both fists for support as he thrust furiously into her with urgency. She'd rather he took his time, but his pace only increased with intensity until he finished quickly and withdrew.

She curled her naked body up on the bed and watching him get dressed.

"Stay," she said, reaching up and grabbing hold of the bottom of his shirt.

"You know I can't."

And with that he was gone.

She lay on the bed, still feeling the sensation of him inside her, sweat trickling off her skin, listening to the sound of his truck fading off down the road till the only sound was the whining hum of the turbines.

CHAPTER FOURTEEN

Oscar didn't know what to think when he left Tatum Gallagher's farmhouse. On his way back to the Darrow farm, he pondered his conversation with her, no need to reference the notes he did not take. Every word she said stuck in his head like a sharp needle. But no matter how he viewed it, he could only arrive at one conclusion. She must be delusional.

It made sense. She suffered the severe trauma of losing her young child; it seemed only natural that her mind could slip a notch or two. Or more. God, how horrifying it must be for her, especially not even having a body to bury. The sea took him, the cruel sea.

Tatum must be in a severe state of depression. Compound that with the lack of sleep she mentioned from the noise of the turbines and it created a cauldron of despair. That he could put in his report. Insomnia compounded with depression bringing on delusions. But the rest? No. That would paint Tatum a lunatic. And Oscar knew crazy when he saw it.

He'd seen it earlier this year when he met Kyle's girlfriend.

Just saying it seemed odd to Oscar. *Girlfriend.* He could have handled Kyle leaving him for another man. But *her?*

Kyle hosted a cocktail party in order to introduce her to all his friends.

Is that what I was? Oscar thought at the time. *Just a friend? After all the time we spent together in the most intimate and romantic moments a couple could share.* But that was Kyle. He thought different, felt different than anyone Oscar ever met. Maybe that's why he fell in love with him. The man had a big heart and felt he could open it up to anyone, man or woman, apparently.

When Oscar got the invitation, it felt like another lunge at his heart. It seemed like some kind of joke. Did Kyle seriously think he'd come to something like this? Of course he did. That was Kyle.

"I still want you to be a part of my life," Kyle told him that day at the café when he broke off their relationship. "You're still important to me. It's just that now, our feelings for each other will take on a different form. But I want you in my life. It's really up to you how much you want to be a part of it."

Sure, Oscar thought. *Make me the bad guy for bailing on a friendship when you're the one bailing on the relationship.*

So Oscar went. It took a few drinks at his own apartment before getting up the nerve to take a cab over to the party on Blossom Street in Boston at the new apartment the couple had just moved into. Claudia Davenport was her name and just the taste of it in his mouth made him want to spit.

He felt a little tipsy when he walked in and was greeted by one of Kyle's co-workers whom Oscar recognized, but didn't remember the guy's name. He never did mingle much with the people from Kyle's office. That seemed another world to him.

The crowd filled the apartment and Oscar couldn't even spot the happy couple at first. But then he spied them over toward the kitchen where Kyle stood before an island opening a bottle of red wine, a big smile on his face. *Do I really want to do this?* Oscar thought, and contemplated leaving before Kyle spotted him and waved, still holding the corkscrew.

There goes my escape plan, Oscar thought. Nothing left but to weave his way through the throng of people choking the interior of the living area, nodding with a smile to those he recognized, ignoring the ones he didn't. Her crowd, most likely. A collision of two worlds.

When he got to the kitchen island, its perimeter bordered by a smattering of laughing smiling people he didn't know, Kyle pulled him in for a great hug.

"I'm so glad you came," he said, his eyes beaming in that way Oscar used to love. "I can't tell you how much it means to me."

"I know," was all Oscar said, an absolute lie. He did not know. He might never know.

"There's so many people here you'll need to meet."

No, Oscar thought. *I don't need to meet any of them.*

Then Kyle turned and waved her over. *Her.*

She had thick light brown hair coifed just over her ears and fair skin with a small mouth and dark eyes.

"This is Claudia," Kyle said. "This is my friend I've told you so much about. Oscar."

Friend. There was that word again. *I can't do this,* his mind bellowed. *I really can't do this.*

"So excited to meet you," Claudia yelled over the din of the party.

"Likewise," Oscar said, feeling like an idiot. Is that what people say to be polite?

She took his extended hand and grasped it lightly. No way did he intend to offer a hug.

"You two chat," Kyle said and grabbed the bottle of wine he had just opened. "I've got to pour a couple drinks for some folks."

No, Oscar thought. *Don't leave me alone with her.* How could anything be more awkward?

"Kyle's got so many amazing friends," Claudia said.

"Yes." He nodded and glanced around the room, looking for someone to latch on to, but most of the people he knew were on the opposite side of the apartment, a seemingly long reach. He turned to her, groping for something to say. "So, I hear you work for Profile Marketing? They're a great firm."

"Yes," she said with a smile. "I love my job."

Oscar only nodded and felt he had no more to converse with this woman.

"Can we talk for a moment?" Claudia asked, leaning in to make sure he heard over the noise of the crowd.

Isn't that what they were doing? "Sure."

"Come with me." She took his hand and led him to the slider door onto the balcony. When she slid it shut, the volume cut down by more than half. The air outside chilled his bones.

"So noisy, I can hardly hear myself think," Claudia said, and then gestured to a pair of chairs. "Sit."

Oh god, he thought. Was it going to last that long that he needed to be seated? Plus it was uncomfortably chilling here in multiple ways.

"I'm glad you came," she started. "I wanted a chance to get to talk."

"It's a nice place," he said, thinking of nothing else to offer.

"I understand this must be difficult for you."

His nerves tightened in his arms and legs, but her soft eyes relaxed him a bit. Her voice seemed soothing. Even the pit of his stomach that held a big knot when he entered the apartment, unraveled a little bit.

"It's a bit awkward," he said, not choosing the right word.

"I'm not surprised." She leaned over toward him. "I just need you to understand how much I love Kyle. He is such an amazing and gentle soul."

"He is." *You can't know the half of it*, he thought. *You haven't invested the time I have.*

"We make each other really happy, and that's the most important thing." Her lips spread in a smile. "I only want to keep him happy. He deserves that. We deserve that. And I don't want anything to keep that from us."

"Of course." *Did she mean me?* "I completely understand."

"Good," she said, her smile stretching even wider, if that was possible. "Then you'll understand why I'm telling you that you are never to have any more contact with him. Ever."

Her smile never broke, which made Oscar think he misheard her.

"Excuse me?"

"I think you heard me." Now the smile did falter. "Whatever disgusting thing you two had in the past is history. And stays that way."

"I beg your pardon." Was she really saying this to him?

"Kyle has a new life. A real life. A normal life. And no faggot is going to fuck that up." Her eyes hardened. "None of his previous life is going to exist for him. You and all your gay friends in there can go on your merry way. Kyle belongs in my world now, and he's going to stay there."

Whatever tension bubbling up inside him now seemed ready to burst through his veins.

"You can't be serious?" His voice seemed calmer than it should, most likely because of the shock that strangled the words in his throat.

"Oh, I am serious. And I have lots of connections, friends in very powerful places. And they can really fuck up your life if you try and interfere."

"And what would Kyle have to say about this?"

"Kyle is happy with me. We are going to be married. And don't think for a minute that he's not going to stand by the one he loves."

Now the words felt like gridlock in his throat and he couldn't push any of them through. As he struggled to get a grip on his composure, the slider door sprung open and Kyle peeked out.

"There you two are!" he said, beaming. "I didn't know you were going to steal my sweetheart away from me."

Which one is he referring to? Oscar thought. But when Claudia bounced up and into Kyle's arms, he saw the look in his friend's eyes and knew he'd lost him forever.

"We were just getting acquainted," Claudia said, the smile back on her face.

"That's great," Kyle said. "Just what I was hoping."

Oscar stood up, his eyes never leaving Claudia's.

Claudia's locked on his. "I was just telling Oscar how much I'm looking forward to getting to know him better."

And as she clung to Kyle as she spoke, her eyes gave Oscar an intimidating stare, almost daring him to say anything different. But Oscar held his tongue, because he knew he couldn't compete with crazy.

It might have been the anger that caused him to take no action against Claudia Davenport. Kyle had ripped his heart out for this poor excuse of a woman. Love wasn't only blind, it had plucked its own eyes out. Let Kyle find out for himself, and see if he comes crawling back. So Oscar chose to say nothing.

He had walked out of that party when Kyle wasn't looking, though he damned well would bet Claudia's eyes followed him all the way out the door. He could almost feel them on his back, penetrating him like the backstabbing bitch she turned out to be. No doubt that searing smile lay below those woeful eyes.

The next day, Oscar got a text from Kyle, saying he didn't get a chance to say goodbye that night, but thanked him for coming. How long after

Oscar left did it take before Kyle realized he was even gone?

Oscar waited before sending him a response, telling Kyle it was a hectic night so he slipped out quietly. Kyle promised to get together soon, but he never made an effort and Oscar felt the strings fraying over the next few months. As much as the pain weighed down his heart, he told himself he'd stay away. He didn't have a fight inside him.

Now, all this time later, these memories still knocked around inside his head. None of it made sense to him, so he stopped trying to figure it out. Time to forge ahead with his life. He consumed himself with his work and the other friends in his social circle – none of them seemed to question why they were no longer a part of Kyle's existence.

Kidney Island provided a great escape for Oscar. Everything seemed simpler here.

At the Darrow farm, Melody introduced Oscar to her father, Tyrus. Oscar felt grateful that Myles Larson was not around. His wife said he worked part-time some evenings at the local beverage store to help make ends meet.

"We do what we can these days," Melody said with a frown.

Oscar jotted down Tyrus Darrow's age, seventy-nine, in his notes as they sat in a living room devoid of the irritating flicker effect from earlier. Though from outside, Oscar could hear a metallic churning sound coming from the turbine blades in the distance. He jotted that down.

"Mr. Darrow," Oscar began, glancing at the pair on the couch.

"You can call him Tyrus," Melody interjected.

Her father turned to her. "I can speak for myself. I'm right here."

"Yes, Dad." She patted his knee.

"How have the shadow flicker effects made you feel?"

"Damn nuisance," he said. "Can't hardly get any work done on the farm."

Oscar nodded. "And what kind of work do you do to help out here?"

"I gather the eggs from the chicken coop."

"Used to," Melody said. "We don't have chickens anymore, or a coop." She looked at her father's face. "Remember, Dad?"

Tyrus sat silent with a puzzled expression.

"That's quite all right," Oscar said, feeling a bit uncomfortable about the man's state of mind. "Do you sleep okay?"

"Okay until the damn rooster starts crowing in the morning."

"We don't have a rooster," Melody corrected. "Though one of the farmers down the road does, but we don't really hear it up this way."

Oscar thought best to not write about that. "What I mean, Tyrus, is do the turbines keep you from sleeping?"

"Don't sleep much anyway," the man said with a grunt.

Oscar hesitated before asking his next question, aware of the delicate nature of it and worried he'd be overstepping his bounds.

"Can you tell me about the incident with the dandelions?"

The old man's brows furrowed and Melody shot him a nervous glance. "Dandelions?"

"Yes," Oscar affirmed.

"I make dandelion wine in the barn."

"I know," Oscar said. "And you were out collecting them a few months back, and something happened." He leaned forward. "Do you remember?"

"They make mighty fine wine," Tyrus said.

Oscar realized this line of questioning remained fruitless. It seemed obvious the man battled against some form of dementia and he doubted anything helpful would come of his interview. He gave Melody a shrug and she projected a silent consent of understanding.

Oscar closed his notebook and stood up. "Is there anything else you'd like to add, Tyrus, about the wind turbines?"

He frowned. "They make everything smell like seaweed."

CHAPTER FIFTEEN

At the northern end of the island stood the remains of the Gull Point lighthouse and the keeper's residence. Its lamp no longer warned boats away from the rocky shore, its light extinguished many years before.

Rigby Lassiter and several other teens pulled up to the lighthouse in two vehicles shortly after sundown. Rigby and his friends Max and Evan piled out of his pickup truck. From an SUV came Whitney Larson and three other girls. Max carried a case of Sea Dog beer while all the others brought camping chairs into the empty house that stood adjacent to the lighthouse.

No lock barred them from entering the front door. It had long been busted. Inside all the rooms were empty save for the litter of empty beer cans and bottles and the occasional discarded potato chip bag and food wrapper.

Rigby hated that some of the kids in town didn't pick up after themselves. This place provided a cool party spot, but he knew if they didn't keep order in place, Constable Jensen would discover the use they made of it and do a better job of keeping the place secured.

They set up chairs in a circle in one of the main rooms and beers were opened and passed around along with snacks they brought. Max Pickett rolled a joint from the baggie of weed he had on him and he lit that and passed it around the circle.

Rigby felt time running short for him and his two buds. Next month would begin their senior year of high school and after that, who knew how many times like these they'd be able to share? Evan had already signed up to join the military, hoping to someday end up in a Special Forces unit. Max had prepared his college applications and would no doubt have a choice of several.

Rigby had no idea what would be in store for him. Neither college nor the military were on his radar. The family farm had ceased to be that, so there would be no carrying on that business. Though he liked the sea, he couldn't see himself spending life as a fisherman or lobsterman like his dad. Other than that, there weren't too many job opportunities on Kidney Island.

He certainly could find something on the mainland, but leaving his mother, especially so soon after losing his brother, Nathan, would be devastating for her. It didn't help that his dad and mom had separated. He had no idea what the result of that would entail. Though he hated the thought of leaving his mother in a state of despair, envisioning himself sticking around this island sickened him even worse.

So on a night like this, he only wanted to relax with his friends, get high and drunk and have a good time. Whitney sat across from him, a blanket around her shoulders to stave off the musty chill in the old house. Most of the windows were broken and a constant breeze from the ocean blew in. He noticed Whitney always flashing her smile at him. He knew she had a thing for him, but he didn't feel that way toward her, or any girl at school.

The girls drank slower than the boys, so Rigby began to feel a pretty good buzz. The weed Max brought wasn't bad either. He munched salt and vinegar chips while everyone talked about the things they wanted to do before summer ended. Rigby just didn't want summer to end at all.

Whitney stood up from her chair. "Rigby, I need to talk to you." She walked over to his spot and offered her hand. "In private."

He looked up at her with puzzlement, and then felt Max nudge him with his elbow. Rigby took her hand and she pulled him up off his seat and led him down a hall.

"Ooooh," the other girls cooed in unison. Max and Evan chuckled.

Whitney took him to another empty room on the other side of the house. She spread the blanket down on the floor and sat on it. He took a seat on the blanket beside her.

"Can you believe summer's almost over?" she said with an eye roll. "I mean it's gone super fast."

"Yeah," he said. "I can't hardly tell you what I even did all summer."

That was a fact. It seemed every day was just getting high and hanging out with Max and Evan.

"I saw you jump off the quarry ledge!" she exclaimed. "That was exciting."

"Sure," he said, but thought back to the bizarre flashing lights under the water.

"Was it scary?"

He smiled. "Kind of." He then wished he retracted that comment. He didn't want her thinking he frightened easily.

"That's so high," Whitney said. "I could never do that."

He laughed along with her.

"Besides," she said. "My bathing suit top would probably come off."

They both laughed again.

She leaned in closer to him. "Of course, it wouldn't take much to get it off." Her head moved forward and before he knew it, she planted her lips on his, her tongue pushing inside his mouth, and he found himself on his back with her on top of him.

It caught Rigby by surprise and when she broke her kiss off from him, he gasped for air.

"I don't think—" he started to say, before her lips were on his again.

Whitney pulled away only to look around the room. "Don't worry," she said. "No one can see us."

Her mouth went right back on his and he felt her hand drift down to the crotch of his shorts. She pulled away from him and even in the darkness of the room, he could see her confused look.

"How come you're not hard?"

"There's something I should tell you," he started to say.

He didn't finish because she began to scream.

Whitney jumped up from the blanket and pointed out the broken window.

"Someone's watching us!" she yelled.

Rigby gathered his wits about him as the others came running into the room; a cacophony of questions filled the air. He stood up and looked out the window. He only saw the tall dark structure of the lighthouse, silhouetted against the night sky. He turned to Whitney.

"What'd you see?"

"There was someone at the top of the lighthouse looking down at us," she said, her eyes wide with fear. "A weird-shaped thing."

Evan went to the window and peered up at the lighthouse. "I don't see anything."

"He was there!" Whitney exclaimed, the other girls huddling around her for comfort. "It was. Some thing."

"Maybe it's the ghost of the lighthouse keeper," Max said, using a deep creepy voice.

"Shut up, Max," Evan said.

"Maybe it's Constable Jensen," Rigby said, also seeing nothing out the window.

"He would have barged in the front door," Max said.

"Let's just leave," Whitney said. "I don't want to be here anymore." The other girls agreed.

Evan turned to them. "I think we should check it out first."

The three boys, with Evan in the lead, led the way out the back door of the house and down the path to the lighthouse. The girls followed with cautious slow steps, not getting too close but not letting the boys get too far ahead of them.

Evan checked the arched door at the base of the lighthouse. It was unlocked. He looked at Rigby with a nod and opened the door.

Max used his cell phone to light up the interior of the lighthouse. The place had the musty smell of the sea. A rusty iron staircase spiraled up toward the top of the tower. Evan went to it and looked up.

"I don't hear anything," he said, looking back at the girls who stood just outside the entrance, but did not enter.

"We should go," Rigby said; his nerves crawled along his skin.

A shuffled sound, something on metal, came from high up in the tower.

Evan's face stiffened. "Did you hear that?"

"Probably just seagulls," Max said.

"Let's go," Whitney said. "I want to go home."

"I'm going to check it out," Evan said, taking charge. He started up the spiral staircase. The structure rattled a bit.

"I'm not sure that's safe," Max warned.

Rigby thought about the other day, when Evan egged him on to jump off the cliff at the quarry. That didn't seem safe either, but it hadn't bothered Evan to dare him.

"You're all right," Rigby said with a nod.

Evan continued up the staircase with slow plodding steps, each one provoking a rusty groan from the structure. If anybody was up there, Rigby thought, they knew by now someone was coming up.

Rigby looked back at the girls, who all seemed to be holding their breath. A cry of metal came from where the staircase attached to the brick wall of the lighthouse. Evan stood about a third of the way up. Rigby's eyes followed all the way up to the top, examining all the spots where the metal bolted into the side walls.

At the very top, he saw a shadow move.

"Hey!" he started to say, but the sound of screeching metal cut off his shout as the spiral staircase began to collapse.

The whole bottom third of the structure sheared off from the side wall, bolts ripping out of bricks with a flurry of stone dust and rust. Rigby had time enough to jump back before the lower portion of the staircase, with Evan hanging on, collapsed to the cement floor in a heap.

Evan cried out in pain. Whitney and the other girls screamed. When the dust cleared, Rigby stepped forward to see his friend lying among the twisted wreckage of the staircase. He saw Evan's right leg bent in an impossible position.

"Oh shit!" he exclaimed and looked to Max for help.

"Fuck!" Max said.

Behind them the girls kept screaming. Evan writhed on the floor in agony as Max stepped forward and began pulling pieces of the rusted metal away from him. Rigby looked up.

For a second, he saw the silhouette of an oddly shaped head looking down at them, and then it was gone.

"Help me!" Max yelled to him, and Rigby broke from his trance and began pulling metal away from his friend whose face was gripped in anguish.

"Someone call for help," one of the girls implored.

"I can't get a signal," Whitney said.

The northern end of the island was often a dead zone for cell service.

"Help me lift him up," Max said. "Let's get him to your truck."

They each grabbed hold of one of Evan's arms and lifted him up.

"Fuck, that hurts!" Evan cried.

Rigby looked down at his bent right leg. "You'll be all right," he said, though he had his doubts.

They helped him out of the lighthouse, but not before Rigby took one last glance up to the top of the tower, but none of the shadows moved.

CHAPTER SIXTEEN

Oscar left his room at the Tides Hotel and wandered down the street to the Raven's Nest. The sign above the front door depicted a raven perched in a crow's nest on a ship's mast, a spyglass to one eye. Inside, dark beams hung above wide pine floorboards. A U-shaped bar anchored the center of the establishment, with pub tables scattered around the perimeter. Odors of fish and grease wafted in the air, circulated by a series of ceiling fans. Country music played softly over the mutterings of conversation broken up occasionally by raucous laughter.

Patrons jammed every stool at the bar, so Oscar took a seat at one of the pub tables. He noticed eyes from the bar soaking up his presence before returning to the glasses and bottles in front of them. A young waitress, dark hair pulled into a bun atop her head, smiled at him from a round face as she brought a menu over.

"Can I start you with something to drink?"

"You certainly can." He smiled and ordered a Washington Apple. He felt in no mood for a craft beer.

"Sure thing," the waitress said and bounded off toward the bar.

Oscar perused the menu with hungry eyes; the long day had worked up quite an appetite. He was in no mood for fish either, wanting something more solid to fill his belly. A nice thick burger, he thought, with some fries. He looked up as the waitress already returned with his drink and he ordered a mushroom burger with Swiss cheese and Cajun seasoned fries.

When she left, he looked around at the other patrons. He judged from the looks of the people in the bar that they were evidently mostly locals. Besides himself, he spotted a few others who looked like tourists, but this place was the only bar in town, so he felt sure the locals regularly filled up the joint.

A man entered the bar and Oscar noticed he carried a white construction helmet and remembered him as the guy he saw riding his bicycle up Haven Road. The man took a seat by himself also at a high-top pub table across the way. Without the helmet and sunglasses, Oscar noticed his handsome face and dark eyes. The man glanced his way and Oscar averted his gaze so as not to appear to be staring.

For such a busy place, it didn't take long for his food to arrive, and Oscar sunk his teeth into the thick crusty bun, cleaving the doughy bread till they struck the firm texture of the beef. Juice sluiced out of the corners of his mouth and he quickly wiped it away with his napkin. It tasted greasy like he hoped and the fries were crisp on the outside and soft and piping hot inside. The meal tasted great and it didn't take long for him to finish. He ordered another drink halfway through.

As the waitress cleared away his plate, and he ordered a third drink, he recognized a man leaving his stool at the bar. It was the guy from the grocery store who had the name tag Brock. The man glanced at Oscar, and then approached a table of three men nearby.

Oscar looked at the trio of men who smelled of the sea even from his table. The man in the center, a tall fellow with blond hair down over his ears and face a brushed sunburned pink, wore a dark blue t-shirt. From under the right sleeve, Oscar saw a tattoo of octopus tentacles spiraling down his arm over a meaty bicep and ending just before his elbow. A gray-bearded man in a black boat captain's cap sat to the blond guy's right. To the left sat a man in a soft cap, thick mustache under a knobby nose and on his left bicep a tattoo of a naked mermaid sitting on an anchor. Oscar noticed the man was missing several fingers on his left hand.

The man from the grocery store spoke to the blond guy in the middle for a brief while. No smiles were exchanged. After a while, Brock went back to his barstool and the blond fellow stared across the room at Oscar with curious eyes.

The Red Sox game played on all the television sets around the pub and most of the patrons' attention drifted to it. Oscar ignored the three fishermen at the nearby table and watched a little of the game himself. Whenever he took his eyes off the screen, the only people in the bar who seemed to pay attention to him were the man with the white construction helmet and the blond guy at the fishermen's table.

I'm not going to feel unwelcome, he told himself, and so ordered one more drink from the waitress and continued watching the game while contemplating his plans for the next day. A few more chats with the turbine neighbors and he should be able to wrap up his investigation here, but he felt no rush to get back to Boston. The city seemed a world away, and not one he craved reentering at the moment. He just wanted to enjoy the tranquility here, or what he could make of it before getting back to the bustle of the city.

When he finished his drink, he paid his tab, leaving a generous tip, and left the pub, noticing but ignoring the several pairs of eyes upon him as he left. The night air had a soothing sea breeze that diminished the earlier heat of the day. He strolled along Main Street, heading toward the marina. He hadn't gotten far when he heard a voice calling from behind.

"Hey, mister!"

Oscar turned and was not surprised to see the three fishermen, the blond guy in front flanked by the other two. He glanced around, as if pretending to see if they were talking to someone else besides him, but also taking a good look at his surroundings just in case.

"Me?" Oscar said, pointing at himself.

"That's right," the blond man said.

Oscar could tell the man was drunk. "Something I can help you with?"

The trio took a couple paces closer and Oscar kept his ground.

"I know why you're here."

"You do?"

The blond guy nodded. "You've been asking lots of questions."

Oscar shrugged, feeling no obligation to respond.

"I don't like nosy people."

Oscar fumed inside but maintained a calm exterior. This all seemed so juvenile. His mind flashed back to bullies like this in college, and he had no tolerance for it.

"I'm not sure my business is any concern of yours."

The blond guy smiled, showing a snaggletooth. "That's where yer wrong."

Who is this guy? Oscar pondered, trying to think of the best solution to extract himself from the situation.

"You stay away from my home."

Now Oscar was completely befuddled. "I don't know who you are or where you live."

"I'm Tatum Gallagher's husband," the blond guy said. "And I don't want you bothering her anymore if you know what's good for you."

Now it became clear. This was Dirk Lassiter. But Oscar thought the guy didn't live with her anymore.

"I thought Miss Gallagher wasn't married," he prodded.

Dirk's mouth opened in a crooked laugh. "I'm not the kind of guy to fuck with, mister."

Oscar sensed the guy meant it and a sudden spasm of fear ran through his body. What the hell was he doing trying to reason with this guy? *Go back to the hotel.*

"I have business with Miss Gallagher." He watched the man's eyes narrow. "I'd like to get a chance to talk to you a bit too, maybe when you're thinking a little clearer." Oscar tried to show no fear, but inside he trembled.

"I got nuthin to say to you." Dirk clenched and unclenched his fists.

"Maybe another time," Oscar said, taking in the looks on all three faces before daring to turn around.

"Don't you fucking walk away from me!"

Oscar's step hesitated as he froze up inside, trying to decide to go or turn back. An unknown voice broke the tension.

"I think we all need to just keep our cool," a man said, stepping out from the shadows of the parking lot of the marina.

Oscar noticed the man wore a police uniform and relief surged through his body. The man stepped in the space between Oscar and the three men, glancing back at him before facing the trio.

"Not trying to make our tourists unwelcome?" the officer said.

Dirk laughed. "He ain't no tourist."

"He's a guest on our island." The officer's voice was stern but even tempered. "He should be treated like one."

Dirk snorted.

"I think you boys had enough to drink tonight. Best you head home."

Dirk glared over the officer toward Oscar, and then the trio turned and walked away.

"Thank you," Oscar said as the officer approached.

"Constable Laine Jensen," the man said, extending a hand, which Oscar took.

"Oscar—"

"I know."

"You do?"

"I make it my business to know who comes to our island. Let me walk you back to the hotel."

"And you know where I'm staying too?" They fell into a leisurely pace.

"Like I said, my business. And pay no attention to those idiots back there."

"Just caught me by surprise." The sea lapped the marina pilings with a sloshing sound. "They anything I need to worry about?"

"Nah," Jensen said. "Just your typical island yokels. They talk big, that's about it."

"Wasn't sure what they had against me."

"You're an off-islander," Jensen said with a smile. "Some of the locals just don't care for them."

"Really?"

"One of the ironies of these small islands. We need the tourists to help the economy, but the natives love to see them leave."

They had reached the Tides Hotel.

"I'm not really a tourist."

"I know that too," Jensen said with a smirk. "You're from Aerosource."

"No, I'm not." Oscar felt defensive. "I'm from Freedom Insurance."

"All the same. Aerosource sent you. Speaking of ironies, that's another bone of contention among the folks here. Most are grateful for the cheap power, but people who live out near the turbines hate the inconvenience."

"I heard that they drove that Dirk guy out of his home."

"There are lots of things that drive Dirk Lassiter."

"Thank you for seeing me safely home," Oscar said, offering a handshake and looking up at the hotel.

"Part of my job's keeping an eye out for people. Locals and off-islanders alike."

Oscar turned to go when something pricked his thoughts.

"Earlier this spring, Aerosource sent someone out here, but no one seems to know what happened to him. Do you know anything about it?"

"It's damn weird. Rented a place out off Haven Road, and then no one's seen him since."

"Aerosource seems to think he got lured away by some rival energy corporation."

Jensen's face tightened. "I told you I keep tabs on things. To the best of my knowledge, that man never left this island."

CHAPTER SEVENTEEN

Barrett Granberry was lying awake in the early morning when he heard the bellow. Of course he was awake most days at this hour, in bed, listening to the whine of the turbines. He went to sleep every night hearing the grind of those damn windmills and the sound never left his ears as the next day arose.

Letty still slept. Thank Jesus. But then her hearing wasn't great these days. The poor woman didn't enjoy enough sleep. He eyed her breathing in the dim light as dawn broke, listened to the air sweep in and out of her nostrils.

The crowing of a rooster from down the road usually signaled his time to arise and greet the workday. Hell, every day was a workday. No such creature as a day off. But this time it wasn't the rooster that stirred his bones.

The sound came from the barn, the ratcheted-up low of a cow in distress. Myrtle.

Against his better judgment, he reached an arm out and shook Letty awake.

"Something's wrong," he said.

Letty wrestled the sleep from her eyes and sat up as he stood beside the bed pulling on his overalls and a fresh t-shirt.

"Call the doc," he said as he grabbed his boots. Then he sat on the edge of the bed while he thrust his feet inside them.

"Do'ya think it's time?" Letty stirred from the bed.

"Must be," he said. "But it sure don't sound right." He experienced enough birthing of calves to gauge the reactions of the mother. This sounded different. He rushed out of the room as fast as his old legs would take him, while his wife dialed the phone.

At the front door, Butch hesitated, as if an invisible barrier prevented him from venturing out. Barrett knew what that barrier was as he looked back before stepping off the front porch. *Never mind*, he thought. *Can't worry about him now.*

By the time Barrett got to the barn, the bellowing from Myrtle drowned out the humming of the turbines and stirred up the other cows. Myrtle stood in her stall, swaying back and forth on wobbly legs like some of the fishermen stumbling out of the Raven's Nest on a Saturday night.

"Easy, girl," he said as he unlatched the gate and entered the stall. He made sure to close it behind him in case Myrtle might attempt to bolt in a frenzy. He grazed the side of her head with a calming caress. "It's okay. You've done this before." Her head bobbed up and down, her mouth opened and her long tongue reached out to seek his hand to return the gesture. She lowed a long bellow and shifted on her legs.

"Doc's on the way," Letty said when she entered the barn. She had bunched her long gray hair onto the top of her head and secured it with a John Deere ball cap.

"Good." Barrett stared into Myrtle's brown eyes, noticing the consternation in them. He brushed along the front of her snout with two fingers, careful not to touch the scabbed-over scar from her incident the other day. "I hope he hurries," he said, though he knew what to do in case he had to. Heck, he'd done it before. But something seemed different this time. He couldn't put a knobby finger on it, but he had a feeling he'd need help on this one. He tried to get the cow to lie down, but he knew they preferred to give birth on their feet.

Outside, Butch yelped from the front door and the turbines whined.

Doc arrived in a jiff, black bag in hand. "What's the situation?"

"She's ready," Barrett said. "But she ain't right."

"Get a good hold on her." Doc set his bag down and looked the animal over. He opened the bag up and pulled on some latex gloves before squeezing some lubricant out of a tube onto the fingers. He rubbed his hands together. "Keep her steady."

Barrett had Letty hold on to Myrtle by the neck, while he went toward the back end, never letting his hand stray from the side of the cow, giving the Holstein a comforting pat every few seconds. He watched as the doc stuck his right hand up inside the cow's uterus and felt around. The grimace on Doc's face told him all he needed to know.

"It's breach," Doc said.

"Of course," Letty muttered.

Barrett frowned at his wife. No need to send the cow bad signals. He gave Myrtle a reassuring pat.

"She can do this all right," Doc said as he worked his other hand inside.

Myrtle howled and shifted her weight, brushing up against Barrett as he tried to steady her.

"Hold her good," Barrett said over his shoulder to Letty.

His wife wrapped her left arm around the cow's neck and leaned the animal's head against her shoulder.

Doc began pulling, and soon Barrett saw two slimy rear legs with tiny hooves poke out of the back end of the cow.

"Keep that end still," Doc said as he tugged.

Barrett leaned into the side of the cow, stroking her hide with his right palm.

Doc pulled more of the calf out. Barrett could see, even through the slickness of the coating on its body, that it was another red-and-white coat. He felt sure Letty noticed too.

"Almost got it," Doc said, drawing in deep breaths, sweat beading up on his forehead. "Just a little stuck at the top."

Myrtle raised her head, with Letty still trying to hold on, and let loose a long bellow. Doc jerked back, his arms strained as he pulled. With a sucking wet sound, the calf dropped from the back of the cow onto the soft hay below.

Barrett felt himself shoved aside as Myrtle turned as if to greet her newborn. He almost lost his balance and pitched over onto the hay, but when he regained it, he stared in horror at the calf.

A cleft ran down the front of the calf's snout, almost splitting its face, and forming what appeared to be the making of two heads. The side facing him had two eyes too close together, and when the deformed head turned, the other side had only one eye that stared out at him.

Letty screamed.

Doc backed up out of the way of the newborn monstrosity. His mouth began to open, but either he didn't say anything, or Barrett was too stunned to hear him.

"A freak!" Letty yelled, hysterical. "We've been damned with a freak!"

Barrett found his voice. "Now, Letty…"

"It's a curse on us!"

"Take it easy," Doc said, but made no attempt to move. "These things occur."

Though from his tone, Barrett didn't think Doc had experienced this before.

Myrtle bent down toward her newborn.

"It's a damn freak spawned from hell!" Letty screamed.

Before Barrett realized anything, his wife had grabbed a spade shovel from the corner of the stall, and moved forward with it raised above her head.

"No!" Barrett called out, reaching an arm forward but too late.

Letty brought the edge of the spade down upon the misshaped head of the calf and it howled as blood spurted from the cleft.

"Stop!" Barrett yelled, but his body froze from the horror playing out before him.

The calf struggled on its wobbly feet, and Letty struck another blow, dropping the creature to the bed of straw, blood spraying out. Myrtle moved toward Letty and clamped her mouth down onto her left forearm. Letty screamed in pain and jerked her arm loose from the cow's jaws, tearing the sleeve of her shirt in the process.

She turned to Barrett. "She bit me!"

Barrett looked at his wife and saw the anger in her eyes. But he saw something else as well: madness.

CHAPTER EIGHTEEN

As Oscar left the hotel and began the drive to the north end of the island, he thought about the email he sent the night before from his tablet. He wrote to his former partner, Kyle, and as best he could without sounding like a bitter ex, explained the incident at the party with Claudia Davenport and the things she said.

The drinks he'd had at the Raven's Nest provided the courage to write the email, but it was all him when he pressed the send button, and a sense of satisfaction overcame him, however brief. Oscar expected no resolution, nor did he want one. Kyle didn't owe him anything, and Oscar didn't want anything from him. All he wanted was to clear the air about his distance since that night. Kyle could take it for whatever it was worth.

It didn't matter if Kyle didn't change his opinion of Claudia. Oscar just wanted him to know who he was dealing with. If he even believed him. The woman's less than subtle threats did not frighten him. No more than those three fishermen from the bar.

That's why he didn't hesitate earlier that morning when he got the call from Tatum Gallagher that she wanted to see him. He agreed to drive out there right away, paying no heed to the warning Dirk Lassiter had given him. Constable Laine Jensen had witnessed the whole confrontation, so he doubted he'd have further troubles from Dirk.

What concerned him more was Jensen's comment about the Aerosource man. If the guy hadn't left the island, where had he gone? Polly Stark had said the man moved out of the rented house at Pickett Fences Estates, but no one had seen him. Had he gotten swallowed up by the ocean the same way Tatum's son Nathan had been swept out to sea? Or did he throw himself off the cliff, like Barrett Granberry's crazed horse?

If Oscar thought Mason Helleson would give him any more information, he would have called the man. But he knew that would prove fruitless. All he could do was continue with his interviews and collection of statements, and be ready to file his report when finished. And Tatum seemed to have some genuine concern she needed to talk to him about.

When he turned onto Haven Road, there again he spotted the hard-hat man on the bicycle pedaling north as well, a backpack strapped around his shoulders. *What the hell is the story with this guy?* he pondered. Maybe he could ask Jensen if he encountered the constable again. The law officer said he kept a close eye on the goings-on around the island. Surely he might know what was up with the bicycle man.

As he neared Tatum's house, he spotted two vehicles leaving the Granberrys, the second being a pickup truck with the old man behind the wheel and his wife beside him. Oscar raised his left hand to wave, but the man's grim face did not respond. A few seconds later, Oscar turned into the Gallagher driveway.

Shadows fell like knives across the land as he stepped out of his car. He glanced over at the turbines, marveling at the smoothness of the rotation of their metal arms. Like clockwork. He spied the three empty campfire chairs out in the yard facing the turbines. He checked his phone, noting the time, thinking one day he should come out here and sit to see how long the effects lasted. It would be good to note that in his report. He could sit with Rigby and his friends, he thought with a laugh.

He didn't get the chance to knock at the front door as it opened when he stepped up to it. Tatum greeted him with worry lines etched across her face.

"Come in," she said, and shut the door quickly behind him as if trying to keep something out.

It did no good. Shadows flickered across the walls, stealing in between the cracks of the closed blinds.

"Is everything all right?" he asked.

She started to speak, and then stopped herself, a nervous hand to her lips. "In here," she said, leading him into the living room.

Rigby sat on the couch, a dour look on his face. He greeted Oscar with an 'oh geez' expression, shaking his head.

"Nice to see you again," Oscar said and took a seat that Tatum offered him by the couch.

"I need to ask you something very important," Tatum said.

"Mom?" Rigby sounded more embarrassed than anything.

"What is it, Miss Gallagher?" He took out his notebook and a pen, hoping there was something worthwhile in her mysterious concern.

"Do you know if the flicker effects of the turbines have ever been known to trigger epileptic seizures?"

Rigby groaned and squirmed on the couch.

Oscar hesitated, thinking back. "I did some research before coming out here," he began. "But didn't come upon anything of the sort. Why? What's happened?" He glanced over at the teenager.

She shot her son a worried glance. "Rigby's had epilepsy since he was young. Used to have seizures from time to time, but they've been controlled with medication and he hasn't had one in several years."

"Till now?"

"It wasn't that," Rigby professed.

"What then?" Oscar asked, looking from mother to son.

The boy told his story of the incident at the quarry and the flashing lights beneath the waters. Oscar thought it over, and jotted down a few notes.

"But the turbine flicker doesn't reach all the way to the quarry."

"No," Tatum said. "But could it be some residual effect?"

"It wasn't like what used to happen," Rigby said with frustration. "It was different."

"How so?" Oscar asked.

Rigby's face tightened. "It's hard to explain." He said no more.

Oscar looked to Tatum.

"I can look into it some more, do some research," he said.

"Thank you," Tatum said. She seemed about to cry.

"Is there a family history of epilepsy?"

Rigby glanced at his mother. "You and Dad never had any issues?"

Oscar saw a look of consternation on the face of the boy's mother.

CHAPTER NINETEEN

When Oscar entered Tatum's house, someone watched them from afar.

In the Pickett Fences Estates development down the road from the woman's farmhouse, a pair of eyes stared out from the open window frame on the second floor of a partially constructed home. The shell of the house had been built, and the roof, but the interior contained the skeletal structure of framed two-by-fours forming an intricate maze that Dirk Lassiter weaved his way through on the way to the upstairs location at the front of the house, where he peered through binoculars across the way to the place he had until recently called home. Where his family still lived. His family. That would always be how he thought of them. His wife, despite the negligence of never signing any official paperwork.

And his wife just let a strange man into her – no, their – home.

Dirk should have been at sea this morning. In fact, he showed up at the docks at 4:30 a.m. as usual to help Jumbo and Brownie load up the gear on the *Seaweed*. They were all island boys, though the others were a bit older than Dirk. He had no idea how Brownie got his nickname, but he'd heard the story about Jumbo's moniker.

When Jumbo was in his early twenties, and just getting started lobstering with Brownie, he hauled up a trap one day to find a jumbo-sized lobster stuck in it. The lobster was at least four pounds, and so big that the critter only made it halfway into the trap before becoming wedged into the netting.

The sucker's claw was bigger than Jumbo's head. When Jumbo attempted to band the claw, the bastard clamped down on the three middle fingers of Jumbo's left hand. Now as the story went, the lobster snipped those fingers right off, but that was an exaggeration. It did mangle the hell out of those three fingers, crushing them so bad and cutting through bone and sinew, that the doctor couldn't save them and had to amputate the fingers.

That left Jumbo with just his thumb and pinky on that hand, now possessing a clawlike appendage of his own, and earning the name Jumbo that stuck with him just as permanently as his deformity.

Brownie owned the lobster trawler *Seaweed* and Dirk had been a deckhand for the past three years. He had replaced Hillbilly, whose leg got caught in a rope from one of the traps he had just shoved over the side of the boat. Before he realized it, the rope snagged his leg around his ankle and yanked him right overboard.

Jumbo tried to cut the rope before it was too late, but in his haste and panicked state, he inadvertently sliced the end that would have given them the only chance to haul the trap and Hillbilly back up, and the poor sucker sank to the bottom of the sea with no chance of retrieving him or the lobster trap.

They say it's bad luck to replace a fisherman lost at sea, and Dirk felt that ever since he signed on to the *Seaweed* he had been marked by a bad spell that led him to the spot he found himself in, spying on his wife.

Dirk could sense trouble, sniff it as well as he could the salt air from the ocean. And before the harbormaster could ferry the trio and their gear out to the *Seaweed*'s mooring, Brownie shared some bad news about the day's work.

"Something's come up." The older sea captain's grizzled face squinted at him in the morning dawn. "Can't go out," he told Dirk without warning.

"What the fuck yer talking about?"

"Something we gots to take care of." Brownie indicated himself and Jumbo. "Can't be helped. Special commission from someone paying a good deal of money." Jumbo didn't say a word, but Brownie scrunched up his face as his eyes bored into Dirk's.

Dirk set down the bucket of knotted rope he held. "What the fuck."

"Can't explain," Brownie said, and spat on the dock. "I'll make it up to you. But we need to do this."

Dirk felt like shit being abandoned by the crew, but Brownie had done this before on a couple of other random occasions. The skipper wouldn't tell him what it involved, and never explained why Dirk couldn't be included in whatever it entailed. That pissed Dirk off. He assumed it had something to do with drugs. Maybe Brownie still handled pot runs on occasions like he did in the old days.

Whatever mysterious shit Brownie and Jumbo were involved with, Dirk watched the *Seaweed* pull out of the harbor without him and that only pissed him off more and gave him an idea of how he could spend his now-wide-open day.

He left the marina in his truck and parked it close to the Tides Hotel and waited. When he saw the dark-skinned off-islander coming out of the hotel and getting into his rental car, Dirk had no doubt where the man was going. Dirk sensed shit like this.

There was no need to follow him closely. Dirk headed in the same general direction toward Haven Road, and pulled over into Pickett Fences Estates before parking behind the unfinished house.

As he scanned the windows with the binoculars after the man entered, he couldn't help wonder what the fuck was going on, though he had an idea. He heard talk that Tatum was sleeping around with someone, and if Dirk found out who, he'd beat the fucker senseless. But he knew it wasn't this guy. No, this fellow was too new to the island. Nothing could have happened that quickly, he hoped.

But this guy wasn't no tourist either. He had some other agenda on the island, and Dirk had a pretty good idea what it pertained to.

Dirk always feared something like this. Ever since Tatum agreed to be with him and pretend her firstborn was his, Dirk thought about the possibility of someday the real father coming back to look for his son. Not that this guy was that fellow. No, he looked too young. But it remained in the realm of possibility that this intruder was a private investigator sent by the real father.

Dirk didn't believe for a second that this guy was interviewing people harmed by the effects of the wind turbines. Hell no. Because the fucker hadn't talked to him yet, and if anyone could tell of the damage those blasted things caused, he could.

Hell, even now, as the shadow flicker fell over the valley below them, he could sense the pain building up behind his eyes. Dirk wore shades, and that mitigated some of the flicker, but it didn't stop the pain. No.

And now he could almost feel it creeping into his skull. He looked away from the machines, but did not turn from the view of his house and the stranger still inside. His head ached dully. It felt like the tentacles of his octopus tattoo unfurled from around his shoulders and weaved their way up the back of his neck, burrowing beneath his hair, suction cups gripping his scalp as the arms curled over the top of his skull – and squeezed.

It began as a gentle squeeze. But then the suckers gripped and the tentacles tightened and his ears could almost pick up the sound of his skull creaking as the bones constricted. It must have been how ole Hillbilly felt as that lobster trap dragged him down to the bottom of the ocean before the cold salt sea flowed into the open mouth of his drowning scream and filled his lungs.

Yes. Pressure. Intense, agonizing pressure that sent bolts of pain into the back of his eyeballs with each flash of the flicker. *Damn you!* Dirk would not pull his eyes away from his vantage point. His mind wanted to scream, but he felt determined to watch his house and see what might be going on.

He could just barge in there and demand to know. But he knew Tatum would look at him with disappointment, and he didn't want that. He'd let her down enough already since he had moved out about a year ago. But she didn't understand. She didn't feel the tentacles squeezing his skull and the bright flashes of pain it brought. Pain he could feel shooting down his body all the way to his balls which tightened inside their sack.

Christ! Jesus fucking Christ, it hurts!

Stop it, dammit! he wanted to scream, but didn't want to give away his presence.

But who would hear him? Not Tatum and that fucking off-islander behind the closed door of his house. Not anyone in this abandoned derelict development that Gavin Pickett in his infinite wisdom thought was a great idea to build in the shadow of those infernal machines with their rhythmic grinding noise and the splintering of light and shadows thrown across the valley.

No! he screamed. Or did he? He couldn't hear anything in his head, his ears consumed by the sound of his skull bones contracting. How much more could he take before it collapsed in on his head and turned his brain to mush?

A door opened. Dirk gripped the edge of the window frame and watched the stranger walk out, Tatum, his Tatum, right behind him. They lingered on the porch and he saw her lips moving while one finger twirled a long strand of her red hair that hung down over a bare shoulder.

He wished he could hear what she was saying to the man. Oh, how he wished. Had the fucker found anything out about Rigby? No. Tatum and Dirk had sworn those many years ago to keep this one secret between them. None other. Just this one.

But hadn't Dirk also sworn to take care of her and stay beside her? He broke that promise when he moved out. She still loved him, he knew, still wanted him. The way she let him fuck her last night was proof of that. He didn't believe the rumor she was having an affair with someone else. No. It couldn't be true. She wouldn't fuck anyone but him. Tatum still belonged to him and Dirk still wanted her.

He didn't like breaking his promise, but it couldn't be helped. The pain in his head became too much to bear. She didn't understand how much it hurt. It wasn't his fault. Blame it on those machines. Ever since they put those fucking machines up to fuck with his head.

But Dirk had a plan to make everything all right again. To help Tatum save the farmhouse and what was left of her land. To get her and him back together where they belonged, but away from the damn machines. It could work. He'd make it work. Just needed to put all the pieces in place.

And hope this fucker with the dark skin wasn't screwing things up. If Rigby's real father sent this asshole, that could spell a whole lot of shit trouble coming his way. He'd have to deal with that.

Dirk couldn't imagine Rigby's father wanted the boy back. No. Dirk wouldn't let that happen. Rigby was his boy now. That jerk gave up his right when he abandoned Tatum that day at the ferry. And Dirk had saved the day. No way would she leave the island now. Not ever.

Dirk was prepared to save the day again. He had it all planned out.

He watched the stranger get in his car and drive off.

Good, he thought. *Now I can get away from this fucking place.* His head throbbed, the tentacles not loosening their grip. The flicker flashed. Shadow, light. Shadow, light. The turbines ground, their rhythmic pulse worming its way into his ears.

Another sound joined them. Screeching. High-pitched screeching.

He looked to the sky to the left of the farmhouse. Seagulls swarmed around in the air. Lots of them, diving down to the ground and swooping back up into the sky, all the time squawking their insane cries.

What the fuck, he thought. It only added to the pain in his head. He turned from the open window, walking toward the stairway. He stopped and rammed his fist into one of the two-by-fours framing what he assumed would be a bedroom one day.

The pain shot through his closed fist and up his arm to join the rest of the misery his body felt. The skin on his knuckles had split open and bled, and he shoved his fist into his mouth to suck on the wound.

Damn stupid!

Dirk stumbled down the plywood steps, anxious to get out of the place. He kept his eyes shielded when he left the empty structure, trying to protect them from the flickering. Once in his pickup parked behind the house, he started the engine.

He didn't notice where the stranger's car went, but Dirk didn't care. He needed to get out and back into town and maybe get stinking drunk. Brownie and Jumbo shouldn't have abandoned him. He belonged on the *Seaweed* with his chums. The hell with their secrets. Heck, he had even spilled to them about Rigby not being his true son. Another promise to Tatum he broke.

But the *Seaweed* crew were his buds. That boat was where he felt most at ease, hauling up traps, emptying the catch and rebaiting them before tossing them back into the sea, down to where Hillbilly's bones lay gathering mollusks.

Dirk sped out onto Haven Road, leaving the screeching seagulls and the grinding turbines with their flicker behind. The tentacles eased up on his skull and withdrew.

CHAPTER TWENTY

When Oscar left Tatum Gallagher's house, he had no plan for what to do next other than research online about epilepsy seizures and any correlation to the shadow flicker effect.

But impulse gripped him when he spotted the sign for Pickett Fences Estates. He had been curious about the residents of this neighborhood because of its proximity to the wind turbines. As far as what information Helleson provided him, the only parties involved in filing an insurance claim against Aerosource were the Larsons, Gallaghers and Granberrys.

But what about the people in this neighborhood? He understood some of the homes were still under construction, though since he had been on the island and down Haven Road multiple times already, there had been no sign of any work being done on the site.

According to the development sign out front there were twenty-four sites for homes in this first phase of the project. Fewer than half that appeared to be finished houses, but as he drove through the neighborhood, there didn't appear to be any sign of life even among the homes that looked finished and ready for occupancy.

A white rusted pickup truck with a missing tailgate sat parked behind one of the unfinished houses that fronted the main road. Maybe a contractor was at work inside, but he heard no hammering or buzzing of power tools.

Oscar turned down the second lane in the development and spotted a For Rent sign on a wooden post in the front yard. On the sign was a face and name he recognized: Polly Stark, the real estate agent he spoke to in Loch Raven village.

The turbines cast their long fingers of shadow even into this neighborhood. Something Polly said crept into his memory bank. The missing man from Aerosource had been renting a home in this development when he disappeared. Oscar decided he should pay Miss Stark a visit.

He turned his car around in the empty driveway in preparation to exit the neighborhood when he spotted an old man walking down the road in his direction. He recognized the man as Tyrus Darrow, Melody Larson's father. It surprised him to find the old man wandering here, but he was even more startled by the fact the man wore no pants.

Tyrus sported a white t-shirt with suspenders clipped to a pair of gray plaid boxers. He wore work boots and gray socks on his feet. At least his socks matched his underwear, Oscar thought with a chuckle. He realized though that this wasn't a laughing matter. Something in the old man's eyes gave the appearance of being lost.

Oscar pulled up beside him and rolled down his window. "Excuse me," he said, but the old man kept walking as if he didn't hear or see Oscar. He put his car in reverse and backed up until he came even with Tyrus. "Do you need help?"

The question startled the old man and he stopped and looked at Oscar with suspicious eyes.

"I don't know you," Tyrus said.

Oscar shifted into park and got out of the car so the old man could get a better look at him.

"It's Mr. Basaran," he said. "From Freedom Insurance. I spoke with your daughter the other day at your house."

Tyrus exhibited no recognition. Oscar noticed that every time the shadow flicker crossed the old man's face, his mouth drew up in a grimace, like some nervous tic. Tyrus tilted his head up and looked around.

"Nothing looks familiar here," Tyrus said. He sniffed the air. "Where did all these houses come from? And why the hell does everything smell like seaweed?"

From the tight rein Melody said she kept on her father, Oscar imagined he didn't stray far from home anymore, certainly not without a chaperone, and without his pants.

"Want me to give you a ride home?" Oscar asked.

The old man shook his head, but it didn't appearto acknowledge Oscar's offer. "Everything's changed," Tyrus said. He looked up toward the hill and the wind turbines. "And where the hell did those blasted things come from?"

Oscar walked around his car to cautiously approach the man. "Your daughter is probably worried about you."

"Daughter?" His brow furrowed. "Do I have a daughter?"

Dementia, Oscar thought. *This man is going senile.* This seemed a much more plausible reason for his behavior that worried Melody than the ill effects of the turbines. Oscar would have to consider that in his report.

"Melody Larson," Oscar said slowly, in case the man couldn't hear well. "Your daughter. Married to Myles. You have two grandchildren." Oscar dug through his memory bank to unearth their names. "Whitney and Troy?"

The old man nodded, but Oscar wasn't convinced he understood.

"I can't have a daughter or grandchildren. I never got married." He scratched his chin. "Always wished I did, but was too busy running the farm."

At least he remembered he had a farm, Oscar thought. "I can give you a ride back to the farm."

"I've got lots of work to do," Tyrus said. "I need to collect the eggs from the chicken coop."

"Then let's get you home, sir." Oscar gently grasped the old man's arm and guided him over to the car and got him settled in the passenger seat. Once behind the wheel, he eased the car out of the abandoned neighborhood, noting the pickup truck he spotted earlier had left.

Tyrus remained silent as Oscar drove up Haven Road, but looked out the window at the scenery as if it was foreign to him. Oscar felt sorry for the old man.

At the Darrow farm, Oscar stopped by the vegetable stand at the end of the driveway. A young teenage girl came out of it when she recognized her grandfather. She approached the passenger window.

"Grampa, what are you doing?" She eyed Oscar with concern.

"You must be Whitney," Oscar said and introduced himself. "I found him wandering over in Pickett Fences Estates."

Whitney frowned and looked down at her grandfather. "Grampa, where are your pants?"

"Is your mother home?" Oscar asked.

Before the girl could answer, a great racket of squawking seagulls filled the sky over the farmhouse.

CHAPTER TWENTY-ONE

Melody Larson panicked when she couldn't find her father.

She had brought him a mug of coffee to his bedroom only to find the room empty. She carried the hot mug into the living room and the back den, calling for him. He did not answer.

That's when she began to get worried and rushed into the kitchen to put the mug on the counter, hot liquid sloshing over the edge and burning her hands. She cried out, swore, and rubbed them on her pants.

"Dad!" she screamed, knowing full well he must have gotten out of the house without her noticing. Damn him.

It was like she needed to keep a cowbell around his neck to know his whereabouts, she thought as she rushed out the front door onto the porch. "Dad!" She hadn't put her sunglasses on yet, and the bursts of light from the shadow flicker caused her to squint. She didn't like the thought of her father out here; she didn't know what harm he'd be capable of doing to himself.

Melody knew Myles was out in the back field collecting corn and hoped he would see Tyrus if her father wandered out that way and not run him over with the tractor. God, what made her think of that? She scanned the yard before her.

Troy twirled on the tire swing under the giant maple tree. He waved at her and pointed into the sky. Melody tilted her head and looked up. In all her panic over her missing dad, her ears hadn't even registered the noise in the air. Seagulls filled the sky and swarmed above the farmhouse in all directions, their screeches and cries drowning out even the drone from the turbines.

She stood frozen, mesmerized by the mass of birds swooping down and up again, heading in one direction and then suddenly reversing, the flock all moving in unison in one fluid motion. *Just like Troy said*, she thought. *The birds are dancing.*

It seemed to her that the seagulls moved to the rhythm of the flicker, almost darting in and around the lines of shadow that swept across the sky. *It's driving them crazy*, she thought. *The flicker is making them mad.*

Melody looked toward Troy, who hung inside the old tire, legs dangling out one end and leaning his head back out the other. He had a broad smile across his face.

For one mad moment, Melody imagined the birds swooping down and grabbing her son and lifting him into the sky. She jumped off the porch and ran across the yard, kicking up dirt and dust behind her sneakers.

"Get in the house!" she screamed.

Troy looked over at her with a bewildered stare, mouth agape.

She reached the tree and yanked him off the tire swing with a little too much force, causing him to fall to the ground. She pulled him to his feet.

"Mom!" He looked up at her like she was the mad one.

"We need to get inside," she said and began tugging him toward the house.

"But Mom! I want to see the dancing birds." He tilted his head back toward the sky.

Melody gripped Troy's wrist tight and tugged him along. "I don't like this," she said, hollering above the screeching seagulls.

"They're just birds," Troy said, twisting around to get a better look behind him.

It's the flicker, she thought. *It's making them act this way.* And she didn't know what else they'd be capable of doing. *Sure, they're just birds. But who knows?* She wasn't taking any chances.

"Just keep moving," she said. She wished the squawking would stop. It hurt her ears and stirred the blood inside her as her heart pumped in rhythm to the flash of light and shadow.

They were almost to the front porch when Melody felt resistance on her arm. She glanced back and Troy had stopped. He was looking beyond the field to the left of the house. She followed his gaze and in the distance, saw the figure of a young boy.

"It's Nathan," Troy said, waving. There was no response from the figure. The shadows fell across the field and gave the boy the appearance of a shimmering mirage. Melody's heart felt heavy as if it solidified into rock. *Who is that?* she thought.

"Come on," she said, tugging at Troy's arm.

"But I want to play with Nathan," he implored.

She shook her head. "That's not Nathan." *It can't be.*

Melody grabbed Troy around the waist, lifted him off the ground and carried him the rest of the way to the porch. She set him down before the front door and looked back across the yard.

The image of the boy was gone.

Gravel crunched under the tires of a car pulling up to the house. She saw her father sitting in the passenger seat of the insurance investigator's vehicle. In her state of fright, she had forgotten about her dad.

"I found someone for you," Oscar said when he got out of the car. He ran around to the other side and helped Tyrus out. Oscar looked up at the sky. "Is this normal for them to act this way?"

"No," she said. "Help him inside."

Once in the house, Melody closed the door with authority and helped her father to one of the recliners in the living room. Troy ran to one of the front windows and peered out.

"Get away from the window," Melody said.

The boy sulked and walked over to the couch, plopped himself down and folded his arms across his chest. Melody looked at her father's distant stare. She noticed his attire.

"Dad, where's your pants?"

He glanced up at her but said nothing. Did he even recognize her?

"What's got into them?"

She turned and saw Oscar looking out the window beside the front door.

"I don't know," she said. "I think the flicker's spooked them."

Oscar looked at her with an expression of disbelief.

"Barrett Granberry believes it spooks his animals," he said.

Melody nodded. "He had a horse that jumped off the cliff at Crooked Cove."

"He told me."

That reminded Melody that it was the same place Nathan Lassiter was before being swept out to sea while fishing off the rocks. She thought about what she saw outside. Or thought she saw. She went to the window beside Oscar.

"Did you see anything out there?" she asked him.

He looked at her. "Besides the birds, you mean?"

"Yes." She paused. "I thought I saw a boy."

"It was Nathan," Troy said from the couch, still pouting. "He comes in the flicker."

Oscar looked from the boy to her.

"I don't know what I saw," she said, shaking her head. "Whatever it was – whoever, it wasn't him."

Oscar went to the door and grabbed the knob. Melody thought about stopping him, fearing it might not be a good idea to go out there. Then she remembered Whitney was still at the vegetable stand and grabbed her cell phone and followed Oscar out to the front porch. She turned to look at Troy before closing the door.

"Stay put and keep an eye on your grandpa." Her father looked dazed as he sat in the recliner. Flashes of the shadow flicker filtered in through the windows, giving the whole room a fun house appearance.

Out on the front porch, Melody looked toward the end of the driveway and the small shack of the vegetable stand. The seagulls still screeched and flew around, but mainly stayed high up in the sky. She dialed Whitney's cell phone and her daughter picked up right away.

"Stay inside the stand," Melody ordered her daughter.

"What's going on? Is Grampa okay?"

"Yes, he's fine." Melody looked up at the sky. "There's just seagulls everywhere overhead, so stay undercover."

"Oooh. No sweat. Wouldn't want them shitting on my head."

"Language!" Melody barked.

"Sorry." And then: "Pooping." Whitney hung up.

Melody watched Oscar as he glanced off into the distance.

He turned to look back at her. "I don't see any boy," he said, frowning.

Melody shrugged. "Probably just some neighborhood kid."

"Are there any other young boys around out here?"

Melody knew there weren't. Not since Nathan died. She shook her head.

To the left, the sun crested the top of the turbines and in an instant the shadow flicker stopped. At the same time, the seagulls began flying off in all directions, as if called away by some unheard signal, until just a handful of the birds remained in the sky over the farmhouse.

"Wow," Oscar said, turning to her with a look of amazement.

"Just like that," Melody said with a smirk. "Back to normal." She glanced at her front door, thinking about her father inside. "Or as normal as it gets around here."

At that moment, the sound of a tractor engine approached, and Myles came by, towing a cart loaded up with picked corn. His eyes shifted between Melody and Oscar and he got off the tractor, leaving the engine running.

"What's going on?" he said as he approached.

"Dad wandered off," Melody answered. "Mr. Basaran found him and brought him home."

"He was over at Pickett Fences Estates," Oscar said when Myles glared at him.

Her husband nodded. "Thanks." He looked at Melody. "Is he all right?"

"He just got him back here when those seagulls went all crazy," Melody said. "Scared the crap out of me."

"I saw them," Myles said. "Just a bunch of birds looking for handouts. Glad they didn't swoop down into the cornfield. We'll have to erect a better scarecrow."

"Would that even work on seagulls?" Oscar asked. "Isn't that just for crows?"

Myles didn't answer. "I'm going to get this load of corn over to the stand. Whitney can help me fill the bins. I'll check back with you in a few."

Melody nodded and Myles got back on the tractor and drove down the driveway.

Oscar turned to her. "Would you mind if I asked your dad a few questions?"

Melody hesitated. She wasn't sure it was a good idea to subject her father to anything more, but she was the one who initiated the claim against Aerosource after the incident with the dandelions, so she might as well see things through, not that she had much hope it would make any difference.

"Sure," she said and led him into the house.

Tyrus Darrow looked up at them when they entered the living room, eyes searching for something. Maybe some understanding? She couldn't imagine what he must be going through. Her heart ached.

Troy sat on the braided rug playing with a toy tractor.

"Go outside and help your father and sister unload the corn at the stand," she said.

He jumped up with glee. "And then can I stay outside after and play?"

"Yes."

He bolted across the room and out the door.

Melody approached her father and knelt down. "How are you feeling, Dad?"

His tired eyes scanned her face. She saw recognition in them and smiled.

"Fine," he said. "Been a busy day. Collected a lot of eggs."

She nodded. "That's good, Dad." She looked over her shoulder at Oscar, who stood behind her.

"Is it okay if Mr. Basaran asks you some questions?"

Tyrus looked up at Oscar. "Who?"

"This is Oscar," Melody said. "From the insurance company. You met him the other day."

"I don't need no insurance." He grunted.

"He just wants to chat with you a bit."

The old man shook his head. "I don't got no time. I have to collect the eggs from the chicken coop."

Melody stood up and turned to Oscar. "Give it a try if you want." She didn't think he'd get anything from her father. She stepped back and Oscar knelt down in front of the chair.

"Hello, Tyrus," Oscar said with a broad smile. "How are you feeling?"

"Tired."

"I understand." Oscar nodded. "It's a busy farm to run. It's good you have family to help you."

"I should have gotten married," Tyrus said. "Then I'd have lots of kids to help me with the chores."

Melody winced. She ached whenever he forgot her mother. Forgetting the rest of her siblings didn't hurt as much. They all left the island for greener pastures in a manner of speaking. Only she stayed behind to help with the farm and now her father could barely remember her. A tear slipped out of the corner of her right eye and she quickly wiped it away.

"Has a lot changed since the wind turbines were put up?" Oscar asked.

The old man's face scrunched up. "The what?"

Oscar raised both his arms in the air. "The big windmills, out behind your property. Do they bother you?"

"You bother me," Tyrus said with a scowl.

"I mean, do they make you sick?"

The old man leaned closer to Oscar's face. "Did you put them there?"

Oscar shook his head. "No. It wasn't me."

"Why'd you do that? That's my property." Spittle formed on the old man's cracked lips.

"They make electricity," Oscar said. "To help power everything. Your lights and stuff."

"Dagnabbit! We've had 'lectricity on this island since 19...19...." He scratched his head. "A damn long time!" Some of the spittle flew off his lips.

Melody couldn't help crack a smile despite the sadness of it all.

"How is the dandelion wine making going?"

Tyrus put his hand behind his left ear and pushed it forward. "Huh?"

"Dandelions!" Oscar spoke louder. "You make your dandelion wine? Does it taste good? The dandelions?"

Melody felt a twinge of concern. A vision surfaced of her father stuffing dandelion heads into his mouth to the point of choking. A shiver rattled her spine.

"What does dandelion wine taste like?" Oscar asked.

Tyrus leaned back in the chair, his face sour. "Seaweed."

"What the hell's going on here?"

Melody spun around and saw Myles standing inside the doorway, his face carved with consternation.

"I told Oscar he could ask Dad a few questions." She had a hard time getting the words out and felt foolish now that she said them.

"Is he in any position to answer anything?" Myles said while gesturing toward her father, his tone elevated. "Christ, he doesn't even have any pants on!"

"I'm sorry, Mr. Larson," Oscar said, getting to his feet. "I'm really just trying to help your family."

"We did file the claim," Melody told Myles.

Her husband glared at her and she felt insignificant. "And we'll talk to our lawyer, and nobody else." He looked at Oscar. "I'd like you to leave."

Oscar dipped his head. "Of course."

Melody felt embarrassed. She walked Oscar to the door. She bid him goodbye, but said thank you with her eyes. As she closed the door after him, she heard her father from the living room.

"Seaweed."

CHAPTER TWENTY-TWO

At the end of the Larsons' driveway, Oscar decided to stop and check out the vegetable stand. Part of the reason being that he hoped Myles Larson looked out his window and watched him. The man's attitude rubbed him the wrong way and prompted Oscar to act spiteful, though he didn't care.

But Oscar also wanted to get a chance to talk to the only member of the Larson household he hadn't spoken with yet. He stepped through the screen door and gazed at the bins of vegetables on either side of the small shack. A central bin overflowed with corn on the cob, while tables along the perimeter held an assortment of tomatoes, peppers, green beans, cucumbers and zucchini.

Whitney sat on a stool behind a small counter at the back of the stand. She held a cell phone in her hand and a frown on her face before looking up at him.

"Hi," she said, recognizing him. She put the phone down with disgust. "Trying to FaceTime my friends, but the service on this island sucks."

He nodded. "I have the same trouble sending emails." He hadn't got a response from Kyle and wondered if his message had even gotten through. "Too bad those wind turbines don't generate cellular service as well as they do electricity."

"Yeah," she said with a smile. "That'd be something."

Oscar wandered up the front aisle, stopping to pick up a tomato, thinking about what he might actually need it for. "How do you feel about those turbines?"

She looked confused. "What do you mean?"

"Do they bother you?"

She shrugged. "You get used to it. I'm stuck in here most of the day

during the summer. I just plug in my earbuds and listen to music mostly.
During the fall and winter, I'm at school, so no big deal."

He nodded, and then felt a firm cucumber and added it to his collection.
"Glad I found your grandfather. Who knows what could happen when an
elderly person goes off wandering?"

"Yeah," she said, as if just remembering. "Thanks." She thought for a
moment. "But then, it's not like he can really get lost. I mean, it's an island.
Where could he go?"

"Good point." He brought the tomato and cucumber up to the counter
and set them down. "Was he like that before those turbines went up?"

She gazed at him with curiosity. "Why? Do you think those things
made him that way?"

"I have no idea," he said. "I'm just trying to decipher what effects they
may have on the people living near them."

"I just figured he was old." She weighed his items on an electronic
scale. "That'll be eighty-eight cents."

He spotted a display of the old man's dandelion wine behind the counter.
"That any good?" he asked as he pointed to the bottles.

"I can't drink," she said with a smirk. "But, I mean, it's dandelions."
She made a sour face.

"Let me try a bottle." He dug some bills out of his wallet as she added
the bottle to his purchase. He handed her the bills. "Keep the change."

She smiled and threw the bills into the till. "I'll tell you something. I
think the noise of the windmills is worse than the shadows."

"Oh really?"

She nodded. "At least the flicker only lasts a few hours. The noise those
things make is constant. All day and night. Sometimes it wakes me up in
the middle of the night and I can't get back to sleep. I put my earbuds in
and try to drift off with some music."

"That can't be good," he said.

"It's better than listening to that constant grinding humming." She
shook her head, hair flying back and forth. "I hear Mom sometimes pacing
the floor downstairs. I know she can't sleep."

"Do they ever stop turning?"

"Not that I've seen. Wouldn't the power go out if they did?"

He laughed at her naïvety. "No, it doesn't quite work that way. The power it generates is stored in a power grid that supplies electricity when needed."

"Oh." She didn't look like she cared. She placed his items in a brown paper bag and handed it to him.

"Thanks," he said and turned to leave. Before he reached the door, he thought of something Tatum Gallagher said and turned back to face her. "Have you ever seen the blades spin backward?"

Whitney looked perplexed. "Is that even possible?"

* * *

On his way back down Haven Road, Oscar once again passed the Pickett Fences Estates development, which reminded him of the first stop he planned to make back in town. Once in the village, he parked in front of the real estate office.

Polly Stark greeted him with a wide smile. "So nice to see you again Mr. Bas—?"

"Basaran."

"Yes, of course."

"But you can call me Oscar."

Her smile widened if that was even possible. He thought her face would break open.

"What can I help you with this morning?"

"I'm interested in a rental property I spotted up at Pickett Fences Estates."

"Why, of course," she said, leading him to a chair in front of her desk. She took a seat behind it. "That's on Tolman Road."

He nodded. "I believe that was the name of the street."

"A cozy little ranch."

"Is that the only one for rent?"

"Yes. There are others for sale, but that's the only rental. It's fully furnished." She told him the weekly cost of the rental.

"That's good. Can I get it right away?"

Polly opened a drawer and pulled out a paper form. "I'm sure there won't be a problem."

While Oscar began filling out the form, Polly got on the phone to speak with the owner of the house. By the time she got off the phone, Oscar had finished with the form and slid it across the desk to her.

"You're in luck. The owner is amenable. I'll just process the paperwork and I can call you when everything is all set and you can pick up the keys."

Oscar stood up. "That'd be great. I'd like to get in there by tomorrow."

"I'm sure that can be arranged. The owner will be excited to get someone in there."

"Been vacant long?" he asked.

"Since earlier this year. The last person to rent it was that man from Aerosource. The one who left without any notice."

Oscar didn't know what to think when he left the real estate office. It kind of spooked him a bit about the missing scientist, but now that he had interviewed pretty much everyone who lived the closest to the turbines, he needed to move on to a different kind of research. Oh sure, he could knock on some more doors of other Kidney Islanders who lived in a reasonable proximity to the wind farm, but the three families he had already reached out to were the ones named in the insurance claim, so Oscar felt he met the obligations of his job here.

But when he saw the For Rent sign in the Pickett Fences Estates development, it occurred to him that he could get a firsthand account of what it felt like living with the effects of the shadow flicker. Sure, he'd seen what the phenomenon felt like during his stops at the farmhouses on Haven Road, but he wanted to experience going to bed several nights to the sound of the machines and waking up day after day to that pulsating light and shadow show. That would give him a better handle of what these people were going through and really add some mustard to his report.

Oscar returned to his room at the Tides Hotel, where he decided to work on his report and make some lunch. Before that though, he made a phone call to Mason Helleson, but a voice message said he was away on business, and gave an alternate number for another Aerosource executive if he needed to immediately get in touch with someone. There was no one else Oscar wanted to talk to so he hung up without leaving a message.

He wanted to know more about the scientist who had been sent out here, such as how long he had been here and what his duties entailed. Mason of course probably would have told him it did not concern him, but if the scientist had been living in that rented house off Haven Road, then he would have experienced the same effects of the shadow flicker and the turbine noise as the others out there, so that would make it his business. If the man had spent a great deal of time in that area, maybe he dealt with sleep disruption or headaches or some of the other symptoms the people complained about. Maybe it had something to do with whatever drove the man away, wherever he went.

Oscar supposed he could find out more about the guy from Polly Stark or Laine Jensen. The constable said he kept an eye on the island happenings; maybe he could be of some help. Oscar made a mental note to try and talk to the law officer later.

He fixed himself a cucumber and tomato sandwich out of the items he bought at the Darrow farm stand and opened the bottle of dandelion wine. He sat out on the small balcony with his tablet and notepad set up on the little table. The few boats out in the harbor bobbed silently on the swell of the ocean water like toy boats floating in a child's bathtub. Down below he could hear the splash of water striking the pilings as the tide swept in. Seagulls squawked as they hovered over the harbor, occasionally landing on a post on one of the docks. It reminded him of the weird incident with the birds over the Darrow farm. That would have to go into his report, but he wasn't sure how he planned to justify it. It seemed the turbines had some effect on the birds, as well as the animals at the Granberrys' farm, thinking of the story of the horse that leapt to its death and the odd behavior of Barrett and Letty's cows.

Oscar bit into the sandwich, savoring the crispness of the tomato and cucumber slices, and wiped the juices from the corner of his mouth with his napkin. He turned on his tablet and created a file for his report, checking over the pages of notes he already generated. He poured some of the dandelion wine into a small glass tumbler from the hotel room bathroom. The odor from the wine, definitely wouldn't call it the bouquet, caused his nose to crinkle. He took a small sip and the sour taste felt like he swallowed salty grass clippings soaked in motor oil.

He jumped up from his chair and ran to the bathroom with the glass still in his hand. He poured the remainder down the sink, turned on the faucet to rinse out the porcelain and took a few gulps to cleanse his palate. God, was it supposed to taste like that? He doubted it. Maybe the old guy's mind was so jumbled that he screwed up the recipe.

Oscar grabbed a beer from his mini-fridge and went back out to the balcony, where he took a long slug of the bottle to wash out any remnants of the nasty wine. He sat down and stared at the blank page on his screen. Where to begin?

A couple hours and two beers later, Oscar had several pages of the results of his interviews with the claimants against Aerosource and the effects they believed the noise and flicker from the wind turbines had had on their health and well-being, not to mention their mental state. It was just a rough draft and he would have plenty of time to polish it up a bit before turning it in to his firm, but it was a good start.

His phone rang and Polly Stark greeted him when he answered.

"Mr. Basaran, everything is all set," the woman said in a gleeful tone. "You can take possession of the rental property tonight."

"That's great," he said and arranged for a time to meet her out at the property. After he got off the phone with her, he began gathering his things and prepared to check out of the Tides Hotel.

CHAPTER TWENTY-THREE

Barrett Granberry tossed the last shovelful of dirt into the hole in the back end of his lot where he'd buried the deformed newborn calf. He paused, leaning on the long handle and wiping sweat from his brow, before looking up at the wind turbines in the distance. The slight breeze coming from their direction down the hill onto his farm lifted a little of the heat from his body.

There was always a wind on the island, coming off the sea, usually sweeping down across Penobscot Bay from Nova Scotia, something islanders got used to. That along with farming on the island made for a tough life. His grandfather used to say the wind chips away at your soul a little bit each day. Maybe that's what happened to Letty.

And Barrett couldn't help thinking that the extra breeze blowing down from the turbines ushered along that process. He patted the dirt on the makeshift grave, tamping it down before walking back to the house. The rest of the cows in the herd meandered around the field oblivious to the calamity of the morning.

He had brought Letty to see the doctor after the incident in the barn. The doctor gave her some sedatives to take and told Barrett to keep an eye on her. If it didn't seem to help, he recommended she see a specialist across the way in Rockland. Barrett hoped it wouldn't come to that. Letty was a tough old broad. Whatever had crept into her noggin so easily could just as quickly make its way out, he pondered.

He set the shovel on the porch next to the front door and went inside. Letty remained in the living room chair where he had left her earlier. Butch lay curled up on the floor nearby. The room was dark with the shades still drawn to keep out the flicker, but now that it was past time, he went to pull them up.

"Leave them," Letty said, her tone caustic.

He nodded and moved away from the window, looking at his wife and how still she sat in the chair in the shadows.

"I'll make you some tea and lunch," he said. "You must be hungry."

Letty said nothing.

Barrett went to the kitchen and put the kettle on. He grabbed an iron skillet from a lower cabinet and made his wife a grilled Spam sandwich with melted cheese and tomato. As he finished preparing it, the teakettle whistled and he poured the boiling water into a cup, then let the tea bag steep while he finished preparing the sandwich. He added a pickle to the plate and brought it out to the living room with the steaming cup of tea. Letty didn't make a sound as he set the plate and cup down on the end table beside her chair.

She did not thank him; she only stared at him with steely eyes.

"Bill from Oakhurst called while you were out in the yard," she said, the words slinking out between tightened teeth.

"Oh," Barrett said, surprised.

"He rejected our last batch of milk." She glared at him.

"What?"

"Yuh," she replied. "He said it was off. The whole lot of it."

He felt her eyes searching out his face for reaction. This was not good, he thought. Oakhurst was their biggest account. They couldn't afford to lose it. The farm depended on it. They depended on it.

"Didn't you check it before sending it out?" Letty said, her eyes accusatory.

"Of course." He wouldn't tell her that he sensed it wasn't quite right. He had hoped it was okay enough to get by. Problem was, he knew most of the milkings lately weren't quite right.

"It's because of her," Letty said.

Barrett knew she meant Myrtle. "Don't be silly."

"I told you that red-and-white devil was a bad sign." Her voice rose. "We shouldn't have kept her."

"What were we to do?" he argued.

"Let her wander off," she said. "Hell, kill her. She's cursed and you know it. Ain't nothing good comes from a red. Look what she spawned!"

"That's just an accident of nature," Barrett said in vain.

"It's the devil's work. Ever since you agreed to sell off some of our land. And now look." She pointed toward the closed windows. "Those blasted machines came and are ruining everything."

"That ain't got nothing to do with it."

"The cows don't feed, and they're spilling out sour milk!" She became so agitated, she nearly lifted herself off the chair. "And the red gave birth to that monstrosity!"

"It's not the machines," he argued back, pointlessly he knew.

"Bad enough it caused our Ash to leap off the cliffs at the cove. Now Butch won't even step foot outside during the morning."

"We got no choice but to deal with it." He turned from her.

"And without Oakhurst, we'll go broke. And what will be left of the farm?"

"The cows will straighten out. It's just an aberration. They'll be fine next milking, you'll see." He headed toward the door. "I've got chores to do. Eat your sandwich. I'll check on you later."

Once outside, he paused. Most of what his wife said was nonsense. But she was right about one thing. If they couldn't keep their milk account, they'd lose the farm. And that was everything.

But the rest of her ramblings made him wonder if he should take her on the ferry tomorrow to Rockland and see one of them special doctors.

CHAPTER TWENTY-FOUR

Oscar met Polly Stark at the ranch-style house on Tolman Lane. She greeted him with a rambunctious smile and jingled a set of keys.

"Here you go," she said as he approached. "It's all set for you."

"Thank you," he said, taking the keys from her. "It'll just be for a week." That's all he paid for up front.

She waved her hand. "Believe me. The owner is thrilled to have someone in here for even the shortest amount of time." She lowered her voice as if afraid of being overheard. "I hear he's strapped for cash."

"Do you know much about the owner?" he asked.

"Of course. He's a schoolteacher." Her smile dissipated. "Or rather, ex-schoolteacher, which is why he's desperate for money. The selectmen didn't renew his contract."

"School population has probably shrunk a bit." In his research about Kidney Island, there was a reference to a declining population. "Fewer kids, fewer teachers." He opened the front door and she followed him inside.

"I suppose," Polly said, flicking on a light switch inside the door. "A lot of the younger generation aren't sticking around on the island, which doesn't help. But I heard there might have been a bit of a scandal at the school."

Oscar wasn't really paying attention to Polly. Instead he surveyed the modest living room furniture. Perhaps he made a mistake coming here, but he wanted a shot at experiencing what the others up the road dealt with every day with the effects of the turbines.

"What's this teacher's name?"

"Norris Squires," she said. "A nice young man."

Oscar nodded. "Did he leave the island?"

"Oh no, he's still around. Apparently fighting to get his job back at the school."

He turned to face her. "So why isn't he living here?"

Polly's face grew grim. "You may notice that there are quite a few empty houses in this neighborhood, at least of the houses that are finished."

"Yes, that seemed obvious."

She walked over to the bay window that looked out onto the front yard. "It's been hard to get people to stay here." She stared outside.

He sidled up beside her and looked out the window, which offered a good view of the wind turbines on the hill in the distance. "Because of those?"

She nodded. "Some people didn't care for the noise or shadows coming from those things."

Oscar thought he could talk to whoever remained in this neighborhood and add it to his report. They might not be a part of the insurance claim, but their input could help substantiate the grievance against Aerosource.

"So people just left their houses, like this Mr. Squires?"

She looked at him. "Some. A few of the properties have gone into foreclosure."

"Who thought building this neighborhood close to the turbines was a good idea?" That was the real question. The farms up the road had probably been here for a hundred years or more, but this place was recent.

"Gavin Pickett, our chairman of the Board of Selectmen, developed this property. He bought the land from the Granberrys. It was part of their farm, but like many of the farms on the island, they've downsized a bit. Just another aspect of the dwindling nature of our little piece of paradise."

Oscar couldn't imagine the financial burden this Pickett guy must have taken on with this property. "But still, to think people would want to live this close to the wind farm."

"It's all within the setback regulations," Polly countered.

Oscar knew that to be true from his research. One-thousand-foot setbacks for wind turbines. But who decided on that figure?

"Let me show you around the rest of the place," Polly said, moving from the window with a return of her big smile. She led him through the small kitchen and the three bedrooms, ending with the master.

"I guess this is where you'll be sleeping," she said, leaning closer to him.

He moved a step away and took in the king-sized bed with a nightstand on one side. A tall bureau stood against the wall opposite the bed. One thing he noticed the house lacked was a bookcase, which surprised him for a teacher's house. Oscar had hoped to relax with some light reading at night before bed. Maybe he could pick up a book in town.

"Very cozy," he said to Polly.

"It certainly is," she said. "Might be a bit lonely out here though." Her smile expanded.

"I like it quiet sometimes," he said.

"Well, if you need some company, you do have my card."

Oscar suppressed a chuckle and thanked her for all her help. After she left, he shook his head and went back to the bedroom to unpack. The master bedroom was situated at the front of the house, which suited him fine since that was where the sun rose and he wanted to get the full effect of the shadow flicker. Sure, he wouldn't be living with it daily for years like the others he talked to around here, but at least it might give him the slightest taste of their burden.

He filled the top few drawers of the empty bureau with clothing from his suitcase. Once done, he stashed the luggage in the empty closet where he also hung up his windbreaker. He hadn't needed it yet on the island with the hot weather and had only worn it on the ferry ride over. He'd heard there sometimes could be a chilly sea breeze, but he had yet to experience that. He stashed his briefcase in the closet as well, on a shelf over the rod where he hung his jacket.

He took a ride into town to get a few provisions at the market for however long he planned to stay at the house. At the market he mostly picked up stuff to make breakfasts and lunches, eggs, bagels, blueberry jam, bread, deli meat and chips. He figured he'd eat out for dinner since it would all be charged as a business expense anyway. At the beer cooler he selected a local state brew, Goat Head Light, which looked appealing. He wanted to watch his calories.

At the checkout line, he made sure to go to Tatum Gallagher's register. She seemed surprised to see him but offered a pleasant smile. She looked down at his groceries on the counter.

"Staying awhile," she said, her smile tightening.

He smiled. "Just some things to get me through the next few days. I've rented a place over at Pickett Fences Estates."

Her whole face tensed. "Why on earth would you do that?"

He shrugged. "I wanted to get a good feel for what it's like to live near the turbines, experience the shadow flicker on a somewhat regular basis."

She frowned. "A few days ain't going to show you much." She began ringing up his purchases.

"I know, but I thought it'd be good to get some perspective for my report."

The scanner beeped as she moved his items along.

"Are you putting in what I said about the day the time stopped?" Her voice cracked as she spoke.

"Do you want me to?"

Her eyes met his. "I know you don't believe me."

"It doesn't matter what I believe." He hesitated. "I'm more than willing to leave it out."

She brushed back a few strands of her hair and nodded. "I think that's best. Don't want anyone thinking I'm crazy."

"Fair enough."

She gave him the total for his items and he ran his credit card through the machine. She began bagging his groceries.

"Just make sure you include the stuff about Rigby and his epilepsy. I want that on the record."

"Of course."

Back at his new abode, Oscar put his groceries away and prepared a sliced turkey sandwich before doing some work. A small patio off the rear kitchen door contained a table and four chairs. He sat there while he ate and began working on his report. He did a little research into epilepsy and discovered that the range of hertz that caused epileptic seizures were in the 5–30 range. The flickering from the arms of the turbines was only in the 0.6–1.0 range, so most researchers stated it couldn't cause epileptic seizures. Lucky for Aerosource.

Tatum would be disappointed. But Oscar kept his promise and included information about Rigby and the flashes of light he experienced, even though the boy was underwater at the quarry and nowhere near the turbines. Maybe some residual effects hampered his brain. That would be for someone more knowledgeable than him to determine.

Oscar spent a couple hours working on the report, trying to make sense of some of the things the neighbors told him. It all seemed a jumbled mess that didn't hold sufficient cohesion. Everyone seemed to have different experiences and effects. Some were bothered by the flicker, others by the noise. Lack of sleep and headaches seemed the only common symptom. Maybe the unsettledness of their minds contributed to the rest.

He could hear the noise from the turbines now, hovering over his little workspace like a faint echo. A constant hum. He closed his tablet.

Enough for today, he thought.

He got up from his seat and went back inside, where the noise diminished, and into the bedroom. He wanted a convenient place to put his tablet where it would be handy and eyed the nightstand next to the bed that held a small lamp. A drawer in the stand looked the right size.

Before putting the tablet away, he checked his email to see if Kyle had responded to his apologetic message. He frowned. Nothing. The silence spoke volumes. Message received, he thought. Claudia Davenport got what she wanted and Oscar felt determined to finally put this all behind him. It did him no good to fret anymore.

He turned the tablet off and pulled open the drawer to place it inside. A book occupied the space. Reading material, he thought with a smile and took the volume out. It had no dust jacket, just a black hardcover binding. The title was emblazed in raised red letters on the front cover: *The Kybalion.*

Oscar hadn't heard of this book and had no clue what the title meant, but he thought it might be worth reading to pass some of the time at the lonely house when he wasn't working. The book looked old with a wrinkled binding and frayed edges on the corners of the cover. A musty smell exuded from it, enhancing as he flipped it open to the first few pages.

He'd hoped for some spy thriller or suspense novel, but it became apparent that wasn't the kind of story these pages contained. In fact, as he perused the table of contents, he immediately realized it wasn't something for him. It seemed more a religious or philosophical tome, though he did not quite ascertain what kind of worshipers or followers this ideology targeted.

The book seemed to be derived from the teachings of the ancient philosopher Hermes and the movement inspired by his principles. As Oscar skimmed it, words and phrases jumped out at him, pages devoted to the existence of physical, spiritual and mental planes and their connection to matter, energy and mind. Talk of Hermetic science and the dividing of time and principles of rhythm and polarity. It all went beyond him and he figured this book must belong to the teacher who owned the house. What had Polly said his name was? Something Squires. Maybe he tried pushing this kind of science on the kids at the school and that's what caused his termination.

Oscar fanned the pages and prepared to return it to its place in the nightstand drawer when a piece of paper fell out and fluttered to the floor. He bent and retrieved it. The lined paper looked ripped from a notebook. Barely legible scrawl was scratched across it in black ink.

At last. My work has been a success. I need to inform the others. I have found the Opening of the Mouth.

It was signed beneath the words by the initials: *B.S.*

Oscar replaced the paper in a random spot in the book, hoping it wasn't marking a special page, and shoved the book back into the drawer. B.S. That must be the teacher, though he couldn't remember what Polly had said the guy's first name was.

If this was what the guy taught the kids, it sure sounded like BS to him.

CHAPTER TWENTY-FIVE

Dirk Lassiter felt the tentacles of his tattoo shifting again, moving up the base of his neck and tightening on his scalp. As pressure built inside his head, he thought this shouldn't be happening here.

He sat in the assembly room on the second floor of Town Hall in Loch Raven, listening to Selectmen Chairman Gavin Pickett destroy his hopes. Dirk felt his blood pressure rise, as if the tentacles squeezing his brain forced a flood of fluids down his arteries into the rest of his body. This never happened away from the turbines before. It had been what drove him to move out of the farmhouse, leaving Tatum and Rigby behind while he shacked up at Brownie's bungalow on Seabreeze Avenue. To get away from the effects that annoyed the hell out of him.

Now it followed him here in the village center. Was there no escape?

Pressure built up in his eardrums, muffling the noise as Pickett spoke from his pompous seat behind the center of the selectmen's bench.

"So you see," Pickett said, his lips moving slow beneath his dark mustache as if he were speaking to a child, "Kidney Island is just not ready for this kind of a proposition."

Dirk felt that's how the prick was treating him, like a child, or an idiot. Maybe he wasn't smart like the three people on the panel. He didn't have their education. He was just a common laborer, working on a lobster boat after the farm failed and the house painting business dried up. But now he had a plan, a chance to turn his misfortunes around and hopefully win Tatum back in the process. Dirk had it all figured out, and with Tatum's help, since she was better with words, he'd drawn up the proposal that he presented tonight before the selectmen.

"That's not the kind of image we want to present to the tourists we strive to bring to the island," Pickett continued.

Dirk's plan was solid, he knew it. He'd worked out all the details. Now that marijuana had become legalized in Maine, he proposed a pot farm to grow enough product to supply one of the local dispensaries on the mainland. It's not like he'd be selling the stuff on the streets. No, only to legitimate, legally approved sellers. A small business loan would help him get started, and he could be up and running in no time. He just needed to rebuild the greenhouse on the farm and purchase the equipment, lights and heaters and stuff and hire some workers. Plenty of migrant farmers in Maine, especially the Somalis up in the Lewiston area. Seasonal workers once the crops were ready. He could even rent rooms to them at the farmhouse so he, Tatum and Rigby could move into a nice place in the village and be away from those damn turbines.

He clenched his teeth as the tentacles tightened and his ears hummed.

"Maybe sometime in the future," Pickett went on, "we could readdress this once we see how this industry is received in the rest of the state." He cleared his throat and closed the folder in front of him. "But not now. Not on Kidney Island."

Dirk left Town Hall feeling like his head was going to implode.

What the hell did Gavin Pickett care about his future? The developer owned most of the property in town. He had all the money he needed, so why make it easy for anyone else to get some? Dirk climbed into his pickup and peeled out of the parking lot onto Main Street, heading west toward Seabreeze Avenue.

Pickett was the prick who brokered the Aerosource deal and scoffed up all that land from Tatum, the Larsons and the Granberrys so he had enough setbacks for those damn wind turbines that now made everybody on Haven Road miserable. And he bought old man Granberry's property south of the road for that ugly development that nobody wanted to live in.

Dirk heard the bastard lost money on that project. *Serves him right. He allows Aerosource to put those turbines up, and now he's surprised no one wants to live in his stupid development near them.* Who was the idiot there? Mr. Smarty Pants didn't think that one through, did he?

But why did the bastard have to shit all over his plans? His proposal seemed sound and profitable. Pot laws were being relaxed all over the country. Damn, the state of Maine legalized it. Places would be selling it and growers would be supplying it. Dirk wanted in on the action while it was early and hot. This would be life changing.

But not on Kidney Island? Why the fuck not? Damn Pickett. Or Prickett, as some people in town called the selectmen chairman. Pickett scoffed at the idea because he wouldn't be making any money from it. It meant nothing to him. But it meant everything to Dirk. And he knew Pickett coveted the Gallagher farm property. The developer wanted to buy the land, probably for another stupid development. The prick probably still resented him because Dirk convinced Tatum to reject the offer. As it was, she still sold a strip of the land for the Aerosource project. But Pickett wanted the whole thing.

He pulled into the driveway at Brownie's bungalow, slamming the door as he got out. His head hurt, his blood boiled. And he swore the ringing in his ears came from the sound of the turbines, impossible though, considering the distance from it.

Brownie's bungalow lay along the rocky south-west coast, almost as far away from the wind farm you could get on the island. But still....

Out of his truck, the drum of the surf beating against the shore stymied the drone in his ears, but still the tentacles tightened on his skull. He entered the bungalow into a room swirling with smoky vapors. Brownie and Jumbo lay back on the couch, passing the glass pipe between them. Jumbo waved the only the digits on his left hand as Dirk entered the room, giving the impression of a distorted version of the Hawaiian hang loose sign.

"Fuck!" Dirk said, still irked by the night's events. He went into the kitchen to retrieve a beer and returned to the main living space of the house where the others eyeballed him with curiosity.

"What gives?" Jumbo asked, taking the glass pipe from Brownie delicately between his two fingers and sucking in a quick toke.

Brownie stared back at him with his usual dull glazed-over eyes set deep within his creased, tanned face like a wizened old Methuselah. He had about twenty years on Dirk, even more on Jumbo, and though Dirk knew bits and pieces of Brownie's history, the man still remained a bit of a mystery.

Brownie had come to Kidney Island by accident as a young man. He had dropped out of high school and ended up crewing on a drug running boat bringing dope into Maine from Canada back in the Seventies. The story was that one night run, the boat was intercepted by a Coast Guard crew and some idiot fired a shot, though no one was sure which side. Brownie jumped overboard in the chaos of the dark night and swam away from the scene. He spent the night clinging to one of the big metal navigational buoys till early morning and then swam to the only land in sight: Kidney Island. He washed up on shore, near exhaustion, and that's where he lay until he got enough energy to get up and walk into town. After a couple nights sleeping down by the docks, he hooked up with a crew on a lobster boat and began learning the trade. After a decade or more, he could afford his own boat and ventured out on his own.

And he'd been here ever since, captaining the *Seaweed* and taking on Jumbo and eventually Dirk. But he still had his dope connections and always liked a good high after a long day on the sea.

"Give me a hit of that," Dirk said, taking the glass pipe from Jumbo. The clear glass was in the shape of a woman, with a bowl jutting up out of her midsection and the opening between her spread legs. Dirk put his lips up to the slot and took a deep hit. After coughing out most of the smoke he inhaled, he told them what happened at Town Hall with Pickett and the rest of the selectmen.

"Damn," Brownie said from the couch. "I thought I'd finally be able to go legit." He took the pipe back from Dirk.

"Them bastards," Dirk said, taking a swig from his beer. "Between them and that asshole sniffing around Tatum, I feel like kicking some ass." The dope did little to ease the tension in his skull.

"Just relax," Brownie said. "Chill out."

"Easy for you to say," Dirk spat back. "I don't want to be on a fucking lobster boat the rest of my life."

Brownie shrugged.

"There's worse ways to make a living," Jumbo said and scratched the edge of his nostril with his left pinky. "At least nobody bothers you."

Dirk shot him a glare. "Ain't going to get Tatum back that way. And if this off-islander is who I think he is, I need to do something quick."

"You really think he's been sent here by—" Jumbo started, but didn't finish.

Brownie and Jumbo were the only two Dirk had told about Rigby's real father, and he trusted them to keep shut about it and they knew he didn't like to bring it up.

"I just got a lousy feeling," Dirk said, draining his beer and reaching for the pipe again.

"Then stop whining and do something about it," Brownie said in frustration before taking the pipe back.

Dirk nodded but kept silent. It was hard to think with the pressure in his skull. But he knew he needed to do something soon. Everything was falling apart around him. Something had to be done.

CHAPTER TWENTY-SIX

Oscar ate dinner at the Porthole, on a seat at the counter. The constant smell of salt air on the island had pushed him off any type of seafood, so he settled for a mac'n'cheese with sausage dish instead. It came in a small crock; steaming and gooey cheese filled his mouth with every bite. *Maybe pizza tomorrow night*, he thought.

A few more days here, and then he could file his report and go home.

Home. His home life felt empty without Kyle in it and the thought of his ex and Claudia Davenport curling up on a cozy couch to watch television sickened him. Now the pasta and cheese he just consumed felt heavy in his belly, the sausage spicy, and he could practically feel the acids in his stomach gurgling as they broke it all down.

He had a home to go to tonight, even as temporary as it was. But as he stepped out onto the sidewalk in front of the restaurant into the cool night air and the sound of the water funneling through the channel into Loch Raven, he felt no desire to return to it so soon in the young evening. Part of that had to do with knowing what awaited him at Pickett Fences Estates.

The noise.

Even here in the village his ears remembered the grinding whirling sound like a faint echo. He knew he only imagined it, but still, it waited back there. Just listening to it today since he'd been at the house made him realize these people shouldn't have to live with that nuisance. It might not be a health risk covered by insurance as they claimed, but it damn sure must be one great annoyance. That he could put in his report from firsthand experience.

His eyes wandered over the dark closed storefronts till he spotted the light of the Raven's Nest at the other end of Main Street. A few drinks, he thought, just to take the edge off before heading back up Haven Road. That would do the trick.

A low mumble of voices greeted his ears when he walked into the bar, and as heads turned to notice him, the murmur grew softer. Once again it looked like most of the patrons were locals. He thought more tourists might pop in for some libations, but that certainly wasn't the case. No, these were island folk unwinding after a long day of work.

At one table, he spotted Tatum Gallagher's husband, Dirk, and the same two cronies he saw him with the other night. Dirk's eyes fell upon him with a fierce look and Oscar glanced away, not wanting to make any contact. He searched the bar for an empty stool, as all the tables looked full, but it appeared shoulder to shoulder around the U-shaped bar.

Oscar felt nervous, like he shouldn't be there, and started to turn to head back out the door. Maybe this wasn't such a bright idea. But as he turned to go, he spotted someone waving him over.

It was the handsome man he spotted last time, the one on the bicycle with the white hard hat, which now rested on an empty chair at his table. The man motioned him over. Oscar had to look around to make sure the guy meant him, but the man nodded and he felt compelled to oblige.

"Full house tonight," the man said, removing his hard hat from the seat and placing it on the table. "You're welcome to join me."

The man had a pleasant smile beneath dark eyes, and though the situation made him feel a bit uncomfortable, the charming appeal of the man convinced him to accept his offer. What was the alternative? Head back to his rental house and listen to the turbines?

"Thanks," Oscar said, sliding up onto the stool. "I'm Oscar." He extended his hand, which the man took in a firm grasp. He looked a couple years older than him.

"I know who you are," the man said.

"Can't keep anything quiet on this island, is that it?" He wasn't sure if he should be concerned or not.

"How could I not know your name?" the man said. "You're renting my house."

"You're the teacher?" It took Oscar by surprise.

"Norris Squires," the man responded. "And it's ex-teacher."

"Oh, right. I heard something about that."

Norris nodded. "For now. I'm fighting it."

The waitress came over and Oscar ordered a drink. Norris likewise.

"So how come I'm in your house, and you're not? I assumed you left the island."

"You haven't spent a night there yet," Norris said. "Give it time."

"The turbines?"

He nodded. "They put them up after I bought the place. Bad timing on my part."

"Is it really that bad?"

"You tell me. You're the one who's been talking to the neighbors."

"That's common knowledge?"

"Small island." Norris took a sip of his beer. "Word gets around."

The waitress brought Oscar's drink and another beer for Norris.

"Just to set the record straight, I don't work for Aerosource."

Norris laughed. "Yes, I heard that too. Not like the last guy."

The situation dawned on Oscar. "That's right! He rented your house before me."

"For a little bit. Till he just up and left."

That seemed to be the consensus. "What happened to him?"

Norris shrugged. "Who knows, who cares? I got my rent in advance and he didn't even stay as long as he paid for."

It still didn't sound quite right to Oscar. "What was the guy like?"

Norris smirked. "Middle age, nondescript. Stocky guy, maybe a few extra pounds. Thinning greasy hair. Average."

"I meant more along the lines of how did he act?"

"I didn't interact with him too much. He did ask a lot of questions about why I was renting my house. You know, curious about how I felt about the wind farm."

"And what did you tell him?" Oscar thought this man could add some input to his report.

"I said I thought they blow."

He laughed at his own joke and Oscar couldn't help but smile along. He liked this guy already. He presented a certain charm.

"So if you're not living at your own house, where are you staying?"

"I rent a yurt on a farm just outside of town."

"A yurt? Isn't that kind of like a tent?"

"It's a little sturdier than that, but more or less. A farmer friend has three of them on his property. Rents them out, mostly to tourists in the summer. Kind of a way to supplement his farm. But since I moved out of my house, I took advantage of one of his vacancies and rent it year-round."

This struck Oscar as odd. It sounded a little too much like roughing it. "Doesn't it get too cold in the winter?"

"It has a pellet stove to heat it up, but yeah, it still has quite a chill to it. It's only a temporary solution."

"Till you can sell your house?"

"Exactly. Renting it brings in enough cash to keep me going for now."

"Especially without a job?" Oscar glanced down at the hard hat. It must mean Norris worked doing something.

"I work part-time at the hardware and feed store, mostly dealing with farm products, fertilizer and stuff."

That didn't really explain the curiosity of the hard hat, but Oscar felt uneasy about asking.

Oscar thought about the book in the master bedroom and the strange note he found inside it. He remembered it being signed B.S., but this man's first name was Norris.

"I want to ask you about a book I found in the nightstand next to the bed, *The Kybalion*."

Norris's eyes looked blank.

"Is it yours?"

He shook his head. "Nothing familiar. What kind of book?"

Oscar thought hard about the pages he skimmed. "Some kind of occult tome about metaphysics and some such crap. Really weird." He remembered the line on the note, *I have found the Opening of the Mouth.* He shivered.

"Not mine. Must have belonged to the previous tenant. The Aerosource guy."

"What was his name?"

"Burton Sikes."

B.S. That was who signed the note, Oscar thought.

"I guess wherever he went, he didn't bother to take the book," Norris said.

It all seemed odd to Oscar. He glanced around the bar and saw Dirk Lassiter eyeballing him with that sour look on his face.

"Don't worry about them," Norris said, noticing.

"They seem to have a distinct dislike of me."

Norris reached over and placed his hand on Oscar's arm. "That's because they don't like people like us."

Oscar caught his eyes. A chill ran through his body. *Could it be?*

"Like us?" Oscar asked, his throat dry.

Norris retracted his hand. "Yeah, off-islanders. They don't like anyone who's not from here."

"Oh," Oscar said, befuddled and a little disappointed. "Wait. You live here."

"Doesn't matter," Norris said. "Unless you're born and raised here, you're still an off-islander. I've been here five years, and I'm still not accepted."

"What keeps you here?" Oscar sensed boredom and isolation would drive him crazy. He needed the arts and culture of the city. Not to mention shopping, entertainment and a zillion other things, like having a few more choices to eat out than this place, the Porthole, the diner or the pizza joint.

Norris's eyes wandered as he gathered his thoughts. "I used to teach at an inner-city school in Brooklyn. I just got tired of the bullying, racism, inconsideration. And that was just among the staff." He laughed. "Finally started looking elsewhere and found a job opening here. It just seemed so peaceful."

"And is it?"

"It really is," Norris answered. "Once you get by the peculiarities of the native folk. I feel much more relaxed here."

"But you lost your job?" Oscar didn't know if he should press the issue, but figured what harm could there be. "What happened?"

Norris hesitated, an expression of consternation sweeping over his face before a half smile cracked the grimace. "I'll tell you that another time."

"Another time?" Oscar wasn't sure what he meant by that.

"What are your plans tomorrow?"

Oscar thought for a moment. He hadn't actually been quite sure. He wanted to wake up in the embrace of the shadow flicker to experience what the others had to deal with on a daily basis, but besides that, he thought about knocking on what few doors might be occupied in Pickett Fences Estates and talk to some of the people there about their experiences.

"Nothing definite," he finally answered.

"Have you ever kayaked before?"

Oscar had, once when he and Kyle rented some in Boston and went up the Charles River.

"Sure," he said.

"Meet me at the municipal lot by the docks, around 10 a.m. We can take a couple kayaks out in the Basin. It's beautiful there. There's a rental place that I can arrange having the kayaks dropped off there."

Oscar felt this was something he needed, a relaxing day to take his mind off Kyle Devitt, Claudia Davenport, Mason Helleson and Aerosource. He could use a break from reality.

"Sounds great."

They finished their drinks and got up to leave. Oscar noticed Dirk and his seafaring pals were gone. Norris mentioned his bike was chained up in the rack at the municipal lot, which was where Oscar had parked, so they walked there together.

"Don't you have a vehicle?" Oscar asked.

"Sort of." He grinned. "I own an old VW bus, but it's broken down right now. There's only one service station in town, so it takes a while to get things fixed, unless you're someone of some importance on the island."

"And you're not?"

"Let's just say I'm not very high up on the list. It just needs a new carburetor, which I can install myself thanks to YouTube. I've ordered the part online. Just takes time to get out here in nowhere-land."

"I'm glad the internet even works out here."

Norris laughed. "It's not as remote as it seems. And you can be on the mainland in seventy-five minutes if you catch the ferry when it's heading out, or hitch a ride with a friendly fisherman."

"Are there actually any of those here?" Oscar asked, being serious.

"There are. They're not all like Brownie and his lot."

"So you ride your bike everywhere?"

"For now. It's great exercise and does wonders for the environment. I don't have far to go, it's a small island."

As they got near to where Oscar parked his car, the stench from the ocean rose strong over the parking lot as if all the boats in the marina had just unloaded their catch. When they reached his car, Oscar saw why.

The hood of his car was covered in severed fish heads.

"What the fuck?"

He heard laughter in the shadows of the parking lot and saw a rusted white pickup with a missing tailgate pull away.

"Chum for those who like cum!" someone yelled out amongst a roar of laughter and the sound of rubber and squealing tires as the pickup peeled out of the parking lot and disappeared down Main Street.

"Bastards!" Oscar yelled, fists clenched. He looked back at his car. *How did they know?* "What a mess!"

"Idiots," Norris said, looking down at the car's hood.

Oscar thought about the comment that was spewed out of the truck, looked at Norris and wondered if it was directed at both of them. Norris met his eyes.

"Don't worry, it'll wash right off. There's a water hose over by the marina." He pointed to the edge of the parking lot by the docks. "Drive your car over there, I'll meet you and help."

Oscar stepped around the pieces of fish scattered on the ground around the car and got in. He drove slowly over to the marina pumps, some fish heads falling off the hood with soft splats, and he pulled up to where Norris already stood with his bicycle leaning up against a post.

When Oscar got out, Norris had the hose running and aimed it at the hood of the car, the burst of water pushing the smelly fish head remains off and onto the ground.

"I'd say you'd want to take it through a car wash tomorrow to clean off any sticky fish gut residue, but there isn't one on the island. You could do it by hand."

"Thanks," Oscar said, not sure what he'd do. "Should I report this to Constable Jensen?"

"You could," Norris said. "But I don't think it'd do much good. He'd have a talk with them, and then they'd only get more pissed off. It's up to you. They're juveniles."

Oscar thought about how nice Tatum Gallagher seemed and wondered what she ever saw in someone like Dirk Lassiter. But then he didn't even know what Kyle saw in Claudia Davenport, so who was he to judge?

"Thanks for your help."

"No problem, I'll see you tomorrow." Norris shook his hand and then turned to his bicycle.

Oscar stared at the construction helmet strapped to a rack on the back of the bike. Norris noticed.

"I have to ask," Oscar said when he met his eyes.

"About that?"

Oscar nodded.

Norris took in a deep breath. "I wear that when I go out to the turbines." He left it at that. Not really an explanation.

Oscar stared, waiting for more before realizing none was forthcoming. "I don't get it? Do you work part-time on the turbines or something?"

Norris laughed. "That couldn't be further off."

"So?"

"I'm studying the turbines. Charting them, measuring the rotation of the blades, timing them, trying to understand their patterns."

This didn't make any sense to Oscar. "And the hard hat?"

"That's for protection. To interrupt the signals they're sending out."

CHAPTER TWENTY-SEVEN

Melody Larson sat in the dark before midnight.

She didn't have to see a clock to know the time. She sat tense in a chair in the living room where she could see the front door. The shades were up on the windows facing the front, providing her a view toward the driveway.

The night felt hot and through the open windows the hum of the turbines filtered in. Her head ached; her hands trembled from jittery nerves. Myles should have been home long ago. What excuse would he have? Inventory again? How many times did he expect her to fall for that? Did he think he was fooling her?

Light cascaded across the lawn as she heard the hum of the truck engine. Flashes from the beams swept across her face, almost blinding her for an instant. Did he notice her when the light lit up the house? Could he see the look on her face as she gritted her teeth? In a second the light flicked out and she heard the truck door open. The key fumbled in the lock before finding its purchase and the door swung open.

Rage building up inside suppressed the laughter at the comical way he stepped into the house with such soft steps to avoid waking anyone.

Too late. If he knew anything about her, he knew she couldn't sleep anyway. And when his eyes latched on to her presence in the living room, he stopped short.

"Melody?" His voice cracked with startled surprise.

"Did you have a good fuck?" Her words came out like venom.

His eyes crossed, his brow furrowed. "What the hell are you talking about?"

"I know all about it," she said. "No need to play dumb, though you do it very well."

He kicked off his shoes and strode across the room toward her. "You know what?" He tried to sound intimidating, but failed.

"You and your trysts with Tatum." She had long suspected, but earlier had heard from Brock, Tatum's co-worker at the market. He felt it was his duty to inform her of rumors that had been floating around town. More likely he just craved the gossip, but it served its purpose all the same.

"You're tired," he said. "Go to bed." He turned to walk away.

She jumped up from the chair. "Don't you walk away from me!" She felt her insides churning, face feeling flush.

He stopped and spun around. "What do you want, Melody? Want me to say it's true? Do you really want me to tell you that?"

Her lips trembled as she tried to speak. Did she want the truth? Could she stand any more pain? She started to cry. "Why would you do this to me?"

He came right up to her, loomed over her, his lips peeled back in a grimace. "Do you have to ask? You know what you've been like for the past year or more!"

Emotions coursed through her body, part anger, part despair. "I can't help it if I don't have any desire for you lately! I can't sleep! I'm always tired! I have constant headaches from listening to those damn turbines. My brain feels like mush." It did. It felt like a bowl of gruel and someone was digging it out with a spoon constantly scraping against the inside of her skull. She clenched her fists. "I'm always worrying about my dad ever since that day he ate the dandelions and almost choked to death. Now he keeps wandering off. I think about locking him in his room at night so I don't have to worry about checking on him and finding him missing." She looked up at eyes that didn't care. "Don't you have any idea how I feel?" Her voice softened to a plea.

"What about how I feel?" he answered.

Himself. That's all he thought about, himself. "Then just leave," she spat out.

He turned to go and she suddenly realized he might leave. She grabbed his arm.

"No," she cried. "Don't go. Come to the bedroom with me. I'll have sex with you right now. You can do whatever you want to me." She felt ashamed for how she pleaded with him. But it felt even worse when she saw him look upon her with displeasure.

Myles walked over to the hall closet and opened it. She thought he was going to grab his suitcase and start packing, but instead he grabbed a blanket off the top shelf.

"What are you doing?" Her whole body trembled.

"I'm sleeping on the couch," he said, bitter.

A voice came from the top of the stairs. "What's going on down there?" Whitney asked. "Is everything all right?"

Melody rushed to the bottom of the stairs and looked up at her drowsy, distraught daughter. "Everything's okay, dear. Go on back to bed."

"Are you two fighting?"

Melody felt her insides slump. "Just grown-up stuff," she answered half-heartedly. "Go to your room, it's fine now. We'll be quiet."

Whitney looked down, an expression of uneasiness etched across her face, but she turned and headed back to her room.

Melody went back to the living room and stared at her husband while he tried to settle his long frame into a comfortable position on the couch, pulling the blanket up to his chin, even though the room was warm from the summer heat. As anger still bubbled up inside her, she turned and went down the hall to their bedroom. Or was it her bedroom now?

She lay there on the bed, the covers bunched in a jumble by her ankles, night air seeping through the screen in the open window behind her. She glanced at the pillow where her husband's head should be and the empty space beside her, imaging what it would be like if Myles did leave, if this was the image she would see every night she climbed into bed, and her heart sank in her chest.

"What's happened?" she asked the empty spot in a soft voice. Her head throbbed in rhythm with the turning of the turbines outside and she knew the answer.

CHAPTER TWENTY-EIGHT

Figures, Oscar thought as he lay in bed waiting to drift off to sleep in his new temporary home. He meets an interesting guy, handsome and athletic, and of course the guy has a screw loose. How else could one explain his comment about the wind turbines sending signals?

Signals?

What the fuck?

Norris appeared so normal, was a goddamn teacher, for Christ's sake. Maybe whatever deep-seated paranoia became imbedded in his mind toward the wind farm led to his dismissal from the school. Who would want someone like that teaching children?

He debated whether he should accept the offer to go kayaking tomorrow. But in spite of the strange comment about the turbines, he enjoyed the company and conversation Norris provided and looked forward to a day of recreation and relaxation. Then he could finish his report over the next couple days and leave Kidney Island. All the pleasant qualities of the quaint coastal community and its nautical charms were washed out by the oddities of its inhabitants. He wouldn't be sorry to leave this place.

Oscar rolled over on his side, burying his head deeper into the pillow. He couldn't be sure whether the disturbing comment from Norris kept him from sleeping or if it was the clacking, grinding noise of the turbines coming through the open bedroom window. But sleep evaded him, and no matter which way he rested his head into the pillow, one ear always remained exposed to pick up the audible hum of the machine.

He could easily close the window, but the pleasant breeze of the night air was a soothing and refreshing respite from the day's summer heat. But damn, the noise. Soft and distant enough to not be overbearing, but just the right amount to always remind you it's there.

Even as far inland as this house was, Oscar could still smell the salty air of the sea. In fact it seemed even stronger than he had previously noticed when he first visited the homes in this part of the island.

When sleep did finally overcome him, it was not restful. Dreams invaded his head, images of fish heads, mouths opening and closing to the rhythm of the grinding clatter from the turbines; Dirk and his motley lobstermen companions chasing him with long fishhooks; and flickers of light and shadows raining down on him, blinding him.

He stirred in his sleep, rolling over onto his back. His eyes opened and he spotted a shadow lurking at the end of the room in the open bedroom doorway. *Another dream*, he thought. *I am asleep, aren't I?*

The shadow pulled away from the doorway, entering the room. *Just a dream, a walking dream.* Oscar closed his eyes, not wanting to see the shadow come any closer to his bed. In the darkness behind his eyes, he could still sense the shadow as it neared him. He felt if he pulled his arm out from under the covers and reached out to the side of the bed, he would grasp the dark shape and it would feel like thick smoke in his bare fingers.

He sensed the shadow leaning over his bed, could feel its dark breath on him as he slept.

Yes, I am asleep. Of course I am.

He heard a soft scraping sound and then he could sense the shadow had retreated.

Oscar opened his eyes. The room remained empty, no shadows about. He had awoken from an intrusive dream and now he lay in bed in the middle of the night, once again hearing the rhythm of the turbine blades. The salty air smelled stronger, as if the tidal waters rose up over the rocky shore and trickled their way inland, flowing down Haven Road toward the house where he slept.

No, I'm awake now. Before I was asleep, but no more. I need to rest.

He closed his eyes and once again sleep overtook him and this time he hoped, even prayed, that dark dreams would not trespass on it.

★   ★   ★

When dawn broke, it brought the shadows. They flickered across the room in sweeping motions. *Shadow, light, shadow, light.* A stroking rhythm like clockwork gone berserk.

Oscar propped himself up on his elbows and watched the shadows. This was what the others felt every morning. He rubbed the sleep from his eyes so he could see clearer. The shadows continued in revolutions sweeping across the room.

He remembered the shadowy dream from the night before and looked to the empty bedroom doorway. As the shadows flickered across the open frame, he imagined the shadowy figure as something that detached from the flicker, dropped inside his room by the turbine blades.

Oscar let loose a nervous chuckle.

Dreams, he thought. They were always senseless in the light of day. He threw the covers off and swung his legs onto the floor. He stretched, raising his arms up to pull the stiffness out of his muscles. He glanced down at the nightstand.

The drawer was partially opened.

Oscar thought that odd. He didn't remember leaving it like that. He felt sure he had closed it. He reached over and pulled it open some more.

Empty. The book was gone.

A chill erupted throughout his body. *Not a dream?* Had someone really come into his room in the middle of the night? He swallowed hard, spit dry in his throat. No. He had locked the front door. Of course he had.

There was only one way to be sure. He threw on a pair of pants and marched out to the front of the house. At the door he checked the knob. Locked. Like he figured it would be.

Oscar opened the door, greeted by the sunrise and the flicker of shadows that broke it apart, spilling it in pieces across the front lawn and his face. He blinked. *I'm not imagining things,* he told himself. But something didn't seem right. He took in a deep breath, but the air was tainted by a strong smell of the sea, much stronger than it should have been in that area.

He looked down at the doorstep he stood on.

By his feet lay a piece of seaweed.

CHAPTER TWENTY-NINE

The noise woke Melody first, like a gentle nudge to let her know it remained out there. The humming. She didn't have to open her eyes to know the light flickered across her bedroom. Even with her eyes closed, her vision sensed the twirl of light and shadow as if the elements seeped through her eyelids.

Time to wake up. Time to face the routine of the day. Time to know it's still there. It's always there.

She opened her eyes.

Before she even had a chance to blink from the flickering effect, she noticed the empty space in the bed beside her.

Myles never came to bed. Her heart dropped as if something gripped it and tugged it down deeper into her chest. She could no longer be mad, only sad. He might have come to bed in the middle of the night and happened to get up before her and head out into the fields. But no. She didn't sleep that deeply to not be able to detect his presence, his warmth, and the sinking feeling of the mattress as his body pressed into the space beside her. She would have sensed that. It would have woken her because she didn't sleep soundly, not with that infernal clockwork sound of the machines.

Melody rose up on one elbow, trying to rub the exhaustion from her eyes. She dragged herself out of bed, threw on her bathrobe and left the bedroom. In the living room, her eyes fell upon the empty couch and the bunched-up blanket and mashed pillow on one end. He hadn't even bothered to pick up, just left it for her of, course. She took care of everything while he played farmer by day, loner by night.

But no, not alone. How many nights did he spend with her? Now the thing that gripped her heart squeezed tighter till her whole chest ached. She picked up the blanket to fold it, but instead dropped onto the couch and buried her face in it, smelling his scent, as tears poured out to be soaked up by the soft fuzzy fabric.

God, what's gone wrong? Everything is messed up. So...fucking... messed up.

But Melody couldn't be. She had to be in control, because she was the one to take care of things. She would take care of Whitney and Troy. She'd watch out for the seagulls in the shadows. And she would make sure her father didn't wander off or stuff dandelions down his throat. Because everyone depended upon her. Because....

Dad?

She sat up. Her father should be up by now, making coffee. She couldn't smell anything. She sprang from the couch and moved down the hall to his first-floor bedroom. The door remained closed and she knocked, gently at first, and then with more force after the lack of response.

"Dad?" she called through the door, before easing it open and peering in.

Gone.

Damn! she thought.

She didn't like him up and wandering about during the shadow flicker. She couldn't trust what effect it might have or what he might be capable of doing. With no time to dress, she checked to make sure he wasn't in the bathroom, and then ventured outside.

Troy swung on the tire swing under the maple tree, spinning it in circles as he gazed up to the sky. It amazed her he had already gotten up and gone outside to play. Had she overslept? That wasn't like her. Myles must have tended to the boy while she slept. Melody glanced up at the sky, hoping and glad there were no gulls in the air.

"Have you seen your grandpa?" she hollered to her son.

Troy paused long enough to give her a puzzling stare, and then shook his head.

She put her hands on her hips and drew in a deep breath. "Keep an eye out for him."

"Okay, Mom," he said, but kept spinning around on the tire.

Melody had no idea where Myles was, maybe out in the fields. Her gaze went to the barn with its partially opened wooden slider door. Could her father be in there working on his press, making the dandelion wine? She didn't like the idea of him operating the machinery himself these days. He wasn't reliable anymore.

She strode quickly over that way, anxious, one part hoping he wasn't at work with the press, but another wanting him to be there so at least she knew his whereabouts. She slid open the door the rest of the way and looked in.

The wine press sat in the middle of the barn. The smell of the sea mingled with the musty earthen scent of the barn and its aged beams. She didn't understand the mixture of odors. She walked over to the press. Its oiled gears glistened. A tin bucket beneath the press held a murky liquid and the smell of salt wafted up. She turned her head, her nose twitching.

Her father had been pressing something in it, but it wasn't dandelions. She grabbed the wheel and gave it a few turns to raise the hammer up from the pad. Something stuck under it reeked of the sea. She reached down and touched it.

Seaweed.

Oh god. What the hell?

She looked over at some bottles on the counter her father had already filled and capped. She grabbed one, uncorked it and sniffed. It stunk of the sea.

He's been making wine with seaweed. God, he's gotten worse. She wondered how many bottles like this had made it over to the farm stand, been sold to customers and taken home. She put the bottle down, wanting to retch from the stench.

"Jesus, Dad," she said. *This has to stop. He can't be left alone anymore.*

But the question now remained, where the hell did he go?

She exited the barn through the door on the opposite side and scanned the fields. She caught a glimpse of movement in the cornfield. Dad? Or maybe Myles. Either way she rushed into the field, running down one of the rows, the stalks towering over her head. She turned and went toward the direction she thought the figure moved. It headed toward the back of the cornfield.

"Hey," she yelled, even though she wasn't sure whether it was her father or Myles. At this point, either one would suffice. "Stop!"

She paused, turned in another direction and continued on. She caught a glimpse of a shoulder, a pair of legs.

"Wait!" she called out.

The figure seemed to move faster, as if sensing her approach and trying to avoid it.

Either Myles was still angry with her, or her father had slipped further into his dementia. She moved faster, trying to catch up.

Melody turned a corner in the maze of cornstalks and came face-to-face with the man.

She stopped short, looking at the stranger a few feet away as he turned to face her. Her heart tripped up in her chest as she was startled by the unexpected appearance of this unknown man she had unwittingly been chasing.

"Who—?" she started to say, not sure if she needed to be afraid.

The man, who appeared to be in his late fifties and a bit heavy, flashed an awkward grin, as if he had been caught being naughty.

The shadows from the turbines swept across the cornstalks, dousing them both in shadow and light, but every time his face lit up in the flash of sunlight, Melody's mind recollected something familiar about him.

It was the man from Aerosource who had visited her earlier that year, the one who never came back to finish talking to her.

The man looked nervous and then turned and fled farther into the cornfield. Melody was too stunned to pursue him. Before he disappeared into the stalks, she noticed him clutching a book to his chest.

CHAPTER THIRTY

As he drove into town, Oscar was conflicted. A queasy feeling settled inside his gut over the missing book and apparent intruder in his house. Not his house of course, but he occupied the place, so he felt uneasy about the intrusion. He couldn't understand why someone had come into the home and stolen the book. If the person wanted it that badly, couldn't they have just knocked on the door and asked? Say they left it behind by mistake?

And how did the stranger even get into the house if the doors were locked? A previous tenant who still had a key seemed a likely candidate. There must have been multiple people Norris Squires rented the place out to, so he should ask him about it today.

After the things Norris said about the turbines sending signals, Oscar contemplated ditching the whole kayaking affair. But now he had a good reason to talk to the former schoolteacher and maybe shed some light on the whole book-napping incident. And possibly Norris could explain to Oscar a bit more about what he thought about the turbines. It probably wouldn't end up in his report to Mason Helleson and Aerosource, but it couldn't hurt to listen to the man.

Plus, he still took a shine to Norris, and sensed the feeling might be mutual. A day out on the water might do wonders to clear his head as well. Oscar had dressed in the only pair of shorts he brought on this trip. It felt good to be out of his work clothes and shoes and into a summer outfit and sneakers. He deserved a recreational day.

Norris was leaning up against a post by the marina when Oscar pulled into the parking lot. The man beamed an enchanting smile and all ideas of his crazy thoughts went right out of Oscar's mind.

"Good morning," Norris said, as he opened the door and hopped in. He had a small canvas sack with him.

"I hope I'm appropriately dressed," Oscar said, indicating his cargo shorts and t-shirt.

"Perfect. And I've brought some sandwiches for us."

"How long are we going to be out there?"

"Believe me," Norris said, "once we get out there, you're not going to want to come back in."

Oscar's new friend directed him down Main Street past the shops and storefronts, and had him turn left onto Whitman Road once he cleared the village district. The winding tarred road hugged the perimeter of the east side of Loch Raven.

Oscar thought about broaching the subject of the intruder as he drove, but the spirit of the moment was too good to disturb. Later, he thought. Plenty of time to talk about it later.

Norris pointed out a dirt turnout beside the water and Oscar turned the vehicle and parked in a gravel lot beside a pair of kayaks nestled off to the side. Lifejackets rested in each, and Norris helped him adjust the straps on his before they carried the two kayaks to the edge of the water.

Oscar felt a bit nervous, thinking about when he used to go boating in the Marmara Sea in Turkey with his uncle, but this looked like a relatively calm body of water and Norris helped him into the kayak and pushed it off. Oscar hadn't learned to swim until he became an adult. Kyle convinced him to take swimming lessons at the YMCA, so when they made beach excursions to the Cape, they'd both feel more secure in the water.

After Norris got into his kayak, they paddled away from shore and out into the center of the Basin. The body of water had a steady fluid motion from where it flowed in from the ocean through the channel, but then eased up the farther north they paddled until it resembled a calm lake. The sun beat down upon them.

Oscar tried to keep up with Norris, but his lack of rhythm with the paddle kept making him drop behind on occasion. The serene environment distracted him from the continual pace of paddling, causing him to occasionally lean back in his seat and admire the scenery around the water. A splash behind him made him turn. A small black face poked up through the surface about ten feet behind him.

"Hey!" Oscar shouted and Norris turned to look back. "It that a seal?" Norris smiled. "Sure is. They swim up into the Basin sometimes."

Oscar beamed at the sight, watching the little critter swimming along behind him. They paddled on and Oscar glanced back several times until the seal swam off in a different direction. They turned a corner around a narrow part of the Basin and Oscar gazed up.

In the distance he could see the turbines.

They rose majestically on the horizon, like alien entities, their blades rotating in an erratic rhythm like cyclopean eyes scanning the land below them.

Norris stopped paddling and Oscar glided his craft up beside him.

"It's like wherever you are on the island," Oscar said, "you can see them."

"Nowhere to hide from them," Norris said. "Always watching."

Norris talked as if the structures were alive. Oscar thought about the comment Norris made the night before, but hesitated to bring it up. Why ruin the pleasant day? But curiosity itched inside him.

"Come on," Norris said. "I'll show you a great spot where we can beach the kayaks and have a nice lunch."

Oscar kept pace, following the direction Norris took him as they headed to the east side of the Basin. Norris aimed for a small rocky cove and beached his kayak on the pebbled shore. Oscar guided his in right beside him, hearing the rocks scrape along the bottom of the craft. After getting out, Norris led him to a cluster of small boulders where they climbed till they found a flat spot to sit down, their legs dangling over the side.

From this spot, Oscar could no longer see the turbines and somehow that gave him a reassuring feeling, as if he were protected from something. Norris set down the small canvas cooler, unzipped it, withdrew a couple of wrapped sandwiches and looked up at Oscar.

"Tuna or turkey?" Norris asked.

"Turkey, please," Oscar said. "I'm not in the mood for seafood already."

Norris handed him one of the sandwiches with a smile. "I was worried you'd tell me you were a vegetarian. I should have asked before making them." He also pulled out a couple of water bottles and handed one over.

They ate in silence for a few minutes. The paddling had worked up an appetite and thirst that the turkey sandwich and water satisfied.

"Nice out here," Oscar said between chews.

Norris nodded. "I try to get out here as often as I can. Helps clear my head."

Oscar gazed at the side of his friend's face, zeroing in on his eyes and the forlorn look behind them. He wondered what muddied up the man's mind that he needed clearing. Once again he thought about his comments about the turbines.

"So why aren't you teaching?" Oscar cringed as he saw a twitch in Norris's eyes and immediately realized he might have crossed a line in his new friendship and regretted speaking. Norris looked off into the distance, but then cracked a smirk that eased the breath Oscar held in.

"Depends on who you ask," Norris said.

"I'm asking you."

Norris took a deep breath and finished the last bite of his sandwich. "I teach science and we were doing a lesson on energy. Of course, naturally I spoke about solar and wind power and discussed the Aerosource impact on the island. Wouldn't have felt right to avoid it. Anyway, some of my students are neighbors of the turbines, Rigby Lassiter, Whitney Larson, just like me. We talked at length about some of the harmful effects of the turbines, you know, the noise, the flicker, same things you're here investigating."

"And someone had an issue with that?"

Norris laughed. "You could say that. As you've probably guessed, I'm not a big fan of the machines."

"But they can't fire you for that." It seemed ridiculous to him.

"Gavin Pickett can do whatever he wants."

Oscar thought for a moment. "Wait, I thought he was the head of the board of selectmen. Doesn't the town have a school board to make education decisions?"

Norris nodded. "Of course, but don't think for a second that anything happens on this island without the stamp of Gavin Pickett on it. His son, Max, was in my class as well."

"But still, to fire you? There must be some way to fight that."

"Oh, I am, which is why I'm still on the island. But it isn't easy. They don't give that as a reason for my termination. In fact, technically, I wasn't fired. They just didn't renew my contract. They claim the budget didn't allow for my continued employment. That's how they get around things like that. And Gavin Pickett has the final say on budget matters for the island and the village of Loch Raven."

It didn't make sense to Oscar, and he couldn't help come back to the comment Norris made the night before about the turbines sending messages. *No, not messages – 'signals'.*

"Was that all it took to piss off this Gavin Pickett and the school board?" Oscar thought about the picture of the man on the Pickett Fences Estates sign and the sly expression on his face. He disliked the man already, even though he'd never had an encounter with him.

"There was a little more to it than that," Norris said with a sheepish grin.

"What was that?"

Norris gazed away again with a shake of his head, and Oscar thought he didn't want to say any more. But he did.

"I had a student come to me after class one day, to speak privately with me about a personal problem. The student had feelings for a boy in class."

"Why did they need to come to you?"

Norris turned to face him. "It was a male student and he was conflicted about the feelings he was experiencing. So he came to me."

Oscar didn't need more explanation to understand his assumptions about Norris were right. "What did you do?"

"I just advised him that his feelings were natural and nothing to be ashamed about. That he should just be who he felt he was inside."

"And let me guess, someone found out about the advice you gave? Gavin Pickett?"

Norris dropped his head. "I told you, nothing happens on this island without Gavin knowing."

"So, that's really why he had you removed from your teaching post?"

Norris shrugged. "Like I said before, depends on who you talk to. But the crux of the matter is, I'm out of a job."

Oscar took a swallow from his water bottle. "And you're willing to fight for it?"

"I have pride," Norris said. "But I guess more importantly, I have a house that I can't unload."

Oscar thought about the vacant and unfinished properties in Pickett Fences Estates and understood. "You could just walk away."

"And let the place slip into bankruptcy?"

"Start over, somewhere fresh."

Norris laughed. "That's what this place was supposed to be." He finished his water and placed the empty bottle in the cooler. "Besides, I have unfinished business."

"Besides your house and your job?"

Norris's eyes narrowed. "You could say."

"Because of the turbines?"

Norris looked perplexed, or maybe just surprised. "Why do you ask that?"

Oscar took a deep breath. "Something you said last night, about the turbines sending signals. It just kind of made me uneasy."

"But you still came out here today."

Now it was Oscar's turn to laugh. "Well, you do seem like a somewhat normal guy." Norris joined him in his laughter. "Besides, I've heard a lot of confusing things from the people I've been taking to about the turbines, and I'm just not sure what to think anymore."

"What kind of things have you heard?"

Where to begin? Oscar thought. He looked out at the peaceful scene of the lake, its surface mirroring the outcropping of trees and shrubs ringing its perimeter.

So, he began to tell Norris about the conversations he had with some of the neighbors of the wind turbines. He spoke about the Granberrys and the effect they said the machines had on their animals and the horse that jumped to its death up at Crooked Cove. He told Norris about Melody Larson's father, Tyrus Darrow, and his lapse in mind and erratic behavior, walking around without his pants and eating a pail of dandelion heads. That he could attribute to senile dementia, even if Melody thought otherwise.

But it was difficult to explain his conversation with Tatum Gallagher. Norris listened intently as he unraveled that story about how she claimed to see time stop, everyone around her frozen in place while she could move around freely. It felt unnerving just relating the tale and Oscar felt bad, as if he were exploiting her weakened state of mind. The woman had lost a child to drowning just a year before. It seemed obvious that her head was clouded with disorienting thoughts. But still, she believed this had all happened. And speaking of her dead boy, Oscar was reminded of Melody Larson's son Troy telling him he saw his dead friend, that Nathan Lassiter appeared to him in the shadow flicker.

Norris tensed and sat upright at this last bit. Something Oscar had said struck a nerve in his friend.

"Let me tell you," Norris said, "about the real reason I moved out of my house."

CHAPTER THIRTY-ONE

Barrett stepped out of the barn and spotted Letty in the field, her back to him, motionless. She looked frozen, staring at the cows before her. She appeared to be holding something in her hands, but her body hid it from his view.

He approached quietly with curiosity and a bit of concern, not wanting to startle her. This was the first time she'd gone outside since the incident with Myrtle's calf. The lines of shadow from the turbine blades swept over the field in progression, sweeping across Letty's frame like a knife.

"Letty?" Barrett called to her in a hushed voice.

She turned.

In her hands she held his shotgun.

Barrett stopped mid-step, startled. Letty's face looked drawn and ashen, as if all the color had drained from it. When each shadow from the flicker swept across it, she didn't even blink. It was then he noticed the cow she had been staring at was Myrtle.

"What are you doing with that, Letty?" Barrett's voice grew hoarse as his throat tightened.

"It's the devil in animal form," she said, her voice filled with spite. "It gave birth to that monstrosity to ruin us."

Barrett felt afraid to move any closer, staring at the double barrel of the gun, grateful it pointed down to the ground.

"You're not well, Letty," he said. "Why don't you give that to me?"

As he started forward, she raised the shotgun. He froze.

"Someone has to save us," she said. "We need redemption."

His eyes locked on the double barrels of the shotgun, which looked like two black eyes staring back at him. His skin crawled.

"Put that away and we can go see the doctor and have a talk." His voice quivered.

"Talking won't do anything." She gritted her teeth so hard he could almost hear them grinding. "The curse must be broken."

Barrett swallowed hard, his Adam's apple sticking in his throat. He began to raise his right hand.

Letty lifted the barrel of the gun, her eyes blank, lost in the flicker that flashed over them. She spun on her heels, tucked the butt of the gun into her shoulder and fired a blast at Myrtle. The recoil rocked her backward and almost knocked her over.

The left side of the cow's head exploded in a shower of red and white as bone, blood and gray matter flew from its skull. The animal staggered on its legs, but remained upright. The other cows moved quickly away from the area in a frenzy, heading toward the back of the property.

Barrett looked on in shock and then lunged forward toward his wife. Before he got there, she fired the second barrel, her aim good, and obliterating the rest of the cow's head. The animal fell to the ground with a loud thud amidst a cloud of dust.

Barrett came up behind his wife, wrapping his arms around her in a bear hug, squeezing her tight and placing his hands on the shotgun, retrieving it from the relaxed grip of her trembling fingers. She began sobbing as he hugged her tighter.

"It's all right," he said, as her head leaned into the crook of his neck. He stared at the unmoving animal on the ground before him and the blood seeping into the soil. The shadow flicker continued to sweep over the corpse. "Everything's going to be all right now."

CHAPTER THIRTY-TWO

Oscar listened with interest while they sat on the bank of the Basin, as Norris told him about what drove him from his home.

The teacher had underestimated the annoyance of the shadow flicker. It seemed at most an inconvenience in the beginning, but something he imagined he'd get used to after a brief period of adjustment. All he had to deal with was the time in the morning before heading off to work. But he hadn't quite accounted for the noise factor. The slow spin of the blades created a whirling hum, steady and rhythmic. Norris found himself tossing in his sleep; even shutting the windows did not seem to hush the distraction.

Sleep-interrupted nights led to tired mornings and crankiness in the classroom. He drank more coffee to keep him focused during the day, but the habit compounded his sleep deprivation at night.

Oscar knew he should be taking notes about all this, but had come out here on this nature excursion for fun, not work. He figured he could easily remember what his new friend told him and jot it down later.

"Did Aerosource ever warn anyone about the annoyance factor of the turbines?" Oscar asked.

"Minimal disturbance to a minimal portion of the population was how it was presented at town meetings," Norris answered with a slow shake of his head. "Of course Gavin Pickett and the other selectmen brushed it all aside, pointing out the benefits of the power derived from the energy source."

Oscar had to laugh. "Pickett probably never realized how damaging it would end up being to his development project."

"No, he certainly didn't."

"So, the noise drove you out, or the flicker?"

The eyes looking back at Oscar narrowed. "A bit more to it than that," Norris said. "It started the day Nathan Lassiter disappeared."

He told Oscar about that afternoon over a year ago when a frantic pounding on his front door disturbed him in his study, where he had been grading school papers. He hurried to the door to find a panicked Rigby Lassiter on the other side, his face ashen and beaded with sweat.

"My brother's missing," the teen said between exhausted breaths.

Norris could tell the boy had run all the way from his house.

"Okay," Norris said, trying to calm him down. "Relax, take your time and tell me what happened."

Rigby leaned against the doorjamb, trying to collect his thoughts. "Nathan took off this morning, before anyone else got up. He wanted to go fishing. I was supposed to go with him, but I overslept. By the time I got up, he was gone." He paused, gulping in heaps of breath. "He usually liked to head up toward Crooked Cove. The rocks there form a nice ledge at the edge of the sea. It's a good spot to cast." As Rigby struggled to talk, his voice hitched. "I went out there when I got dressed, and he wasn't there, but...."

"Yes?"

"His tackle box was sitting on the ledge." He sucked in a breath. "But no sign of him, or his fishing pole. Mom's called Constable Jensen. He's gathering some people to head out there to search for him."

"Okay, let's go then," Norris said, grabbing a light jacket since it had been quite breezy the past few days.

Norris told Oscar it was more than breezy as gusts of wind swept across the northern end of the island. While heading out toward the coast, Norris noticed something about the turbines. Normally in high winds, the blades rotated faster than normal, but that day they appeared to be moving slower. It seemed unusual.

By the time he and Rigby had gotten out to the area by Crooked Cove, the seas were pounding the rocks along the shore with a ferocious surge, water pushing its way along the crevices, farther up than the normal high tide mark.

Nathan's tackle box was floating out in the surf, bouncing around like a buoy cut loose from its mooring. Soon after, Constable Laine Jensen used a fisherman's hook to snag a fishing pole from the edge of the shore. Sure enough, Rigby identified it as belonging to Nathan.

Tatum Gallagher stood up on the rocks in the arms of Nathan's dad, Dirk Lassiter, sobbing and burying her head in his shoulder. Jensen called the Coast Guard and then with the help of others, continued to search the shoreline.

"They never found him," Norris told Oscar. "Swept out to sea they say. Not even a body to bury."

It was a horrid tale and made Oscar sick to his stomach thinking about it. But he didn't understand what it had to do with the wind turbines and Norris moving out of his house. The only connection that occurred to him was that Crooked Cove was the same spot where Barrett Granberry's horse leapt to its death. He shivered.

"Is that it?" Oscar asked, still confused.

"No," Norris said, shaking his head. "There's more."

About a month after Nathan's disappearance and presumed drowning, though no funeral was ever held, Norris said he went out one morning to tend to a small raised garden bed on the side of the house where he attempted to grow a meager parcel of vegetables to disappointing results. The bed of kale, green beans, spaghetti squash and cherry tomatoes were badly in need of rescue from the weeds smothering the wilting crops.

Norris thought it'd be a good idea to grow some of his own vegetables, organically and economically. What seemed a brilliant idea in the early spring turned disastrous as he found little time to keep up with the burgeoning crop in the small ten-by-ten bed. So early one Saturday morning, he grabbed his garden trowel and hand rake and went out to do battle with the virulent weeds.

He tried to ignore the shadow flicker thumping across the front of his house and casting its streak of shadows over his lawn. Though he knew the shadows made no sound, the rhythmic cadence of the turbine blades made it seem like the dark shades thumped like the beats of a heart.

Another sound joined the noise of the turbines, the wail and squawk of seagulls. He knelt beside the bed, digging up the roots of the weeds with the rake and dumping them in the wheelbarrow he had set beside the garden. He looked up, shielding the glare from the flicker with a gloved hand.

Seagulls filled the sky, more than he had ever seen gathered in one spot. Sure, along the harbor and coastal rocks they'd hover, but never so many inland. They darted back and forth in the sky almost in a choreographed pattern, and he could swear they were dodging the strips of shadows sweeping across the sky, as if playing a game of chicken with them.

Norris stared for the longest time, amazed at the sight, surprised the frantic flights of the birds didn't cause them to crash headlong into each other and drop from the sky. They weaved in and out of the shadow flicker in intricate patterns. It mesmerized him.

Then he realized someone else nearby was watching. But not watching the birds. Watching *him*.

Across the street in the front yard of one of the unfinished homes in the development, barely a skeleton of wooden framework, a young boy stood staring at him.

Norris froze as his heart tightened in his chest. It looked like Nathan Lassiter. From the distance, it was hard to be certain, and the shadows from the flicker fell across where the boy stood.

But every time the brightness came across the boy, Norris recognized the face and the strawberry-blond hair. The child did not move, with the exception of his mouth. He appeared to be saying something, but Norris couldn't hear from this distance and the groaning of the turbines.

Norris stood, his legs shaking, and called out, but the figure did not stir, so he started across his lawn to the road. It was Nathan, he saw as he approached, of course it was him.

"Nathan!" he cried, dazed by this sudden miracle, his heart racing. Norris moved quickly across the street. At the edge of the opposite lawn he stopped.

Nathan began to disappear.

A trick of the shadows, his mind told him. But the strangeness of it mired his feet in his tracks, afraid to come closer. It seemed every time the shadow flicker passed, the boy was there, but when the bright light followed it, he was gone.

What the hell?

When Nathan was there, his mouth still moved, appearing to shout something, but Norris couldn't hear. It was as if the child were talking underwater, his voice muffled.

"What?" Norris yelled, leaning forward, straining to hear, but afraid to move closer.

Finally, he realized Nathan was saying the same thing over and over, but the voice was faint. Then the sound broke through.

"Seaweed!"

The sun peeked above the top of the wind turbine blades, and just as if someone hit a switch, the flicker stopped and the birds scattered.

The boy was gone.

CHAPTER THIRTY-THREE

Tatum Gallagher was shocked when she opened the front door of her house and saw Myles Larson standing there. She didn't know what to say. He had never come to her house in the daytime. Before she could find words, he brushed past her into the house.

"Myles?" She remained at a loss for what to think or say.

"I can't stay," he said, appearing agitated.

"Not even for a cup of coffee?" she finally managed, still bewildered.

"No." Now he seemed upset. "I don't mean here, now. I mean on this island."

She came up to him and put a gentle hand on his arm. "What are you going on about?"

"Melody knows." His eyes looked stern, digging into hers as if accusing her of something. "Somehow she knows about us."

"But, how?" Tatum felt deflated and even embarrassed, like how she felt as a schoolgirl when she got knocked up by handsome Braydon Lane at the University Marine Research Center. Now all these years later, here she found herself being naughty again.

Myles began pacing. "It doesn't matter how."

Tatum couldn't think; her mind felt scrambled in many directions.

He stopped in front of her. "I've been out driving around all morning trying to sort things out in my head." He sucked in an angry breath. "I'm ready to get off this damn island. Find an attorney in Rockland, file for divorce and start over somewhere."

No, she thought. This wasn't the plan. But did she really have a plan or more scattered schoolgirl daydreams like the ones she had those many years ago when she was pregnant with Rigby? But those plans evaporated in an instant and here she remained, her son almost grown up now.

"But Rigby," she said. "He starts his last year of high school next month. I can't go now. We talked about waiting."

Myles's hands balled up into fists and his face grew flushed. "I'm tired of waiting, of putting up an act in a marriage I can't take anymore."

Tatum felt like crying, as if she was losing control of everything. Just like Braydon slipped away seventeen years ago, and Dirk last year after Nathan died, now Myles was slipping from her grasp, her one last hope for happiness and security.

"I don't know what you expect me to do," she said in panting breaths, tears welling up behind her eyes. "Tell me."

He shook his head, his face a mix of anger and disgust. "I can't tell you what to do."

She stared at him, her eyes pleading for some answer from him. *Help me*, she wanted to cry out. *Don't just stand there, give me some help. Tell me what to do.*

Before she thought she would burst into tears on the spot, a pounding came on the front door. Tatum felt frozen, unable to move. Myles stood still for a moment, then turned and flung open the door as if expecting to yell at an unsuspecting solicitor. But instead, Melody Larson stood on the front porch.

Tatum gasped. Melody shot a volatile gaze over her husband's shoulder at her and Tatum shrunk back in defense.

"I don't give a shit right now about what's going on here," Melody said, venom in her voice. "But right now my father is missing and I need help."

Myles glanced back at Tatum with a forlorn look, almost as if to say goodbye. When he turned back to Melody, he said one word: "Fuck," and then followed her out the door, leaving Tatum alone.

Now she did begin to cry.

She retreated to the sofa in the living room, sank down in the cushions and grabbed a throw pillow for comfort, squeezing it into her belly as if to fill the hollow feeling in her gut. What could she do now? Everything felt like it was falling apart.

She brooded on the couch for the better part of the next hour before another knock came at the door. She leapt from the couch, nearly tripping in her anxiousness to answer the door. *He's back,* she thought. She imagined old man Darrow was found safe and sound and now Myles was back to figure out their future.

But when she opened the door she got her second surprise of the day. Board of Selectmen Chairman Gavin Pickett stood on her porch, and she didn't like the smile on his face.

"What a pleasure to see you, Tatum," he said.

She felt sure it was a pleasure for him and she instinctively clutched a hand at the top of her blouse, pulling the fabric together.

"What can I do for you?" she asked, sniffing back the remains of the tears she'd shed earlier and hoping it wasn't noticeable.

His smile widened. "Oh, it's not what you can do for me. It's more like what I can do for you."

"What are you going on about?"

"May I?" he asked, gesturing for permission to come into her house.

With a sigh she stepped aside and reluctantly let Pickett into her house, hoping whatever he wanted wouldn't take long.

"I'm very busy," she said, following him into the living room.

He turned and looked at her as if studying her. "Are you?" he asked. "Are you really busy?"

He knew the answer to that but she didn't want to give him any satisfaction, so she stayed silent, letting her expression show how impatient she felt.

Pickett glanced around the room. "Such a lovely place, lots of history."

Tatum kept silent.

"Must have been a grand old farm in its day," he continued. "You must be very proud of your family heritage."

"What do you want, Mr. Pickett?"

He chuckled. "Oh please, Tatum. We've known each other so long. Of course you can call me Gavin." He watched her and she gave him no response. He nodded. "Okay, down to business. What if I said I could help you bring this farm back to its glory days?"

She had no idea what he was getting at. "And how would you do that?"

"We," he emphasized, stepping closer to her. "I have a grand plan to turn your fortunes around."

She was slightly intrigued, but cautious considering whom she was dealing with.

"I have a business plan for renovating your greenhouse and getting this farm a license to grow marijuana for some of the legal dispensaries on the mainland."

Her face flushed with anger and she stepped toward him. "You bastard! That's Dirk's plan. He presented it to you at the selectmen meeting and you and your cronies shot it down!"

He nodded but still didn't drop his grin. "Yes, Mr. Lassiter presented a very raw proposal before us that certainly didn't meet any realistic guidelines. I merely took his idea and extrapolated it out into a real serious business model. One that the board of selectmen couldn't help but grant an ordinance to allow." His eyes twinkled.

"He worked hard on that plan. It was his dream to start something really profitable."

Pickett laughed again. He took another step closer to her. He discarded the grin. "Do you really think he has the brains to achieve something like this? Get real. It would fail before it even got off the ground. No financial institution would bankroll his plan with his background."

She put her hands on her hips. "But you could get it done, of course."

Pickett spread his hands. "It's what I do. I make things a success. I brought the wind turbine project here, bought land at a good dollar value from you and your farmer friends on this road. It's helped keep all of you going in these lean times."

Now it was Tatum's time to laugh, but there was spite in it. "What about your failed housing development down the road? Not much success there."

He frowned and shrugged. "A minor complication I expect will turn around. Times can be tough for even the best of us."

Her face tightened as anger welled up inside her. "I'm not selling you my farm."

"It's not a farm anymore," he said, taking a step closer. "Hasn't been for quite some time. But it can be something again." He took another step, bringing him face-to-face with her.

She quivered at his closeness.

"And you don't have to sell me the whole farm," he said. He reached a hand out and placed it on her left shoulder. His smile returned and it made her queasy. "We could form a partnership and take on the venture together." He trailed his fingers down her arm past the end of her sleeve and over the goose bumps on her flesh. "With my financial input and your considerable charm, we could make quite a successful merger." His hand dropped onto her left hip and lingered there.

Her whole body wanted to shake but she felt frozen inside. Her lips parted but she couldn't speak.

Pickett removed his hand and walked past her toward the front door. He opened it and she heard his voice from behind her.

"Don't take too long to think about it," he said. "You're in danger of defaulting on your mortgage. I've seen your bank statements and I do have to say you are in quite the conundrum." He knocked on the side of the doorframe as if testing its sturdiness. "Hate to see this old place fall into bankruptcy. Might even think of bailing it out myself."

The door slammed and he was gone. Tatum exhaled a deep breath she had been holding, one expelled with the anger she had also withheld. *Bastard! Damn fucking prick!* She paced around, wondering what to do. God, if Dirk knew what that asshole was up to, he'd....

What? What would Dirk do?

Something drastic.

Her mind spun, a flurry of thoughts racing around inside. Dirk, Myles, Gavin....

Her breathing deepened and she felt she might have a heart attack and drop dead right there on the floor. That would solve her problems.

She thought again about Dirk and how his rage would be tenfold hers. She went into the kitchen and grabbed her cell phone. Dirk would be out on the lobster boat with Brownie and Jumbo. They would be maybe halfway through their day. Not drunk yet, but certainly having a few in between hauling up traps.

She called him, holding the phone to her ear, and hoped he would be just as enraged as her. No. *More.*

CHAPTER THIRTY-FOUR

They paddled back in silence to the spot where Oscar had left his car. He wished he could enjoy the serenity of the natural surroundings but couldn't push away the thoughts spinning through his mind. He felt glad they were out of sight of the turbines that seemed to be the source of so much consternation among the people he interacted with on the island.

Were they all crazy, driven nuts by the constant whine of the turbine blades and the nauseating flashing of the shadow flicker? Could it be as simple as that? Maybe the lack of sleep those machines inflicted on the people who lived near it altered their thought process. Because none of the other options made any sense to Oscar.

When they pulled the kayaks out of the water and stashed them to the side of the gravel clearing, he decided he needed to break the awkward silence.

"Did you ever see him again, Nathan Lassiter?" He hesitated when he spoke, not sure he wanted to hear the answer.

Norris looked at him with sheepish eyes, seemingly afraid to speak. Then he nodded sadly. "A couple times, but always from a distance and only during the flicker." He cast his eyes down. "I could never be sure it was him. It just looked like a lost boy wandering around the shadows. I tried to go after him once, but the flicker stopped and he went away. I thought maybe it was my mind playing tricks on me."

"But you left, moved out." He could see the fear in Norris's eyes and knew it was strong enough for him to take such drastic measures.

"It scared me. I felt like I had no control. I didn't like that, wanted to do something about it."

"What could you do?" Oscar didn't really mean it as a question, but Norris decided to respond anyway.

"I needed answers, I mean, I teach science, for Christ's sake. Things have to make sense."

"Did you ever tell Tatum Gallagher about seeing her son?"

"Hell no!" He shook his head. "She was depressed and crazy over it enough without adding that."

There's that word, Oscar thought. *Crazy*. Just like he felt when Tatum told him the story about seeing time stop and people frozen in place. But she had lost a child, so crazy could be considered acceptable. But what had Norris really seen?

"So what did you do?"

"I began studying the turbines."

"Studying? How?"

"Taking measurements. Timing them. Documenting everything about them. The revolutions of the blades, the speed, the patterns. I'd go up there almost every day, in the morning especially, and note everything I could about them."

This all sounded too weird to Oscar and once again he found himself conflicted between liking this man and being somewhat unsure about him.

"What did you expect to find?"

"An explanation."

Yeah, Oscar thought. *That's what I'd really like. An explanation. Someone to tell me why birds dance in the sky, animals try to hurt or kill themselves, an old man eats a bucket of dandelions, a woman sees time stop and a dead kid walks in shadows. Explain that to me. Someone please.*

"And did you?" he asked.

Norris laughed and to Oscar it sounded like a madman's laugh.

"I have a theory, but you might not believe it."

No, Oscar thought. *I might not. But what the hell.* "Give me a try."

They walked over to Oscar's car and Norris leaned up against the back.

"Besides the studying I've done about the turbines, I've also been doing a bit of research into Aerosource. As a renewable energy developer, they receive funding from the federal government."

"Yeah, a lot of companies do."

"Just got me thinking. I've noticed specific patterns sometimes when the turbine blades rotate. Even the flicker itself seems very regulated at times."

"And what do you think that means?"

He sucked in a deep breath. "I think they create a hypnotic effect."

"What?"

"I know it sounds farfetched. But it does seem like these things are messing with people's minds. Mine included. Of course Tatum Gallagher didn't see time stop, but what if the effect of the turbines made her think she did? Hypnotism can have an amazing effect on people. It's been demonstrated plenty of times."

Oscar tried to keep a straight face so as not to insult his friend. "So you think the turbines are hypnotizing people?"

"Why else would I see a dead boy walking around?"

It seemed so preposterous that Oscar was at a loss for words. It made less sense than Rigby Lassiter and his friends tripping over watching the flicker.

"I know it sounds crazy on the surface, but if you dig down deep, it is entirely possible."

"For what purpose?" Oscar asked, still bewildered.

"Fuck if I know," Norris said. "I mean, it could be just a scientific research, funded by the federal government. An experiment."

"And the people of Kidney Island are the test subjects?"

"At least the ones living near the turbines."

"You think the US government is testing the ability to hypnotize people with windmills? And how would that benefit them?"

Norris shrugged. "Maybe they'll place them all along the Texas border aimed into Mexico to make the Mexicans think it's not better to come over the border."

Now Oscar burst out laughing, almost doubling over, and grabbed at his sides. "You can't be serious."

Even Norris began to chuckle. "I know it sounds ridiculous when I say it out loud. But you haven't had much time to feel the effects. It's pretty unnerving."

Oscar thought for a moment. "Is that why you wear the construction helmet?"

He nodded. "And sunglasses. Just to try to deflect some of the effects. As a precaution. I figured it couldn't hurt."

Oscar didn't know what to say next, only he didn't have to because at that moment, Norris's cell phone rang.

Whoever called, it seemed serious because Oscar watched as Norris went through a series of facial expressions from surprise to confusion to concern before succumbing to an attempt to soothe the person on the other end. When he ended the call, Norris looked at him.

"That was Rigby Lassiter," he said. "He got a frantic call from Whitney Larson. Her grandfather's gone missing. The constable's on his way."

Oscar didn't question whether a teenager having their teacher's private phone number was normal; he only concerned himself with the seriousness of the situation. He remembered the other day when he found old man Darrow wandering around Pickett Fences Estates without his pants. Sounded like they needed to keep the old man on a leash.

"I hope they find him okay," Oscar said.

"I think we should help."

Oscar agreed and they hopped into his car and headed out toward Haven Road, all thoughts of the calm day kayaking on the water dissipated while the conversation about hypnosis and scientific experiments turned like a cog in his head, interrupted only by images of Tyrus Darrow wandering around lost. Was the old man hypnotized too? Was that why he kept wandering off? And what about the incident where he stuffed a bucket of dandelions down his throat? It all really pointed to senile dementia or the onset of Alzheimer's, not some fantastic theory about a secret government-subsidized program to control the minds of innocent townsfolk with the spinning wheels of a group of wind turbines. It sounded like lunacy.

Sitting beside him, Norris kept quiet, concern etched on his face, and all Oscar could wonder was if his friend thought his conspiratorial ramblings would frighten him away. At the moment, they hadn't, but Oscar wasn't sure how much more he wanted to be sucked into the paranoia of the island inhabitants. Maybe it would be best for him to finish his report and cut this business trip short. It might be time to finally leave Kidney Island before he succumbed to the contagious madness.

When they arrived at the Larson farm, Oscar spotted a small gathering of people in the front yard. He pulled down the long drive, hesitant a bit, feeling as if they were intruding on a private moment. He parked next to the constable's car and they got out. Constable Laine Jensen addressed the group as they approached, talking about the need to canvas the area. Nearby Melody Larson looked distraught, her face drenched in anguish. Her husband, Myles, stood a few feet from her, oddly not offering any comfort.

Rigby Lassiter stood beside the Larsons' daughter, Whitney, his arm around her as she silently sobbed. Oscar noticed Rigby exchanged glances with Norris, who offered a comforting nod.

Constable Jensen finished instructing the gathering of volunteers and they all fanned out in different directions. Oscar and Norris headed across the fields toward the east. The beauty of the warm sunny day seemed lost in the moment of their task. Oscar glanced up the hill toward the turbines, drawn by the hum as the blades spun, and thought more about the things Norris suspected. He couldn't fathom how any of it made sense. But it was harder to understand that Norris believed it all.

As they approached the Granberry farm, Oscar couldn't help but think about the story Barrett told him regarding his horse that ran off and leapt to its death off the rocks of Crooked Cove, the same place where Nathan Lassiter got swept out to sea. He hoped Tyrus Darrow hadn't been drawn to that same spot and felt glad that he and Norris hadn't been given that assignment in the search field. Constable Jensen took that one himself. He thought about asking Norris if his hypnotism theory had any explanation for the attraction of Crooked Cove, but decided he'd rather not bring the subject up under the circumstances.

Norris stopped and Oscar drew up beside him.

"What's that?" Norris asked, pointing toward the Granberrys' pasture.

Oscar scanned the area, seeing only cows milling about doing whatever cows normally do. But then he spotted one cow on the ground, lying on its side.

"What the hell?"

They headed in that direction, their pace slowing as they got closer. When they were within about ten feet, they both stopped.

"Jesus," Norris muttered.

Oscar gazed at the dead cow on the ground, flies buzzing around the mess of what remained of its mangled head, looking more like the ground beef its brethren were someday destined for.

"What happened here?" Oscar asked, not expecting an answer. He turned to look over at the house, hoping everyone was okay.

"Let's see if they're home," Norris said.

As they approached the farmhouse, Oscar could see the farmer's truck was gone. Norris knocked on the front door regardless. As he waited to see if there were any response, Oscar looked over at the barn with its door slightly slid open. A dog padded softly out of the darkness of the barn interior and stopped. Its skin drew back from its mouth, baring its teeth. A low growl came from its throat.

We're intruding, Oscar thought. "Let's go," he said to Norris. "I don't think Barrett's dog wants us here."

"Nobody's home anyway," Norris said, descending from the front porch. "Let's continue our search north, into the conservation land."

As they left the yard, Oscar couldn't help looking back at the Granberry farm with the angry dog and the dead cow with its head blown off and wondered what the hell happened here.

They skirted the turbines; it was apparent that Norris did not want to tread very close to the machines. Beyond the Granberry pasture, they hopped over the split-rail fence at the perimeter of the property and proceeded north. Once in the conservation sector of the northern end of the island, they picked up some of the hiking trails and called out Tyrus Darrow's name every so often in case he wandered nearby.

They didn't see anyone else during their search and weariness set in. They paused to take a break, grabbing a seat on some rocks near the trail. Norris had their water bottles in his backpack from their kayaking excursion and he handed one to Oscar.

Oscar took the bottle with gratitude. He hadn't realized how thirsty the search had made him. The sun still beat down with warmth despite the breeze sweeping over them from the north. He couldn't remember the last time he had this much exercise in a day. Probably back when Kyle was always encouraging them to take weekend hikes and get out of the city.

Looking north, Oscar spotted the top of a tower beyond the next hill.

"What's that?" he asked, pointing.

"The Gull Point lighthouse," Norris said after taking a swig from his bottle. "We should probably check it out just in case."

"Are we that close to the shore?"

"We've been walking quite a ways," Norris said with a laugh.

Oscar felt amazed. No wonder his legs ached. He knew the island was small, but didn't realize how easy it was to traverse the area from the homes on Haven Road to the northern shore. Still, he wondered if the old man could have wandered this far from home.

"Is there anyone there?" he asked about the lighthouse.

Norris shook his head. "It's been decommissioned for several years, long before I got to the island."

"Why's that?" He thought it would still serve some purpose to boats at sea.

Norris shrugged. "Most boaters and fishermen use electronic navigation these days. A lot of lighthouses are more scenic sites than anything these days."

"It's a shame," Oscar said, still looking toward the lighthouse.

"Let's check it out."

They got up and continued down the trail. When they reached the lighthouse, Oscar saw a two-story white wooden frame house beside the tall white tower of the lighthouse. As they approached, he could see most of the windows were broken. A green wooden front door flapped open and closed in the breeze, as if gesturing to them to come inside.

Oscar followed Norris into the house. The rooms were vacant with the exception of empty beer cans and bottles littering the floor.

"Teens use this place sometimes for a party hangout," Norris said as they moved from room to room. Enough light entered through the windows to allow them to see around the interior. The rooms were devoid of furniture. "Nothing to see here."

As they stepped outside, Oscar glanced at the lighthouse.

"Should we check that too?"

"Sure," Norris said and led the way. He opened an arched door at the base of the tower. Little light made it through the tiny windows high up in the brick walls of the tower and it left the inside of the shaft in grim grayness.

Oscar spotted metal debris at the base of the lighthouse, a heap of twisted black steel. Looking up, Oscar noted the spiral staircase to the top was missing its bottom third. Seeing nothing else worthwhile in the lighthouse, they stepped back outside.

"I think we've searched enough," Norris said. "Let's head back. I hope someone else had luck finding Mr. Darrow."

As they started heading out along the trail, Oscar glanced back over his shoulder at the lighthouse.

"If the local teens abuse this place, why don't the authorities keep it locked up?" he asked.

"They try, but the kids keep breaking in. Constable Jensen chases them out from one place, and they just find another spot."

Oscar gazed around the dilapidated structures. "Maybe they should just tear the whole thing down," he said.

"Oh, no. Gavin Pickett has plans for all this. He wants to renovate the buildings, save them as a historic landmark, operate it as a tourist spot."

"He's the one who terminated your teacher position."

"That's the one. Asshole extraordinaire. Prick thinks he runs this whole island." Norris turned to him. "Which he kind of does."

"What's stopping him from renovating this place?" Oscar asked. "If you say he runs everything."

"It's in the works. Pickett just refuses to use money funded by the town. Last I heard, he was proffering a deal with Aerosource to donate funding to support the renovation. Kind of as a nice gesture for allowing them to put the turbines up."

They continued on in silence, and before long Oscar could see the turbine towers up ahead and was grateful he was almost home. The day had exhausted him. He just hoped someone had located Tyrus Darrow. He liked the old man and didn't want anything to have happened to him.

CHAPTER THIRTY-FIVE

About twenty-five miles off the east coast of Kidney Island, the lobster boat *Seaweed* approached a smaller pleasure boat stopped alongside one of its buoys.

Poachers, Dirk Lassiter thought as they gained on the other boat. It was something they dealt with from time to time and the main reason Brownie carried a shotgun on board.

"Jumbo!" Brownie yelled. "Take the wheel and bring us alongside."

A cackling Jumbo, jacked up from the impending excitement, bolted into the wheelhouse and took control of the boat while Brownie reached under the front cabinet to bring out his shotgun. He joined Dirk on the portside while they closed in on the pleasure craft with what looked like two young couples in their twenties, the boys in long board shorts and tank tops, the girls in bikinis.

The two boys had a lobster trap up on the edge of their craft and were in the process of emptying its contents when the *Seaweed* approached. The boys saw the boat coming and immediately dumped the trap over the side.

"Grab the boat hook," Brownie told Dirk and he went to the back of the boat, grabbed the long pole they used to haul the traps on board, and rejoined his captain's side.

As the *Seaweed* pulled up alongside the other boat, the taller of the two boys jumped behind the wheel and started its motor.

Brownie put his left foot up on the side rail and leaned out, raising the shotgun.

"Shut that engine down, you little prick, unless you want a hole in the side of your daddy's pretty boat!" Brownie yelled.

Dirk saw his captain's eyes flare up like hot coals and the boy did as he was told, the motor sputtering out. Dirk felt Brownie would rather the kid had disobeyed so he'd have an excuse to unload the shotgun on the frightened youngsters.

Jumbo had pulled the *Seaweed* right alongside the other boat and Brownie instructed Dirk to grab hold of it with the lobster trap hook and hold it tight.

"That's my buoy and my trap you cocksuckers hauled up," Brownie said, spitting a wad of chew into their boat at the feet of the shorter of the two boys.

"We didn't mean anything," he said, as the girls cowered behind him, covering their bikini tops with their arms as they looked up at the imposing man with the shotgun. "We were just being—"

"Fucking stupid?" Brownie finished.

The boy nodded.

"I'm going to give you thirty seconds to put those little darlings you took from my trap into my boat, if you know what's good for you."

Both boys quickly scrambled to gather up the lobsters and started tossing them over the side onto the deck of the *Seaweed*. Jumbo joined the others on the deck and helped gather the lobsters. Brownie kept the shotgun trained on them the whole time, following their nervous movements. When they were done, Brownie straightened up.

"You don't ever want to let me catch you pulling this shit again," Brownie said, before spitting. "Now you haul your asses out of here before I really lose my shit."

Dirk unhooked their boat and the tall boy started up the engine and they watched as the boat sped off. The driver raised his right hand, middle finger extended.

"Fuckers!" Brownie said.

"Should have sunk them," Jumbo said.

"I've got their boat number."

"You going to report them?" Dirk asked.

Brownie didn't answer.

"Should have made those girls take their tops off before you drove them off," Jumbo said. "Get a good look at their titties." He cackled again, flashing his crooked teeth.

Brownie eyed his mate silently. "Let's haul that trap up and see what's left in it. Then finish up this fucking day. I need to get wasted now." He returned to the wheelhouse and put away the shotgun.

Dirk used the hook to snag the buoy and the rope attached. He and Jumbo hauled up the trap and emptied it of only two more lobsters.

After gathering the last of the lobster traps, Brownie turned the *Seaweed* around and guided it back toward Kidney Island. Dirk and Jumbo grabbed beers from the cooler and were relaxing on the deck when Dirk's cell phone rang. He pulled it out of his pocket and looked at the screen to see Tatum's beautiful face.

"Hey girl," he said, surprised at the call.

His joy turned fitful as she told him about the visit by Gavin Pickett and his proposal to her about the farm property.

"That fucking bastard!" Dirk yelled into the phone, startling even Jumbo. Brownie turned and gazed back from the wheelhouse with curiosity.

"And that's not all," Tatum said, detailing the lecherous suggestions Pickett made to her.

"I'll fucking kill him!" Dirk felt the octopus tentacles of his tattoo once again creeping up the back of his head, squeezing his skull, sending pressure pain along his whole scalp. He didn't even have to be near the windmills anymore to feel its effect, he thought. *It's in me now. It's always there, lurking, waiting to grip me.* The muscles in his arms tightened. He thought he might crush the phone in his hand. "He can't do this to me," he said to Tatum.

"He can do whatever he wants," she replied. "He's got the money and the control of the selectmen. He's got it all."

"We'll see about that!"

"What are you going to do?" she asked.

The tentacles tightened on his skull. "I don't know just yet." He wanted to punch something.

"Well, you need to do something," Tatum said and rung off.

"What the fuck's going on?" Jumbo said when Dirk got off the phone.

Brownie kept looking back listening as Dirk explained what that prick Pickett had planned.

"Christ," Brownie said, "you've been working on that plan for a shit-long time."

"That's damn right!" Dirk said, tossing his empty beer bottle out into the sea.

"What you going to do?" Jumbo asked. He opened a fresh beer and handed it to him.

Dirk chugged half of it and wiped some drool off his chin with the back of his hand.

"I'm going to do something. But first I need to get fucking drunk and high and figure this out."

Jumbo glanced into the wheelhouse at Brownie. "Maybe we can help him out," he said.

The captain looked back at him. "Now's not the time, Jumbo."

Dirk looked back and forth at the two of them, aware there was something they knew that they weren't sharing with him. The tentacles squeezed his skull again.

CHAPTER THIRTY-SIX

A somber mood hung in the air at the Raven's Nest. The place was crowded but the din was low. Even the background music filtered out of the speakers at a dull volume. Chatter among the patrons was soft, almost as if everyone were whispering to one another.

The search party found no trace of Tyrus Darrow, and several hours after the sun set, it had been called off for the night. No use having people wandering around in the dark with flashlights, Constable Jensen had told everyone. He would patrol the back roads throughout the evening, but sent everyone else home.

Most had come to the Nest to imbibe and wallow with the sullenness of the day's events, Oscar and Norris among them, sitting together at one of the pub tables. There was a thought of ordering a bottle of the old man's dandelion wine that the bar stocked, but Oscar remembered how horrible it tasted when he tried it earlier in the week and they decided to resort to other options.

Norris drank rum and Coke, while Oscar favored a special Maine blueberry martini. They were several drinks in already and the night still remained young.

"I don't understand how an old man can get lost on an island," Oscar said, frustrated. "It's not that big."

"Bigger than you think," Norris replied. "Lots of open conservation land north and west of their farm."

"I can't see how he'd get that far. He was old and waddled more than walked." Oscar gazed around the bar, imaging the other patrons held similar conversations. He felt glad that Dirk Lassiter and his motley fishing buddies weren't here tonight. He didn't imagine he could stand another encounter with that trio.

"Nathan Lassiter wandered off and was never found," Norris said, as if that were some excuse for what happened to Tyrus.

"But he drowned," Oscar countered. "Do you think that's what happened to Mr. Darrow? Do you believe he made it all the way to the shore on such a hot sunny day?"

Norris shook his head. "Nah, doesn't seem likely."

They ordered another round of drinks.

Oscar had so hoped they would have found the old man down around Pickett Fences Estates when they got back from the lighthouse. The streets were empty and eerily quiet, giving Oscar the feel of a ghost village. The two of them had checked all the unfinished and empty houses with no luck. They had then worked their way south of Haven Road, wandering through the fields, hoping to stumble upon some kind of evidence Tyrus had come that way. But nothing.

Before nightfall, they had returned to the Darrow farm and got a chance to talk to Constable Jensen. They told him about the dead cow at the Granberry farm and Jensen informed them that he had gotten a message from the town veterinarian. Apparently, Letty had an incident, whatever the hell that meant, and Barrett took her over to the mainland to see a doctor. A dead cow with its head blown off? That certainly qualified as an incident, Oscar guessed. The constable didn't go into any further details. Oscar hoped the old couple was okay.

The futility of the search left them distressed and hungry and he and Norris decided the Raven's Nest was the best place to quell both needs. But after his fifth drink, Oscar began to feel a bit lightheaded, and he still needed to drive Norris home, or to his yurt, if that's what he called home these days.

Oscar pondered whether he felt brazen enough to invite Norris back to his own house and spend the night, but even in the alcohol haze he experienced, he doubted the man would want to be anywhere near the neighborhood given the present circumstances.

"I think we need to go," Oscar said, realizing any more drinks and he wouldn't make the drive all the way up Haven Road.

Norris nodded, chugging one last swig down and crunching the remnants of his ice. "I believe you're right. This day started out terrific, but turned to crap real quick."

They paid their tab and exited the bar. Outside the air cooled a bit, the night dispensing with the heat of the day. They walked to the parking lot by the marina. Oscar was grateful not to find a heap of fish heads on his rental car. Once the two of them were buckled in, he drove off down Main Street, Norris guiding him toward his temporary home.

As the car turned onto Pequot Road, Norris pointed out a grand house overlooking the south shore.

"That's Pickett's place," Norris said.

Oscar stared at the big home, admiring its grandeur, but making no comment. Nor did he notice the rusted white pickup truck parked across the street from it, the one with the missing tailgate, nor the shadowy figure of the man slumped down behind the wheel.

As they headed out of the village and toward the western end of the town, Norris told him where to turn onto Sunset Road, which swept through open fields with views of the ocean. The farm where Norris rented his yurt was a couple miles down the road on the right.

Oscar concentrated on his driving, feeling the buzz that suddenly settled in his head. He felt assured, and grateful, that Constable Jensen was most likely still patrolling on the other side of the island, looking for any sign of Tyrus Darrow.

Norris pointed out a narrow dirt lane before a big farmhouse and Oscar turned into it, following it as it led through a field. In the distance, he spotted three large humps.

"I can't believe you live in a yurt, instead of the nice house you own," Oscar said, hoping not to offend him.

Norris laughed. "Does make me seem odd, don't it?" He smiled back at him.

Oscar parked before the one with an old VW bus beside it and looked at Norris. "Not odd," he said. "Maybe unique."

They stared at each other with a long pause.

"Come on in," Norris said. "Let me show you the place."

They got out and before going in the door in the center of the hut,

Norris stooped to pick up a small package left on the ground by the door. He used his cell phone to light up the address label and grinned.

"Oh great," he said. "My carburetor's arrived." He turned to Oscar with a childlike expression of glee.

"Now you don't have to ride all over the island on your bicycle."

"It's good exercise though. Keeps me in shape."

Oscar had to agree, but didn't say so.

Norris led him inside and flipped a switch. An overhead light bathed a glow over the interior.

"Wow, electricity even," Oscar said as he scanned the room. "All the modern conveniences."

The yurt was one large round room. On one side stood a queen-sized bed up against the curved wall between a pair of long narrow windows. A picture of a lighthouse hung on the wall above the bed. To the right of the bed stood a tall dresser, on the left a table lamp. Opposite from the bed was a bistro table with a pair of stools, one either side. Around the perimeter of the room were a small bookcase, wine rack, wooden chair with red leather cushions, a little wooden bench and a small pellet stove.

As Oscar scanned the circumference of the room, he began to feel dizzy, as if the room itself were spinning. He stepped inside, made his way over to the end of the bed, and sat down to steady himself.

"You okay?" Norris asked, setting his mail package down on a small narrow decorative table by the front door.

"Yeah, just those martinis snuck up on me."

"Rest a bit," Norris said. He turned on the table lamp and switched off the bright overhead light.

Oscar squeezed his eyes shut, and then reopened them. He noticed across the room a trio of large barrels. "Is that your water supply?" he joked.

Norris stared at the barrels with a grim look before he sat down on the bed next to Oscar.

"No," Norris said. "That's ammonium nitrate."

Oscar stared at the barrels through fuzzy eyes. He turned to Norris. "Ammonium what?"

"Fertilizer," Norris answered, his mouth slack.

"What the hell are you fertilizing?" Oscar laughed. "You got a weed farm out back here?"

Norris shook his head. "No. But if I combine that with some nitromethane, it makes one hell of a bomb."

Norris turned to him and the expression on his face cut off Oscar's laugh.

"You can't be serious?" But the look on Norris's face didn't alter. "What the fuck do you want to blow up?"

Norris didn't answer. He didn't have to. Oscar knew without having to think hard, but still had a difficult time believing.

"Wait a minute," he said, trying to make sure he could think clearly. "There's no way—"

Before he got another word out, Norris's mouth was on his, and his lips parted and the tongue entered with such masculinity that Oscar put all other thoughts out of his mind.

CHAPTER THIRTY-SEVEN

In the night....

Melody Larson's heart wrenched as she crawled into bed next to her daughter. Myles decided to stay on the couch again. In all her distress and torment over the disappearance of her father, her husband still couldn't manage to find the means to comfort her. He could join her and Whitney in the king-sized bed, but no, that would be too much like a family. She wished he would just leave altogether.

As she lay there, listening to the sound of the wind turbines through the screen of the bedroom window, she had no idea how she expected to sleep. *He's out there somewhere, wandering, lonely, scared. Or maybe even....* *No!* She would not allow that thought to penetrate her mind. *He will be safe. He will be found.* She would lie there all night awake and await the call when someone would find her father.

At the Gallagher house, Tatum also lay in bed awake. She'd heard nothing more from Dirk and wondered if he'd taken any action. She figured she would hear something, anything. But the phone didn't sound. She pulled the covers up to her chin.

The house was quiet. Rigby was sleeping over his friend's house, as usual. This summer he never seemed to want to stay at home. Nobody did. Braydon left her, Nathan left, Dirk left, Myles was leaving. Soon it would be Rigby's turn to leave after his senior year of high school. He'd go away to college, or into the military like his friend Evan wanted. Either way, Rigby would be gone. And where would Tatum be? Alone. It seemed like she was always alone.

She wished Myles would come over and surprise her in the middle of the night. But she knew that wasn't going to happen. She knew he wouldn't leave his wife's side in her time of crisis. But what about Tatum's crisis? She couldn't afford to keep up this place. Dirk wasn't much help and hadn't stuck around. Myles wanted to leave, but she needed more time.

Outside, the noise from the windmill sounded like a clock, the hands sweeping around and around. Time was running out.

At the Granberry house, Barrett sat in a chair in his living room, TV off, small table lamp on, Butch on the floor by his feet. Letty was staying overnight at the hospital in Rockland for observation. She had a sudden break from reality, the doctor had said. Maybe a sign of early onset dementia. Barrett fretted over her condition. Where was his Letty? He wanted her here. No, needed her here. All their kids had left the island and now it was just the two of them to tend to the farm and the cows.

When he got home from the mainland, there was a message on his answering machine. The representative from Oakhurst had called to tell him the company was severing their contract due to his not being able to fulfill the agreement. It was just sour milk, he thought. Then he began to laugh. No use crying over sour milk. The laughter turned to tears.

What would they do now? How was he going to tell Letty? Maybe she was right. Maybe Myrtle had cursed them with the deformed offspring. They had sold some of their land to Aerosource for those infernal wind turbines and they were paying the price. They lost Ash, they lost Myrtle and her calf, and now they'd lose the farm.

And it looked like he was losing Letty.

Then what?

Outside the window, he could hear the cause of his destruction as the machine ground on through the night.

In a rusted white pickup truck with a missing tailgate outside a stately home on Pequot Road sat Dirk Lassiter, a twelve-pack of beer on the seat beside him and a shotgun on the floor behind the seats. The grip of the octopus tentacles squeezed his skull with full force and he thought he heard the grinding of his bones. But he knew that was just the sound from the wind turbines, even all the way from the opposite end of the island. That's how powerful its reach was, he thought, just like the tentacles on his back, it could stretch beyond anything imaginable. It reached out to him now and his head felt about to implode.

Earlier in the evening, Dirk had hung out with Brownie and Jumbo at the captain's bungalow after dropping their load of lobsters off at the marina. Dirk felt too pissed off to venture out to the Raven's Nest, not wanting to chance running into Pickett or any of the other town elders, afraid of the public spectacle he might make.

So instead, the trio got drunk and high at Brownie's place. But the more Dirk drank, the less weed he smoked and the less mellow he became compared to the other two.

"Let it go," Brownie said, taking a big hit off his naked lady glass pipe, letting the smoke seep out his nostrils. "Pick your fuckin' battles."

Dirk couldn't sit still. He paced back and forth, only stopping to take a swig from a beer can. "That bastard can't do this to me. Someone needs to put him in his place."

"Take a hit, man," Jumbo said from the couch, after Brownie passed him the pipe. He offered it to Dirk, holding it in the only two fingers of his left hand. "You need to mellow."

"Fuck that," Dirk said and chugged the rest of the can, then tossed it toward the recycling bin shoved in one corner of the kitchen. The can missed, bouncing off the edge of the bin, and skittered across the linoleum floor with a rattling sound. He went to the fridge and grabbed another cold one.

"Listen," Jumbo said, looking back at Brownie first. "Things will look up soon. I'm tellin' ya."

Dirk noticed that Brownie glared at Jumbo.

"What the fuck you talking about?" Dirk asked.

"He ain't talking shit," Brownie said. He got up from the easy chair he had been relaxing in and grabbed the pipe from Jumbo. He turned to Dirk. "Don't get all worked up. Keep your shit together and let it go."

"Let it go!" He couldn't believe what he heard. This from the guy who earlier threatened to blow a hole in some kid's boat over pilfered lobsters. "I got a right to be pissed. I ain't letting nothing go. If I could, I'd take a lobster and shove it up Pickett's ass and let the thing claw its way out."

Jumbo rolled on the couch in laughter.

"Someday I'd like to see that," Brownie said. "But today's not the day."

"Maybe we should just tell him how things are," Jumbo said when he stopped laughing.

Brownie turned and glared back at Jumbo. "We ain't got nothing to tell him, you fuckface."

"What the hell's going on with you two?" Dirk asked Brownie.

"We're just trying to have a good time," Brownie said with as much a smile as his craggy face allowed.

"Pretty soon, there's going to be nothing but good times," Jumbo said with a cackle.

"What are you talking about?" Dirk asked.

"Can't we just let him—"

Before Jumbo could finish, Brownie spun around, grabbed the two pincer fingers on Jumbo's left hand and squeezed them tight. Jumbo screamed.

"Shut your fucking cunt hole!" Brownie yelled. He let go and Jumbo slumped into the couch.

"Someone better tell me something," Dirk said, feeling pissed. These were his friends, but it seemed obvious something was going on that he wasn't in on, and he didn't like that. It seemed everyone conspired against him these days.

"There's a time for everything," Brownie said, winking. "It's not up to me to say, but we may be able to let you in on a venture that will more than make up for everything. I just need you to sit tight for now."

The tentacles tightened on Dirk's skull and he felt his whole body might cave in. "Yeah, well, when you want me, you come fucking find me."

He turned and left the bungalow, sensing no attempt from either of his friends to stop him. The first thing he did when he drove off was head to the beverage store in the village to pick up a twelve-pack of beer. The next thing he did was stop at the marina, where he got onto the *Seaweed* and retrieved the shotgun Brownie kept stashed there. He made sure it was loaded.

Dirk drove around while drinking the first couple beers, his whole body feeling anxious and unsettled and his head aching. He knew where he wanted to go, but delayed getting there till he had enough alcohol in him to muster some bravado. He turned the pickup onto Pequot Road and parked on the street on the opposite side from the great white mansion: Pickett's place.

No lights were on in the house, just one bright onion-shaped lantern over the double front doors. Dirk didn't exactly know what he wanted to do, but felt a confrontation with the bastard was due. The shotgun could stay in the truck, only to be used if he absolutely felt he needed it. But whatever the outcome, he had no plans to stand for this prick trying to steal his idea, or his woman.

He wondered where Pickett was now. Out on the town with some of his other rich cronies, maybe? He still couldn't believe Brownie and Jumbo had the audacity to even attempt to justify this asshole's actions. Maybe Pickett had something on the two of them, something he could hold over his so-called friends. Pickett reigned as the most powerful man on the island, so it would come as no surprise if a lot of people owed the man some debt.

Dirk tossed the empty beer can over into the back floor and grabbed another, popping the tab. He needed to drink faster before they started getting warm. He watched the house and its dark windows.

Come on, you bastard. Show yourself. He scanned the second-floor windows. He frequently gazed up the road, and then into his rearview mirror to see the opposite direction, getting excited every time he saw headlights, only to be disappointed when some random car passed by. *Fuckers.*

He chugged some more beer. *Where the fuck could Pickett be?*

The tentacles tightened and he winced from the pain inside his head. Despite the hollow feel, a thought crept inside. What if Pickett was out at Tatum's place? Maybe he was the guy she was running around with. No. Couldn't be. He tried to shake the thought out of his head, but it only made the pain in his skull rattle like a ball bearing.

She wouldn't go for an older guy like that, he told himself. But… but. Someone like Pickett could give her the security she desired, security Dirk had not been able to provide. But she told him about Pickett's visit. Tatum wouldn't have done that if he was the guy she was whoring with, would she? Unless. Yes, unless she told Dirk so he'd do something stupid, something that would get him sent away so she'd have a reason to desert him.

But he had been the one who deserted her, left her when the pain got so bad from the flicker and the turbines grinding away throughout the night, nonstop, just like the pain in his head from the tentacles. It wasn't his fault! It was Pickett's. He brought those damn machines here. He got the farms on Haven Road to sell off chunks of their lands to Aerosource. Valuable land, now worth shit.

Dirk crushed the empty beer can in his right hand, wishing he could squeeze the aluminum into mush, and then tossed it over his shoulder. He couldn't help it if he left, even though Tatum still drowned in the sorrow over Nathan's death. But it was his boy too and he suffered as well. But the headaches and the insomnia were too much. He begged her to sell the farm – hell, it wasn't even a farm anymore – and rent an apartment with him in the village so they could start fresh without the burden of that behemoth money pit.

But no, she wouldn't. It was Tatum's family legacy, she said, and the place her children were raised. But Nathan was gone, and Rigby…. Well, Christ, Rigby wasn't even his kid. Sure, he helped raise the boy and cared about him, but he was spawned by some snooty university fucker over at the marine research station. Rigby didn't even bear any resemblance to him, or his own mother, for that matter. That dark hair and dark complexion, that all came from that college asshole.

Dark complexion? Dark hair?

Dirk thought again about the off-islander who'd been snooping around and stopping in at Tatum's house. *Fuck!* Maybe he was the college asshole, come back to claim his seed. Dirk's left hand squeezed into a fist, while his right hand crushed down on the half-full can of beer, causing some to squirt out the top. He tipped it back and downed the rest.

It must be him! The fucker came back. Maybe he wants his boy and Tatum too, take them both away. The tentacles flexed, creeping along his scalp and adjusted their grip before squeezing tight. He could see the resemblance, the darkness of the foreign guy. Tatum never told him much about the guy or that he was a foreigner. Looked like a fucking A-rab. A ring of pain engulfed his head and he closed his eyes.

Bright lights behind him forced his eyes open.

A car had pulled up behind him and stopped, lights shining through the rear window of the truck cab. He heard a door open and someone get out, then footsteps coming his way.

Dirk looked at the keys in the ignition and thought about starting the truck up and speeding off, but then he glanced in his side mirror and saw it was Constable Jensen approaching.

The law officer came up to the driver's side door and shone a light in the open window that blinded Dirk and sent shivers of pain into his brain.

"Whatcha doing?" Jensen asked as he gazed inside the cab of the truck.

Dirk shielded his eyes with his left hand. "Can you get the fucking light outta my face before you blind me?" He felt more concerned about the constable spotting the shotgun lying on the floor in the back.

"Sure," Jensen said and pulled the beam away. "But why you sitting out here, Dirk? Is there a problem?"

"No, no problem," Dirk said, trying to speak clearly. The beer on the passenger seat remained in plain view, so there was no sense hiding the fact. "Just felt I shouldn't be driving, so decided to pull over and rest a bit."

Jensen nodded. "I see. I see."

Dirk shrugged. "You know how it is."

"Of course," the constable said. "Smart thing. Don't want to drive off around a corner and end up on the rocks or in the ocean."

"That's right," Dirk said. "Just figured a little catnap till my senses come back."

Jensen licked his lips. "Sounds like a good idea. But first, can you just take those keys out of the ignition and hand them to me?"

Dirk was caught off guard. "Oh, yeah, sure." He removed them and handed them over to the constable.

"Thank you very much, Dirk." He deposited the keys in his pocket. "You just sleep it off and I'll swing by in the morning with your keys."

"Thank you very much," Dirk said. Then he added "sir" as an afterthought.

"Don't go wandering off," Jensen said and left.

Dirk released a sigh of relief, and then grabbed another beer. He still had another spare key in a magnetized hide-a-key box under the rear bumper. But for now, he was content to sit tight and wait for Pickett.

He poured more beer down his throat, hoping it would ease the pain in his skull and release the tentacles.

CHAPTER THIRTY-EIGHT

Oscar awoke disoriented, gazing up at an unfamiliar curved ceiling. *Where am I?* This didn't look like his room at the Tides Hotel. No, wait. He'd moved out of that place into the house on Tolman Lane he rented from Norris. But this didn't look at all like that bedroom either.

He looked around.

Norris.

He was in the yurt Norris rented; that's why the ceiling looked obtuse. The night came back to him with a smile. He reached a hand across the bed and turned.

Nothing.

No one lay beside him. He sat up, but the sudden movement caused a rush of blood to his head that made him feel dizzy. *The drinks last night, too many.* He brought a hand to his brow, feeling damp sweat. He sucked in some deep breaths of cool morning air that felt refreshing and soothed his dry throat. Water. That's what he needed.

But where was Norris? Did he leave to fetch coffee for them or maybe a touch of breakfast? Oscar threw the covers off and swung his legs over the side of the bed. He looked around for his clothes and spotted them bundled in a heap on the floor.

He got up and began dressing, wondering where one goes to the bathroom in a yurt. He had to piss. After getting his clothes on, he sat on the edge of the unmade bed and began putting his sneakers on. He gazed around the room.

Something about the room seemed off but he couldn't quite figure out what. His eyes stopped on the bench beside the door. A small opened package lay discarded. Oscar walked over and picked up the empty box. He looked at the return address label from an auto parts dealer.

Something for his VW bus, Oscar remembered, a carburetor or some such part. The strong urge to piss distracted him and he hurried outside, looking for a porta potty or some type of facility. He didn't see anything like that, but also noticed the VW bus was gone.

What the hell? Had Oscar slept that long and soundly that Norris got up and repaired his VW and took off? But where? Maybe Norris indeed decided to get him breakfast. Or at least coffee, he thought, as he rubbed his head, hoping the fuzzy aching feeling in it would subside.

No time to ponder his friend's sudden absence, he thought, there were more urgent matters. He walked around to the back of the yurt, making sure to stand far enough away from it, and looked around to make sure he couldn't be seen. Then he unzipped his pants and began to urinate into the grass in front of him. A wave of relief settled over him. About halfway through, something dawned on him and he tried to hurry.

He knew what looked out of place in the yurt. Or rather, wasn't in its place. When he finished peeing, he zipped up and rushed back inside.

An empty space remained against the wall where the barrels of ammonium nitrate had been.

"Fuck!"

Memories from last night flooded back, along with talk of bomb making.

"Jesus Christ!"

He can't be serious, Oscar thought as he grabbed his keys off a counter and hurried outside. When he got behind the wheel of his car, he still couldn't believe what might be happening. Was Norris crazy? Did he really plan to blow up the wind turbines? He thought about what Norris had to say about hypnotism and government experiments. *The man can't really believe that enough to commit an act of destruction, can he?* At times Norris seemed as sane as anyone, but other times he talked about things that made him seem as much a lunatic as some of the other people on the island he'd interviewed.

Had the shadow flicker really driven them all mad?

Oscar sped off down the dirt road, hoping he wouldn't be too late to stop Norris.

When he reached the paved Sunset Road, he sped up, carefully negotiating the sharp turns that followed the jagged coast. He rolled through the stop sign that put him on Pequot Road, slowed down a bit as he entered a more residential area, but still kept a steady pace. He didn't know how much of a head start Norris had on him. Damn, why hadn't he heard him get up this morning? He remembered Norris pouring them each a glass of wine before they went to bed. Could he have drugged the wine? The idea disturbed him, but he couldn't dismiss it.

As Oscar continued driving down Pequot Road, his mind remained deep in thought. He did not notice the rusted white pickup truck parked on the side of the road, nor the man behind the wheel who perked up when he went by. Nor did Oscar even bother to glance at his rearview mirror, or he would have seen the pickup pull out and begin following him, keeping a bit of a distance behind.

When Oscar got through town at a slow drag and reached Haven Road, it allowed him to pick up speed and he raced toward the northeast end of the island, He bore right at the juncture of Crockett Road and pressed harder on the gas pedal, hoping he would be in time to stop this insane plan by Norris. He felt himself breaking into a sweat. *God, please let it not be too late.*

He only slowed when he spotted the dirt road turnoff on the left and eased his car into it. His heart tightened in his chest when he saw Norris's old VW bus parked near the base of one of the turbine towers.

Christ, he's really here, thought Oscar. He'd hoped he had been all wrong and his friend was indeed out getting him coffee and a bagel. But no, there he was, connecting some wires to one of the barrels Oscar had seen back at the yurt, so immersed in his task he didn't even look up as Oscar parked near the VW and got out.

The silence of the interior of the car was broken when Oscar stepped out. The grinding noise from the turbines pulled his gaze up the long cylindrical towers to the blades, each rotating with their own rhythm. Another sound carried in the air, as if from a distance, and Oscar's eyes followed his ears down the valley beyond the turbines where the sky was filled with seagulls. A cacophony of screeches engulfed the area as the birds weaved in and out of the staccato cadence of shadows being splayed across the land.

The display dazzled him as he watched, transfixed, thinking the little Larson boy was right when he stated it looked like the birds were dancing. It was an ominous, yet beautiful sight in the clear blue morning sky, marred only by the reflecting waves of shadows.

Maybe it is hypnotism, Oscar thought, almost feeling like he couldn't move. Then he pulled his gaze away and tried to regain his composure and focus on the task at hand. Norris could be onto something with his preposterous theory, but that still didn't justify what he planned to do.

He approached Norris cautiously, worried that startling him could have unexpected consequences for them both. His friend did not hear him, too embroiled in the task at hand. When Oscar got closer than he felt comfortable with, he cleared his throat.

Norris looked up. "Damn."

"You can't seriously be doing this." What else could he say? He wanted to shout and scream, but thought better to attempt to keep the man calm.

"You should have stayed away," Norris said, and bent back down to the wires he was hooking up to some device on top of the barrel.

"Are you crazy?" *No*, he thought, *not the right approach.* "This is insane." *Not much better.*

Norris ignored him.

"The only thing you're going to accomplish is blowing yourself up... and maybe me with you."

Norris didn't look up or stop. "Then I suggest you leave."

"Just think for a minute, will you!" Oscar raised his voice, though he tried not to. "Do you even know if this will work?"

"I've done my homework."

Like a good teacher, Oscar thought. "But what do you think this will accomplish? Even if you do manage to knock these things down. They'll just put them back up. You're fighting a multi-billion-dollar energy conglomerate. You can't win."

Now Norris did look up, with anger on his face. "Someone's got to fight them. If you don't see the need, then get the hell out of the way."

Oscar let out a deep breath, wishing it would calm his nerves, but he could still feel them sparking inside his body. "There's got to be something else, a better way."

"What? Your stupid report?"

Oscar felt insulted and his fear turned a little to anger. "Let me bring my findings back to Aerosource. Maybe there's some way they can resolve the issues."

"They're the problem," Norris said. "They're not going to resolve anything." He finished what he was doing and took a couple steps away from the barrel. "There." He almost smiled.

Oscar's eyes followed the wires that linked all the barrels placed at the base of each tower. *He's really going to do this*, he thought, exasperated. He approached Norris, trying to think of some way to reason with the man. As he got close, he could see Norris shaking with nerves. *He's scared*, he thought. *Maybe there's some lingering doubt.* He dared to reach out and lightly place his hands on Norris's shoulders and look deep into his blue eyes.

"Listen to me," Oscar pleaded. "We can find a better way. But this?" He gestured to the bomb apparatus spread out before them. "This isn't going to help anything. It'll land you in prison and what would that accomplish?"

He saw Norris's eyes shift, his face contract. *There's doubt*, Oscar thought. *He's starting to doubt.* Another idea crept into Oscar's head. Norris needed help; psychological help. Maybe the shadow flicker drove him to this point, or maybe there was something else not right in his brain. Whatever the cause, Oscar had to make him realize it.

"Oh god," Norris said, and looked around at his handiwork. "I don't know."

That was the opening Oscar needed. "Dismantle it. Undo what you've done here and get it away. No one needs to know."

Norris began laughing. Not a thundering funny laugh, more like a hysterical nervous one.

"What is it?" Oscar asked.

Norris looked at him with a mad grin. "I'm not sure I know how." He laughed some more.

"Just do what you did, but backward," Oscar said, incredulous. "It must be as simple as that."

Norris scratched his chin, deep in thought. "I think I can." Then he nodded. "I'm sure I can." He looked at Oscar. "There's only one problem."

"What's that?"

"I'm just not sure how stable this all is." He looked back at the barrels.

"Take your time," Oscar said. Then he saw movement down below in the field.

"What the—" He turned his head and looked. Norris also turned.

A young boy walked across the field toward them, his features diluted from the shadows of the flicker that swept over him.

"It's him," Norris said. "He's come back again."

Oscar looked at Norris's face and saw a glaze over his eyes. "Who?"

"Nathan Lassiter."

Oscar looked back at the boy. "Of course not. Nathan is dead."

"They never found him," Norris said. "He's just lost."

Oscar felt annoyed by this distraction. Just when he thought he had the situation under control. "Whoever it is, we need to get him away from here. It's too dangerous with all this unstable stuff you've got."

"He comes in the flicker," Norris said, a dazed look on his face.

"Listen." Oscar grabbed him by the arm. "Start taking this bomb apart, and I'll get the boy away from here."

Norris gazed at him and nodded. He turned and walked hesitantly over to the closest barrel.

Oscar strode past the turbine towers toward the field, still perplexed by the sudden arrival of this boy, whoever he was. The shadows flashing over the field gave the boy the appearance of a phantom. When the light was there, Oscar could see him plain as day, but the next second when the shadow washed over him, he almost appeared to fade, like some kind of mirage.

In the sky above the field, more seagulls gathered. Their screeching increased in pitch as they flew to and fro. The boy did not even look up, as if he accepted this behavior from the birds.

Oscar hurried his pace, not wanting this boy to get too close. A fright rose up in him as he realized the danger of the situation, especially if Norris was not careful dismantling the explosives. This whole thing could literally blow up in their face. It suddenly occurred to Oscar how scared he really was.

When Oscar reached the boy, they both stopped. In each wave of light, Oscar could see the long mussed locks of strawberry-blond hair and a small smattering of freckles on the bridge of the boy's nose. He swallowed hard, a cold clammy feeling coming over him.

The boy did look like the pictures he'd seen in Tatum Gallagher's house, though his hair was much longer.

No, he thought. *It simply can't be.* But it looked like him.

Oscar bent down to be eye level with the boy. "Nathan?" he asked with some trepidation.

The boy gazed back at him with a curious look.

"How do you know my name?"

A lump stuck in Oscar's throat. *Oh my god.* His mind spiraled in a dizzying frenzy.

"Where have you been?" He couldn't believe he was asking this.

The boy looked back the way he came. "In the land of seaweed. I lived with the lighthouse man." He returned his gaze to Oscar, a blank look on his face.

"What are you talking about?"

"Where's my mom?"

Oscar didn't know what to tell this kid. Something terrible happened to him, and maybe it made him mad like everyone else.

"How did you get here?"

"I followed the flicker."

Oscar stood up, not sure what to do or say. He looked back up the hill, seeing Norris hard at work trying to deactivate the device he had built. He looked back to the boy.

"Listen, it's not safe here." He felt a sense of urgency. "You need to get away from here. It's dangerous."

"I just want to go home." The boy looked sad.

Oscar glanced down the hill. "Look, you can see your house right there," he said, and pointed toward the Gallagher farm. "I bet your mom is waiting for you."

The boy looked back at the house, though Oscar couldn't tell if he recognized it. He gazed back up at him. "But what if I get lost again?"

"I'll watch you the whole time," Oscar said. "I can see you from here. Just walk a straight line for your house, and I'll make sure you get there. Don't go anywhere else, just head right for it."

The boy hesitated, but then began walking down the hill. Oscar felt a sigh of relief for getting the kid away from the area, but wondered if he was doing the right thing to let him go off by himself. He wasn't really sure who this kid was (*he couldn't be Nathan*), but he needed to get him far from this spot.

As Oscar turned to head back up the hill toward the turbines, he heard a rustle in the field grass behind him and turned, thinking the boy had come back.

Through the dizzying stutter of the shadow flicker came another figure, a man. It took a while for Oscar to recognize Dirk Lassiter because he was too busy noticing the shotgun the man carried.

"I know why you're here!" Dirk yelled. His eyes appeared blood red, as if the whites of his corneas had streaks scratched across them. He looked like he hadn't slept in days. He held the shotgun up, occasionally letting go with his left hand to wipe some invisible object away from the air in front of his face, as if trying to brush the shadows aside.

"Easy," Oscar said, taking a step back, shocked by his sudden appearance. "Watch where you're waving that thing." The man seemed drunk and Oscar's heart skipped a beat as he stared at the dark barrels pointed toward him.

"You're here for the boy!" Dirk screamed.

Did he mean Nathan? Or whoever that kid was? "Put that thing down for a minute, will you!" Oscar yelled, scared the shotgun would suddenly go off.

"You can't take the boy!"

"Nathan just went down to your house." Oscar pointed in the direction the kid had gone.

Dirk's eyes nearly crossed. "What the fuck you talking about? Nathan's been dead for a year."

"I don't know, man," Oscar said, trying to remain calm. "But some little kid just went down the hill if you're looking for someone."

"I'm looking for you, fucker! You ain't taking Rigby and Tatum away."

Now Oscar was really confused. *This man is drunk and crazy and got some disturbed notion in his head.* But he held a shotgun pointing in his direction, so Oscar had to find some way to reason with him.

"I'm not here to take anybody away." He glanced back up the hill to see Norris still working on his device. Oscar looked back at Dirk. "You need to trust me. This isn't the place to be right now."

"You're the one who ain't knowin' his place to be, you little prick."

A seagull dipped low and almost skimmed the top of Dirk's head. He looked up with surprise and anger at the bird.

Oscar gazed up and saw the birds in what looked like a spiraling funnel, still weaving through the bands of shadows.

"I need to help my friend up there," Oscar said, taking a cautious step backward.

"You ain't going nowhere," Dirk said, raising his shotgun.

Oscar froze, scared, his legs weak.

A pair of seagulls flew low and one of them clipped the left shoulder of Dirk with its talons, tearing at his shirt before flying off.

"What the fuck!" Dirk screamed, looking up at the sky.

The seagulls screeched louder, drowning out his voice.

Oscar wanted to turn and run up the hill while the man seemed distracted, but he didn't dare. Fear had gripped his body and he couldn't move.

A few more seagulls swept down toward Dirk and he swung madly at them with the shotgun. "You sons of bitches!" He looked at Oscar. "Did you bring these gulls here?"

Mad, Oscar thought. *The man is mad.* He took another step back.

"Don't you go anywhere, fucker!" He raised the gun.

A swarm of seagulls swooped down on Dirk, one lashing him across the cheek with its talons, drawing a streak of blood. Another nipped his left hand with its beak as he tried swatting it away. The shotgun waved wildly as Dirk tried to fend off the gulls that now were attacking him.

Oscar panicked and turned to run, and looked up at the hill where Norris now saw what was going on.

"Watch out!" Norris screamed and pointed.

Oscar looked and saw Dirk staggering, seagulls clinging to his shoulders, head and arms, blood running down his face from a laceration across his forehead. He raised the shotgun despite the attack on him.

Oscar dropped to the ground with his hands over his head.

A loud blast roared from both barrels of the shotgun, and Oscar felt something whizzing in the air above him. At the top of the hill, a second blast sounded, and then the whole top of the hill by the turbines roared with a tremendous explosion.

CHAPTER THIRTY-NINE

In the shadow flicker....

Melody Larson sat on her front porch. She hated being outside in the morning when the flicker whipped across her front yard. But she didn't want to be inside the house right now. Myles was in the bedroom packing his suitcases.

Just some time away, he had told her, to sort things out.

What the hell did that mean? She'd be stuck trying to run the farm by herself? Meanwhile her father remained missing and all she could think about was what happened to Nathan Lassiter last year when he went fishing. What if her dad wandered down to the shore in a state of delirium and fell into the sea? All she could think about was him having the same fate as that poor little boy.

At least her father had lived a long life. But still, she ached inside, grieving at his loss even though she didn't know whether he was really gone. Constable Jensen had called first thing this morning to tell her they'd be out searching again today. *It's a small island, there can't be too many places for him to hide.*

No, Melody thought. But it's a big sea and it could swallow up an old man in the wink of an eye and drag him down to its murky bottom.

She wiped a tear from her eye.

Out in the front yard, Troy swung on the tire hanging from the maple tree. He had been excited about the birds in the sky again. Melody would have had him come inside, but this time the seagulls were farther away from the house, in the sky up the hill doing their zany dance.

She wished they would fly right into the propeller blades of the turbines and be chopped to pieces. That would put an end to their incessant squawking that drove through her head like rusty nails. But despite all the screeches from the gulls, she could still hear the whine of the turbines as the blades spun and the shadows swept over her.

At the Granberry farm, Barrett stood in his pasture staring at his cows. He had buried Myrtle yesterday right next to her deformed calf, for whatever it was worth. It had taken almost every ounce of his energy to dig a hole deep enough and he had to use the tractor to haul her body over to it.

But the area where Letty had shot the animal still held a bloody spot turned brown and dry from the sun beating down. The other cows avoided that area, as if they sensed something.

Barrett watched the cows as the shadows from the flicker fell over them, wondering if the sour milk had indeed been an effect of the turbine torture, or a curse as Letty believed. He had a restless sleep last night, feeling separated from his wife, who spent her own night alone in the hospital in Rockland. The doctor had called him last night, telling him it would be good to have a family consultation to decide what to do about Letty.

Family consultation? There was no more family, at least not here. No one but him. All their children had moved away. They all had busy lives and kids of their own. They had no time to drop everything and come back here. Not for two old folks whose days were growing short.

Barrett heard a bark and looked back to his porch to see Butch standing there. His dog seemed to plead with him to come back to the house. Butch wouldn't venture out here, not during the flicker. He didn't blame the dog. The flicker had ruined everything. Spoiled the milk so that he could no longer sell it to any of the local dairies. The cows were too skinny to sell for slaughter. Not enough meat on them bones. The bills were going to start piling up, and now if Letty needed long-term hospitalization....

What could he do? What choices did he have?

He lifted his face up, staring straight into the flashes of light and shadow that seemed to send slivers into his mind.

Barrett turned and walked toward the barn. Butch barked at him some more but he ignored the dog. He slid open the barn door and walked inside. He paused and scanned the interior, into the stalls and up to the rafters. Empty milk jugs were stacked against one wall, probably never to be filled again.

His eyes caught a length of rope hanging from a wooden peg by the first stall. Behind him, Butch still barked and waves of shadows fell into the open doorway of the barn.

*　*　*

Tatum Gallagher sat in the living room of her house, wearing her sunglasses and wondering why she hadn't heard from either of the men in her life. Myles Larson had not returned any of her messages and that infuriated her. She needed to talk to him before he did anything rash. She needed to make him understand that she needed time.

Time for what? she wondered, looking around the room. Even with the blinds closed, the flashes of shadow and light seeped through the slits between each blind filling the room with a rhythmic cadence of brilliance and darkness.

She had also heard nothing from Dirk since her phone conversation the night before about her visit from Gavin Pickett. She expected more fallout from Dirk and didn't understand why there had been nothing from him. She wasn't sure what she expected, but silence wasn't it.

Tatum got up from the chair, feeling restless, her stomach turning over inside, making her nauseous. Air, she thought. She needed air. She opened the front door and stepped outside. Out here the flicker was stronger and the sunglasses felt useless. She glanced up toward the hill wishing the sun would hurry up and peak above the windmills so the flicker would vanish.

As she gazed in that direction, a silhouette appeared in the field beyond her house. It moved in her direction with a slow steady pace. She took off her sunglasses to get a better view.

It looked like a boy.

Before her mind could register anything further, a tremendous explosion erupted from the top of the hill.

CHAPTER FORTY

One lone gull cried in the sky.

Oscar heard it when he pulled his hands away from his ears, the sound still muffled while the ringing in his ears subsided. He opened his eyes and looked up, spotting the seabird circling overhead in a swirl of smoke, and wondered where all the other birds had gone. He stood up in the haze that encircled him; his head throbbed from the deafening roar of the explosion.

The bomb!

He looked up the hill as the smoke cleared. The turbines still stood.

The white metal of the bases for all three structures was charred with black streaks that ran thirty feet high, as if the turbines had been licked by a giant blackened tongue. They stood rigid on the hill. The explosion had no effect.

As Oscar stared, he noticed something.

The blades rotated counterclockwise.

Norris!

Oscar ran up the hill, seeing no movement from above. *Jesus*, he thought, panicked, his heart racing inside as the muscles in his legs propelled him toward the top. *Please God, be okay.*

Thick smoke hung around at the clearing when he reached it. He heard the groaning of the turbine blades as they rotated backward, sounding like the pain of a wounded beast. Oscar's eyes stung from the smoke and watered, tears trying to flush out the acrid vapor. He spun around, looking for Norris. He tried to call out, but when he opened his mouth, smoke choked him. He backed away a bit and brought the neck of his shirt up to cover his mouth.

Nearby the two vehicles, his rental and Norris's VW bus, were charred ruins, smoke pouring out of them and a few flickers of flame flapping in the wind.

Oh god, he thought. *What the fuck!*

More of the smoke began to dissipate, as if the slow spinning blades propelled it down the hill toward the pastures below. As the area cleared, Oscar spotted something. He fell to his knees and picked up a sneaker he recognized belonged to Norris. Its weight told him there was something in it.

He dropped the sneaker, turned, and leaned over the ground, feeling the urge to retch, not sure if it was from the smoke he inhaled or what he saw inside the sneaker. *No,* he cried inside. His eyes watered, perhaps from the stinging smoke or the realization of what happened to Norris.

Above, the seagull screeched again. Oscar got to his feet, dizzy and wobbly, and wondered why he wasn't hearing sirens. Surely the explosion had been seen and heard by others on the island. Constable Jensen and the fire department should be on their way by now.

But Oscar listened and heard nothing. He whirled around, not knowing what to do, trying to figure out what the hell happened. The cry of the seagull above reminded him.

Dirk Lassiter. Where was he? The lunatic had been waving his shotgun around and the birds had swarmed over him. The gun had gone off. The stupid idiot must have fired wildly up the hill and set off the rigged explosives.

But where had Dirk gone?

Oscar felt the need to get away. Though the smoke was clearing, it still made it hard to breathe. And the thought of accidentally stumbling upon more of Norris's remains made him nauseous. Plus, that lunatic Dirk could still be somewhere out there. Oscar needed to get help.

He looked back at the destroyed vehicles, knowing he'd have to hoof it. He started down the hill, glad to get away from the smoke and the horror it obscured. His legs felt weak and a couple times he thought he'd stumble and pitch forward into the long grass. But he maintained his balance as he worked his way down the hill.

Oscar spotted something and stopped.

Something lay in the grass before him. He approached with trepidation, not sure what he saw until he got closer.

Dirk's body lay on his back, arms flung wide from his sides, legs splayed. His face was a ruined bloody mess, pieces of flesh stripped from it where the seagulls had torn at it with their beaks and claws. One eyeball was missing, the other hung down by his check from a thin piece of muscle.

What the fuck.

Oscar turned and this time did vomit into the grass; his stomach heaved several times before nothing more came out. He wiped spittle away from his chin with the back of his hand.

This is nuts, he thought, looking around and then glancing up at the sky, almost afraid to see if more gulls were near. But even the lone bird had flown off, seeing nothing more of interest here, and the only thing remaining in the sky were trails of smoke pushed along by the turning of the turbine blades.

Off to the left, Oscar spotted Dirk's white pickup truck stashed behind a copse of trees. He ran over to it, wanting more than anything to get away from here, still not understanding why no one had come to the scene. The explosion had been deafening and his ears still rung. More than half the island should have heard it and many more would have seen the rising cloud of smoke. It just didn't make sense.

Oscar got to the pickup and opened the driver's side door. No keys in the ignition. He looked in the center console and above the visor. He checked under the floor mat and in the side door pocket. Nothing. Damn.

He slammed the door. The keys were probably in Dirk's pants pocket. Oscar shook his head. No way was he going back and touching that body. He gazed around, finally looking down the hill at the farmhouses, his quickest place to find help. The pastures and farmhouses were bathed in a layer of what Oscar assumed on first glance to be smoke drifting down from the explosion at the turbines. But as he set off down the hill, it dawned on him that a morning fog lay spread out over the landscape, seeping in from the distant coast, and he could even see a glimpse of the village on the horizon mired in its grasp.

The Granberrys' farm was closest and that was the direction Oscar targeted. The old man was sure to be around as Oscar spotted the cows scattered about in the pasture. It puzzled him that he still heard no sound of emergency vehicles heading up toward the scene of the explosion. Had everyone down there gone deaf and blind?

He glanced behind him, back up at the hill at the turbines and the blades on all three structures rotating in the opposite direction. He wondered if the explosion caused that, jarring the machines' mechanisms and sending them into a corrupt rotation.

Poor Norris. What were you thinking?

Oscar continued down till the field leveled out. He came upon Barrett's split-rail fence that lined the back end of his property and he ducked between the rails to cross into it. He kept his eyes focused on the ground as he made his way through the field, careful to watch out for cow dung. The cows before him paid him no attention as he walked by. Too interested in grazing, he figured, and....

He stopped.

His head swiveled and his body turned to and fro as he examined the cows around him. They weren't grazing. They were standing still. Absolutely still.

Oscar rubbed a hand across his eyes, in an attempt to wipe his vision clear. He spotted one cow in front of him and kept all his attention on it. It stood upright on its legs, head bent toward the ground, mouth open as if ready to grab a clump of grass.

But it stood motionless.

Frozen.

His mind came back to Tatum Gallagher's story. *"I saw time stop."*

Oscar spun around, looking at the other cows in the field. None of them moved.

Many times living in New England he had driven by fields of cows and they always appeared to be standing still, but he knew that was because sometimes they didn't move much. But this was different. These cows were different. They did not move at all.

Oscar ran a hand through his hair as his scalp tingled. He realized he held his breath and released it, but felt he needed to suck another one back in. He needed to find Barrett. He needed to find someone, anyone.

He turned and almost bumped into the side of a cow before him. It looked like a statue placed out here in the pasture to resemble a real cow. He avoided its gaze and moved around it, giving it a wide berth, in the direction of Barrett and Letty's home. He only got a few steps when some sensation compelled him to turn and look back.

The cow stared right at him.

Not possible, Oscar thought, as he felt the hairs on his arms stand up. The cow had been looking the other way before. *So its head moved.* It had to be.

But it stood still now, like the others.

With caution, he approached the cow in slow shuffling steps. When he got close enough, he stepped back in horror, a gasp catching in his throat. He brought his hand to his mouth to suppress it.

A cleft ran down the center of the cow's face, dividing it in two and giving it the appearance of having two faces, each pointing in different directions. Two sets of eyes occupied one half of its face, one lone eye staring out at him from the other side. No wonder it had appeared to be looking at him from both sides.

What madness is this?

His heart thumped to the beat of the turbine blades at the top of the hill.

He turned and ran toward the house, no longer worried about where he planted his feet. He had to find somebody. When he reached the Granberrys' house, he pounded on the front door.

"Hello!" he cried out, looking over his shoulder at the disturbing scene of the motionless cows. "Is anyone home?"

No answer. No sound from inside the home. He stepped away from the door and looked around. The door to the barn stood open and he headed over that way, hoping he'd find Barrett there, but also wondering why the man hadn't heard his cries and come out to investigate.

Something's wrong, Oscar thought. *Something's very wrong here.*

He hesitated before entering the barn, calling out Barrett's name in a soft voice as if afraid to disturb whatever the man might be doing. Once inside, he realized he needn't have worried.

Oscar saw the dog first. It stood in the middle of the barn, its tail pointing out straight behind it, its ears perked up and its jaws open in a silent bark. Like the cows, it looked like a statue and it scared him.

But what frightened him more was what drew the dog's attention.

Barrett Granberry stood on top of a milk can, a noose around his neck, the rope running up to the rafters above and then down to a post and cinched there. One foot stood firmly on the can, the other in mid-stride off it, the can tilting forward ever slightly. The old man's eyes looked sad and fearful, as if with this sudden step he was about to take, he might have second thoughts.

But he stood frozen in place, not yet having taken that fateful leap.

"Jesus Christ!" Oscar exclaimed, horrified by the sight. His head felt dizzy as the dreamlike state of everything around him caused him to question his own reality. "What the fuck is going on here?"

He approached the old man, almost thinking he could catch him before he fell off the milk can. But Barrett remained suspended in that position, held frozen in time.

I saw time stop.

Norris's theory came to mind. *Am I hypnotized? Could that really be what's going on?* Oscar looked down and touched his left arm with his right hand. *I feel that*, he thought. *My body is here. I'm not asleep. The explosion didn't send me into some kind of subconscious coma. I'm alive, I know it.*

He looked up at Barrett, seeing the anguish on the old man's face.

But what the hell is this then?

Oscar had no explanation except Norris's absurd theory. He approached Barrett and reached out a hand, but stopped short of touching the old man, afraid of what might happen if he knocked him off his precarious perch. But he felt helpless, wishing there was some way to stop this insane act.

His eyes followed the thick rope as it rose from Barrett's neck and looped around the rafter above, and then angled down and was tied off at one of the beams in the barn. Oscar went over to the rope.

If I can just cut the rope, he thought. He didn't have a knife, but he could find something around here. He reached out and touched the rope, expecting the frayed fibers to be rough. But the rope felt cold and hard, like metal. There would be no cutting this. He tried untying it, but the solid nature of the rope made it impossible.

He looked back up at Barrett. What had driven him to this? And why did everything stop in the middle of it?

Oscar had no idea, but his nerves felt frayed and he wanted to get out of there. This place felt too creepy. He left the barn in a hurry, but took one last glance at the frozen image of Barrett Granberry about to step off the milk can into…what? The last act of his life being held hostage by time. Everything seemed unfair. He wished he could help somehow. A pain worked its way along the muscle walls of his heart.

He fled the barn and headed up the road to Tatum's house, hoping to find help there. His mind was scrambled. Thoughts raced around in circles, maybe going backward like the wind turbine blades. Nothing made sense. His reality had been distorted, all out of whack. If he didn't feel the ache in his chest and the pain in his skull, he would believe he lay back up the hill, unconscious from the explosion, and this was only some shell-shock nightmare.

But he felt the road beneath his feet and the strain on his lungs as he struggled to breathe. He slowed to a walk, unsure of any urgency, hesitant as to what he expected to find. And even a bit afraid. Yes, an undercurrent of fear lay just beneath the surface, yet too deep to scratch.

He didn't get far up Tatum Gallagher's driveway before realizing no help would be found there. But he continued forward, right up to the edge of the front porch. His heart relaxed a bit, and the sensation felt good.

Before him, Tatum's suspended figure knelt on the porch, her arms wrapped around the young strawberry-blond boy, her face a mask of euphoric shock, mouth spread wide in a glorious grin at the sight of her son, Nathan. Tears, frozen in time, looked like icicles on her cheeks, and drops of them hung in midair, glistening in the morning sunlight and waiting to plunge to the floorboards of the porch.

Oscar stared at the suspended scene before him, thinking that if one good thing had come out of this whole weird phantasmagoric experience, this was it. Tatum's lost child, long thought dead and swept out to sea, had come back to her. Oscar thought his heart would burst, and had to wipe away a tear of his own. He looked at its wetness on his hand. *Why me?* he pondered. *Why aren't I frozen in time like everyone else?* It didn't make sense. Nothing did. The boy had appeared out of the shadow flicker, but from where? And Oscar had sent Nathan back home and somehow he had arrived, only to be caught up in this frozen landscape. At least he found his way back to his mother's arms.

Oscar saw the open door to the house, probably left that way in Tatum's rush outside when she discovered her son had returned. He walked inside and made his way to the kitchen. He looked around for a landline, but found nothing. He left the house. It probably wouldn't have done any good. Would there be anyone to call? Would the line even work?

He looked up the hill. The turbine blades still functioned, albeit in the wrong direction. But power must still be generated somehow, somewhere. Something must work. He left the yard and continued up Haven Road.

At the Larson home, he saw Whitney Larson in the farm stand at the edge of the road. But she wasn't really working. She sat on a stool behind the counter, cell phone in hand, not moving. Had she been talking to someone? Texting someone? And what happened to the person on the other end of the line?

Oscar entered the farm stand and walked over to the counter. With tightened nerves, he reached over and tried to pull the cell phone out of the girl's hand. It would not release. It felt like trying to pry an object off a statue. Solid.

A cold spasm ran down his spine. He looked at the vegetables in the bins, almost daring himself to pick up a tomato or a pepper and take a bite. But he feared it would be like biting a rock and decided not to try. He left the stand and continued down the Larsons' driveway.

Myles Larson stood by the open door of his pickup truck, a suitcase in his hand, raised in midair as it appeared he was about to put it in the space behind the front seat, but the stoppage of time had halted his progress. Oscar spotted what looked like a ferry ticket poking out of the front pocket of the man's shirt.

Leaving? Oscar looked to the front of the house where Melody stood in the open doorframe of the front door, leaning against it as if for support, one hand reaching out, her face frozen in anguish. Oscar glanced back at Myles, putting a mental picture together. He thought about these neighbors he had come to know during his brief stay on the island and felt stricken with voyeuristic guilt at intruding on all these people's private moments of joy, sadness, and in the case of Barrett Granberry, desperation.

He shouldn't be seeing this. These people weren't even aware of his presence. He had no right to move about them like some spectral observer.

Oscar looked inside the cab of the pickup. The keys were in the ignition. He climbed up into the seat and tried turning the key and pressing on the gas pedal.

Nothing. The key wouldn't turn; the pedal wouldn't press.

It all felt like props on a movie set. None of it real.

He got out of the truck and walked over to the house, thinking maybe Melody would have a landline he could try, though he hadn't much hope. He probably would have no more luck than with Whitney's cell phone, most likely wouldn't even be able to lift the receiver.

Oscar had to turn sideways to get by Melody through the doorway, not wanting to brush up against her frozen form. He examined her face as it came inches from his own. She too had a streak of tears running down her cheek like a frozen river on a mountain. The trail ended at the end of her jaw with one teardrop clinging to the edge, about to release.

He went inside, working his way to the kitchen. There on one end of the counter was a cordless phone resting in its stand. *Might as well try*, he thought. He walked over to it and grasped the receiver. It wouldn't lift. *No, of course not. Nothing works*, he thought.

Out the kitchen window he could see the turbines in the distance. *Except those. They worked. Why?*

His mouth felt dry and he looked at the sink. He needed to quench his thirst. Oscar reached out and tried to pull on the faucet handle, tugging hard, and then wrapping both hands on it and yanking. It didn't budge.

"Damn!" he said, surprised at hearing his own voice in the quiet, the only sound he had heard since the lone gull that had been hovering above him up the hill and the grind of the turbine blades. The quiet unnerved him and he felt like screaming to disrupt the silence.

Instead he left the kitchen, and once again turned his body sideways to ease himself out the front door. Face-to-face with Melody once more, something seemed odd. He stared at her, trying to understand what felt out of place. He studied the lines of her face, the tear trail down the side of her cheek. Then he saw it.

The teardrop that had been clinging to the edge of her jawline was now in midair just below her chin.

It moved!

The teardrop had moved.

The thought slammed into his head like a hammer.

Time hadn't stopped. It was just moving at a fraction of its normal speed.

He thought about Barrett Granberry in his barn precariously stepping off the top of the milk can with the noose around his neck.

Oh my god! There might still be time to save him.

Oscar raced down Haven Road, his legs and arms pumping as hard as he could though he felt he ran in slow motion, as if an invisible force pushed back against him, as if time were slowing down. And isn't that what happened? he thought, time had slowed. Not stopped like he first assumed. Not like what Tatum had told him during her first interview. It had crept at a pace barely discernible to the naked eye, except for the smallest chance that he had seen that teardrop fall.

Oscar felt like his time slowed for him. No matter how fast he tried to run, his body felt like it struggled to move, as if he weren't gaining any ground. He passed Tatum's house, but didn't pause to see if anything had changed about the loving embrace she gave her young son. He didn't dare take his eyes off the road as he ran down it, almost afraid it would interrupt his pace.

His lungs strained, burning hot inside as if he were sucking in fire instead of air, the cavities filling up with hot ash making it a struggle to breathe. He felt he could collapse at any moment and sprawl out across the road. But he didn't stop. Somehow he found extra energy reserves deep down inside the most remote spots of his muscles and that momentum carried him along until he reached the Granberry farm.

As he turned into the drive, the barn seemed even farther away than before. Had it moved? Wasn't it closer to the house? His body felt overcome with exhaustion; the muscles in his legs stinging and stiffening, as if turning to stone.

Am I freezing up now? he wondered. *Maybe this is what happened to everyone else, it just took a little longer for me and soon I'll be like a frozen statue like the others.*

But no. They weren't frozen. He knew that now. They moved, just at an imperceptible pace. Something the naked eye could not see. But he saw it. Yes he did. He noticed the teardrop had fallen.

At the open barn door he stopped, his body bent over, his lungs spitting out hot breath, his legs throbbing with intense heat. He thought he might pass out. Everything started getting dizzy; the ground moved beneath him. He squeezed his eyes shut for a second. *You didn't come all this way to stop now.*

He opened his eyes and stepped into the barn.

His gaze was drawn up. Barrett Granberry's body hung from the rope, the milk can tipped over on its side, his feet hovering more than a foot over the ground, his eyes bugged out wide, his tongue hanging out from the corner of his mouth.

Too late, Oscar thought, his heart sinking into his gut. *There wasn't enough time.*

On the ground beneath the dead body, Barrett's dog lay curled up, its eyes closed, jaws resting in its paws, guarding its master's lifeless corpse.

Oscar turned away, his body weak, his breathing deep. He walked out of the barn and looked around the pasture before him and the motionless cows scattered about. Something drew his attention to the top of the hill.

A man stood in the distance before the turbines.

Oscar stared in puzzlement. At first he thought it might be Norris, somehow still alive, but then he remembered the sneaker and what he saw in it. Even from the distance, he could tell this man looked older, with a heavier build. The man appeared to be looking down at him.

Then the man turned and walked away.

Oscar's first urge was to shout out.

It had been weird walking around feeling all alone here, not understanding why everyone else seemed to be held in some state of suspended animation. It freaked him out and scared him. Now here was somebody else, walking about just like him.

But somehow he was still afraid. Who was this mysterious man and why could he move around? Oscar thought he should be a bit discreet and not let the man see him. But when the guy turned to walk away, a sensation crept inside Oscar's gut that made him not want to lose track of this man, a feeling of urgency. *Don't let him out of your sight*, his mind screamed. *Follow him.*

The man disappeared over the hill and Oscar ran through the pasture in a state of panic. He raced up the hill. When he reached where the turbines stood, he spotted the man off in the distance walking into a heavy fog. At first Oscar thought it was smoke from the explosion settling over the back side of the hill. But no, it clearly was fog, enshrouding the valley below, swept in from the northern shore.

It had been a bright sunny morning earlier, but now this hazy fog had settled over everything and the skies had become overcast. He even felt a chill in the air that raised goose bumps on his arms, or maybe those were the result of the fear still festering inside his body. But he shook his discomfort off and focused on this new stranger whom he could see walking across the field to the north.

Oscar began to follow at a safe distance, close enough to keep his eyes on the man, but back enough so the stranger wouldn't sense he was being followed. Sometimes it seemed he lost the man in the fog, but spots cleared enough to keep tabs on him. If anything, this strange fog helped protect Oscar from being discovered, though the man never turned around to look behind. He marched forward with determination and Oscar kept pace.

The only time Oscar looked back, he became startled to discover he couldn't see the turbine blades anymore. Odd, he thought, but had no time to contemplate it. He had only this unknown man to pay attention to and maybe find some answers to what the hell was happening on this island. He had no idea if this man knew any more than he, but his sudden appearance and being the only other living creature to be moving about, must have some meaning.

They crossed into the conservation land on the north side of the island, with the mysterious man walking along the hiking trails that crisscrossed that tract of public land. The route seemed familiar to Oscar from just the day before when he and Norris helped in the search for Tyrus Darrow. How much had changed in such a short course of time, and though the fate of Norris filled him with melancholy, he wondered whatever happened to Tyrus.

Oscar knew exactly where this trail led and as it brought them closer to the northern shore of the island, just west of Crooked Cove, he smelled the strong salty odor of the sea and could hear the surf rolling up against the rocks in the distant foggy horizon. He heard another sound too, one that assured him he was heading toward the destination he'd assumed: the throaty bellow of a foghorn.

He ducked behind some shrubs as the structure came within view, and peered around a branch to see the strange man approaching the Gull Rock lighthouse. Something wasn't quite right. The lighthouse structure itself appeared as Oscar had seen it yesterday, only the white painted bricks seemed fresher and the light shone out from the top of the tower. This made no sense. The lighthouse had been decommissioned, Norris told him yesterday. But here it was in working order.

The old abandoned house beside it also looked different. It no longer had broken windows, and the gray cedar shakes weren't cracked and weathered. The man walked up to the front door of the house and knocked.

What's going on? Oscar wondered, confused. This place was abandoned yesterday, but now looked fine. Of course this was the same place. He recognized the lighthouse. Its beam filtered out through the foggy morning in tune to the blare of the foghorn. But the house had been an unlivable wreck, long abandoned, Norris had told him, when the last keeper had moved out and the lighthouse shut down.

But as Oscar watched the unknown man knock again, the front door opened and someone let him in.

Thoughts ran through his mind like a whirlwind. So whatever

happened back on Haven Road must be some kind of aberration. There were others moving about on the island and someone was living in the lighthouse keeper's home. But how could this structure look like this in a day's time, as if someone from HGTV came here and renovated the whole house overnight?

Oscar wanted to get a closer look. He moved along the shrubs toward the left side of the house, before he had to cross open ground. The stench of the salty sea grew stronger the closer he got. When he reached the side of the house, he looked out toward the ocean. The rocks below were covered in straggly seaweed, as if the ocean had vomited up the dregs deep within its belly onto the shore. The stench made him gag.

A rickety-looking wooden pier stretched out from the edge of the shore. A dinghy tied to it rocked with the swell of the waves. Oscar crept up to the side of the house just beneath a window. He wanted to peek inside and see who his mystery stranger was meeting. He reached up, gripped the edge of the windowsill, and pulled himself up to take a look inside.

He spotted furniture, a couch, chair, coffee table. A bookcase stood in one corner. Someone indeed lived here. Though the place looked tidy, he noticed seagulls inside the house. Three sat still on the mantel, while several more were perched on the bookcase and the coffee table. They didn't move, so he wondered if they had become frozen like the late Mr. Granberry's cows. He wondered how they had gotten in. Maybe someone left a window open.

It seemed obvious someone lived here. But yesterday the rooms had been empty. He didn't understand. As he rose to get a better look inside, a reflection appeared in the glass, a hideous distorted face.

Startled, he started to turn to see behind him, when something heavy struck his head and everything went black.

CHAPTER FORTY-ONE

He returned to consciousness with blurred vision and a throbbing pain in the back of his head that rippled out across his skull. As the fuzziness in his eyes cleared and things came into focus, he noticed he sat in a kitchen with his hands and feet tied to a wooden chair at a table.

An odd metallic scraping sounded from his left and the noise irritated the pain in his skull.

"I see you're finally awake," said a voice.

A man came into view, the same man he had followed from the wind turbines.

Oscar squinted up at him, his vision still adjusting. The man looked to be in his late forties or early fifties with thinning gray hair combed over the top of his head. He was a bit overweight and wore a white shirt and dark pants.

"You took quite a knock on the noggin," the man said.

Oscar tried to remember what happened. "You hit me?"

The man shook his head. "Oh, no, not me. I'm not the type for physical confrontations." He then pointed off to the right. "He whacked you."

Oscar looked, spotting a strange man sitting on a stool, an ax across his lap and holding a sharpening stone that he rubbed repeatedly along the edge of the blade. The sound drove pain into Oscar's head with each stroke.

"Lucky he only hit you with the blunt end," the gray-haired man said.

Oscar looked back at the first man. "Who are you people?"

"That's Creigh," the man said, pointing to the fellow with the ax. "He's the lighthouse keeper here."

Oscar always imagined a lighthouse keeper would be tall and thin, kind of like the structure of the building itself. But this man stood barely over five feet tall with a stocky thick frame. What made his diminutive stature even more so was the fact he barely had a neck, so his large head seemed to rest on the top of his broad shoulders. His wide face held a thick nose, the bridge of which rose up into his forehead, leveling off with his dark eyebrows. His big round fish eyes looked like they'd have a hard time seeing over the protuberance of his nose, so that he'd have to turn his head to look in either direction. His hair, wispy and scraggily, hung down over his ears. His mouth hung open as he sharpened his ax.

"And I'm Burton Sikes," the first man said.

Oscar looked back at him, thinking that name sounded familiar. Where had he heard it before? Then he remembered the note in the book at Norris Squires' house signed by B.S.

"You're the missing Aerosource man," he exclaimed.

The man laughed. "As you can see, I'm not missing."

Oscar's head hurt too much to think. "But where have you been?"

"Right here," the man said.

His grin maddened Oscar. "And where exactly is here?" He felt confused. "I was at this house yesterday, it was abandoned and dilapidated. And I was told the lighthouse had been decommissioned. There was no keeper."

"That will take a little explaining."

"More than a little," Oscar said. "What are you doing here?"

Sikes pulled up a chair and sat across the table from him. He put his hands on the table and drew in a deep breath. "You're not going to like anything I say, and you may not even understand it."

Oscar grew agitated. "Try me."

"I belong to a special group of people, sort of a consortium. People of science, but more than that. A sort of science others don't really understand. Science that pushes the boundary of reality itself."

The man talked gibberish. It made Oscar think of Norris and his crazed theories. Was everyone on this island mad?

"Are you familiar with the Hermetic sciences?"

Oscar gazed back with a puzzled look.

Sikes frowned with a somewhat pouty expression. "It's sort of a lost field from the age of philosophers. It's a science that investigates the hidden nature of alternate planes of reality."

Oscar thought back to the strange book he discovered in the nightstand in Norris's house and the note inside. *I have found the Opening of the Mouth.*

"You stole that book!"

Sikes scowled. "I'd hardly say stole. It's my book to begin with. I just left it behind by mistake."

"What do you mean left it behind? Where did you go?"

Sikes shook his head. "You have no idea where you are."

Oscar felt the muscles in his body burn with rage, as if he could rip through his bindings like they were paper. But of course he couldn't.

"I'm on the north shore of the island at a lighthouse keeper's home. And for some reason, I'm being held hostage by a pair of lunatics."

Sikes disregarded him and continued. "Hermes and his disciples studied alchemy and magick and astrology. That book you found, *The Kybalion*, delves into the Hermetic principle of rhythm and polarity. The dividing of the astral plane."

None of this helped the pain in Oscar's head, only exacerbated it. And the constant scraping of the sharpening stone on the ax blade didn't help. He turned to Creigh.

"Can you stop that please?" he yelled.

The man's hand stopped mid-stroke. His mouth still hung open and a piece of drool flowed out onto his lower lip. His head turned so his eyes could shift to Sikes, who nodded. Creigh put the stone into his front pocket, but kept the ax on his lap.

Oscar looked at Sikes. "He's not planning to cut my head off with that thing?"

"Not as long as you behave."

Oscar was somewhat joking, but now felt on edge. This whole day started out like a dream, but evolved into a nightmare. He sifted through all that Sikes had said.

"Are you talking about the occult?"

Sikes shook his head. "Science, Mr. Basaran, but a science most people don't understand."

"Does Mason Helleson know you're here?"

At that Sikes laughed. "Who do you think I work for?"

Oscar had disliked Helleson from the beginning, not really understanding why, except for a feeling of distaste for the man. He thought back to all his questioning of the missing Aerosource man and Mason's dismissal of it.

"Does he know you're here?"

"I keep him apprised of all my whereabouts."

Oscar glanced across the room. The fog out of the kitchen windows gave the effect of the house floating among the clouds. Outside the foghorn blared and the salty air seeped in through the open window. The light flashed out against the misty bank like heat lightning and the surf roared when it splashed against the rocky coast.

On a shelf against one wall were a couple of seagulls, frozen in place. He thought of the cows and the people down on Haven Road.

"Are those real?" he asked, hoping maybe for some explanation of what he saw in the valley.

Sikes glanced over his shoulder at the shelf. "Oh, heavens no. Those are carved from wood. Creigh does that. All lighthouse keepers need a hobby or two to bide their lonely time."

Oscar shifted his gaze to Creigh. He had no desire to know what other hobbies this man might have. He thought about what the boy who looked like Nathan Lassiter said to him before the explosion. *I lived with the lighthouse man.* Could it be that this cretin kidnapped the boy and held him captive here? But still, that didn't explain why this place looked deserted just yesterday. *Unless they were somewhere else.*

"Where exactly are we?" he asked.

"That may be difficult to explain to you."

"I've got nowhere else to be."

Sikes drew in a deep breath. "Have you ever heard of aeromancy?"

Oscar shook his head.

"Wind has power," Sikes continued. "More than just providing electricity. It's its own energy, powerful. Aeromancy is the study of that. The power of the wind can actually divide planes of reality."

"What the fuck are you talking about?" Oscar squirmed in his seat while his arms struggled against the restraints, subtle enough not to draw concern, but hopefully to ease the tightness of the ropes that cut into his wrists.

"It's science, Mr. Basaran, though a type of science known to only a few select groups. We've been practicing this and studying it for quite a long time, experimenting."

Oscar thought again of the people and animals he saw in some form of suspended animation. But, no, not suspended. Because they moved. Barrett Granberry finished hanging himself.

"What are you messing with?" he asked, though his immediate thought was that Sikes was screwing with his mind.

"We're explorers and scientists. With the wind turbines, we've been able to use the energy to achieve our goals."

"And what is your goal?" *Madness*, he thought.

"It took time and lots of failures, but we found the right formula, the right way to harness the wind energy." Sikes leaned forward. "You see, as wind moves through the blades of the turbines, a wake is formed, similar to turbulence, though not as chaotic. With the turbines set in the right pattern, one tower downstream from the first would suffer encountering the wake and altering it."

"To what end?" This made no sense, Oscar thought. The gibberish of a madman.

"To achieve what we intended." Sikes beamed. "We created a rift in reality."

The words came back to Oscar again. *I have found the Opening of the Mouth.*

Oscar felt his skin crawl beneath the ropes. It was a mouth all right, and it seemed to be swallowing him. He felt trapped in a place with a man whose mind had splintered and his odd companion with an ax. His head throbbed from where he had been struck, compounded by all the nonsense this so-called scientist had force-fed him. He started to fear for his life. He was at the mercy of these two, but he didn't want to let on how scared he was. He needed to go along with their absurd notions even if only to buy himself some time. Who knew what plans they had for him?

"And Aerosource has been backing this experiment?" Oscar asked.

"No," Sikes said, and leaned back with a shake of his head. "We are a private consortium. Mason uses the money and opportunity Aerosource has to invest in our endeavors. The higher-ups in the company have no clue what we're up to."

"And what happened to the people in town?" Oscar asked. "The ones who seemed frozen in time?"

"When the rift opens, there is some blurring of the planes. You just saw the effects of that. Those people are just fine in their own world."

"Their own world?" What the hell was he talking about now?

"Oh yes," Sikes said with a smile. "I'm afraid, Mr. Basaran, that you have inadvertently crossed over into an alternate world."

The pain in Oscar's skull intensified. He felt as if he had been hit over the head again.

"You're not fucking serious?"

Sikes's smile widened. "I certainly am."

Oscar glanced around the kitchen; his eyes rested on Creigh sitting on his stool, also with a crazed grin.

They're all mad here, he thought, and wondered what he stumbled into. "I'm here, on the north end of Kidney Island at a lighthouse keeper's home. Where else do you think we are?"

Sikes shook his head. "They actually call this Serenity Island here."

"And who are they?"

Sikes's eyes narrowed. "They call themselves the Trident, the people who live in this part of the world. Our group has been making contact with them for the past year since I've first crossed over."

Humor him, Oscar thought. *Play along to buy some time till you can figure out what to do and how to get out of this mess.* He fidgeted in his chair some more, trying to loosen his bindings a bit.

"And what is the point of coming here?"

"Opportunity," Sikes said. "A world that can offer us so much more. Our consortium has big plans for us."

"And these Trident people, they have something to offer?"

"We are very open to working with them. This is just the beginning."

Oscar couldn't care less about what Sikes and Helleson were trying to do here. There was only one thing that concerned him.

"So what are your plans for me?" He cast a glance toward Creigh.

Sikes stood up from his chair. "You're something of a problem. I'm going to need to consult with my superiors to see what to do with you."

"You mean Helleson?"

He ignored the question. "I'm going to leave you for now in the capable hands of Creigh as I have some things to prepare for." He started to leave the kitchen.

"What's that?"

Sikes stopped and turned back.

"Company is coming."

CHAPTER FORTY-TWO

Oscar sat in the kitchen alone, still strapped to the chair. He managed to loosen the bindings somewhat, but not enough, and worked diligently now that he had time to himself. He didn't know where the lighthouse keeper went, and wasn't sure how long he'd be gone.

His mind raced with everything going on. It had been bad enough with what happened back at the turbines, but now the predicament he found himself in seemed even more surreal than the people down on Haven Road stuck in the suspended animation. If the explosion from the homemade bomb knocked him into a sort of hallucinatory state of delirium, that could explain a lot. But what about now? Either he was experiencing a continuation of his mind-warping trauma, or this Sikes guy had suffered his own brain fracture. Something had happened to him that caused his disappearance, and wherever he spent the interval till now had only succeeded in deepening that fissure.

All this talk about an alternate world had been so much drivel. But Oscar needed to play along for now, until he could find a way out of this mess. He wondered if anyone would notice him missing. Probably not. He worked alone and Helleson was the only one he had been reporting to and he had no specific timeline for his investigation to wrap up and be filed. He paid a week's rent at the house, so it would be several days before anyone would worry about that, especially now that his landlord was dead.

He thought about Norris, and it exacerbated the pain in his head. He certainly hadn't hallucinated that knock on his noggin Creigh inflicted on him. No, the pain was very real. The constant blare of the foghorn didn't help matters. When the hell would this damn fog lift anyway? It must be almost noon.

A knock came at the door.

Startled, Oscar leaned back in his chair, almost to the tipping point, but enough to gain a view down the hall toward the front door. Who could that be? What had Sikes said? *"Company is coming."* But he left the house to prepare for whoever he expected to meet, so who could this be at the door?

The knock came again and Oscar yelled, "Hey! Help!"

Footsteps sounded from outside the back door of the kitchen. He turned in time to see Creigh come in from outside, his face twisted in frustration. He held the ax in his hands and his disturbing eyes shot darts at Oscar. He held a finger up to his cracked lips. He glanced at the door after another knock and then pushed Oscar's chair in toward the table and out of sight of the hallway. He bounded down the hall toward the front door.

Oscar heard a voice when the door opened and craned his head back to get a peek.

"Hello," a familiar voice said. "Can you help me? I seem to have lost my way."

Over the top of Creigh's misshapen head, Oscar caught a glimpse at the man in the door. Tyrus Darrow.

"I was out looking for dandelions," Tyrus told Creigh, "but got turned around in the fog and can't find my way home."

Oscar looked on, stunned at first, but then wanted to yell out. He stopped himself. Creigh still had the ax and Oscar didn't want to put Tyrus in danger. He had nearly forgotten about Melody's father's disappearance and the search for him yesterday. But at least now this proved Sikes's story was nonsense.

"Can you help me?" Tyrus pleaded.

Oscar had never heard the lighthouse keeper speak and wasn't even sure if the man could, but then he did.

"No help for you here," Creigh said. His voice sounded deep and strained, as if having no neck had forced his Adam's apple down into his larynx to clog it. "Go away!"

"Please," Tyrus said, his old wrinkled face sinking. "I can't find my way home. If you could just point me in the right direction. I live on Haven Road."

Oscar leaned back a little more, trying to catch the old man's attention. He thought he saw Tyrus lift his head and his eyes look over the top of the lighthouse keeper's head.

Oscar mouthed the words: *Help me.*

He couldn't be sure if the old man's eyes were even able to see this far or if he understood his message, but as long as Creigh held that ax, he didn't dare speak out.

"Go away, old man," Creigh said, pushing Tyrus back with his left hand and slamming the door. He turned to look back at Oscar with a twisted grin.

Oscar felt his heart sink and hope fade.

About a half hour after Tyrus was abruptly shoved out the door, Creigh went out the back again, but not before stopping in the kitchen and tightening the ropes around Oscar's arms.

Damn. He didn't know where Creigh went, perhaps to tend to some business in the lighthouse. But now Oscar had to start all over again trying to get his bindings loose. He worked slowly and methodically, not knowing how much time he had but wanted to give himself some kind of chance for escape.

Oscar heard the back door of the kitchen open and silently cursed, figuring Creigh had returned. He turned to look and saw Tyrus Darrow step through the doorway. His heart leapt.

"Tyrus!" he said, trying to temper his excitement.

The man approached in a slow shuffle and pointed at him. "I know you."

"Yes, yes, you do. And you've got to help me."

The old man looked down at the ropes binding him to the chair. "Why are you tied up?"

"The lighthouse keeper is mad. And there's someone else with him. They're holding me captive. Please hurry and help me get out of this." Oscar pulled up on the ropes, nearly lifting the chair and him in it in the process.

"Oh goodness," the old man said and tried to undo the knots in the ropes with his gnarled hands. He fumbled for a bit, and then stopped. "I'm afraid these old hands ain't much use anymore."

Oscar looked around the kitchen, panicking that this rescue attempt would be fleeting. "Check the cabinets. Find a knife."

Tyrus moved over to the counter and began pulling open drawers. Oscar looked through the glass of the back door, watching out for Creigh. Through the fog he could glimpse the base of the lighthouse, but no sign of its keeper.

"Aha!" Tyrus said and pulled a long knife out of one of the drawers. "Will this do?"

Oscar's eyes widened at the size of it. "Yes, get over here."

The old man approached and bent over to begin sawing at the fibers of the rope. Oscar's nerves tightened and his throat went dry. He imagined the knife slipping, slicing open the veins in his wrist, and himself bleeding to death strapped in the chair.

"Easy," he cautioned.

The old man continued to work with slow deliberate draws of the serrated blade on the rope. The last fibers snapped and the binding dropped to the floor. Oscar flexed his fingers, getting full feeling back as the numbness in his hand subsided.

"Give me that," he said, taking the knife from Tyrus. He began to cut the rope holding his left arm to the chair. Once free, he began working on the legs. He freed the right leg first. Just as he was cutting the last bit of rope on his left leg, the back door burst open.

"Intruder!" Creigh rushed in with a roar, his face enraged and red, his arms lifting the ax over his head.

Oscar cut through the rope on his leg and leapt up off the chair. He shoved Tyrus out of the way as Creigh swung the ax down on the now-empty chair, shattering it with one blow. Creigh pushed Tyrus to the ground and swung his ax toward Oscar. The blunt end of the ax struck Oscar's arm and the knife went flying. It clattered on the floor out of sight.

Tyrus tried to stand up and Creigh turned to face him. Oscar looked around for the knife but couldn't spot it. He searched for some type of weapon and grabbed the only thing nearby: one of the wooden carved seagulls on a shelf.

As Creigh began to raise the ax again, Oscar came up behind him and used his full force to bring the wooden seagull down on top of Creigh's flat head. A crack sounded and the little man dropped to the floor in a heap.

Oscar looked down, not sure if he had killed Creigh or just knocked him unconscious. He looked at the seagull in his hand and noticed the wooden object had nearly split in two. He dropped it to the floor.

"Are you okay?" he asked Tyrus.

The old man nodded. "I think so." He pointed down at Creigh. "Is he okay?"

"I don't know, and I don't want to stick around to find out. We need to get out of here."

He grabbed Tyrus's arm and led him out the back door. The salt air smelled strong and stung his nose, but felt good after the stale air in the house.

Now what?

Oscar guided Tyrus along the path that ran from the house down to the lighthouse about fifty yards away. The light at the top flashed its beam out across the foggy ocean. If Creigh had only been knocked unconscious, Oscar didn't know how long he had before the man awoke.

The best thought seemed to be to get to town and find help, report what went on here. But looking at Tyrus made him realize the old man was not fit for a long trek across the island. The stench of the sea drew his gaze down below the lighthouse. He saw why the smell of the ocean seemed so strong here. The rocks at the sea's edge were covered in heaps of seaweed. The waves rolled and crashed onto the rocks, the surf sluicing its way up through paths between the stones only to recede and slink back into the ocean leaving behind more seaweed.

The other thing Oscar spotted below was the dinghy tied up to the long narrow dock. The idea of getting in a boat in these rough waters didn't thrill him, but it might be easier to travel with the old man this way. *If I stay close to the shore*, he thought, *I could follow the coastline around to the other side of the island and Loch Raven village.* He looked at Tyrus's weary face.

"We're going for a boat ride," he told him.

Holding onto one arm, he guided Tyrus down the long wooden staircase that led to the dock.

"Are you sure this is a good idea?" Tyrus asked, hesitant but not resisting.

"Don't worry," Oscar said. "We're not going out too far." No, he thought, looking at the breakers. They only needed to get the boat out beyond the waves and then head around the island. It would be arduous for himself, he knew that. It would be no joyride for sure. The sea was rough, and it would be a long way around. But Tyrus would be okay. All the old man had to do was sit in the boat. It was the best way to get both of them to safety.

Oscar looked out at the sea and felt grateful the fog seemed to be dissipating. Tyrus lurched and almost pitched forward down the stairs.

"Easy, fellow," Oscar said, steadying him. "Almost there."

Tyrus wheezed for air when they reached the dock at the bottom.

"Rest," the old man said, his voice a whisper.

"You can get plenty of rest in the boat," Oscar said, and led him to the end of the dock where the dinghy was tied up. It took great effort, but he managed to lower the old man into the boat, despite it bobbing and weaving on the roiling sea. Oscar went to the piling and began untying the rope that lashed the boat to the dock.

"Stop!" sounded a voice from above.

Oscar looked up and saw Creigh standing at the top of the steps. The sight startled him, though he was somewhat relieved that he hadn't killed the man. Creigh held his ax and descended the steps. Oscar tossed the rope into the bottom of the boat and clambered down.

Tyrus looked up at Creigh. "I don't think he wants us to take his boat."

"Too bad," Oscar said and grabbed the oars. He pushed off from the dock and began pulling on the oars, riding up over the crest of a wave and down the other side. He would probably get sick, but couldn't worry about that now. The surface of the water was thick with seaweed, making Oscar's initial draws on the oars heavy as if he were rowing through a stew. The farther he got out to sea the clearer the ocean became.

By the time Creigh reached the dock, the two of them were nearly a hundred yards away from it. Creigh raised the ax over his head and yelled something unintelligible. Oscar paused long enough to wave back and chuckled to himself.

"Asshole," he muttered under his breath.

He continued to row, already feeling the strain on his upper arms. Once he got past the breakers, he steered the dinghy parallel to the shore.

"Where are we going?" Tyrus asked, looking around the boat like a little lost boy.

"We need to get to town," Oscar said, "and find help. Or maybe we'll come to a house or something." He paused and glanced over at the barren coastline. It was going to be difficult since most of the north shore remained conservation land. They hadn't gone far and already his body felt sapped of energy, his arms like elastic bands, the wood of the oar handles coarse on his palms, raising calluses that stung as he rowed.

"Why did that man tie you up?" The old man's eyes narrowed suspiciously in his wrinkled face.

"There were two of them. I think they're delusional." Oscar shrugged. "I don't really know what they wanted with me."

"Lots of crazy things these days." Tyrus hugged his arms. "Cold out here."

Oscar felt the chill of the sea air too, but his exertion with the oars kept up his body temperature so he didn't mind a bit of a cool breeze, but he understood how it must be affecting Tyrus. He was grateful the old man had pants on this time.

"How long till we get where we're going?" The old man shivered with a spasm that shook his whole body.

"I don't know," Oscar said, wheezing. He knew it could take a while. It didn't help that he rowed against the ocean current, making it twice as hard to get somewhere. But this would be the shortest distance to the village center on the other side of the island. But he knew deep down inside they probably wouldn't make it that far. He always kept physically fit, but even this much exertion taxed his strength.

He lifted the oars out of the water and paused, resting for a moment, trying to recharge his battery. If he had someone younger than Tyrus with him, they could take turns, but he knew the old man would be no help. He glanced again at the coast, praying for the sight of a house or building, anything that would give them hope of rescue.

As he leaned forward, bent over the oars and drew in a deep breath, a sound in the distance caught his attention. He turned and looked to his left, out past the dissipating fog. He heard a boat engine. He scanned the horizon and spotted it. A small boat chugging along the water. It headed in the opposite direction, but farther out to sea.

Hope, he thought. *If I can get the boat's attention, maybe they can bring us back to town.*

"That could be our ride," Oscar said and put the oars back in the water. He bore down on the starboard side oar to change direction and then pulled hard on both to propel them in the direction of the oncoming boat.

Tyrus said nothing, only craned his neck to see what Oscar was talking about.

Oscar dug deep with the oars, straining his back and shoulders, feeling a flame burn through the muscles. *This might be their best chance,* he thought. He continued rowing, often turning his head to look over at the boat to make sure he was on line to intercept it.

It still looked too far away. His arms felt like giving out. He stopped rowing and turned around. He stood up and waved his hand over his head and yelled. There was no way anyone on the boat would hear him, but it felt good to yell for help.

Suddenly, the boat changed direction.

It sees us! Oscar turned to look back at Tyrus. "They've spotted us!"

He waved a few more times and then sat down. *No sense rowing anymore. Let them come to us.* He let out a deep breath, on the brink of exhaustion. He hoped he could make whoever piloted the boat understand the gravity of their situation. Maybe they could even radio the Coast Guard or state marine patrol. Or Constable Laine Jensen back at the Loch Raven police station. Anybody who could help.

As they sat in the dinghy waiting for the arrival of rescue as the boat drew closer, Tyrus uttered one word.

"Seaweed."

Oscar's eyes widened when he saw the name written on the side of the approaching lobster boat and spotted the bearded man behind the wheel and the laughing first mate standing at the bow with a boat hook in his hands.

"Oh shit." Oscar grabbed the oars and began rowing. He turned the boat around and started pulling for shore. He was frantic with sudden renewed energy. If they could get beyond the breakers and into shallow water, the *Seaweed* couldn't follow.

But the boat gained fast, its engine more capable than the muscles in Oscar's arms. It loomed larger as it approached. And it didn't look like it would stop.

"Watch out!" Oscar yelled, his heart leaping up into his throat as the prow of the boat smashed broadside into the dinghy, shattering the wood and sending splintering pieces of board flying.

Oscar got flung into the water before he could react, sucking salt water down his throat and hearing the rumble of the *Seaweed*'s motor above him. He surfaced and gasped for air, his throat and lungs stinging with the salty brine of the sea.

I'm going to drown, he thought. *I don't have the energy to swim.*

He dropped under water; the wake of the boat pushed him down like great big hand. He held his breath, the water churning around him. He waved his arm in an attempt to drive himself up to the surface. When he rose above it, he opened his mouth to get air but a rush of water flowed in instead. He slipped under again, gagging and unable to breathe.

Suddenly, he felt a sharp pain under his right arm. Something had grabbed him and he was lifted into the air. He coughed out water and sucked in air, grateful to breathe. The pain dug into his armpit and he realized he had been caught by the boat hook.

Oscar glanced up and saw Jumbo leaning over the gunwale of *Seaweed*, holding onto the boat hook and lifting him up. The man reached down with the two pincerlike fingers of his left hand and grabbed the scruff of Oscar's shirt and hauled him up and over the side rail of the boat.

The man stood over him, laughing. "Have a nice dip?"

Oscar lay on the deck, spitting up water and drawing in deep breaths. He felt dizzy and nauseous; his stomach roiled.

Then he thought of Tyrus.

Oscar rolled over onto his side and despite the total lack of strength in his body, managed to push himself up to all fours. He crawled over to the edge of the boat, grasped the side of the rail and pulled himself up to his knees.

He spotted Tyrus floundering in the water nearby.

"There he is!" Oscar yelled. "Help him!"

Footsteps sounded on the deck as Brownie stepped out of the wheelhouse and walked over to where Oscar clung to the rail. The captain stared out into the sea at the old man.

"Help him!" Oscar implored.

Brownie glanced down and then spat into the ocean. "We only got orders to bring you back." He turned and walked back to the wheelhouse.

The engine revved and the boat moved away. Oscar looked out, helpless and saw Tyrus sink beneath the surface and then bob back up again. Beside Oscar, Jumbo continued to cackle.

Tyrus sunk beneath the surface again, but this time did not come back up.

CHAPTER FORTY-THREE

Few boats were moored in the harbor as the *Seaweed* pulled in. Oscar stood at the bow, shivering under a blanket Brownie had given him, his teeth chattering. Murderers, he thought. They let the old man drown without an ounce of concern. What would they do with him now?

As Brownie guided the boat up to the dock, Jumbo jumped off with a rope in his hands, which he quickly wrapped around the cleats. Brownie cut the engine as Jumbo tied off the other end.

"Let's go," Brownie said to Oscar, motioning for him to disembark.

Oscar glared at him with accusatory eyes before reluctantly stepping over the gunwale onto the dock, his feet a bit wobbly. He planned to bide his time until he could find someone to help him and report what happened out at sea and at the lighthouse. They were all in cahoots, he figured, but still had no idea why. Were they all mad? He hoped to find Constable Jensen.

A group of fishermen stood on the opposite side of the marina admiring a large fish hanging from a hook. The fish looked unlike anything Oscar had ever seen. It appeared to have an armored exterior, and large pectoral fins. Its bloody mouth hung open, displaying a beak-like jaw.

The fishermen turned to look at Oscar and his companions, their large eyes gazing at them with curiosity. One of the men had rather long droopy ears. The fishermen took particular notice of Oscar and he hugged the blanket around him a little tighter.

"This way," said Brownie, and prodded him in the back. A man of few words.

As they walked from the marina into town, the two lobstermen flanking him, Oscar looked around at the buildings. The layout of the town seemed the same, but some of the buildings looked different than he remembered. He turned to gaze up at the granite block structure of Town Hall, wondering why he thought it had been a brick building. A flag flapped in the breeze on the pole out front of the building. Instead of the state of Maine flag flying on top, there was a red flag bearing the gold symbol of a trident.

"What's with the flag?" he asked, turning to Brownie.

"The island and the mainland are part of the Kingdom of the Trident," the captain said, annoyed at having to answer him.

Burton Sikes mentioned that name, but Oscar couldn't remember the context. The man had spoken so much nonsense, Oscar struggled to understand any of his sputtering.

The two men led Oscar down a deserted Main Street, which seemed odd for the middle of the day. They stopped before the Raven's Nest Tavern. Oscar looked up and noticed the sign had been changed. Instead of the raven standing in the crow's nest with a spyglass up to one eye, the sign had a seagull with a sea captain's hat on and the bar was now called Gull's Grill and Bar.

"What happened to this place?" Oscar asked, confused. He had just been here the night before with Norris. *God, was that only last night?* It didn't seem possible. So much had happened between then and now, most of it strange, some of it tragic.

"Stop with the fucking questions and get inside." Brownie shoved him in the back. Jumbo had the door open already and Oscar stumbled in.

The interior of the place looked darker with round tables instead of the square ones from before. The smaller bar positioned nearer the back held only one long row of stools in front. The only two other patrons in the place, two older men, looked up at them with wide round eyes set in pasty faces. They sat hunched over a table and after a moment returned to the beer steins clutched in their hands.

Oscar's eyes widened when he saw a very beautiful dark-skinned woman with long thick dark hair that hung in ringlets down over her shoulders behind the bar. The woman was naked from the waist up, her large breasts fully exposed.

What the hell is going on here? He looked away, embarrassed, and clutched the blanket around him even tighter.

"Over here," Brownie said, grabbing his arm and nearly dragging him to a booth with red vinyl seats up against the side wall. He shoved Oscar onto the bench on one side and took a seat on the other.

"Couple of pints, Lexann!" Brownie barked. "Put them on the institute's tab."

"Coming right up," the dark-haired woman said with a smile and began pouring a dark amber lager from one of the beer taps into a stein.

Jumbo walked over and leaned across the bar. When the bartender finished pouring the second beer, she grabbed the steins and set them down in front of Jumbo.

"Thanks, toots," Jumbo said with a leer. "Got a nice tip for you." He reached out with his left hand and grabbed the nipple on her right breast between the pincers of his two fingers and gave it a little tug.

Lexann broke out in a grand smile and playfully pushed Jumbo's hand away with a laugh.

Jumbo cackled and grabbed the mugs. On the way over to the table, beer slopped over the tops and splashed onto the floor. He set the steins down on the table and slipped in next to Oscar.

"How about something for me?" Oscar asked, his throat raw from the sea water he had swallowed and still shivering from his dunk in the ocean. "Maybe some hot tea."

"Lexann!" Brownie shouted. "Some hot tea for the pansy." He winked.

Oscar shook his head, bewildered by everything. *This is insane,* he thought. *I'm still trapped in this nightmare with these madmen and there's no end in sight. What the fuck's going on?* He looked at the two men at the table as they lifted their steins to their mouths to take a swallow of the frothy substance. The steins both had an intricate carved pattern of a giant squid, its tentacles reaching out and wrapping around a lighthouse.

The bartender came over to the booth with a steaming cup of tea in a scrimshaw decorated cup. From the waist down she wore a short black leather skirt and thigh-high matching boots. She smiled as she set the cup down in front of Oscar, who averted his eyes from her nakedness. As she turned to walk away, Jumbo slapped her on the bottom. She didn't flinch and returned behind the bar.

"Behave yourself," Brownie said to Jumbo.

Oscar brought the cup of tea to his lips, relishing the warmth from the steam on his face. He blew on it and then took a sip. He coughed at first, the hot liquid stirring up the salt in his throat. The tea felt good though, sinking down into his stomach with a warm soothing sensation.

"What are we doing here?" he asked Brownie.

The captain wiped froth from his mouth with the back of his hand. "Waiting for the boss."

After two more pints of beer, the door to the bar opened and a man stepped in and walked over to their table. Oscar recognized his face from the picture on his sign at the housing development.

"Jesus Christ, what a fuckup!" Gavin Pickett said when he got to the booth. "What the hell did you bring him here for?"

"We were thirsty," Brownie said, his voice undeterred by Pickett's agitation.

The selectmen chairman looked around the bar, taking notice of the only other two patrons in the place.

"Still wasn't a smart idea," he said. He looked at Oscar for the first time. "How the fuck did Sikes let this happen?"

"Bad enough some fucker tried to blow up the turbines back home," Brownie said.

Back home?

"Damn," Pickett said. "The boss ain't going to like this mess. Not with all the strides we made with the Trident. They ain't going to like it either."

"I thought you were the boss?" Oscar asked, more confused.

"Shut up, asshole!" He looked at Brownie. "Finish your drink and let's get down to the docks. He should be arriving from the institute anytime now."

As the three men led him outside, Oscar tried to figure out what Pickett meant about the institute. More mysteries without any answers. The only institution he knew of on Kidney Island was the old University of Maine Marine Research Institute, but that had been abandoned more than ten years ago he had been told.

Heading back down Main Street toward the docks, Oscar wondered how the two lobstermen cretins managed to be hooked up with the selectmen chairman. He couldn't imagine Pickett's type even associating with this motley crew, never mind them working for him, which appeared to be the case. He wished someone would give him an explanation, and not the cock-and-bull story Burton Sikes tried to feed him. Speaking of the Aerosource scientist, where had he gone off to? Creigh must have alerted Sikes by now of his escape. Was that how the lobstermen had come after them? No, that was too quick. Sikes had mentioned company was coming before he left, was this trio who he meant? Or was it whoever this boss happened to be that they were expecting at the docks?

Upon reaching the marina, Oscar heard the powerful rumble of a boat engine and watched as a forty-foot cabin cruiser idled its way toward the docks. As it eased up alongside one of the empty slips, Brownie and Jumbo stepped forward to catch ropes tossed to them by a well-tanned man with dark hair who looked to be in his late thirties.

When the engine cut off and the boat was moored, the figure of Mason Helleson stepped out of the cabin and onto the dock. He surveyed the group at the dock and shook his head. "This is what happens when you enlist scullions to do your work."

It felt incredible to Oscar that less than a week ago he sat in Helleson's office receiving the particulars of the assignment that sent him to Kidney Island. A lot had happened in the interim that led to his coming face-to-face with the Aerosource executive once again.

When Mason approached, he scowled and shook his head. "I didn't expect you to screw things up this badly."

"What is going on here?" Oscar asked, frustrated. "Why am I being treated like a prisoner? What's this all about?"

"I thought Mr. Sikes explained everything to you."

"He just rambled on about the wind turbines being used to split planes of reality and some such nonsense."

Mason grinned. "The consortium wouldn't have invested millions if we thought this was all nonsense. Look around you. What do you see?"

Oscar glanced around at the marina and the town. "Kidney Island and the village of Loch Raven. What am I supposed to see?"

"Subtle differences, Mr. Basaran. We have achieved a remarkable feat here. Lots of research and hard work is beginning to pay off."

This wasn't helpful, Oscar thought. Even Helleson spouted gibberish. "What do you want with me then?"

Mason shrugged. "You've presented us with an unfortunate situation, so now we must deal with you somehow."

He looked past Oscar to the others. "Follow us to the institute," he said to Brownie. "We'll take him on our boat." He looked at the dark-haired man and gestured Oscar toward his cabin cruiser. "Take him aboard, Braydon."

Oscar followed the man onto the deck of the cabin cruiser, with Helleson right behind. Brownie, Jumbo and Pickett boarded the *Seaweed*. Both vessels were unmoored and pulled away from the docks and motored out of the harbor. The cabin cruiser led the way up the coast, Braydon at the wheel, with the *Seaweed* tailing behind.

Oscar took a seat on deck, his clothes still damp and feeling chilled. The breeze blowing over the boat made the cold worse. Mason opened a cabinet and took out a bottle of Scotch and two glasses.

"Maybe this will help warm you up," Mason said and poured the two of them a drink.

Oscar wasn't much of a Scotch drinker, but felt it might help raise his body temp.

"To the future," Mason said and clinked glasses with him.

"What kind of future are we talking about?"

"For you, it's a bit uncertain," Mason said in a glum tone. "But for the consortium, it remains extremely bright."

Oscar frowned and took another sip. He had to find a way out of this predicament, but had no idea what to do. "What is this consortium all about?"

"Science, Mr. Basaran. Using it to explore the unknown. What we have achieved here is beyond remarkable."

"You realize your men killed an innocent old man?" The image of Tyrus Darrow sinking beneath the water flashed through his mind.

Mason shrugged. "Collateral damage in the name of science. I can't help the ineptitude of some of our followers." He glanced at Oscar. "I didn't expect you to stumble into our endeavors."

"Why did you send me here?"

Mason grimaced. "To do your job. To deal with a nuisance among a few villagers who were stirring up unnecessary negative attention to our operations on this island. A few days on the island to interview a few inhabitants and then write up your report. You should have been back in Boston in no time and filed your findings with me."

"And would you have done anything about the problems those people were having?"

Mason shot him a sour look. "Those people were of no concern to me. Our consortium had more important things at hand. They were just a distraction."

Oscar took the last swallow of his drink, wincing at a bitter taste at the bottom. He started to get queasy again from the motion of the boat as it glided across the water. His head also felt dizzy. He kept silent, tired of his useless conversation with Helleson. His stomach lurched and his head ached.

"We're almost there," Mason said.

Oscar looked across the bow and saw a long dock up ahead. Onshore were a large two-story building flanked by a small grouping of cottages, a long one-story building and a metal Quonset hut. As the boat approached the pier, he spotted Burton Sikes standing on the dock.

Company's coming, Oscar thought. His eyelids drew heavy, his muscles limp. He looked at Helleson.

"Did you drug me?"

Then everything went dark and he felt his body slide out of the chair onto the deck.

CHAPTER FORTY-FOUR

Oscar awoke, blurry eyed, and tied to a chair again.

Damn! Why the fuck does this keep happening?

He pulled on the straps to no avail. They were much tighter than the bindings at the lighthouse. He scanned the dark room around him, turning his head as far as his restraints would allow. He sat in the middle of the first row of seats laid out in a semicircle pattern, like a theater or classroom. The seats faced a black curtain.

Oscar cursed himself for not trying to run off when they left the bar. None of the men appeared to display any weapons. Somehow the absurdity of his situation hampered his ability to think straight. If he got another chance, he would have to make sure he didn't waste it.

A door opened behind him and he heard footsteps approaching. He craned his neck, but couldn't see who it was until they came down the aisle to the front of the room. Helleson and Sikes.

"People will come looking for me," Oscar said in a tone he hoped sounded threatening.

Both men grinned.

He wished he could slap those expressions off their smug faces.

"And they would probably find you," Mason said. "If they were looking for you in this world."

"You're still going with this alternate dimension theory, huh?"

"I tried to explain it to him," Sikes said to his boss. "He was reluctant to listen."

"I'm here," Oscar said, infuriated. "You're here. That's all I know."

Mason leaned in. "But here isn't here, anymore. We've cracked a scientific breakthrough the world has never seen before."

"Using occult science and magic wind? That's what you want me to believe."

Mason shrugged. "You can believe whatever you want. We've achieved our goal and opened up a path to a new world."

"So you're trying to tell me this other world has an abandoned marine institute just like our world? And a village that looks just like Loch Raven? Seems a bit preposterous."

"The worlds are almost mirror images," Mason explained. "They just evolved in a different manner. Different forces shaped them."

This was pointless, Oscar thought. "And what do you want with this other world?"

Mason smiled. "A chance to achieve more than we could imagine. Power and riches beyond compare." He leaned closer to Oscar's face. "A better world, where people like you know their place."

His biting words made Oscar flinch. *Megalomaniac. That's the term for Helleson*, he thought. *A delusional demagogue.*

"And where is my place?"

At that Mason released a hearty laugh. "That's the point," he said, trying to suppress his amusement. "You don't have one."

"Then what do you want with me?" He understood they had no intention of letting him go. But they couldn't keep him forever, could they? Somehow, it would be up to him to find his own way out of this mess.

"I have no use for you. I'd just as soon toss you in the sea along with your elderly friend." He gave a nonchalant shrug. "But you may have some experimental value to others. So, I'll leave you with them. There is someone special who wants to say hello to you." He turned to leave. "Farewell, Mr. Basaran."

"You can't keep me here!" Oscar yelled, as he strained against his bindings. He turned as much as he could, but the old man was no longer in sight and he heard his footsteps heading up the aisle.

Sikes walked over to a panel in the wall and opened it.

Behind Oscar, he heard a door open again and more footsteps of someone who approached down the aisle, but they were lighter clicking steps. When the person came into view, he looked up into the face of

Claudia Davenport.

Oscar's eyes widened and he felt the color drain from his face as his words nearly caught in his throat. "What the fuck?" A mirage, he thought, from the stress of his ordeal. Then she spoke.

"I warned you not to interfere with me," Claudia said.

Oscar opened his mouth, too stunned to form intelligible words. "How...who...?"

"I told you I knew people in very powerful places," she said.

He remembered that conversation on the balcony the night of her and Kyle's engagement party. She told him she'd ruin him if he tried to get between them.

"I don't understand," he said.

"I've handled the marketing for Aerosource for quite some time. They're one of my biggest and richest clients. That led to my introduction to Mason Helleson and the invitation to join the consortium. They've given me goals I'd never imagined." She leaned closer to his face. "And as you know, I get what I want."

If she had come any closer, he had the urge to bite her nose off. "Does Kyle know anything about this?" No, of course he wouldn't. Not naïve Kyle, who somehow lost his way with this woman for some inexplicable reason.

"Don't you worry about my Kyle," she said, acid on her tongue. "I make sure he's very happy."

"I regret ever trying to accept you," Oscar said with his own dose of bitterness.

"Oh, you're going to regret a whole lot more," Claudia said with a smile.

Sikes, still standing by the panel in the side of the far wall, pressed a button and the black curtain opened to reveal a large turbine blade that covered the whole wall.

"We've been doing our own experiments on shadow flicker," Sikes said with a childish grin. "All in the name of scientific exploration." He hit another switch and a light came on behind the blades. He pressed a button and closed the panel door. The turbine blade started with a hum and began to turn. Claudia and Sikes left the room with laughter.

Before Oscar, the blades fell into a rhythm, and the shadow flickered across his eyes.

CHAPTER FORTY-FIVE

Shadow light shadow light shadow light shadow light.

Oscar shielded his eyes against the trio of wind turbines on top of the hill and turned away. Slivers of pain shot through his skull. Down the hill, cows gathered, at least a couple dozen, restless, and looked up at him. The one in front had a cleft running down its face, splitting its head and giving the impression it had two heads. It bellowed a long, low moan.

The cows charged toward him.

He turned and ran up the hill with the cows in pursuit. The flicker cast its beat across the pasture stirring their frenzy. In the sky above him, seagulls gathered, swirling in circles in the sky, their cries piercing the air.

The cows gained on Oscar, but he couldn't run any faster. He continued north, toward the roar of the surf, his lungs straining, ready to burst. The closest cow to him bent its head down and nipped him on the leg. He stumbled and fell.

They swarmed around him, biting him. He pushed himself to his feet and broke away from the herd toward the cliff's edge, the cows still in pursuit. He spotted the lighthouse to his left. Creigh stood atop his tower, waving his ax above his head.

Oscar glanced back at the cows charging toward him and then down below the cliff at the ocean thick with seaweed. His heart thudded in his chest as he took a deep breath and leapt off the edge.

During his fall the wind sucked the air out of his lungs. He thought he might pass out before hitting the water, but when he struck, the icy sea enveloped him like a cold steel trap. His muscles stung with hot pain and his body collapsed in on itself. His lungs felt ready to burst. He tried to swim to the surface but the thick seaweed blocked his way. He pushed at it, trying to create a path to the surface. When he broke free, he opened his mouth wide and his lungs grabbed at the air available.

Oscar treaded water as best he could without getting mired in the seaweed. He looked up and saw the cows lining the ridge of the cliff's edge. Then, one by one, they began jumping off into the water.

The cows hit the ocean with the force of artillery shells, shooting up great spouts of spray. Oscar turned to swim away, but as each cow rose to the surface, they came after him. His arms felt like rubber as exhaustion took hold of him. Soon the cows were nipping at his legs, his arms, his torso, causing great welts of pain. He began to sink beneath the water.

Oscar's head came up out of the water.

He saw a ceiling above him and lights. He looked around and saw he lay in a shallow tank of water. Something nipped him in the calf.

He glanced down and saw the tank was filled with lobsters. A claw pinched him on his right forearm.

"Jesus!" he screamed and grabbed the side of the tank, pulling himself up and over the side where he fell onto the cement floor. He looked down at his body, naked except for his drenched boxer briefs, and saw welts all over his legs and torso. "What the fuck?" He heard laughter behind him and turned.

Jumbo stood off to the side, nearly bent over from laughing so hard.

"They were going to eat you," the man said, holding his belly and barely containing himself.

"What the fuck is wrong with you?" Oscar said, dazed. He got up, wobbly. "And where the hell are my clothes?" *This is insane*, he thought. What had they done to him and why did they leave this deranged asshole in charge of him?

"Miss Claudia said I could have some fun with you," Jumbo laughed. "And that's what I'm doing."

Oscar glanced around the room. "Where are we?" The place looked like some kind of maritime museum. Historical objects of marine equipment lined the walls and shelves: ancient oars, wooden harpoons, a diving helmet, a ship's bell, a wheel, sextants, spyglasses, compasses, brass lanterns, maps, sailcloths, rigging ropes and various-sized anchors, including a large one leaning up in the corner of the room.

"This is the arty-facts room," Jumbo said with a grin. "From when the institute was active. And it's where we keep the lobster tank for our dinners. But you ain't going to enjoy that. Miss Claudia wants me to bring you to her when I finished having my bit of fun."

"Can I get dressed first?" he asked.

Jumbo pointed. "Your clothes are over there. Sorry you don't have an extra pair of dry skivvies." He chuckled.

Oscar walked over to the nearby counter where his clothes lay in a rumpled pile. He wasn't about to put his shorts on over his wet briefs so he figured to discard them. He turned to look over his shoulder.

"Can I get a bit of privacy at least?" He said it more as a command than a question.

"I suppose," Jumbo said with a shrug. "Not like I want to see your cock and balls, or your skinny dark ass." The man turned around. "I like my asses a bit rounder."

Oscar looked up at the artifacts gracing the wall before him, seeking something he could use as a weapon. He spotted an old wooden harpoon on the display and grabbed it. It felt heavier than he thought it'd be. He turned and started toward Jumbo.

"Just don't try anything stupid," Jumbo said, his back still turned.

Oscar crept up to him, planning to club the man over the head with it. Jumbo must have heard his wet bare feet slapping on the concrete floor and turned. "Bastard!"

With a sudden lunge, Oscar rammed the point of the harpoon into the man's stomach.

Jumbo gave a ghastly cry and fell back, clutching the end of the pole sticking out of his gut. Oscar still held his end, stunned at what he just did, not even sure why, but now wondered if it could be undone. As Jumbo lay on the floor squirming and squealing with pain like a stuck pig, Oscar pulled back on the harpoon, trying to remove it. The barbed end came out, bringing some of Jumbo's intestines with it.

Oscar jumped back, horrified, as blood puddled out onto the floor around the twitching man.

Shit, he thought. *What the fuck did I just do?*

Now what?

Get out!

He ran to the counter and grabbed his clothes, not caring as he put his shorts on over his wet underwear and threw his shirt on over his head. He didn't know if he'd have time to put his sneakers on, but with Jumbo still crying and gurgling on the floor, he didn't think it wise.

When Brownie came into the room, he knew it didn't matter.

"What the hell's going on?" Brownie yelled, looking at his first mate lying on the floor in a pool of blood.

Oscar didn't even think the man noticed him standing there and took advantage of the distraction. He reached down and picked up the bloody harpoon, this time wielding it like a club and smacking Brownie across his right shoulder. The blow drove the man to his knees. He looked up at Oscar with squinting eyes.

"We're going to your boat," Oscar said, brandishing the harpoon. "And we're getting the hell off this island. And if you don't do what I say, I'll ram this thing down your fucking throat."

Brownie eyed the bloody point of the harpoon and looked down at his sea mate who had now stopped thrashing. One last gurgle of blood poured out of Jumbo's throat and then he became still, his eyes open wide.

Brownie nodded.

"Get up," Oscar commanded.

Brownie took one more look at Jumbo, as if to reassure himself Oscar meant business, held his right hand out, palm up, and slowly got to his feet.

"Lead the way," Oscar said, pointing with the harpoon.

"We won't get far," Brownie said and began walking toward the door in the back of the room he had entered through.

"Never you mind, just go." Oscar wished he could put his sneakers on, but didn't want to take the chance of taking his eyes off the captain.

When the two of them stepped outside, Oscar noticed it was nearly nightfall. The sun dipped just above the horizon toward the mainland. He gazed around the area. No one appeared to be about and most of the buildings were dark except for the one they had just exited and the larger main house.

"Let's get to your boat," Oscar said.

He kept a close eye on Brownie as the captain led the way to the *Seaweed*. Oscar gripped the harpoon tight in sweaty palms, realizing the weapon remained the only advantage he held at the moment. Once on the boat, Brownie started the engine, which came to life with a low rumble.

"Make it quick," Oscar said, nervous the sound of the boat would alert the others.

Brownie proceeded to untie the mooring ropes from both the stern and bow, but appeared to take his time, pretending to struggle with the knots.

"Hurry," Oscar said, irritated. He heard voices in the distance and looked up toward the buildings. Figures approached in the darkness. He glanced over at Brownie. "Let's get out of here."

Brownie went back into the cabin and started guiding the boat away from the dock just as Mason, Sikes, Claudia and Pickett showed up.

"Don't be stupid, Mr. Basaran," Mason said, his voice flat with a tone of annoyance. "Where do you think you're going?"

"Away from this lunatic asylum," Oscar said through clenched teeth. He tightened his grip on the harpoon.

"There's no place for you to go," Mason said.

"Once I get to the mainland and report what's going on here, you'll be in the same boat, pardon the pun."

None of them laughed. Braydon came running out of the main building to join the group.

"He killed Jumbo," the young man said.

Oscar hoped that made it clear to them that he meant business.

"You'll be sorry," Claudia said.

Oscar looked back at her, despising the smug look on her face. He caught movement out of the corner of his eye and turned. Brownie, one hand still on the wheel, reached down with his other hand toward a flare gun secured below the engine panel. As Brownie grasped the handle of the gun, Oscar swung the harpoon down on his wrist. The flare gun clattered to the floor and Oscar bent down and grabbed hold of it while Brownie nursed the pain in his arm.

"No more shit," Oscar said. He felt a bit more courageous now that he held two weapons. His whole body pulsed with excited nerves.

Brownie straightened up behind the wheel and kept one eye on Oscar and one on the way in front of him as the boat pulled out of the small harbor and headed out to sea. The others back on the dock diminished from view.

"Where to?" Brownie asked, casting a glance at him.

"To Rockland," Oscar answered. He figured he'd rather get to the mainland than try and find help in town on the island. Get real help, he thought, marine patrol and state police.

"It ain't Rockland over there," Brownie said.

"Still playing that game?" Oscar shook his head. "Let me ask you something that doesn't make sense. If we're in some other world, how the hell did you get your boat here? Huh?" He felt proud thinking he'd found a hole in their bullshit story.

"There ain't just a rift on the island," Brownie said without hesitation. "Sikes found it stretches out into the sea, just beyond the Gull Point lighthouse."

Oscar felt his face flush.

"Shut up," he cried. "No more from you. Just drive the damn boat."

Oscar glanced out toward the bow of the boat. They continued on in silence for about a half hour. An uneasy feeling crawled up into Oscar's stomach as he saw nothing but ocean water out the cabin window of the lobster boat.

What if there's nothing else out here? What if the island is all there is? Goose bumps erupted along the skin of his arms, raising his hairs. His throat grew dry and he tried to swallow. He felt a sensation of being alone and cast off. He thought of his friends back home, his colleagues, and even Kyle. *Are they out there somewhere?*

Then he saw lights and breathed a sigh of relief. He spotted the flashing light of the Rockland lighthouse that stood on the end of the mile-long granite breakwater guarding the harbor. Beyond that were lights of the town.

He looked at Brownie and flashed a sarcastic smirk.

The captain grinned back, displaying his crooked teeth, and jerked the wheel.

The boat swerved and Oscar felt himself tumbling to the deck. The harpoon slipped from his left hand, but his right still gripped the flare gun. His left elbow slammed hard onto the deck and sent a shiver of pain up his arm to his shoulder. He looked up and saw Brownie standing over him. The captain had grabbed the harpoon and held it over his head in both hands.

Oscar saw the mad expression on Brownie's face and the bloody tip of the harpoon he was about to plunge down into him. Oscar trembled with fear as he raised the flare gun, closed his eyes, and pulled the trigger.

Even with his eyes closed, Oscar sensed a great flash of sparks and wave of heat. When he opened them, Brownie's entire body and part of the cabin were engulfed in flames. As the captain roared in intense pain and his body thrashed around, Oscar madly scrambled in a backward crawl out of the boat's cabin toward the rear deck. He didn't stop till he hit the back wall of the stern.

Oscar looked on in horror as fire engulfed the whole cabin. He searched around him for some type of life preserver or jacket but saw nothing but a coil of rope. He worried the flames would reach the engine and gas tank soon, and knew he didn't have a moment to spare. He stood and got up onto the back washboard of the boat. He turned and stared out at the dark sea, fearing it almost as much as the blazing boat he stood on. With a silent prayer, he dove off just as the boat cabin exploded, spattering him with broken fragments of wood before his body hit the water and disappeared under it.

He rose up and opened his eyes as he broke the surface. What remained of the boat still burned and lit up the area around him as he treaded water. Pieces of the boat surrounded him and he tried to find one large enough to support him. The main part of the boat began slipping beneath the water, the flames hissing as the sea doused the burning hulk.

With what little light the last remaining flames provided, Oscar spotted a large plank and swam toward it. He reached it, gasping with relief and spitting out the stinging water. He relaxed, trying to catch his breath.

The water erupted around him as a large shape shot up out of it.

The burned form of Brownie loomed over him, his face charred and blistered, hands with flaps of peeling skin reached for him, grabbing him by the scruff of his shirt. His mouth opened in a hoarse roar.

Oscar flinched back, pounding on the man's face, feeling the skin oozing. Brownie's grip released and the charred body slipped back into the sea. As the last piece of the burning boat sank, the flames extinguished and Oscar found himself in darkness, still clinging to the wooden plank.

He floated for a brief moment, trying to catch his bearings. A light reached out toward him and he realized his body floated toward the Rockland lighthouse and its revolving beam flashed over him. It made him think of the shadow flicker. *Light, dark, light, dark.*

But this time it gave him hope.

He clung to the plank and began kicking his legs, aiming for the lighthouse, carried along a bit by the current that helped push him in that direction. When he got closer, he ditched the plank and began swimming. The waves pushed him to the right, toward the breakwater.

As he approached, a big wave seemed to scoop him up and toss him onto the seaweed-covered rocks on the side of the breakwater. His whole body vibrated with pain when he struck the rocks, but the seaweed helped cushion the blow and he clung to the rocks and felt a wave of relief. He heard voices and lifted his head a little.

He couldn't move. It didn't matter though. Dark shapes of people were running from the shore end of the causeway toward him. Others came out of the home attached to the lighthouse.

Oscar looked up at the great structure. Something looked different.

When he first came to Kidney Island, he remembered the ferry passing the Rockland lighthouse. The home attached to the lighthouse was a two-story structure painted white, the lighthouse a square brick tower.

But even in the darkness and the light cast from the top of the tower, he saw the whole entire structure was a massive granite building with a circular stone tower. As the figures on the breakwater scrambled down the rocks toward him and he felt hands grabbing him and lifting him off the rocks with a flurry of incoherent voices, he looked up to the top of the lighthouse tower and saw the red flag flapping in the wind with the golden symbol of a trident emblazoned on it.

CHAPTER FORTY-SIX

Oscar awoke in a small room.

He surveyed the bare surroundings. He lay on a bed with a pancake-thin mattress, the wire of the springs beneath poking up and aggravating his already sore muscles. A lone toilet nestled in one corner appeared to be the only other furnishings in the room. No. Not a room. A cell. The only door had no handle or mechanism to open it on this side.

Am I in jail?

He sat up and quickly grabbed the side of his head with his right hand as the blood rushing to his brain caused a throbbing pain. His clothes were gone and in place he had been dressed in a gray one-piece type of jumpsuit. On the floor was a pair of shoes, socks stuffed inside them. He remembered the sinking of the *Seaweed* and swimming for the lighthouse.

The lighthouse?

Against the back wall of his cell was an octagonal window, the glass embedded with a wire security screen. He put the socks and shoes on, got up and went to the window, having to stand up on the edge of the toilet seat to peer outside. He saw the ocean, the marina down below and out in the harbor was the lighthouse at the end of the breaker. *Must be Rockland*, he thought.

But then why am I locked up? A precaution?

Oscar examined the solid steel door at the front of his cell. It also had a security window, this one rectangular. Beneath it was an open slot. He felt compelled to bang on the door for help, but as he approached, the face of an attractive young black woman appeared in the window, her brown hair untamed and wiry.

"Hey," he said, surprised.

"Hello," she answered in a soft, polite voice. "I've brought you breakfast."

She slid a tray through the slot beneath the window. He took it, puzzled. The tray held toasted bread with scrambled egg chunks, raw flaked salmon and topped with sprigs of dill.

"Why am I in here?" he asked. "Can you help me?"

"You are to go before the council at the assembly," she said, before starting to leave.

"Wait!"

She turned back.

"What's your name?"

"Arrie."

He smiled. It sounded like a pretty name. "Can you help me?"

"They say you came from another world."

He looked down, exasperated. "I don't know anymore." He glanced back up at her beautiful eyes. "Is this Rockland, Maine?"

Arrie's eyes grew confused. "This is the village of Neptune."

"I've never heard of that." Could the *Seaweed* have drifted off course? Or maybe Brownie had purposely led him astray? "Is it in Maine?"

Again she gazed upon him as if he were mad. "It's in Vinland, a province of the Kingdom of the Trident."

He put his hand against the glass window. "I need to find someone to help me."

"The council will decide what you need."

Then she was gone and he slinked back to his bunk and sat down. He stared at the food on the tray, not feeling much of an appetite, his throat still raw from the sea water. But he had no idea when his next meal would come or how long he'd be in here, so he began to eat and surprised himself by devouring every crumb. The salmon felt salty and greasy in his gut.

He set the tray on the floor and lay back on his cot, reflecting on his ordeal and trying to remember everything he'd need to tell this so-called council when the time came. Everything from the moment he woke up in Norris Squires' yurt till he washed up on the rocks at the Rockland lighthouse. Even he thought the story sounded unbelievable, but what remained true was that several people had died, a couple by his own hand.

So why wasn't he being brought before the police? What authority did this council have? He thought his nightmare would be over when he reached shore. Now he doubted it.

A couple of hours later, his cell door opened. Two men in uniform entered and placed manacles on his wrists in front and escorted him out to the hall where a third officer waited.

"I'm Police Chief Kolbeck," said a thin man with a narrow face and beady eyes. "You're to be brought before the council."

Oscar looked at the unfriendly chief. "Can you tell me why I'm here, what I've done?"

"Save it for the council."

They led him outside where the bright sunshine hurt his eyes. The manacles rattled as he raised them up to shield his vision from the glare. When he came to Rockland to catch the ferry nearly a week before, he hadn't paid much attention to the town, but the layout of this village seemed familiar.

Overhead, seagulls called out as they circled over the roofs of the granite buildings. Chief Kolbeck motioned him toward the back of a nearby police truck. The other two officers opened the rear doors and he climbed into the windowless compartment. One of the officers got in also and sat across from him on a bench seat. Kolbeck and the other officer got in the front.

The drive was short, barely five minutes. It seemed they could have easily walked. When Oscar stepped out of the van, he saw they were in front of a majestic building next to the marina. The structure was constructed of white marble and twin spires rose above either side of a grand arched portico. Written on a sign above the entrance doors were the words: *Neptune Yacht Club*.

Oscar turned to the chief. "Are you serious?"

"Keep your trap shut till you get before the council," Kolbeck said and shoved him forward. The two police officers each took one of Oscar's arms and led him through the entrance into a grand foyer. They ascended a set of stairs and then down a hall and through a set of double doors into what looked like some sort of function hall.

Five empty high-back chairs sat upon a raised platform at one end of the room. The space immediately before it was empty, but rows of chairs were set up about thirty feet from the stage and many of them were filled with spectators. Other people stood along the side walls, even though there were still plenty of empty seats.

Oscar spied Arrie and she caught his gaze, a cautious look upon her face. The two officers led him to a spot in front of the stage and stayed by his side. Chief Kolbeck took up a position by the side of the stage next to a flagpole. Oscar noticed the Trident flag hanging off it. Rumblings of conversation ran through the crowd but hushed when a squat man entered from the side of the stage.

"Please rise," he said, "for the Council of the Assembly and the Grand Regent Cain Crogan."

The audience stood as five men entered in procession and marched to the chairs on the stage. The tallest of the five, one with a wild mane of gray hair and beard that encircled his head like a ring of fire, took the middle seat, which had a taller back than the rest.

This must be the Crogan guy, Oscar thought, *the one they called the grand regent.* Once the five men sat down in unison, the rest of the audience took their seats. Oscar felt nervous and the manacles on his wrists seemed to gain extra weight with the tension and pulled his arms down.

Crogan cast his eyes at him and Oscar's nerves cringed. He bellowed with a cavernous depth, "You've crossed the whale road and arrived here without proper authority."

It wasn't a question but Oscar felt the man expected him to answer.

"I escaped on a boat from murderous men," he said, trying to maintain a steady voice. "I was in a desperate situation."

"What were you doing on Serenity Island?"

That again. Could it be that everyone else was right and he was the one living in a delusion? He shrugged and his manacles shook. "I don't know. I was lost and then became captive." What else could he say? He didn't know how to navigate this strange world.

"Did Mason Helleson send you?"

Oscar looked up with surprise at the mention of the name. This man knew Mason. How should he proceed?

"He was the leader of the group holding me captive. I don't know what they wanted from me, but I had to escape for my own safety." *And sanity.*

The man named Crogan looked perturbed and Oscar worried he'd made a mistake. Crogan turned to the men on either side of him and spoke softly to them. Oscar couldn't make out the whisperings. At one point, Crogan lifted his hand and the conversations stopped. Once again he glared down at Oscar.

"Tell me everything that happened to you."

Oscar took a deep breath and as articulate and careful as he could be in choosing his words, he began to spin his tale, starting from his meeting in Mason's office at the Boston headquarters of Aerosource and up until his arrival on the shores of what he thought was Rockland, Maine, but now he wasn't quite sure.

The speech exhausted him and when he was finished, the chief let Arrie bring him a glass of water, which he gulped down and handed back to her. His eyes met hers and she gave him a reassuring look. After it was done, Crogan leaned forward in his chair.

"We shall take a short recess and reconvene after lunch." He turned to Chief Kolbeck. "Bring the intruder to a secure room and make sure he's fed."

Intruder? Was that what they considered him? Not a victim, not a suspect, but an intruder, as if all he did was trespass in their community.

Kolbeck and the two officers led him out of the room and down the hall. They brought him through another set of doors to what had the appearance of a doctor's waiting room. A couple of chairs and a small couch were the only furnishings. Oscar sat down at the instruction of the chief, who departed the room, leaving the two officers behind with Oscar.

About a half hour later a knock came at the door. One of the officers opened it and Arrie entered, carrying a tray with three steaming bowls and three glasses of water. Oscar smiled upon seeing her, the only pleasant face amongst all these surly strangers.

"Thank you," he said when she handed him a bowl. He looked down at it, stirring its contents with a spoon. It was a stew with chunks of herring, potatoes and leeks in a broth seasoned with dill. *Fish again*, he thought with dismay. He was sick of fish. He glanced up and smiled.

She brought bowls and water to the two officers, who seemed excited.

"Any news?" Oscar asked.

Arrie looked at him, nervous, as if afraid to speak in front of the lawmen.

"Your friends are coming," she said in a low voice.

"Friends?" He didn't know what she meant.

"From Serenity Island. They've been in contact with the authorities. They're arriving in a boat under escort."

"No chatter with the prisoner," one of the officers said, after slurping some of his stew.

Arrie nodded, gave Oscar a frightened glance, and left.

So was he a prisoner or an intruder? Oscar wondered if there was even a distinction. And now Mason and the others were coming here? And what was their relationship with Crogan and the council? None of this seemed to bode well for him, and he ate his stew with distaste.

Not long after lunch, Chief Kolbeck came to the room and took them all back to the assembly room. When the officers led him in, the council members were already in their chairs. Oscar was stunned to see Mason, along with Claudia Davenport, Gavin Pickett and Braydon. Only Burton Sikes was missing from the so-called consortium.

Oscar grimaced at the group, noticing Claudia taking particular pleasure in his restraints. They all seemed confident and self-assured, with only Braydon showing signs of nervousness.

Crogan pointed at Oscar and turned to look at Mason. "Is this the man you unintentionally allowed into our world?" he asked angrily.

Mason took a step forward. "Yes, an unfortunate accident. He inadvertently got caught in the rift when my scientist opened the portal between our planes."

"Just like that little boy a year ago?"

Oscar perked up at that. The Lassiter boy.

Mason nodded. "Glitches in the aeromancy that we are attempting to iron out. Minor problems."

"Harrumph!" Crogan's voice boomed. "Our man Creigh at the lighthouse informed us another intruder has gotten through. An old man."

Mason spread his hands wide and smiled, as if trying to belie the situation. "These unfortunate incidents are being handled. The old man is no longer a concern."

"And the boy?" Crogan bellowed.

Mason shrugged. "He's just a boy who got lost. I understand he's back in his world."

Crogan's jaw tightened. "These incidents are unacceptable!" he roared. He pointed at Oscar. "This is unacceptable! A boat exploded and sank. A charred corpse washed up on shore."

Oscar looked at Mason, whose smile never left his face. But Claudia and Pickett now looked as uncomfortable as Braydon.

"I assure you there will be no further complications," Mason said.

"When your people reached out to us a year ago, we agreed to an arrangement based on your assurances that we could trust your discretion and protect the portal." Crogan stood from his chair. "You've broken that trust. And for that, there must be consequences."

Oscar swallowed, his throat dry, his nerves tingling. He looked out into the crowd, catching Arrie's eyes with a pleading glance. She looked down.

Mason stepped forward. "We are prepared to do anything to make amends." His tone still sounded like a man in charge, but Oscar knew who ruled here.

Crogan signaled to Chief Kolbeck, who left the room and quickly returned. He carried with him a handheld speargun and handed it up to the grand regent. Crogan took it and walked to the edge of the platform.

The two officers on either side of Oscar grabbed his arms and held tight. Oscar felt the color drain from his face. He looked over at Mason, who wouldn't let go of that sickening smile.

"Come forward," Crogan said to Mason, and waved him to the stage.

When Mason got there, the grand regent handed him the speargun.

"As a demonstration of your good faith, I ask you to sacrifice one of your people. It makes no matter to me who."

Mason's smile dropped and he glanced down at the weapon. "One of my people?"

"Yes," Crogan said. "And I don't mean him." He pointed at Oscar. "One of your own people."

A huge wave of relief swept over Oscar.

"But why?" Mason said, confused.

Pickett, Claudia and Braydon looked at each other in stunned silence.

"To prove your loyalty to our collaboration," Crogan said.

Mason looked up at the grand regent, mulling over his orders with consternation, and then turned to face the others.

Pickett took a step forward. "Wait a minute," he pleaded. He looked at Claudia. "She's no real value. Make it her. I'm too important back on Kidney Island. I have too much value."

Claudia turned to him. "You despicable bastard!" She faced Mason, her eyes wide. "He's not even a part of the original consortium. We brought him in only because we needed things from him."

Mason stepped toward the trio.

"That's right," Pickett said. "I brokered the deal for the wind turbines. If it wasn't for me, you would never have gotten a foothold on the island."

Braydon said nothing. He stood there, his whole body trembling, his face sweating.

"None of you really matter," Mason said. He raised the gun and fired a spear into the throat of Gavin Pickett.

The crowd gasped.

Pickett's eyes grew wide as his body dropped to the ground, the spear impaled through the front of his throat and protruding out the back. His hands grasped it, as if trying to pull it out. Blood spurted from his throat and pooled on the floor of the assembly room. His legs kicked several times as his body squirmed in the bloody pool. In a few seconds, all movement ceased.

Mason turned to Crogan.

"Satisfied?"

Crogan nodded. "Good enough." He signaled to Chief Kolbeck. "Take the other two away and lock them up."

Kolbeck moved forward as did several other officers from the back of the room.

"Wait!" Claudia yelled. She looked at Mason. "Do something!"

One of the council members, a short toad-looking fellow, called Crogan over and spoke quietly to him.

The officers had begun to drag Claudia and Braydon away when Crogan held up his hand.

"Wait!" he commanded. "Apparently, Councilor Westergard has taken a liking to the woman and wishes she be placed in his servitude. Bring her to his quarters."

The man named Westergard looked on with a salacious grin and rubbed his hands together.

Claudia screamed as the officers dragged her off. "You can't do this to me!"

Crogan looked at Mason. "Mr. Helleson, we will have one of our finest rooms prepared for you for the time being."

Mason nodded with a smile.

Oscar looked dazed at the unmoving body of Pickett. He watched Braydon being led away by several officers. Mason handed the speargun back to Chief Kolbeck.

"What about me?" Oscar asked, looking up at Crogan.

Crogan studied him. "The council will retire to private sessions to discuss your situation. In the meantime, you will be returned to your cell at the station house." He signaled to Kolbeck. "Take him away."

CHAPTER FORTY-SEVEN

"Hey, Oscar."

The voice came from outside his cell door. Oscar had been reclining on the bunk recovering from the shock of what happened in the assembly room. The horror of Pickett's body twitching in the pool of blood spewing from his neck; the callousness Mason demonstrated in agreeing to execute one of the members of his trusted circle, and the barbarity of the grand regent handing over Claudia to one of the council members like some common trollop.

As much as he loathed Claudia, he would never wish such degrading lecherousness be forced upon her at the hands of the sleazy-looking councilman. *Who are these people?* What in god's name kind of place did he end up trapped in?

When the voice called out, he got off his cot and went to the window in his door, but saw nothing out in the hall. Then the man's voice came again and he leaned down to the food tray slot beneath the window and peered out. Across the hall he saw a pair of dark eyes looking out at him from the slot beneath the window in the cell door opposite his.

"It's Braydon," the man said.

"So they've got you locked up too?" He relished some satisfaction in this, though he hadn't had any substantial interaction with this member of Helleson's callous consortium.

"Yeah, shit's gone all to hell." His voice sounded dejected. "It's not what I expected."

"What did Mason think was going to happen?" Oscar asked. "What did he want from these people?"

"Helleson promised me power and prestige when he enlisted my services in his organization. He told us this alternate world would be a better place, where powerful people could achieve more than their wildest dreams." The man's eyes dropped. "I think he underestimated these people."

Oscar felt sorry for the guy. "How'd you get involved?"

"I used to be a marine biologist grad student at the institute when it was in operation. After it shut down, Helleson's group purchased it with the help of Gavin Pickett. They recruited me for what I thought would be a private marine research center. At the time I didn't realize that Helleson's group was undertaking a different kind of research. I ended up just being a glorified boat chauffeur for members of the consortium. So much for my marine biology degree."

"Sorry to hear that," Oscar said. He thought for a minute. "Have you been over on this side before?"

"Yes, a few times. But we've never left the island. We've only had radio contact with Crogan and the council from the institute. This was our first time going over to the mainland. As you could see, it didn't go well."

"Damn." Oscar had a hard time wrapping his head around things. "How do you get back to our world? There's no wind turbines on this side that I could see."

"I don't understand a lot of this aeromancy stuff myself," Braydon said. "That's Sikes's department. But from what's been explained to me, the turbines create the rift, and the opening exists on both sides of the plane regardless. It's just a complicated formula to get the right wind flow and turbulence to open the rift. But once it's there, we can go back and forth." He paused. "I guess that's how you got sucked in. You just happened to be at the wrong place at the right time."

Oscar was grateful that Norris's attempt to blow up the turbines didn't work. Or maybe if it had worked, he wouldn't have gotten stuck here in the first place. He didn't know for sure. It hurt his head to think about it.

"What do you think they're going to do with us?" Oscar asked.

"I don't know. But it can't be good. I can only hope Mason can reason with them."

Oscar was irritated knowing his fate was in that man's hands. "Damn you all for your occult science."

"I'm sorry," Braydon said. "I made a mistake. Seems my life's been full of them."

"I know how you feel," Oscar said. "My big mistake was taking this assignment to investigate Kidney Island."

"Had you been on the island long?"

Oscar thought back, trying to remember not only what day he arrived, but also what date today actually was. "Less than a week."

"Do you know Tatum Gallagher?"

The mention of her name drew him back. He thought about how crazy her talk of witnessing time stop had sounded, at least until he experienced it himself. He had chalked it up to grief over losing her youngest son. Now he had the satisfaction of knowing the boy made it back to her.

"Yes, I met her. How do you know her?"

His voice grew sullen. "I met her a long time ago, when I was a grad student at the marine institute. She was just a teenager then, not even out of high school yet."

"I see."

"No, I don't think you do. How is she? Have you met any children she might have?"

Oscar was puzzled by the man's curiosity. "Yes, I met her son." He reflected more. "No, two sons. She has two boys."

"What are their ages?"

Oscar tried to remember exactly. "One's a teenager, late teens, still in school though. The other is a young boy, about nine or ten."

"What's the older boy like?" His voice sounded sad.

"Seems a nice polite kid." Oscar thought back to the day he met Rigby with his two friends, getting high and tripping to the shadow flicker. If they only realized how dangerous it really was. "Why the interest?"

"I think I'm his father." His voice cracked.

"What?"

"I had a summer fling with Tatum when I spent time doing grad work at the institute. She came to me one day and told me she was pregnant." His words got caught in his throat and he had to clear it. "I promised I'd take care of her and take her with me when I left the island."

"But you didn't."

"No. Obviously. When my studies were done, I left without telling her. Haven't had any contact since. I felt like such a coward."

Oscar thought about Rigby and his dark hair and complexion. He thought about Dirk Lassiter's dirty blond hair and Tatum's red locks. He could see the resemblance between Rigby and Braydon.

"It's a shame," Oscar said. "He seems like a real good kid."

"I hope he had a better father to raise him than I would have been."

Oscar thought about Dirk and his threatening rants and horrifying end. "Maybe."

"I hear someone coming," Braydon said, and his despondent eyes moved away from the open slot.

Oscar retreated to his cot, nervous about the approaching footsteps, but relieved when he saw Arrie's gentle face at the window.

"Dinner," she said in a soft voice.

Her lack of smile worried him and he wondered if she knew his fate, or if she just felt unsettled by the disturbing events in the assembly room.

"What is it?" he asked as he moved to the door.

"Wild mushroom soup," she said as she slid the tray in.

Oscar took hold of it, grateful it was something other than seafood.

"Have they said anything about me?" he asked.

She shook her head. "I haven't heard anything."

He wondered if she would tell him even if she did know. "Do you work for the police department?"

"Sort of," she said hesitantly. "I'm in servitude to them."

"What do you mean? Are you a servant? Does this place have slaves?"

"No, not like that." Worry lines crisscrossed her brow. "I get paid a stipend. Our world has a class hierarchy. People like me can only attain a certain level. That is our place."

Oscar started to understand. "And people like Crogan and the council are the ruling class."

"That is their birthright."

"No wonder Helleson felt this was a better world for him."

She turned away and delivered food to Braydon's cell. Before leaving, she looked back at Oscar. "I wish I could help."

Oscar brought his soup to the cot and sat down. He had little appetite, his stomach churned and felt knotted, but he ate all the soup, which tasted bland. He needed to keep his energy up, though all seemed hopeless at the moment.

After dozing on the cot for a while, his dreams restless and fretful, he awoke to noises outside. He went to the window at the back of the cell, standing on the edge of the toilet to peer out. Crowds of agitated people roamed the streets. Boats filled the marina, maybe fishermen returning from their day at sea, or day-trippers docking for the night. Fog flowed in from the ocean, casting the whole area in a wispy haze.

Footsteps, several of them, sounded down the hall toward his cell. Oscar got down from his perch on the toilet. Keys rattled in his cell door and he saw uniformed men through the meshed window. The door flung open and Chief Kolbeck entered with three officers. Kolbeck flashed a sly grin.

"What's going on?" Oscar asked, taking a step back till he came up against the wall and could go no farther.

"Take him," Kolbeck said.

The three officers came forward, one holding a set of manacles.

"Tell me what you're doing with me!" Oscar yelled.

Two of the officers grabbed his arms to prevent a struggle while the third locked the manacles on his wrists.

"Grand Regent Crogan has ordered a Blot," Kolbeck said, and then signaled to the officers, who began dragging Oscar forward.

"I don't know what that means!" He struggled slightly, only to show defiance, though he knew he was no match for the three officers.

Kolbeck didn't answer, only smiled.

"What the hell's a Blot?" Oscar demanded to no avail.

When they brought him into the hall, he noticed the cell door across from his was open, and Braydon was not there.

Oscar looked back at Kolbeck. "What have you done with him? And what are you doing with me?"

"All in good time," the chief said, and the officers led Oscar down the hall.

He ceased struggling, knowing it served no purpose. He'd have to plead his case to Crogan, but he wished he knew what their intentions were. Before they led him out the front door of the station, he spotted Arrie.

"What's going on, Arrie?" he yelled to her. "They said something about a Blot? What are they talking about?"

Her eyes dropped before she spoke. Her face lowered.

"A Blot is a sacrifice to the gods."

CHAPTER FORTY-EIGHT

Oscar struggled as they brought him outside, but the two officers held firm grips on his arms and the third prodded him in the back with his nightstick. Kolbeck led the way as they marched him down the street. Onlookers lined both sides yelling and cursing him.

This is insane, Oscar thought, his heart pounding in his chest in rapid fire beats. *This place is a madhouse!*

As they led him down the street along the marina, his mind was ablaze. *They can't do this,* he thought. *This is barbaric.* What kind of people were these? His pleas to Chief Kolbeck were ignored.

"I've done nothing wrong!" he screamed to the crowd, who seemed to want his blood. These people didn't even know anything. They didn't know what he'd been through and how he got here. "None of this is my fault!"

Where was Braydon? he thought, remembering the empty cell. What had they done to him?

Through the wispy fog that seeped over the moored ships in the harbor and into the streets, he could tell where they were taking him: the breakwater that led out to the lighthouse. The great stone structure stood at the end of the breakwater. Its spire appeared to pierce the fog like a sword through a cloud. Its bright light flashed out into the darkness of the sea.

At a small parking lot by the entrance to the breakwater stood Cain Crogan and the other members of the council. Mason stood with them, a smirk on his smug face. Also in tow was Claudia, looking a hell of a lot less pleased. She had been stripped down to what looked like a black leather skirt and a matching bathing suit top. A studded collar was wrapped around her neck and connected to a leash held by the slimy councilman named

Westergard. Her eyes caught Oscar's and looked sorrowful. He wondered if she felt bad for him, or for herself. He felt a tinge of empathy for her.

"Crogan, please," Oscar pleaded when they reached the group. "You must listen to reason."

"The gods demand a sacrifice," Crogan said, his voice bellowing so the surrounding crowd could hear. "The sea will be angry if the gods aren't appeased. You have crossed the threshold into our world and you do not belong."

"Then send me back!" Oscar screamed, tears flowing from his eyes. *This can't be real*, he thought. *This can't be happening.*

"Soon, you will be where you belong." He looked at Kolbeck. "Take him away."

"No!" screamed Oscar. He caught a glance at Mason. "Mason, do something! This is all your fault! I didn't do anything!"

The officers lead him down the granite breakwater causeway. The sea churned on either side, sending misty spray up into his face. The boats in the harbor to his right rocked on buoyant waves in water choked with seaweed. The ocean indeed seemed angry.

The council, along with Mason, followed behind. Some townsfolk proceeded along the breakwater; others took up vantage points along the shore. Oscar looked back and spotted Arrie in the crowd. She saw him, but offered only a sad glance. He looked away, knowing she'd be no help.

At the end of the breakwater they came upon the large granite building and circumvented it to the lighthouse on the other side. The tower seemed to go on forever. At its peak, the light flashed.

The officers led him to the side of the lighthouse facing the open water to the harbor. A large metal ring was anchored into a block of stone about seven feet off the ground. Kolbeck took out another pair of manacles and attached one end to the chain linking Oscar's restraints. The officers raised his arms and attached the other end to the ring embedded in the lighthouse wall.

The muscles in his arms strained and pain shot down into his shoulders. The officers stood back. Crogan stepped forward, locking eyes with Oscar.

"I'm sorry, young man," Crogan said.

"Please," Oscar said, his words pained inside his tightened throat. He could say no more.

Crogan walked to the edge by the sea and gazed out into the foggy surf. He raised his arms.

"For the infractions of the intruders," he screamed into the ocean, "we offer you this sacrifice!" He turned and looked up at the top of the lighthouse. "Call forth the Jormungandr!"

He stepped back to join the others.

Above Oscar, a foghorn bellowed out into the dark sea, its deep roar long and drawn out, echoing in his ears.

The sea rolled; the surf crashed onto the rocks below him. He saw nothing.

Oscar glanced over to Mason, who only gave a callous shake of his head.

Waves broke out in the harbor, white surf churning over. Oscar braced his back up against the cold damp stone of the lighthouse. Every nerve in his body felt as if it were on fire. He could feel the thumping beats of his heart, the pulse of his blood.

The foghorn blared again. Something in the fog stirred.

Dark gray movement just beneath the surface, barely discernible in the dark water. It seemed like the ocean were alive, thriving, rising up.

What is it? Oscar couldn't tell. But it seemed large.

The foghorn roared from above.

It's calling it, Oscar thought. Calling it to him.

The bulk of something broke the surface and Oscar spotted a pair of saucer-sized eyes.

"The Jormungandr has arrived!" Crogan bellowed. "Bring forth the sacrifice!"

At that, the officers grabbed hold of Mason.

"Hey!" Mason yelled. "What are you doing?" He looked at Crogan in confusion. "What is the meaning of this?"

"You have violated our trust," Crogan said to him. "You have allowed intruders to cross the threshold into our world and jeopardized our existence. You have angered the gods and punishment must be served."

Mason looked at Oscar, and then back to Crogan. "But him! Not me!"

"This is all your doing," Crogan said, unsympathetic. "Take him!"

The officers dragged a screaming, struggling Mason to the edge of the breakwater, his face a mask of panic, and threw him down onto the seaweed-covered rocks by the water's edge.

In the water, something rose.

Once it broke surface, the sea creature took shape. Oscar looked down in the water at a giant squid, a sight to behold. He had seen images of one online before, but to see one in the ocean amazed him with its massiveness.

Mason looked out at the creature as it moved toward the rocky shore. He turned and began scrambling up the rocks, slipping on the seaweed and falling down. The squid's two long tentacles reached up out of the water, feeling their way along the rocks till they found their prey. One of the tentacles wrapped around Mason's right leg, the other gripped him by the waist, the serrated rings of the suckers attaching to him.

Mason screamed.

The tentacles lifted him off the rocks and carried him to the sea. He pounded on the tentacles to no avail, his screams rising above the roar of the ocean surf and the blare of the foghorn.

When the tentacles brought the struggling man closer, the arms of the squid grabbed hold and drew him toward its waiting mouth. Mason kicked and screamed as the mouth opened and the beak bit down on his legs.

Oscar wanted to close his eyes, but was mesmerized by the spectacle before him. Mason's struggles and screams lessened as the squid sucked him farther into its mouth and soon he fell silent. Oscar watched up until Mason's head disappeared down the beast's throat.

After witnessing such horror, Oscar braced himself, thinking the same excruciating fate awaited him. The squid, satiated with its meal, slid back beneath the murky waves.

Crogan approached. "I needed a distraction," he said, "so that Mason Helleson wouldn't suspect what we planned to do. Sorry for the display we put you through."

Oscar looked at him, confused.

Crogan motioned to Chief Kolbeck. "Unchain him. Take him back to his cell till we decide what to do with him."

A wave of relief rushed through Oscar. He felt he might pass out.

CHAPTER FORTY-NINE

Asleep in his cell, Oscar suffered dreams of tentacles reaching for him, the serrated edges of the suckers securing to his flesh and gripping tight, trying to drag him into the sea. He woke in fits several times only to drop back into sleep and the same nightmare.

He awoke for good when a voice whispered to him.

Oscar gazed up from his bunk to see a shadowy face at the window of his cell door. He got up and crept softly to it. Arrie stared at him from behind the glass.

"What's going on?" he whispered in nervous excitement. He wondered if it was his turn to be sacrificed. "What time is it?"

"Just after midnight," Arrie said, looking back down the hall for a second. "I've come to get you out."

He heard a clink of a key inserted into the lock, and then the door opened.

"How did you get the key?" he asked.

"Don't worry," she said. "Doesn't matter. We must be quick and quiet."

He stepped out into the hall, his body trembling with nervous excitement. Braydon's cell door was closed, but he couldn't tell if he were inside. He hadn't seen him since their earlier conversation.

Arrie led him down the hall to a back staircase. He couldn't believe how quiet the police station seemed. Where were the night duty officers? He wanted to ask Arrie, but was too afraid of alerting someone if he spoke. She took him down the stairs, their footsteps soft on the steps, and out a door at the bottom that deposited them in a parking lot in the back of the station house.

"What's the plan?" he asked.

"Ssssh. It's all worked out. Come along."

He followed her down the street and across to the marina. The sea must have calmed since earlier because the water only lapped softly along the wooden hulls of the boats docked there.

Maybe the gods were satiated, he thought.

"I've secured a sailboat that you can take back across the whale road to Serenity Island," she said.

"Are you coming with me?" he asked, concerned about her safety.

"No," she said, as they walked along the pier. "My place is here."

"But what if they find out you helped me escape? I don't like to think what they'd do to you."

She stopped and turned to him. "You don't need to worry about me. I'll be all right."

He wasn't sure about that. "But how am I going to make it back to the island? I don't know how to handle a boat." He thought about all those times back in Turkey when his uncle tried to teach him to sail. If only he had paid attention to those lessons.

"I've arranged that." She smiled, continuing to lead him to a small boat at the dock. "I have an experienced sailor for you."

They stopped and Oscar looked down at the boat. Braydon sat in the cockpit, smiling up at him.

"How'd you get here?" Oscar asked.

"I let him out of his cell earlier, to help get the boat prepared. Now you must go quickly, before the guards discover you're missing."

Oscar stepped into the boat, unsure, but knowing he had little choice.

"I'm just as anxious to get out of here as you," Braydon said.

Oscar looked up at Arrie. "Are you sure you can't come with us?"

She shook her head. "No. My place is here."

Oscar looked back at the port town. "I don't think this is the best place for you."

"I don't belong in your world as much as you don't belong in mine. Bon voyage."

She bent down and untied the rope from the cleats for both the bow and stern. Oscar took a seat on the deck toward the bow. Braydon set the mainsail and the boat caught wind and glided away from the dock. Oscar looked back at Arrie.

"Thank you," he said, trying not to call out too loudly. She only waved and watched them from the pier.

Braydon effortlessly guided the sailboat out of the harbor. "The seas are calm and the wind is steady. The fog's lifted. We got nearly a full moon. A good night for sailing."

Oscar looked at the lighthouse at the end of the breakwater and then down at the water around them, thinking about the giant squid. He hoped it was satisfied with its recent meal of Mason Helleson and wouldn't be searching for more prey. This boat wouldn't be much of a challenge for the creature. His stomach felt queasy and he didn't know if it was from thoughts of the sea beast gorging on Mason or the rocking motion as the boat's hull bobbed along the ocean surface.

"How do you know how to find the island?" Oscar asked.

"Using the stars to guide us," Braydon said with a smile.

Oscar looked up. "Are they the same stars as in our world?" he asked.

Braydon laughed. "Yes."

Oscar looked back as the lights of Neptune grew dimmer. The farther out into the ocean they sailed, the more nervous he felt. The sea seemed so quiet, desolate in the darkness. What if they missed the island and continued sailing out into…wherever? Whatever lay beyond *this*.

He wouldn't feel safe till he reached land. The ocean felt too large and ominous. He didn't belong here. Another thought crept into his mind. He turned to look back at Braydon.

"How will we find our way back to our world?"

"Sikes will help us," Braydon said.

Oscar had nearly forgotten about the Aerosource scientist with all that had taken place back at Neptune. "What if he won't?"

"We'll make him. What choice does he have? Helleson's gone, Pickett's gone, Miss Davenport's…." At that his voice trailed off.

Oscar thought about Claudia and wondered about her fate. He looked back the way they came but the mainland was no longer in sight. She would be stuck there. He wondered what would become of her and how

Kyle would handle her mysterious disappearance. Oscar could tell him, but would Kyle believe any of this? Oscar barely believed it himself.

"There!" Braydon shouted and pointed.

Up ahead, Oscar could make out a form on the horizon, a dark humped shape. No landmarks were discernible. As they got closer, he could see the flicker of a beam from a lighthouse. He wasn't sure which lighthouse. He wanted it to be the one at the entrance to the harbor and the village center.

But what if the townsfolk were just like the ones back at Neptune? Would he be any safer? He thought maybe it would be best to land somewhere else on the island, possibly the institute. But Braydon was the one in control. He glanced back at him.

"Where are we going to dock?"

Braydon pointed out. "Look and see."

Oscar looked in the direction he indicated, and as the island drew closer, he could make out which lighthouse they approached. Creigh's lighthouse.

"I don't think this is a good idea," Oscar said, turning back to look at Braydon.

Braydon was pulling on the furling line and reducing the mainsail. The boat slowed but continued in a straight line for the lighthouse.

"What are you doing?" Oscar asked.

"This is as far as I go." Braydon's face looked grim.

"What are you talking about?"

Braydon reached down into the cockpit and pulled something out. It looked like the same speargun Helleson had killed Pickett with. He pointed it at Oscar.

"What the fuck is going on?" Oscar asked. He swallowed hard, not taking his eye off the tip of the spear.

"You don't think getting out of the police station was really that easy?"

Oscar should have known. Now he knew why there were no officers in sight.

"Crogan had it all set up," Braydon continued. "He actually felt bad for you and realized none of this was your fault. So he made a deal with me to take you out to sea and…." He hesitated. "Dispose of you quietly. He didn't want the townsfolk to think he was unreasonable."

Oscar noticed the speargun quivered in Braydon's hand.

"And what do you get out of this?" Oscar asked.

"Crogan promised me a place in this world." He shrugged. "It's better than what Helleson got."

"You can't honestly want to stay here? Did you forget you have a son back there?" Oscar pointed to the island. "Back in the world where you belong?"

Braydon shook his head. "I've never been a father to him, so it's no use starting now."

"You can't be serious about this."

"Besides," Braydon said, "do you really think Crogan would let us go back? With all that we know? He wouldn't. So I made the best deal I can. I get to live, only here with them."

Oscar stood up. "And I get to die?" He thought about making a lunge at Braydon, but the point of the spear aimed at him unnerved him.

Braydon hesitated. "I'm not a killer." He lowered the gun. "Do you know how to swim?"

"What?"

Braydon swung the boom toward him and it caught Oscar in his midsection, knocking the wind out of him and pushing him off the deck of the boat and into the sea.

For the third time in the last twenty-four hours, Oscar found himself fighting for his life in the unfamiliar sea. He broke through the surface in time to see the sailboat cutting across the water in the opposite direction. Oscar treaded water for a few minutes, trying to catch the breath that the sailboat boom had knocked out of him.

When he felt stable enough, he began to swim toward shore. He aimed for the end of the long pier that jutted out into the water. The undercurrent pulled at his legs and made it hard to maintain his course. He constantly had to adjust his direction and it felt like the ocean fought against him. Several times he stopped and floated, giving himself some time to regain his strength, but every time the water drew him away from where he wanted to go.

Oscar was determined to not let the sea win this battle, and he forged ahead with each stroke of his arms, lifting his head from time to time to spit out sea water and gather his bearings. The pier drew closer and it gave him incentive to push his body to the max even though his arms and legs felt like giving out.

You can make it, he told himself. It became a mantra that he repeated over and over in his mind. Just a little farther. The closer he got, the more seaweed he encountered, pushing through it as he swam.

As the rickety wooden structure loomed ahead, a wave picked Oscar up and pushed him toward it. He reached up and tried to grab hold of one of the pilings, but his hands slipped on seaweed clinging to its side. A swell came and lifted him up a bit and he lunged for the edge of the pier, taking hold and clinging to it.

His arms felt weak and he could not lift himself up. He hung there, clinging to the side of the pier, resting and hoping he could find the strength deep inside to raise himself up onto the dock. He reaffirmed his grip and prepared to try again when he looked up and saw someone standing above him.

Burton Sikes stood on the dock.

"Welcome back, Mr. Basaran," Sikes said, and proceeded to step on his fingers.

The sole of his shoe crunched down on his hand and Oscar screamed out in pain but refused to let go. *I've come too far,* he thought. He stared up at Sikes's face.

Oscar heard a thunk and Sikes's eyes went wide, an ax blade embedded in the top of his head. The ax was withdrawn and Sikes pitched forward off the pier into the water. Creigh stood on the dock holding the bloody ax. He reached down and offered a hand to Oscar.

Oscar gratefully accepted the gesture and Creigh pulled him up onto the dock. Wheezing and gasping, and flexing his mashed fingers, Oscar gazed into the water at the corpse of Burton Sikes floating on the water and pushed around by the swells. That could end his last hope of making it back home.

He looked at Creigh, not sure if he should thank him or not.

The diminutive man looked down at him and smiled. "Crogan's orders," he said, indicating the bloody ax.

Oscar wondered what that meant for him.

"Come," Creigh said and helped him up.

Oscar had to lean on the shorter man as he helped him walk back along the pier. All life in his leg muscles seemed to have left him and he relied on Creigh to escort him up the stairs and into the house.

They sat at the kitchen table and Creigh got two large steins and poured a pair of dark amber beers from a glass growler, then placed the container back on the table. Oscar looked at the stein, noticing the same engraved image of the squid and lighthouse he had seen back at the tavern in the town. He stared down at the liquid and then looked at Creigh's misshapen eyes.

"Don't worry," Creigh said and raised his own stein.

Oscar smiled and brought the drink to his lips. The beer was warm and bitter but washed away the stinging salt from the sea water in his throat. He drank half the drink in one long gurgling gulp and then set the stein down, drawing in a deep breath.

"Tell me everything Burton Sikes told you about this rift between our worlds," Oscar said.

Creigh took another swig and then set his stein down.

"He talked about the windmills on the island on your side." His voice was clunky, the words coming from deep in his throat. "He said he monitored the wind currents, adjusting the windmills to catch the air, to create the effect he called...." He thought for a moment and scratched his large head.

"Aeromancy?" Oscar prompted.

Creigh's eyes went wide. "Yeah. That's what he called it."

"Did he say how often the opening would occur?"

Creigh shook his head. "No. He said the winds were fickle."

Oscar looked down, dejected. Creigh poured more beer from the growler into both their steins.

"There is one thing I can tell you."

Oscar looked up. "Yes?"

"The wind wasn't the only way."

Oscar felt hopeful. "What do you mean?"

"Sikes talked of other openings. The use of other elements."

"Elements? How so?" Oscar lifted the stein to his dry lips.

"Like water."

"The sea?" Oscar remembered something Brownie said about the rift stretching out into the ocean and that's how he got the *Seaweed* through.

"Let me tell you a story," Creigh said before taking the growler and pouring the rest of the contents into both their steins and setting the empty glass jug down on the table. "I went out fishing late one day in my dinghy and hooked a big tuna." He stretched his hands wide. "I fought long and hard and it dragged my boat farther out into the sea. But it was stronger than me and my line broke." He paused and gulped some beer. "I gone far enough out to sea I barely see the island. And it gut dark. I saw no light from the lighthouse. I gut scared. My job to keep the light shining. So I rowed back in the direction I hoped was right. It took long time, and hard without beacon to guide me, but I made it back to pier and tied my boat up. I ran to the lighthouse and went up the stairs. But something weren't right. The iron stairs were caked in rust. The bolts holding it to the brick walls loose and the staircase wobbled. I got to the top to see if the motor had run out of kerosene, but...."

"But what?" Oscar didn't understand where Creigh was going with this story. It seemed he had gotten off track.

"No motor. Nothing the same. And I heard voices coming from my house. I looked down and could hear and see shadows of people in the house. And then a girl screamed. I got scared. Voices came. The intruders came to the lighthouse. I heard one climbing up the stairs, and then I heard the sound of wrenching metal and the staircase collapsed. I heard more screams." He paused and took a deep breath and another swig. His voice sounded scratchy. It seemed like he wasn't used to talking so much. Oscar imaged being a lighthouse keeper was a lonely life and one not given to conversation.

"Go on," Oscar prodded. "What happened next?"

"I heard lots of yelling, and then the people, they seemed like young kids, got in trucks and cars and drove off. I came out of the top of the lighthouse and saw the bottom half of the staircase had broken off. I got a rope, went down the stairs as far as I dared go, and then used the rope to tie off to the most solid piece of iron I could find and lowered myself to the floor. I went to the house and saw it was empty."

"The people had all left?" Oscar asked.

"Yeah," Creigh said, "but that's not what I mean. The house was empty. No furniture, no belongings. My whole house empty, like it wasn't my house no more. Then I looked inland and understood."

"Understood?"

He leaned forward. His eyes grew wide. "I saw the shadows of the windmills."

"You had crossed over."

He nodded.

"What did you do?"

"I was afraid. I didn't know. But I remember Sikes talking about there being an opening in the sea. So, I got back in my boat and rowed out to sea. I drifted around for a while. I thought about throwing myself in the ocean and letting the sea take me. It would be a fitting end. But then I saw something."

"What?"

He pointed out the kitchen window. "The light."

Oscar followed his gesture to the lighthouse outside.

"The beacon signaled to me, and I followed it back home."

Oscar looked at Creigh's curious face and then at the empty glass growler on the table. A thought came to mind.

"Do you have a pen and some paper?" he asked.

CHAPTER FIFTY

At the gravel-strewn cove that passed for a town beach on Kidney Island, Nathan poked along the shoreline seeking seashells while Tatum watched from a spot away from the water and the chilling breeze. It still felt dreamlike to see her boy at play after he'd been gone for so long. It was a miracle and made her glad she never believed he was truly dead. God had sent him home to her.

But in exchange, he took the boy's father, and she realized with every joy comes a bit of anguish. Dirk was gone now, and Myles Larson had left the island without her, so now she would be stuck here forever. But she had both her boys now, and that's all she needed. Maybe Rigby would stay after his senior year of high school and they could revive the farm like Dirk had hoped.

A car door slammed but she did not turn to see who it was. She did not like taking her eyes off Nathan, especially with him being so close to the water. She didn't want to bring him here, but he loved the ocean and she couldn't let what happened ruin that. After all, it turned out it wasn't the sea that had taken him anyway. Besides, they lived on an island in the ocean; there was no escaping the sea.

"How's he doing?" Constable Laine Jensen said as he came beside Tatum. She did not turn to face him. "Good. Like nothing ever happened."

"That's great to hear."

She knew that was not the only reason he came to see her.

"Did you go out to the lighthouse?" she asked.

"Yes," he said. "Nothing there. Not a sign anyone had been living there. Not one speck."

She sighed. "But Nathan said he was there for the past year, with a funny-looking tiny man who was the lighthouse keeper."

"I know, Tatum. But I tell you, there's been nobody there. Not for quite some time."

Down on the shore, Nathan kicked off his sneakers and stepped into the water.

"Nathan!" Tatum hollered, taking a couple steps forward. "What are you doing?"

He turned to look back at her with a smile. "I see something!" he said, excited.

"Don't go past your knees!" she yelled back. Probably spotted a starfish or crab.

"Boys will be boys," Jensen said.

Yes, Tatum thought. She knew boys well, and men too. "How's your investigation going?"

"Well, it's really the state police in charge," he answered. "I'm just the local contact. But from the evidence gathered up at the wind turbines, it seems I can draw the same conclusion."

"Which is?" She knew the answer could affect the legacy of both her boys.

"Seems that Norris Squires and that off-islander Oscar Basaran were trying to blow up the turbines for god knows what reason. Some kind of protest I guess." He scoffed. "And it appears Dirk Lassiter came upon them and attempted to stop then, but was killed in the ensuing blast."

Now she did turn to face him.

"Dirk died a hero is what I gather," Jensen said.

Some compensation, Tatum thought, for her sons now being fatherless.

"There's just one trouble the investigators are having," Jensen said.

"What's that?"

"Squires' van and Basaran's rental car were both destroyed in the blast. So that places them at the scene. But the people from the forensics lab have only come up with the remains, what was left of them, of Norris." He scratched his head. "Not one scrap of anything from that Oscar fellow. It was a tremendous blast, just seems strange not to find anything."

"Hey!" Nathan shouted as he ran up from the shore carrying something.

Tatum smiled at the excitement in her boy's voice.

"What is it?" she asked.

"Look!" he exclaimed when he reached them. "It's a bottle with some paper in it."

Tatum and Jensen looked down at the corked glass growler and a rolled-up bundle of papers inside it.

"It's a message in a bottle like you see in movies," Nathan said, excited. "Maybe someone needs help."

Jensen took the bottle from the boy and pulled out the cork. He shook the papers to the opening and gently removed them with his fingers. There were a handful of sheets rolled up. The constable unfurled them and began reading.

MESSAGE IN A BOTTLE

I hope someone finds this. My name is Oscar Basaran and I am an insurance investigator for the Freedom Insurance Company. I have been on assignment on Kidney Island off the coast of Rockland, Maine. People probably think I have mysteriously disappeared, but that is not the case.

This will sound unreal to whoever finds this, and understand me when I say it has been hard for me to believe it, myself. A group of people have been delving into some type of occult science involving the use of wind to create a rift between planes of existence. These people include Aerosource executive Mason Helleson, scientist Burton Sikes, Loch Raven Selectmen Chairman Gavin Pickett, and Profile Marketing agent Claudia Davenport and others. Somehow this group has managed to open a rift between two alternate worlds, the one we know of and one beyond this one though it looks similar.

I have inadvertently become trapped in this other world on an island they call Serenity off the coast of a territory named Vinland and the town of Neptune, part of a kingdom known as the Trident. Neptune is run by a council who made some kind of pact with Helleson and his group. Things did not go as planned and now most of them are dead.

I have escaped and am stuck on Serenity Island in this alternate world. I am being helped by a lighthouse keeper named Creigh. I am trying to find my way back to my own world. Every day I go out to the hill where the wind turbines stand in my world, hoping to find my way through the opening in the rift. I will keep trying. It's all I can do. Creigh says there is also an opening out at sea and that has led me to cast this message in the bottle into the ocean to hope my message finds its way to somebody.

I'm not sure what help anyone can provide, but I am praying for a miracle. I will keep trying to find the opening and hope that eventually I will find my way home.

ACKNOWLEDGMENTS

While shadow flicker is a real occurrence, I have exaggerated the effects for the purpose of this strange tale. I want to thank the crew at Flame Tree Press for making all this possible, especially my editor, Don D'Auria, for his enthusiasm for this book and guiding it to its finished form along with copy editor Imogen Howson and all the rest. And Flame Tree Studio for designing the fabulous cover art.

I thank my wife, Rhonda, for her amazing support in my writing endeavors and encouraging me, along with her sister, Dawn, to explore the topic of wind turbines. Rhonda's love and devotion makes everything so much better and I feel blessed to have her by my side.

My daughter, Jenna, champions my books, even if she doesn't read them, and I love making her proud, just as I know my own dad was proud of my achievements. This will be the first book of mine he won't be able to read. He is sorely missed by all.

There are more than 4000 islands off the coast of Maine, but Kidney Island does not exist, so don't go looking for it. But if you do find it, don't say you weren't warned.

FLAME TREE PRESS
FICTION WITHOUT FRONTIERS
Award-Winning Authors & Original Voices

Flame Tree Press is the trade fiction imprint of Flame Tree Publishing, focusing on excellent writing in horror and the supernatural, crime and mystery, science fiction and fantasy. Our aim is to explore beyond the boundaries of the everyday, with tales from both award-winning authors and original voices.

•

•

Join our mailing list for free short stories, new release details, news about our authors and special promotions:

flametreepress.com